Where Nightmares Walk

Lucifer's Halo – Book I

By Phineas Delgado

ISBN: 979-8-9948540-0-6

Cover design by: Lil Hazell
Library of Congress Control Number: 2025910199
Printed in the United States of America

DEDICATION

For all the people who helped me along the way:

*For my sister, Anne, who always believed, and wanted more
than anything to read my book. I'm sorry I was late.*

*For my best friend, John, creator of the original LeapStryke,
who graciously let me use the name of a character he loves.
Without you, none of this would exist.*

*For my friend, Ron, who planted the seed of what became Lucifer's Halo
when we talked about comic books in his dorm room at McGuire.*

*For my brother, Joey, who taught me faith is a powerful tool, and with it,
you can accomplish anything.*

*For my high school Literature teacher, Mrs. Benington,
who made me believe that people would read what I wrote.*

*And finally,
For my family. Always for my family.
Thank you. I love you all.*

God, who foresaw your tribulation,
has specially armed you to go through it,
not without pain but without stain.
- C.S. Lewis

Chapter 1

Every night when Tim slept, he would see them again; they were soulful eyes, as silver as the full moon and as haunting as a mist-covered moor. They were so pervasive he didn't even need to be asleep to see them. They were ever-present in his mind, and he hated that he didn't know whose eyes they were. He was certain he should. That's why, deep down, he felt he probably deserved the torment, even if he didn't know why.

Tim wasn't sure of many things anymore, but he trusted his instincts, and they told him the eyes belonged to someone he loved. He didn't know her name, and it broke his heart because those same gut feelings told him she was unforgettable. In his heart, he felt that this woman and he had been close, though, because every time he saw those eyes, his soul cried out in pain. He ached to know more, but he was convinced he never would.

Anyone in Tim's position would have felt the same way, but it's difficult to imagine or relate to. Most children have played blind or deaf, or even pretended to be lame or forget something. But it's impossible to know how it really, truly, feels to lose your most important memories. They make us who we are, and we fear their loss more profoundly than any other thing. It's a fear so ubiquitous that we devote tremendous time and resources to enshrining them with pictures, written words, and memorials of stone and metal.

Tim's situation was unusually severe, and it wasn't just his head and brain that were broken. The accident that robbed him of his recall also made off with a great deal of his body as well. Between the two, though, Tim lamented the loss of his memories the most. Overcoming his physical disability was something Tim knew he would eventually do. Breaking out of the prison of his mind, though, was a challenge he wasn't sure he could overcome, even if he had the motivation. He was starting to believe that he'd died and that this was his personal version of hell.

Despite their taunting nature, it was those remarkable eyes that were Tim's only source of lasting strength. Those attending to him felt differently, though. It was their opinion the constant stress of focusing on the eyes was hindering his recuperation. They tried, on several occasions, to shift his focus away from their elusive owner toward more practical, tangible things. They believed the eyes weren't a real memory at all, but rather a conflation of the eyes of those he'd been working with during his recovery. But Tim knew better; his gut told him to cling to the sliver of optimism that one day, like on TV, the flood gates would open, and he'd remember everything.

What truly made the effort Sisyphean was Tim's short-term memory wasn't in any better shape than his long-term memory. Nearly every morning, he had to start over to some degree. Sometimes, he wouldn't remember anything from the day before. Other times, he could remember things for days on end. Either way, just as he started to see a glimmer of hope, he'd forget something while recalling it—the thoughts dissipating like a ghost before he could grab hold of them.

Thankfully, everything wasn't gone; some memories were indelible. Tim never forgot his name, his age, how to write, or advanced math and science. But he didn't know where he was from, what he did, or who his friends and family were. And those things never wanted to stick. It was infuriating and demoralizing. He was starting to feel like an Etch-a-Sketch that had seen too much use, and all he could do was sit there and wait for someone to draw the next picture before his brain erased it all again.

Tim wasn't sure how long he'd been in his bed, but as far as he was concerned, it might as well have been his whole life. He was a helpless lump, and his anger and frustration at the situation fueled his work to be free of the damned bed and the confines of the horrid room. But the effort was exhausting, both for him and those helping him.

Keeping Tim positive and focused on his recovery was a full-time job. The rehab team reminded him, ad nauseam, that he was lucky to be alive, and that literal miracles had been performed for his benefit. The damage to his nervous system had been so extensive, the surgeons had to develop new, untested techniques for him to have any hope of recovery. Even with those, they had only hoped to restore *some* of the use of his extremities; it was doubtful he'd ever walk normally, and living independently would take a great deal of work. But all of it hinged on healing his brain.

Tim was keenly aware that the people in charge of his rehabilitation, namely the Chief Surgeon, Dr. Stephen Samuels, and the Head Nurse, Francine Marcum, hadn't taken any time off since he arrived. They'd been there every day, at least by his reckoning, but he wasn't sure how long that had been. Their demeanor, at least, suggested that it had been far longer than he knew. It certainly felt like ages for him, so he could only imagine how they felt about it.

Since he was essentially trapped in his room, what Tim wanted more than anything else was to break the monotony. He asked for something to read, and they brought him some Reader's Digests from the '60s and '70s. He asked for a television, hoping for news from the outside world, and instead, they piped in decades-old TV shows. He even asked for a mirror, and the staff summarily refused. The environment was being strictly controlled to keep his fragile mind from being further damaged.

With nothing else to occupy his mind, Tim found other things to do. Recently, he took up eavesdropping to pass the time. He was sure that he should have felt guilty—he might have heard something private, after all—but he found that most of the staff spoke among themselves as if he weren't there anyway. Besides, it came naturally, and it was better than watching another episode of *My Mother the Car*.

This new distraction was helped by Tim's discovery of an uncanny ability to hear even the most hushed conversations. It didn't matter where they were, or how quiet they wanted to be, he could hear them without difficulty or even much concentration.

Just that morning, he heard something about a war, some tidbits about the President, and that the price of gas had broken six dollars a gallon. None of it meant anything, of course, because he lacked any context. For all he knew, he'd heard those things before and had just forgotten. Not that it mattered. Even this guilty pleasure didn't help the time pass any more quickly. Nor did it help make sense of the endless waking nightmare in which he found himself. Every day was the same thing, over and over.

Until it wasn't.

Chapter 2

There was no reason for Tim to think that day would be different than any other. Granted, while he didn't remember any of the previous days, he knew they were all the same, nonetheless. He was lying in bed after another grueling physical therapy session, waiting for his usual dinner of tasteless grey sludge. The ruckus of the evening shift change came from the hallway, indicating he didn't have long to wait.

Then, without warning, the routine was interrupted by a loud and insistent **DING-DING-DING DING-DING-DING** of an alarm bell. Tim didn't remember ever hearing it before, and he was fairly sure he would. It was decidedly annoying and loud enough to wake the dead. It didn't take a genius to know something important was happening; a realization that was reinforced by the sudden flurry of activity and raised voices from the hall.

Sensing an opportunity to break the cycle of boredom, Tim decided he would listen in on what was happening. He lay as still as he could, focusing on the commotion outside his room. He didn't need to strain to understand what was said at the nurse's station, which was some distance down at the far end of the hall. Nurse Marcum was giving someone a dressing down the likes of which he'd never heard. She had a rather distinctive voice, and it was one of the few things that didn't need reintroduced repeatedly. Probably because he was always exposed to it.

Eager to hear more, Tim focused on the voices. His heart raced as he listened to the furor at the other end of the corridor. Nurse Marcum was quite angry, and he felt sorry for whichever poor nurse she was letting have it. He just needed to hear the voice to know who it was, and once he did, a startling realization settled in.

It was someone new; it was someone he didn't know. Tim's heart leaped into his throat. He was certain one of the voices in the hall was one he'd never heard before. Listening intently, the reaction of Nurse Marcum and the other staff reinforced Tim's belief and implied this unfamiliar visitor was also not welcome.

As the yelling escalated, Tim noted they were talking about him. His pulse quickened, his mind racing with the possibilities. Why would someone come to see him now? Who were they? Could they tell him more about what happened to him? Whoever it was seemed insistent on seeing him. It was the first sign that anyone outside of the hospital knew or cared that he was there. The idea of there being a world beyond the four walls of his room, a world that missed him, exhilarated him.

The commotion moved closer, down the hallway toward Tim's door. Nurse Marcum's hard-soled shoes clicked furiously on the tile, echoing off the walls. Tim also made out the slower, more deliberate steps of the visitor as both stopped in front of his door. If there had previously been an attempt to keep the altercation to a dull roar, that pretense was long past.

"Listen, I don't care if the Chairman of the Joint Chiefs wrote those orders himself, Commander," Nurse Marcum shouted, confronting the uninvited guest, "Doctor Samuels oversees this facility, and he has the final say on who gets access. He's made it clear," she added, in a voice that outsized her diminutive frame, "that no one sees the patient until…"

"*Patient?*" the stranger snapped, cutting her off in mid-sentence. "Are you listening to yourself, Major? That's a superior officer in that room and a damned fine one at that. And that officer *has a name!*" he shouted.

The outburst was enough to bring about a stunned momentary silence. It was a severe contrast to the previous shouting. The nameless stranger took advantage of the break to bring the argument to a quick close.

"Listen, *Major,*" the man continued, this time emphasizing the nurse's lower rank, "as I said before, I'm here to complete a Medal of Honor workup on Colonel Andrews. I don't think I need to tell you who authorizes those, or how highly visible this is. I'd hate to report back to the President that her authority doesn't carry the weight it used to. I *will* see Colonel Andrews, and I will see him *immediately,*" the stranger added forcefully. "Now, if you don't mind, Major," the visitor moved toward the door, his shadow visible to Tim through the small window of frosted glass.

Tim suddenly realized that he'd been holding his breath since he'd heard the stranger refer to him as *Colonel* and the Head Nurse as *Major.* He had no idea that he was in the military, or that he was in a military hospital. There were no uniforms, no one wore ranks, and no one ever referred to him by *his* rank. He was curious what he did to warrant receiving the Medal of Honor, and if it was connected to what put him there. He knew that the staff didn't tell him everything under the pretense of protecting his recovery, but he wondered why they kept something so important from him. His stomach churned, and he started to feel uneasy.

Tim's excitement was turning into apprehension. He trusted his instincts, and they told him that something was terribly wrong. Things that he questioned before, but dismissed, gnawed at the corners of his mind again. Nothing made sense now, and the only way he would get answers was for the disagreement in the hall to be resolved. Instead, Nurse Marcum slammed her hand on the door, preventing the stranger from opening it.

"Honestly, Commander, I don't care if he's being sainted by the Pope or he's the second God-damned coming!" the small Major roared. "My orders are clear, and a patient's *doctor's* orders trump everything and everyone else. Or did you miss that one at the Naval Academy, Commander?" she added curtly. "Yeah, I know who you are. That bullshit confidence routine might work in the O Club with the Lieutenants, but it doesn't work on me."

The tension was almost visible, seeming to seep through the door as waves of heat. Tim was dizzy from the mounting anxiety and from the revelations outside his room. It frustrated him that he didn't know who the visitor was and angry that so much was kept from him. He wasn't the only angry one. Tim heard the visitor sigh audibly and change his tone as he replied.

"I'm going to say this as nicely as I can, *Major*. Even if I didn't outrank you, and I most certainly do, we both know that this isn't a—what did you call it?—a 'bullshit confidence routine,' and if I wanted you out of my way, there's very little you or anyone else in this building could do to stop me. Now please, step aside before I move you aside. I don't want to hurt you." As the man spoke, his tone lowered, and the formality melted away, which made room for a subtle drawl.

Tim felt the rage radiating off Nurse Marcum. He'd heard her yell before and he'd seen her angry, but he'd never heard her this livid. He knew enough about her to know she was someone not to be trifled with, and he wasn't sure he wanted to meet the person who had. There wasn't much he could do about it now, though, since he saw her shadow move aside and heard the door handle moving.

With the press of a button situated near his right hand, Tim raised the head of his bed so that he could sit up as much as possible. Then, using a small analog stick next to his thumb, he maneuvered a rolling table over to his bedside. The lights in the room were turned off because they hurt his eyes, so he braced himself for the inevitability of his visitor turning on the overhead lamps. His heart raced; it pounded so relentlessly he heard nothing else. As expected, the stranger opened the door and turned on the lights with a loud click.

Tim lifted his right arm and covered his eyes as he winced against the harshness of the fluorescent bulbs. As he slowly adjusted, he saw a man move across the room and toss a leather briefcase onto the chair next to the bed. Tim focused as well as he could against the stinging brightness and looked up at his visitor.

The man's demeanor shifted as he came to the bedside and looked over Tim's unsightly condition. It seemed to Tim that he wasn't prepared for what he found. Gathering himself, the stranger looked around the room, then back to Tim, and mustered a weak, but sincere, smile.

"It's…," he began before he cleared his throat to start over, "uh, it's good to see you again, buddy. If that's really you under all those bandages," the man joked, trying to ease the tension, which was palpable. Tim wanted to smile, but that part of him didn't work yet. So, he just nodded and gave a thumbs up.

The stranger's smile widened as he moved closer to the bed and leaned against the rail. "There's a lot we need to talk about, but I don't think we'll have time to go over everything. Something tells me Major Spitfire out there won't waste any time calling for help. You see," he said, leaning over and whispering, "I'm not s'posed to be here."

Standing back up with a wink, he added with a wry drawl, "But I reckon you already knew that. After twenty-five years, I think we're pretty much always on the same page."

Tim's only reply was to stare back blankly. There was no denying there was a nagging familiarity, but Tim had no idea who this man was or why he would be there. He must have telegraphed his unease and confusion because his guest backed away from the bed with a frown.

"Good Lord, man," he said, dejected, "she wasn't lyin'. You don't remember me, do you?"

Tim's brain was in full revolt. Despite his utter certainty that he did not know this person, he felt similarly confident that he *should*. But he was only familiar in the way déjà vu was; as soon as Tim got close enough to put his finger on it, the recollection slithered back into the fog. With no context, he was just another person Tim didn't know. Tim felt lost and disappointed and shook his head slowly, his eyebrows raised in apology. His head was starting to ache.

The man pulled the chair over from the corner and placed his bag on the bed so he could sit down. He lowered the rail and leaned close to the edge of the bed. "You remember anything at all?" he asked hopefully.

Tim shrugged and held up his fingers in a pinch, then gestured to the dry-erase boards across from his bed. One contained the information Tim remembered regularly or without prompting; things like his name, the names of the staff, his age, and his learned skills like math and reading. The other had a much shorter list of things Tim recalled from the previous day. Neither held information relevant to Tim's life before he arrived.

The man stood up and regarded the boards with a frown and furrowed brow. "She told me you wouldn't know who I was, why I was here, or why you mattered. But I didn't believe her. I mean, why would I? How could you forget your oldest and best friend? She said you were…gone," the visitor's voice trailed off as he lost himself for a moment.

Then, in a flash, the man started pacing the room frantically, crossing his arms as he slid deep into feverish thought. He walked over to the bed and grabbed the footrail with firm hands before speaking.

"I guess we better get started before we're interrupted, and I get carried off to make little rocks out of big rocks. First, an introduction. I am Nate Lange, a Commander in the United States Navy, and your best friend. I've known you since you were old enough to spit and we grew up together in Ohio. So, when I found out you were alive…," Nate paused, "well, let's just say that I knew if the shoe were on the other foot, you'd have dick-punched every general in NATO if you thought it meant finding me. I had to come," he said with chuckle and a wide smile.

Tim wasn't smiling, though. His heart sank at what he heard. This random stranger, who was apparently not-so-random, created more questions than answers, much to Tim's dismay. Mountains of them, in fact. Why did he think Tim was dead? Why wasn't he allowed visitors? What was so important that this man was willing to risk everything to see him? Tim's concern once again showed on his face.

Nate looked at his friend, his smile gone, and said "Jesus, it's worse'n I thought. I don't have time for this." On cue, Nurse Marcum's distinct voice carried down the hall interrupting the reunion. Time was running short.

"All right, boss, we don't have time to rehash everything. We got important shit to discuss, and I didn't expect…this," Nate said, motioning at Tim's circumstances. "It don't matter what they told you. Just forget all of it and I'll give you the crib notes. You were…are…an Air Force officer—an Academy grad and pilot—just like your dad. You were the youngest person to make O-6 since '43, and one of the most decorated. Hell, they awarded you the Air Force Cross…" Nate choked, eventually spitting out the word, "posthumously. They gave it to your wife."

Tim's head reeled at the exposition. He stewed in the realization that the rehab team kept these things from him: his career, his achievements, his family. They lied to him endlessly. Nate continued, as quickly as he could, so he didn't notice the nearby table tilting up. Tim's eyes darted back and forth, scanning over the screen wildly. When Nate finally looked over, he saw the same word repeated, over and over.

STOP.

Chapter 3

Tim's head felt like it would burst. He tried to wrap his brain around everything he'd heard since Nate first appeared. It all begged the question; how long had he been there? It was clear they were keeping a great many things from him to the point of being outright dishonest. More questions; why were they lying to him? Why couldn't they just tell him the truth? A wave of disturbing suspicions charged to the forefront of his thoughts.

Then a stark insight hit Tim like a freight train; if they lied about everything else, they were also lying about the eyes. They *did* belong to a real person, someone he knew and loved. This sudden awareness cemented a fear Tim avoided thinking about; whoever the eyes belonged to was dead because of him. This inevitably led to the conclusion he was responsible for it all: her death, his convalescence, who knew what else. What else had he forgotten?

The Amnesia Trope has been used so often for comedic or melodramatic effect that it's taken for granted. Someone gets hit on the head and they forget everything; they get hit on the head again and it all comes back as if nothing happened. It's usually not so neat and tidy in real life, but it does happen. After all, that was what Tim and his recovery team were working for. Or so he thought. Sometimes, though, the dam would burst, just like in a soap opera.

Without warning, Tim thrashed about on the bed as much as his broken body would allow. Despite his limitations, he still made a tremendous racket, which caused Nate to panic and run to the door. He paused, looked back at Tim in the bed, and wondered if he should call for help. He couldn't know what was happening.

Tim's previously foggy mind was suddenly clear and flooded with images that crashed and collided like too much water poured too fast into too small a bucket. It wasn't just the missing pieces of Tim's past either; it was also everything that his rehab team had been telling him over the past weeks. Not weeks, months; no, not months…years. He had been here for years.

Tim's mind was bombarded with as many as four different versions of the same event. He remembered a wife and daughter very clearly, but he also remembered being told about a son, and never being married or having children. He thought he knew which memories were real, but he couldn't know for sure. Why would he have all these other memories of other lives that weren't his? Why would they have lied about so much? Still more questions than answers. The truth of his life was now becoming clear. He just didn't understand why there was so much more than there should be.

Tim settled down and caught his breath. The waves of conflicting memories subsided, and his heart rate slowed. Seeing that his friend was out of danger, Nate peeked out the door, then locked it and made his way back to the bedside. He checked the monitors and breathed a deep sigh of relief before he looked over at the table to see a new message.

We are SPARTAN—I am Orion—You are Argus—What happened?

Nate's smile returned when he saw the name of their unit, and their call signs, on the screen. He grabbed Tim's shoulder in relief before he reached for the bag at the end of the bed. As he rummaged through the case, he spoke at a frantic pace, obviously excited by the turn of events and the impending interruption by Nurse Marcum.

"You missed a hell of a lot, and we're outta time. This is what's important. Our last mission wasn't on the books, not that many of 'em were. But that last one was just…diff'rent; somethin' was off, and we knew it. Workin' with civilians was always messy, and we'd never been asked to operate on US soil or work with other non-military agencies. Hell, we were forced to tag in a CIA spook you weren't allowed to vet. The brass made it seem like a milk run, but we didn't get assigned to jobs like that. Naw, this was somethin' more," he concluded with a frown.

Nate finally found what he'd been looking for and pulled out a nondescript envelope from his bag. He turned the envelope so Tim could see the front. It was yellowed with age and had only a date on it; typed, not hand-written. Tim looked over to the screen on his tabletop and then back to the envelope to confirm the dates matched.

Nate turned the envelope back toward himself and continued, "In the end, it wouldn't'a mattered how easy it was, not that it coulda been. Claire was a handful, even when she got her way. She didn't appreciate us bein' called in and was upset that we was messin' with her routine."

"She told us constantly she didn't need protecting. But there was a trail of bodies ever'where she went. That's why we were called in. We were the best, running by the numbers. You expected no less. Lives depended on it. This one wasn't supposed to be any different. We ran the perfect op, and it still blew up on us…literally," Nate remembered quietly.

Nate sat in the chair again, continuing his explanation. "We traveled with Claire as she gave seminars 'round the country. We begged her to cancel, but she refused. And she had friends in high enough places that we couldn't force the issue. We was at the University of Cincinnati, and she just ran off. You took off after her 'fore we even knew what was goin' on, and it was two hours 'fore we caught up. We got there and…," Nate's voice trailed off.

"It all went to hell," he continued after composing himself. "It fell apart so fast. The whole thing 'as over 'fore any of us knew what was goin' on. The both of you were in an abandoned building downtown, near the highway. After we arrived, we confirmed you 'as inside and geared up to come help you."

Nate shuffled in the chair, glancing at the door as he spoke, "There 'as a gunshot from outta nowhere, and ever'thin' just went…white. Once the light faded, we saw the building collapse near the top floor 'fore exploding. It was the damnedest thing I ever seen, and we seen some shit," Nate added with a quiet chuckle.

"It took us over an hour to count heads; the destruction covered something like ten acres. Luckily, it was early morning on a Saturday, and the area was mostly empty buildings and garages. She knew exactly where to be. She always knew. Once we could, we made our way to the building where you both'd been. There 'as Claire, lyin' in a cleared circle, the rubble fanned out all around her. We originally thought that the shot hit somethin' explosive, like a gas line or somethin'. But it looked like *Claire* was the source of the explosion. When we got to her, we saw the gunshot had hit her in the head," Nate paused again, briefly, as he struggled to hold back tears.

"You were just gone, man. Not a trace. Not a stitch of clothin' or a smear on a hunk a' concrete. Nothing. We called in crews to clear the debris. It took weeks and we never found a single trace of your body. We assumed whatever happened when Claire was shot vaporized you. It didn't make any sense, but we 'as already way past a place where science or traditional forensics could explain.

"The official story was somethin' about an errant cigarette butt and a gas leak. Two other members of the team died and that dick from the CIA was also missin'. You were declared dead, and we buried an empty coffin a couple weeks later. After that, we all tried to move on with our lives."

Nate cried openly now as he struggled to continue against the torrent of emotion. He kept his voice low and carried on, knowing time was of the essence. "Man, that was *five* years ago. FIVE YEARS! Claire's daughter, Emma, caught up with me last week and gave me this," Nate said, holding up the envelope for emphasis before he opened it carefully.

"Emma said Claire had a flair for the melodramatic—which sounds about right—and since she knew she wouldn't be 'round, she'd given a bunch of sealed letters to the family lawyer for safekeeping. They 'as given instructions to deliver them to Emma at specific dates and times. This one, though, this 'as meant for me. Well, for me to give to you. Can you see well enough to read it? You need to know what it says," Nate said gravely as he offered the letter.

Tim motioned Nate to place the open letter on the flat part of the table to his right. Once the letter was there, the surface lit up and the contents appeared on the screen, exact in every detail and large enough for both men to read with ease.

> June 14th, 1977
> Dear Commander,
> I wish I knew your name so that I could address you properly, but I don't always get to see everything I want. My name is Claire, and we will be well acquainted when we're older. I can see that you're a very sad man, Commander, and since I know I can help you, I feel I must. I have to warn you, though. If you choose to do the things I say in this letter, it will make your life harder than you can imagine. You'll be giving up everything to save someone you hold very dear. Someone that we will both hold dear. But it will set events in motion that will

give him the chance to start his life over
again, and maybe even more. It won't happen
right away, but I can assure you that his
life will change for the better, and you'll
be the reason for it.

I have faith you'll do the right thing.

Since you work at the Pentagon, you'll know
that the government likes to hide things in
plain sight. In a small, unmarked building
on the outskirts of Washington, D.C., you'll
find the man you didn't know needed found.
He thinks he's in a hospital, but he's being
kept for bad things. They've robbed him of
himself so that they can make him into their
mechanical puppet, killing and destroying as
they pull the strings. Please help him,
Commander; you're the only one who can.

Sincerely,

Claire Thibodeaux

*PS - Please make sure the man reads the
letter. I know it seems odd, and you may
think this foolish to do, but it's important.*

Tim felt the urge to cry, but that part of him still didn't work. But he felt his throat tighten; that lump and pain you only feel when the heartache is true. He wanted nothing more, at that moment, than to get out of bed and run away as fast as his legs could carry him. He understood now that the haunting silver eyes were Claire's, and why they tormented him. He tried to save her and failed.

When Nate was sure Tim was done reading, he continued speaking at a frantic pace. "My gut told me this letter 'as about you. I drive by this place ev'ry single day – hell, I know people who worked here. I did some askin' around, but no one knew what this place 'as for, only that it 'as here. So, I devised a brilliant plan to get in. And since I owe you my career, and my life, three or four times over, I fig'r'd the least I could do was put it all on the line to find you. And now that I know you're here, I won't stop until we get you home. You have my word."

Nate leaned over and grabbed Tim's right hand and held it tight with both of his while he smiled at his friend. They were so caught up in the moment, they didn't realize they were out of time. They didn't hear the key turn the lock, so they were caught off guard when a well-trained Marine boot kicked the door open with a raucous slam. Nate gave Tim a quick wink and pretended to be confident. But Tim saw the fear hidden just below the surface. Whatever happened next, it was going to be bad, and they both knew it.

Nurse Marcum pushed her way past the armed men in the front, a smug and satisfied smile etched onto her face. "I'll give you credit for having the balls to still be here, Commander, but you lose points for being too stupid to know when you're beaten," she said sarcastically.

The MP's moved in quickly to secure Nate and his bag, but Nate kept calm and collected and offered little resistance. Though he still pulled his arms free from their grip, chiding, "There's no need for that Marines. I'm still an officer in the United States Navy and a gentleman. I'll go quietly."

Nate turned to regard his diminutive adversary, saluting her curtly, "I wish I could say it's been a pleasure, Major." She just frowned in reply.

Nate's smile instantly faded as he turned toward the door. A large, thin, shadowy figure blocked his path and stopped him short. Nate's casual self-assurance melted like frost in the sun. As the figure entered, the room darkened noticeably. Even the harsh overhead lights dimmed, and Nate reflexively withdrew, bumping into the Marines behind him.

There was no mistaking when Stephen Samuels entered a room. His countenance was supernaturally dark and menacing, features enhanced by his permanent scowl. Upon meeting him, no one's first guess would have been that he was a doctor. No, he had the look of a banker or politician about him; the kind that turned down loan applications or passed legislation that ended free lunches for school kids.

Samuels walked into the room at a deliberate pace. His torso barely moved as he strode across the floor, his hands clasped firmly behind his back. His face, long and narrow, framed tightly pursed lips that were so thin as to be almost nonexistent. The deeply etched lines on his face only reinforced his dour expression, and his dark eyes affirmed his sinister intent. Tim watched Samuels anxiously as the Chief Doctor regarded Nate the way a hyena would a wounded lion.

"I'm actually quite surprised to see you here, Commander Lange; I really am. I knew, of course, that our subject's past would come calling eventually, despite all my security precautions. I had hoped it wouldn't, though," Samuels said in a thick accent Nate couldn't place. "At least not until I was finished. But here we are," he added with an insincere smile of sorts.

"Now, if I recall correctly, you had a nice, comfortable office job at the Pentagon, far away from anything stressful, or exciting, or…meaningful. Tell me," Samuels asked, edging closer to Nate, "how did you find out that we were here in this building?"

Nate looked over to Tim and winked again, then back at Samuels, hiding his discomfort as best he could. "I guess y'all just ain't as good at keepin' secrets as you thought you were. 'Sides, ferreting' out rats like you is what we do," Nate added, motioning at Tim, "and we're the best."

Samuels roared, leaned into Nate, and raised his hand as if to slap the undesirable intruder across the face. But before he did, he noticed something out of the corner of his eye. In the rush and commotion, Tim and Nate both forgot about the letter on Tim's table. Samuels narrowed his eyes to focus on the words which still appeared on the screen.

"I see now," Samuels said calmly as he straightened himself, "If the hero can't get to the oracle, bring the oracle to the hero. The mystic speaks from beyond the grave. That explains a great deal. What a clever woman she was," Samuels' lips curled into a smile that could curdle milk. He was impressed.

"What you don't seem to understand, *Mister* Lange," Samuels continued as he turned back to face Nate, "is that you failed before you even began. You came here to save Colonel Andrews, but Colonel Andrews is not here. He died five years ago. You were just telling us that you were there. What you see in the bed," Samuels added without bothering to look in Tim's direction, "is a piece of well-funded government property. One into which, I might add, I've put a great deal of time and energy. I will not let you destroy what I've built. You will not take what is mine," he added with a low growl as he leaned in close to Nate's ear to add, "And he *is* mine."

Nate's face turned bright red and twisted with rage as he erupted violently. The MP's grabbed him by the arms and dragged him, literally kicking and screaming, into the corridor, down the hall, and out of the ward. Samuels waited for Nate's protests to fade before he moved to the end of Tim's bed while Tim just stared at the empty doorway. Nurse Marcum rushed over to check the monitors.

"What should we do now?" she asked as she checked Tim's leads. "He knew too much to have just used a letter from some dead woman. He came in here like he owned the place. How did he even know we were here? It's not like we're in the DOD Directory. We have to have a leak. And I think it's safe to say the patient had another recall event. This will set us back months. Someone inside had to have helped," she reiterated insistently.

Samuels didn't answer, instead looking over to the screen and the letter still displayed on it. Moving around the bed, he reached out and plucked the yellowing page off the surface with his long, knobby fingers. His scowl deepened as he read the letter more thoroughly and looked at Tim when he finished. Tim just continued to lie there, staring at the door, and sobbing tearlessly.

"Let's not sell the man short, Major," he finally said after a long silence. "Our over-zealous friend was a member of an elite Special Forces unit, and he had access to all the information he needed to find this place, even without this," he added, waving the letter. "This was just the nudge he needed to get started, and it presents an unexpected complication. I think Phase Three has run its full course. It's time to move the Beta Project to the Phase Four facility. And while a leak seems unlikely, we shouldn't risk it. We wouldn't want any further interruptions, would we? I think we can afford to purge this site. Begin the preparations right away."

Nurse Marcum nodded and started back toward the door. Samuels, without looking at her added, "Oh, and Major, I'm extremely disappointed. I expect you'll take care of everything and oversee it personally so that nothing else goes awry. Am I being clear?"

"Y-Y-Yes, my Lord," she replied, a slight quiver in her previously stern voice. "I'll take care of it all myself." Without another word, she hurried out of the room, her shoes clicking desperately into the distance until they faded out of earshot.

Tim still stared at the doorway, lost in his thoughts. He hadn't paid much attention to the exchange between Samuels and Nurse Marcum, so he didn't even blink as she rushed out of the room.

Samuels moved back around to stand in Tim's line of sight while he folded the letter and put it into his pocket.

"I am sorry that Commander Lange disturbed your rest, Beta 3. Don't worry, though. Tomorrow, this will all have been just a bad dream. Maybe not even that. You can rest easy now, your past will never come back to haunt you again." Samuels said with a wicked grin.

Tim closed his eyes as Samuels moved out of the room and turned off the lights. He wanted to cry, but that part of him didn't work anymore.

Old age is not so fiery as youth,
but when once provoked cannot be appeased.
- Thomas Fuller

Chapter 4

Two years had passed since the horrifying event at the small medical research laboratory in Arlington, Virginia. It was widely reported that a Naval officer broke into the complex after being paid by a foreign power to sabotage a project there. One of the pathogens they were attempting to isolate was released during the break-in, and only the infiltrating officer escaped alive. The man was captured at the scene, but any physical evidence of his sabotage was destroyed when the site was purged to protect the public. He was court martialed, but there wasn't enough evidence to convict him of any crime more than abusing his clearance. He was retired without ceremony and disappeared from the public eye.

Far to the south, an old man who once knew that Naval officer slept in a well-appointed but modest bedroom, his only sleeping companion a large shaggy dog. Drake paid little attention to the story when it was in the news, but he made some calls to some important friends. He was owed enough favors that when he asked for something, which wasn't often, it was usually given. Keeping Nate Lange out of prison, though, took all his clout. But that didn't matter to him. The truth mattered.

Drake was around long enough to recognize a lie when he saw one, and the story about Nate's alleged espionage was more obvious than most. But it happened just before Finals Week, so he didn't pay it the attention it was due. Once he knew Nate wouldn't be sent to prison, or worse, he was satisfied. He had enough on his mind as it was. He didn't want reminded of old times.

If he was asked, Drake would have said he was fine, but anyone around him often knew he wasn't getting enough sleep. What they couldn't know, and what he wouldn't tell anyone, was the reason why. Every time he closed his eyes for more than a few minutes, he would have nightmares. One nightmare, actually; the same one on endless loop.

Drake was a lucid dreamer, so nightmares weren't something he'd dealt with since he was a child. More unusual than the nightmare itself was the fact that Drake was unable to escape it. Normally, he could navigate his way out of any dream he didn't like, but not this one. So, to avoid the dream, he avoided sleep. He could sleep when he was dead, he assured himself. Merlin, his furry cohort, disagreed with that sentiment, and slept enough for both of them.

Drake wore his age well, though he was much older than he appeared. He would often quip, "I'm old, and it's not the years, it's the mileage," though he didn't deny that he was well past middle age. Despite this, he wore his years like most people wear a coat, shrugging them off whenever it was inconvenient. He had a well-earned reputation for being able to go from doddering fogey to man of action in the blink of an eye.

RING-RING-RING

Drake opened a single, groggy eye and scanned the nearby nightstand for his alarm clock. The pale phosphorescent glow of the hands told him that it was either 2:20 or 4:30, neither being reasonable hours for a phone call. Somewhere in the back of his mind, he remembered that it was Rush Week, and he was often the target of prank phone calls from hopeful pledges. That was enough reason for him not to pick up.

RING-RING-RING-RING

Of course, it might not have been a pledge. Drake was notoriously unpopular among the first-year students, likely because his Paranormal Studies 101 class was a requirement, regardless of a student's major. While they didn't need to pass the class, and Drake didn't teach all the classes himself, he was nevertheless blamed for more than one ruined GPA. Drake, for his part, didn't see failure as a character flaw, and instead encouraged his students to learn from the process.

Failure was a common occurrence. So much so that there was a long-standing rumor that if you aced the exam, you'd get a free pass on all your other classes. It wasn't true, of course, but it was widely believed. In consolation, Drake offered a free dinner to anyone who did. After all these years, only one student had received the honor, and she was quite special.

RING-RING-RING

The phone was getting harder to ignore. Drake reached over and pulled the other pillow over his head, trying in vain to muffle the annoying noise. The old Western Electric telephone was a classic desktop model, the kind with a real metal bell inside. A bell that was suddenly more of a nuisance than it was worth, at least as far as Merlin was concerned. The sleepy dog lifted his head and whimpered disapprovingly at his bedmate.

Drake scowled in reply. "The bloody phone can ring itself into oblivion for all I care. I won't give them the satisfaction!" Merlin barked a weary, but angry retort before he hopped off the bed and plodded slowly out of the room. On his way out, he grabbed a short piece of rope tied to the handle and pulled the door closed with a soft and annoyed growl. He'd find his repose elsewhere.

RING-RING-RING-RING-RING

Drake was now cursing the persistent caller. Even under the best circumstances, it didn't take much to test Drake's patience. Anyone who had him as a professor could verify that fact. As he hid under the pillow, he wondered what sort of savage would let a phone ring so many times, particularly at that hour. He added a second round of expletives aimed at himself for not having an answering service or voice mail like everyone else. In fact, he was questioning the intelligence of having a phone in the bedroom in the first place.

RING-RING-RING-RING

Thirty-three rings was his limit. Either this was the most determined prankster in college history, or the call was legitimately important. He couldn't think of anything *that* important. At least nothing that couldn't wait until coffee was brewing. So, he erred on the side of 'prankster.' There was only one way to know for sure.

Drake tossed aside his blankets, slid into his slippers, and shuffled sleepily over to the desk where the phone was still ringing relentlessly. Picking up the handset silenced the infernal bell, which was intensely satisfying. Drake considered placing the receiver down on the desk and going back to sleep. But only for a moment.

Drake regarded the handset with disgust, sighed, and held it up to his ear. He prepared to give the caller a piece of his mind, something which was considerably more than most could handle. He cleared his throat, ready to unleash his righteous, drowsy fury. He didn't even give the caller the honor of a greeting.

"Listen, I don't care who you are. I don't even care what time it is. Since I can't smell the divine scent of my morning coffee wafting into my bedroom, I know it's not a decent hour for phone calls!" Drake exclaimed. "I'll have you know you interrupted a very pleasant dream where I was being attended by scantily-clad, large-breasted women. So, you have exactly fifteen seconds to tell me what's so bloody important!"

Drake often used tactics like this to scare off potential pranksters. No one wanted to think about Drake in any state of undress, and most were too embarrassed to mention it to anyone else. He found it effective against telemarketers as well. He hoped the caller would be shamed into hanging up. That would at least allow him to struggle for a bit more rest. He waited impatiently for the tell-tale CLICK in the receiver which would signal his success, but it didn't come. Drake was in no way prepared for what happened next.

"Yes, Doctor Sullivan, I know it's very early in the morning, and I apologize for interrupting your, ahh…," the female caller paused, clearing her throat before continuing, "rest. However, this call is to inform you that a Code Grey event has happend, and your services are needed and have been requested at the *highest* level."

Drake's stomach fell to his feet when he heard the distinctly feminine voice in his ear. He could be as crass as the next person, even rude when he felt he needed to be, but he always considered himself a gentleman. He was so taken aback and disappointed with himself he barely registered what she said. He was too busy trying to come up with an adequate apology.

"Doctor Sullivan, I said there was a Code Grey. I need your response, please," the caller pressed impatiently.

Brought to his senses, Drake replied sheepishly, "Oh yes, of course. The Raven will fly."

"Thank you, Dr. Sullivan, Since the need is immediate, I've taken the liberty of sending a car to pick you up. It should arrive in…," she paused, checking the time, "about fifteen minutes."

Drake had been a consultant with the U.S. Government on paranormal events for some time, but there hadn't been a Code Grey called in seven years. He tucked the handset against his ear with his shoulder and walked over to the nightstand, then grabbed his glasses and cleared the gunk from his eyes before putting them on.

"As I've gotten the 'make an ass out of myself' portion of my day out of the way," Drake attempted what he knew was an insufficient apology, "can you tell me anything more? I'm hardly on the first-call list, these days. What I mean to say is, am I truly needed, and if so, was it so important that it couldn't wait for a later hour? I'll barely have time to pack. You see, I don't keep a suitcase ready anymore…"

"Dr. Sullivan, I assure you that no one would want to bring you on-site unless it was absolutely necessary. You'll have to trust me when I say that this requires your full, immediate, and *local* attention. I've told you all I can on an unsecured line, Doctor, so if you don't mind, I have other things to do this morning," she curtly concluded. Drake heard the caller's impatience in her tone, showing that both his apology and attempted recusal fell short.

Drake didn't appreciate being brushed off by anyone, though, even if he deserved it. "I'll have you know, I am still a man of some importance, and I have responsibilities. There are arrangements to make, classes to reschedule, proctors to assign; who's going to take care of my dog?" Drake asked urgently, irritated that someone thought he would drop everything and leave at a moment's notice.

With a sigh that could sever a steel cable, the caller showed she had moved from impatience to annoyance. "I promise, Doctor, that everything will be taken care of," she replied sharply. "We've already notified the University administration, and they're making arrangements to cover your upcoming classes. We also have someone coming to watch your home and take care of your dog. It's all been arranged. Like usual."

Drake wanted to protest, but he couldn't. This woman knew exactly how to handle him, and it had him off his footing. He knew how important a Code Grey was, and that he'd be needed, he just didn't care for having his presence demanded. He would have preferred to have been asked, not ordered about like a common lackey. Despite this, all he could muster in reply was a dry, "Is that all?"

"Oh yes, I nearly forgot," the caller added spryly. "Dress for cold weather; you won't have a chance to change before departure. And pack lightly. We'll have cold-weather gear on-site for you since you won't have time to gather your own. Once you arrive, make a list of things you'll need, and we'll make sure you get them. Safe travels, Dr. Sullivan."

Without another word, the mysterious caller hung up, leaving Drake dumbfounded as he held the receiver and stared into the distance. After a few moments, the line reset, and the sound of the dial tone roused him from his trance-like state. He hung up the phone, turned around and stood with a hand on his hip, pondering what just transpired.

"Dress for cold weather?" Drake asked himself. "It's late August. Where the hell are they sending me?"

The act of contemplation then created the thing contemplated.
- Isaac D'Israeli

Chapter 5

Drake sat in the back of the inconspicuous black sedan and stared out the window silently. At that moment, he sped toward an unknown destination, though a short twenty-five minutes earlier, he was still in his nightclothes frantically packing. Drake drummed his fingers on the armrest of the door, nervously watching as the world sped by. He hated feeling rushed; rushing upset his stomach, and the Code Grey had him unsettled enough.

Drake was a calculating man, one who chose his actions carefully, even if he wasn't so mindful with his words. Most people would say he was too slow, that he spent an inordinate amount of time mulling over possibilities before he acted. But once his mind was made up, there was no doubt the decision was the right one. At least to him.

Everything about this situation moved too fast for his liking, and he needed to slow things down. In his considerable experience, when things were rushed, it meant someone didn't want people looking too carefully. That was never a good thing. He made a mental note to quickly figure out who it was.

More than that, it was all a bit too cliché for Drake. A random phone call in the wee hours, a mystery caller who used code words and gave secret instructions, and now an unmarked government car traveling at breakneck speed to an undisclosed location. He was sure he'd seen this movie before, and he hated it.

It occurred to Drake that his anxiety was as likely caused by his third cup of coffee than any mysterious conspiracy. All traces of his earlier grogginess were gone, but his mood hadn't improved. Initially, the driver resisted Drake's request to stop, but Drake insisted and had, in fact, already called the order in so it would be ready. The driver relented, and when Drake returned to the car with a tray full of large coffees, the driver reached for one. Drake pulled the tray away.

"If you wanted one, you should have gone in," he scoffed.

The driver frowned, reached over, and took one anyway. Drake thought of rebuking the theft, but his driver's stern look discouraged any argument. "You're welcome," Drake said quietly through gritted teeth. The drive was rather quiet after that, so Drake was left with his caffeine-fueled thoughts. He decided he would use the time productively.

Everything up to this point indicated Drake was heading into something frightening and unprecedented, and it had happened recently enough it hadn't made it into the news. Code Grey events, by their nature, were massive and difficult to manage. Usually, these were more about damage control and mitigation. The cover-ups came later. That's what happened in Cincinnati.

Out of habit, Drake looked to his left where Merlin would normally have been. Drake didn't like to leave him behind, but the driver was adamant that Merlin wasn't invited. Drake didn't press the issue, and he was glad he hadn't. Things were tense enough, despite him feeling Merlin's presence reassuring. This was the first time in ages that they would be apart more than a day.

Drake looked back out the window and shifted awkwardly in the seat. With his thermals, heavy flannel shirt, and down parka, he sweltered in the late summer heat. The hot coffee didn't help either. He was certain that the young lady at the coffee shop thought he was insane, considering when he'd stopped, it was already a muggy eighty-one degrees. He thought that maybe the whole thing might be a joke at his expense, but he wasn't comfortable with the idea of being in the Antarctic wearing nothing but linen. He hated being wrong more than he hated looking foolish.

Unable to take the deafening silence any longer, Drake decided to try to get more information from his only source. the surly driver. He was beside himself with boredom and he thought talking might help stifle his anxiety. While Drake was usually seen as a contrary person, he often found himself in conversations he didn't start, with people who hadn't intended to talk to him; it was something he used to his advantage.

"Well then, Sergeant…," Drake piped up before he paused in embarrassment. "I don't think I caught your name, actually," he said with a sheepish smile.

"The coat says De Loach, Dr. Sullivan," came the terse reply. The driver didn't even bother taking his eyes off the road. It seemed that the incident with the coffee hadn't done Drake any favors.

"I see," Drake replied apologetically. "Sorry about that. Well then, Sgt. De Loach, where are you from? How long have you served?" Drake inquired. He hoped to break the rather thick ice between them. There was no reply.

Undaunted, Drake cleared his throat and continued, "Fair enough. Maybe help a bloke out, let me know where we're heading?" Drake was doing his best to mask how perturbed he was. Again, there was no reply from the front seat, which just irritated Drake further. He was not someone who was used to being ignored.

"Listen, Sergeant, can you at least tell me why I'm dressed like an Arctic whale hunter?" Drake asked desperately. He felt like this was a more-than-reasonable question and one he deserved an answer to.

Sgt. De Loach sighed heavily as he looked in the rear-view mirror. "I'm sorry, Dr. Sullivan. I don't have any other information for you. I was ordered to secure transport and to bring you to the base, and that's what I'm doing. As for your final destination, that's above my pay grade. I assume you're heading somewhere cold," he added with a forced smile, finishing with an obligatory, "sir."

Drake slumped back into the seat, defeated. To say he was disappointed was a massive understatement. He was positive that this man had been hand-picked because he hated talking. He knew he shouldn't be upset, and his behavior had been something less than admirable. He was starting to feel ashamed. It seemed he wasn't done making an ass out of himself after all.

With no alternative left, Drake milled over what little information he had. His thoughts wandered to the Code Grey, and he wondered what could have happened to prompt such a response. A Code Grey meant that something phenomenal, paranormal, peculiar, and perilous had occurred, and it was Drake's misfortune that no one understood *phenomenal, paranormal, peculiar, and perilous* better than he did. No one ever had and no one ever would.

Drake didn't flaunt his knowledge or use it as a bludgeon. He didn't need to. He enjoyed educating people about the things he knew, and if they weren't interested, he didn't force it unless lives were at stake. Certain information, though, he kept to himself and only shared when absolutely necessary. He understood a simple, basic truth better than most people; some things were best left forgotten.

Drake's position as the Dean of the College of Paranormal Arts and Sciences at Duke University made him the paramount authority in his field. It also meant he was the primary source of information on anything that fell outside the purview of traditional science. Centuries of fear and superstition, however, often led to Drake not being taken seriously.

Even after the Awakening, when the unexplained and paranormal became more common. Especially after the Awakening. History was filled with charlatans and con men who claimed to have powers beyond those of mortal men. It didn't help when they started to actually have them. The distrust and paranoia had grown into fanaticism and persecution.

That's how he came to find himself in that car, traveling to who-knows-where. The first and most important Code Grey was commonly referred to as the Cincinnati Incident. At least that's what most people called it. It was what made the government take the Awakening seriously and forced the set-up of the Code system. After that, Drake's services were in higher demand, particularly with foreign governments that had no one with Drake's experience to rely on. They all knew what was going on, the dangers these incidents posed, and that they were wholly unprepared to deal with them. And when they didn't, Drake made sure they did. He could be incredibly persuasive when needed, and more than a little intimidating.

On the home front, it helped that one of Drake's early protégés worked for the government. He recommended from the beginning that no one was better suited to help sort everything out than Dr. Drake Sullivan. He was even given an official title: Special Advisor to the President on Paranormal Events. That's why everyone at the White House called him "sappy." Just not to his face.

Notwithstanding his current attitude, Drake enjoyed his extra-curricular work. It gave him immense satisfaction to help people understand how the world was changing. Most of that work was dispelling rumors and superstitions that surrounded the Awakened. Witches, freaks, monsters, abominations: these were the nicest of the names they were called. Drake was the first to call them *Awakened*, and he had the clout and visibility to make it stick.

The Awakened started to become more and more common, as were the accidents and occurrences they invariably caused. Since

Cincinnati, there had been ten Code Blacks, and about two dozen or so Code Reds, all involving newly Awakened individuals, and they all needed Drake's help. That didn't even cover the nearly countless Orange, Yellow, and White events he also consulted on. It had been a very busy seven years, though things had slowed down considerably in the past year or so, though not because there were fewer people Awakening.

Drake pushed back in the seat and rubbed his temples to alleviate the looming headache before it set in. Being overheated seemed to make it worse. He leaned his head back into the headrest and closed his eyes, rifling through the file cabinet of his mind. Memories were almost always a comfort for Drake, though today that comfort was fleeting.

Drake looked over again to the empty seat to his left, feeling more alone than ever. This time, he wasn't thinking of Merlin. Instead, he was remembering that rather special young woman who aced his exams all those years ago. The only one to win the dinner. Claire Thibodeaux was the reason why he wanted to help so many people. He failed her, and he vowed never to fail anyone again.

Drake was so deep in his self-reflection he hadn't noticed the car stopped. It wasn't until he heard the abrupt slam of the driver's door that he came to his senses and looked around. He could hear Sergeant De Loach talking to someone, and he patiently waited for his door to open. He heard the trunk lift, then he could feel someone rummaging around in the space behind his seat. But the commotion stopped, and the conversation faded. Drake peered out the back through the small gap left by the open trunk and saw Sgt. De Loach walking away from the car with another airman.

Irritated by the continued lack of courtesy, and more so by the fact that he brought it on himself, Drake threw open the car door and exited. Instantly, he was slammed with a wave of hot, humid air which fogged his glasses; the feeling was so abrupt that Drake lost his breath. Looking out over the tops of his frames as he gasped, Drake looked for the person he expected to greet him. He was alone except for a distant ground crew that prepped a large helicopter.

Sgt. De Loach turned and shouted back to Drake as he pointed to the aircraft, "You better hurry, Dr. Sullivan. That's your ride, and they *will* leave without you."

Drake huffed and cursed, mostly at himself, while he pulled his bag from the car. "Where the *hell* are they sending me?"

Chapter 6

The flight from Durham to Fayetteville was faster than Drake expected. He only ever drove between the cities and wondered to himself how much it would cost to fly it regularly instead. He didn't enjoy the trip, though, partly because of the heat—the military helicopter wasn't air-conditioned—and partly because he hated not knowing what was going on. He was concerned because whatever happened couldn't wait an extra hour for him to be driven rather than flown. The whole experience had been overly dramatic from the start, and he wasn't a fan of theatrics…unless they were his.

Before long, the door of the UH-60 opened abruptly, and Drake was escorted out of his seat and onto a bustling tarmac. This airfield was quite a bit busier than the last was, even at this early hour. As the morning sun peeked through the trees on the horizon, Drake winced and hissed a little, like a Victorian monster reeling from the burning rays. His head pounded as the budding ache developed into a full-blown migraine.

Drake gathered himself and did his best to look like he had some idea of what was supposed to be happening. Once again, there was no one to meet him, and he had no idea where to go.

With the morning he was having, Drake was reluctant to seek help, not that there was anyone nearby to ask. So, he stood there, looking like a lost child at the airport.

Just as Drake convinced himself this was all a cruel prank and pondered what a cab ride back to Durham would set him back, he noticed a beautiful young woman approaching. He wondered if she was part of a caffeine-induced hallucination and quickly looked around to see if she might have been walking toward someone else. But he was alone in that part of the flight line. Drake took a moment to compose himself, stood up straight, pulled down the hem of his coat, and ran his hands through his mussed hair before calling out to her.

"Excuse me, young lady," he exclaimed, waving his hand to get her attention. She nodded, acknowledging that she had seen him, and continued walking his way. As she approached, he put on his best smile and turned on whatever remained of his charm.

"My dear, I don't know who looks more out of place here: me for being so old and ridiculously dressed, or you for looking so smart and beautiful," he complimented, still smiling. He was trying his best to hide his mood and discomfort.

Without as much as even a slight grin, the young woman raised an eyebrow, replying curtly, "Wow, Dr. Sullivan, I didn't expect such a warm greeting, especially after how you treated me on the phone earlier."

It took a special kind of person to stun Drake into silence once, let alone twice in the same day, and this woman had done it. For half a second, he considered trying to recover with a snappy retort, but he realized with the way his day was going, it would likely blow up in his face. He decided it was best to keep quiet.

Sensing that she had Drake adequately subdued, the officer introduced herself. "My name is Captain Sarah Heighton, and I will be your handler for the duration of this incident," she said directly, offering her hand formally.

Drake shook her hand and figured now was as good a time for an apology as any. "Young lady, I had no idea…," he began.

Capt. Heighton pulled her hand quickly away, surprising Drake. "Excuse me, Dr. Sullivan, but you can address me by my rank, as 'Captain Heighton,' or by my call sign, which is *Athena*. Calling me 'young lady,' or anything similar, is both disrespectful and patronizing. Not to mention completely inappropriate and unprofessional. Now, if you don't mind, sir, we need to get you boarded. Everyone else has already arrived and is seated. We're just waiting for you."

Even through the noise on the busy flight line, you could have heard a pin drop. Drake hadn't been so thoroughly dressed down in years and he didn't consider defending himself. Besides, a nearby C-130 was starting pre-flight, so continuing the discussion there would have been useless. Drake frowned a little and sighed in resignation, picked up his bags, and followed her with his head down. As he walked, his thoughts drifted to Cincinnati again; this young captain reminded him of a colonel he knew of there. It took a sharp tug on his shoulder to bring him to his senses.

"Please be careful, Dr. Sullivan, you nearly walked right into the…," Capt. Heighton stopped, mid-sentence. "Oh, I see. You weren't given your eye wear," she noted with a slight grin. It seemed that Sgt. De Loach wasn't finished making Drake regret his stinginess.

"Here," she said, offering him a small case, "I always carry an extra pair. I'll have a chat with Sgt. De Loach later. I'm sure he just forgot."

Drake took the case from Sarah's hand and opened it slowly. Inside were a pair of lightly tinted glasses in a modern frame. He looked them over suspiciously and noted that they looked unremarkable, their tint not enough to be protective. He looked at Capt. Heighton confused and opened his mouth to speak, but she raised a hand to stop him.

"Before you say anything, just put them on. They won't hurt you, Dr. Sullivan, I promise," she added with a wry smile.

He set aside his skepticism, realizing that it was his ego fueling it. Reckoning that he couldn't look more foolish than he already did, he put on the glasses as he'd been asked. As the frames settled on his nose, he expected them to be pre-made to his prescription, and was a little disappointed when the world was blurry. But after a moment, the lenses began to adjust themselves, and soon, he could see more clearly than with his own glasses.

Once the world was in focus, Drake looked up and saw why Sarah had grabbed his shoulder. There, not two feet in front of him, was the side of an aircraft he knew wasn't there a moment prior. Not trusting his own senses, Drake gazed out over the top of the frames, then back through the lenses, trying to process what he saw. He even reached out to touch the side, just to make sure he wasn't going mad.

Sarah tried, unsuccessfully, to stifle a chuckle, alerting Drake to how silly he must have looked. She'd seen a dozen or so people use the glasses that morning, but Drake's response was by far the best.

"The lenses are made with a polymer that can be controlled with a slight electric charge. When you put them on, a beam scanned your eye and adjusted the shape to meet your needs. They are also paired to the aircraft, which has a light-scattering skin. Without the glasses, it can't be seen," she proudly explained.

Drake looked over to Capt. Heighton with a deep frown. His fears about the nature of this incident grew rapidly. "This seems a somewhat extreme measure, even for a Code Grey, don't you think, Captain? What the bloody hell are you pulling me into?"

Sarah's smile slid from her face as quickly as it appeared. "I'm sorry for all the cloak-and-dagger, Dr. Sullivan," she offered somewhat apologetically. "I'm going to ask that you believe me when I say this mission is extremely sensitive and urgent, and it's crucial that we get you to the scene as quickly and quietly as possible. You'll be fully briefed once you're aboard."

While Sarah spoke, Drake had put the glasses back on and was investigating the plane. He didn't intend to object; he'd had his fill of being put in his place for the day. He just nodded his understanding and reached out to touch the surface again. He didn't trust technology. It was his opinion that technology made people lazy, and too much of it was designed to be replaced often.

In his mind, simple tools were the best tools. Capt. Heighton saw his continued unease, so she continued with the explanation.

"Well, since you can see it now, allow me to introduce you to the crown jewel of the United States Air Force: the Douglas-Curtiss-Lockheed Mark 16. The official designation is the AC-75 Spectre II, but we call it the Demon. This one was an original protype, configured mostly for carrying pax and cargo, though it can still hold its own in a fight. The production models are a bit smaller and are going into service later this year. We could have really used these a few years ago," she lamented, looking at the jet almost reverently, her voice trailed off a bit before she continued.

"What you're seeing here is still highly classified, Dr. Sullivan, and despite being ready for service, it still doesn't exist on paper," Sarah said directly while Drake looked on with a mix of awe and fear.

"While it's unusual for the Air Force to use a prototype in service, we saw an opportunity with this advanced technology. Especially since we don't have any other supersonic, covert aircraft designed for transport," she concluded.

Drake, listening intently, hung on every word. But something raised the hairs on the back of his neck. It took him a bit, but he settled on it being the *Demon* moniker that he found off-putting. Most American aircraft were named after altruistic concepts, weapons, powerful animals, or birds of prey: things like daggers, sabers, mustangs, thunderbolts, and falcons. Sarah noticed Drake's continued disquiet, but they were already behind schedule.

"If everything is satisfactory, Dr. Sullivan, I need to get you boarded. We're running late," she mentioned, extending her arm toward the front.

Drake, still ruminating on the source of his unease, and reserved from his earlier behavior, simply replied with a quiet, "Yes, of course."

The pair walked toward the nose until Sarah motioned for Drake to stop. She raised her right hand as if she were going to touch the fuselage, but instead, a holographic keyboard appeared out of thin air. She tapped out a long sequence, which then elicited the familiar hiss of the pressure seal on the door breaking. As the hatch opened and the stairs lowered, Drake grabbed his bags and climbed the stairs. Suddenly, out of nowhere, he stopped short and turned toward Sarah.

"Just one last thing, if I may?" Drake asked rhetorically. "Why Demon? It seems decidedly…well, un-American, if I'm being frank. You lot tend to be the holy-roller types. It's just so atypical."

Sarah smirked a little, muttering under her breath about losing a bet. "We had an over/under on how long it would take you to notice," she said wryly. "Secretary Blake bet me ten dollars that you'd notice before you boarded. He knew it was right up your alley," she quipped. "You're right, it *is* unusual, but so is the aircraft. When the commander of the original test crew saw the designs, he noticed that the abbreviated designation from the design firm was DCL-XVI…"

Drake's eyes widened noticeably as he exclaimed, "You can't be serious!"

"That's almost exactly what the colonel said," Sarah laughed. He noticed at once that it was six hundred sixty-six in Roman numerals. It wasn't intentional, of course, but there it was, in blue and white. And once he mentioned it, it was all we could talk about," she smiled at the recollection. "Anyway, since these were intended to replace the aging out C-130's, they had already settled on officially calling them *Spectre II*, but the colonel and the rest of us continued to call it the *Demon*. The name stuck, just like with the *Warthog*," she whimsically noted.

Drake was dumbfounded and took a moment to reply. "Oh yes, quite right. I can see why you'd do that," he said flatly, still shocked at the revelation. He climbed into the cabin and made his way to his seat. They took off just as the sun was clearing the tops of the buildings, but Drake's stomach was sinking instead.

He no longer cared where he was being taken, and he barely paid attention during the in-flight briefing. He knew many of the other passengers, mostly from their work, or having consulted with them in the past. All of them were renowned experts in their particular fields, but he knew none of them held the answer to whatever caused the Code Grey. He'd never felt as alone as he did on that flight. He berated himself silently, and not for the last time, for answering the phone in the first place.

> Power is not a means; it is an end.
> One does not establish a dictatorship in order to safeguard a revolution;
> one makes a revolution to establish the dictatorship.
> *- George Orwell*

Chapter 7

After what felt like a day of endless and meaningless meetings, Drake settled in for what was bound to be a fitful sleep. The briefings convinced him that whatever happened did indeed require his full and undivided attention, but the overt military presence only made him more anxious. He knew that the military's involvement would only stifle his ability to help in the ways he was best suited. It also meant that he wouldn't be able to prepare properly for whatever came next, and Drake was a man who *needed* to be prepared.

Halfway around the world, a man who also had a fitful sleep watched the sun rise. To the casual observer, these men might have appeared to be quite similar, though they both would have taken exception with the comparison. However, they both spent most of their time alone, did so in lovely, though austere surroundings, and mentally mapped every outcome of an action before committing. And neither of them was quite the man they appeared to be.

Where they were different were in the ways that truly mattered. Drake might be easy to annoy, and could appear irritable or arrogant, but he was compassionate and slow to anger. He was filled with a basic desire to help people and understood that patience worked far better at getting what he wanted than antagonism and ego. Put another way, Drake understood the value of other people, even when he knew more than they.

This other man, though, was quite the opposite. While he held the outward appearance of being calm and introspective, he was quick to anger and held on to his rage like a child would their favorite toy. He would spend weeks planning and implementing his vengeance, seeking the most damaging and destructive ways to exact his pound of flesh. He measured people by how much they could give him, or rather how much he could take. He knew he was better than other people, and he made sure they knew it too.

They were similar, yes, but they couldn't be more different.

The man watching the dawn was Ying Qi, and he held absolute power over a quarter of the world's population. After he appeared on the world stage two decades earlier, he claimed the long-vacant Imperial Throne of China. It was like something out of a movie: the unknown orphan raised by monks secretly being the king. Only it was real.

At the time, no one took his claim seriously. According to the Communist Party, the Chinese people didn't need an Emperor, nor did they want one. There were repeated attempts to arrest him, but all invariably failed. The efforts were halted when the arresting agents and officers stopped returning. After that, it was decided that a less direct approach was needed, so they worked to counter his claims using the state-controlled media.

The rest of the world had their own opinions, as expected, but they were driven by corporate news sites which were more interested in clicks and views than in the truth. American outlets speculated that he would establish a new government based on the principles of Kung-Fu. Following suit, the BBC had taken to calling Ying Qi by the moniker, *The Quiet Monk*, both for his political naïveté, and his unusual background. It wasn't long before the name stuck, and internet searches for "quiet monk" and "kung-fu emperor" far outpaced those for Ying Qi's actual name. His opponents tried to use it against him, but it only amplified his image as a man of the people.

Ying Qi had successfully made himself out to be a different kind of leader; a leader who was compassionate, present, soft-spoken, humble, and wise beyond his years. He commanded respect, not from the threat of force or violence, but because of his patience and willingness to listen. Unlike his Communist adversaries, he made no attempt to counter the media's characterizations of him. In fact, he avoided consuming news through the media altogether and didn't use them to spread his message. He preferred interacting directly to the masses.

It worked. The Chinese people responded to his tactics and messaging and fervently accepted his leadership. Reports from local gatherings—what few there were since media were turned away—noted that his charisma was "surely akin to that of Jesus of Nazareth" and "inspiring in a way not seen since Caesar." When asked, the locals said that he brought joy, pride, and happiness long dormant in their homeland.

The Communists, who feared the loss of their power, panicked at the prospect of an open revolt. They did everything in their power to diminish his appeal, even reaching out to their global rivals for help. But after decades of state-controlled media telling them the West was wicked, the people of China saw their government's actions as a betrayal. They lacked faith in the Communists and their words, and no threats from the Party could change that.

One short year after he debuted on the public stage, despite all predictions and expectations, and without a single shot fired, Ying Qi assumed control of the most populous country in the world. As bloodless coups went, this was probably the fastest and smoothest in history. Overnight, the political landscape of the entire world changed. Unlike his Communist predecessors, Ying Qi didn't execute or imprison his opponents. Instead, he offered them the opportunity to continue working in their posts, provided they publicly acknowledged him as their Emperor. All of them did; every last one of them.

Initially, it seemed that this change could only be a positive one. China had long stood as an adversary in the world economy, choosing to steal ideas and rebrand them instead of opening trade. People were oppressed, and China's attitude toward the rest of the world was undeniably combative. World financial markets rallied even at the chance that Ying Qi would lift the trade barriers and end decades of humanitarian crisis.

It didn't take long for that optimism to fade, though. It quickly became clear that the new Emperor had other plans. One month after taking power, the new government of China released an official statement to every member country of the United Nations and every major world media outlet. It read:

> Effective immediately: the People's Republic of China is hereby dissolved, and control of all government facilities and processes have been assumed by His Imperial Majesty, Third Emperor of the Qin Dynasty, Son of Heaven, Lord of Ten Thousand Years, Qin Tian Zi. To restore stability and peace to a region still tense from decades of conflict and oppression, we regret to inform you that the government of China is discontinuing formal relations and trade with any country with which we do not share a common border. Once we have established productive relations with our neighbors, we will again take our place at the world table.

With his first official act of diplomacy, Ying Qi, addressed by the formal name of his office, became the most powerful man in the world. He didn't just pull China from the U.N., which would have been disruptive enough on its own. No, he pulled China into severe isolationism the likes of which hadn't been seen in centuries. No trade, no communication, nothing in or out of China except to its immediate neighbors. Even then, nothing passed through them to the rest of the world. Chaos ensued.

The financial markets that had risen to dizzying heights came crashing down just as quickly. Overnight, the United States, Japan, Great Britain, Russia, and the European Union were brought to the brink of financial ruin. Within a week, a world-wide economic depression was settling in, a crisis the world was still recovering from. Worse still, China owned a great deal of the US's debt in the form of bonds; bonds the new government cashed in. America was crippled. It had taken Ying Qi a short forty-five days to do what the Communist Soviets and Chinese hadn't been able to in nearly a century: bring the West to its knees. By isolating China, he had ensured that no one could ignore China.

Any hope things would go back to the way they were, or even that the situation would improve, were dashed in short order. After a decade absent from international affairs, it seemed that Ying Qi had no intention of opening China to the world. More surprising, it was revealed that the Chinese people themselves demanded and welcomed the continued isolation. This presented a whole other issue, one more difficult to address.

As soon as the Americans realized China wasn't going to resume relations, they started working to force a change in regime. They were well-practiced at this as they'd been doing it with some success since the 1940's. But those efforts relied on the participation of disillusioned locals, something they weren't going to find in China. Any hope of inspiring another revolution was crushed. Without local help, there was no hope of destabilizing the regime.

Other conventional avenues similarly failed. Diplomatic envoys were invariably turned away. Attempts to use third parties also failed; China's neighbors had either closed their borders or refused to act as liaisons. Even emissaries who were Chinese expatriates were denied entry. Because of this, the Americans and their allies tried to use covert means to get what they wanted. Those also proved equally fruitless.

China became an informational black hole. Making matters worse, Ying Qi was extending his influence beyond China, reuniting nations that had been traditionally subject to, or directly under Imperial Chinese rule. The first to succumb was Tibet, which had resisted Communist Chinese governance from the start. In a stunning turn, the people of Tibet asked to join the Empire. Mongolia was next, followed soon after by Korea, which had set aside decades of hostility to reunify and join China together. It was like watching Nazi Germany steamroll over Europe, except this time, the invaders were welcomed with open arms and cheers.

Despite all of this, the U.S. Government continued to try to get any information it could about what was happening behind what they called the Silk Curtain. But, as before, each attempt was unsuccessful, sometimes spectacularly. In the years since Ying Qi assumed power, twenty men had been sent into China covertly. Of those, only one returned. It was this level of unprecedented failure, and the anxiety it fueled, that led the Americans to get creative.

That's how Claire Thibodeaux became a government asset, and why she was important enough for a Special Forces team to protect her. She sent a letter by courier to the childhood home of the Director of the CIA that had been dated ten years prior. That was an attention grabber on its own. Aside from putting Claire on a watch list, it wasn't paid much mind until the final mission into China failed. The letter described—in exact detail—everything about the mission, including who was in the situation room and the name of the surviving agent. The Director became an immediate believer.

Claire's involvement changed everything. Up until then, the stories coming out of China were eerily identical. At the start of his reign, Ying Qi allowed anyone who wanted to leave the opportunity to. Most were people who had family abroad they wouldn't be able to see again. Even *they* still referred to Ying Qi reverently by his preferred honorific, *Wànsuìyé*, Lord of Ten Thousand Years. In fact, they refused to say anything negative about Ying Qi, even casually or when prompted to read something prepared by someone else. There was an unwavering loyalty to him that was unlike anything ever documented. It was the first "mass loyalty" event.

It was hoped that Claire's unique skills would give an answer to the question everyone was asking: how was Ying Qi able to pull it off? To Claire, the answer was obvious, and she was shocked no one else had thought of it. Ying Qi was one of the Awakened, and an immensely powerful one.

What came next was an insight only she could provide; everything they knew about Ying Qi was, in fact, a lie he planted in their minds. The only nugget of truth, because all lies have them, was that he'd been raised in a monastery. Everything else was a carefully crafted and controlled piece of propaganda created by the most powerful telepath that would likely ever be born. Claire theorized that the reason he preferred large public appearances was that it was easier to control the people if they were close to him. The more people he controlled, the easier it was, and his influence spread like a virus.

Claire also insisted Drake be consulted, and he agreed with her assessment. Ying Qi was likely among the first to be Awakened, making him what Drake called an Apex; an extremely powerful being that was a threat to be taken seriously. He added that it was his opinion that while Claire, who was also an Apex, might be able to give them insight, she wouldn't be able to help them deal with Ying Qi directly. He doubted any one person could.

The Americans shared what they learned with their allies, though they took great pains to keep their source a secret. The Awakened were still regarded with a certain amount of distrust. Besides, psychics had a history that predated the Awakening, and it wasn't flattering. It was assumed Claire's information wouldn't be trusted. It didn't matter, though. Claire had her own contacts, and other governments were doing what the Americans had. And they were all in agreement.

It turned out, though, that knowing the truth wasn't all that helpful. You couldn't save people who didn't want to be saved, and you can't protect against an enemy that can make you think he's a friend. It was the *Red Scare* all over again, but this time, the danger didn't have to be exaggerated or invented.

Claire was convinced that if Ying Qi was powerful enough to directly control the minds of two billion people, and plant a contrived origin story in the rest, he could do things they couldn't even begin to imagine. She used the refugees as an example. They left before Ying Qi was in power and still, they could only view him with reverence and awe. And they hadn't been under his direct influence for years.

The breakthrough they needed appeared in the least likely of places. A Japanese fishing boat in the East China Sea picked up a small dinghy carrying a handful of Chinese and Korean refugees unlike any who had come before. This ragtag group of accidental sailors told horror stories about what was happening behind the Silk Curtain. Apparently, there were thousands of people in China who were immune to Ying Qi's mind-altering powers, and they'd been unseen by Claire for the same reason. These few people were all that managed to escape, but many more still needed help.

The truth was finally clear. Ying Qi ruled China and its annexed territories with an iron fist, and he was hiding the reality of it with the use of his mental powers. Those who were immune, people Drake would later call *Concealed*, knew exactly what was going on, though, and how poor their lives had become under Ying Qi's leadership. To keep them in line, the emperor had created a specialized group of enforcers. They weren't a normal police or military force, but rather monstrous creatures that were more machine than man. They patrolled relentlessly for any signs that Ying Qi's control was anything but complete.

The refugees were doggedly hunted and only escaped by sheer luck. Their stories were all similar: mandatory relocation of millions of people, forced labor with little or no pay, limited access to media and no access to the internet. Even cell phones were forbidden for most citizens. Where other former Chinese nationals referred to China as "mother," and the emperor with unwavering deference, these poor souls called their once-beloved homeland *Èmèng Zǒu Dì Dìfāng*, The Place Where Nightmares Walk.

The American and Japanese governments shared everything they'd learned, but many refused to accept the truth of it. It all sounded so impossible. They argued that the lack of corroboration from other expatriates made it difficult to know which of the conflicting accounts were truthful. Claire grew concerned, especially when her own colleagues doubted the reports or called them outright lies. She realized that Ying Qi discovered what was happening and was altering their perceptions of what they'd seen and heard.

That's when people started dying. First, it was another of Drake's students who was a member of the French government. Then it was a close friend of Claire's that she'd helped through her own private training practice; he worked for the Germans. The refugees told her that it was the work of the *Èmèng shouwèi* – the Nightmares, Ying Qi's enforcement unit. In short order, Claire was the only mentalist involved that wasn't in hiding, being mentally controlled, or dead.

Claire never reported Ying Qi's attempts to pry into her mind. She was talented enough to keep him at bay and even shield those around her. She knew that the only way Ying Qi could attack her this way was to have someone under his influence in her immediate presence. She just didn't know who it would be. She knew, though, that eventually he'd be able to get to her, just not through her mind. She had already seen it. So, while she walked the path to her own demise, she took comfort in knowing it was a path she chose, not him.

Claire was right, of course. Once Ying Qi realized that he couldn't get to her himself, he made sure he had someone on the inside. It wasn't difficult. He only needed that pawn to touch her once, and he would have an unfettered path into her mind. It was a challenge he relished, and one he was certain he would win.

He was so committed to not having his plans ruined by a "meaningless woman" that he didn't notice she was in control. But, in the end, he didn't win, though he thought he had. Claire made sure that everything would happen just the way she wanted, but that meant she had to die first. And die she did.

Chapter 8

Ying Qi, like any high-functioning sociopath, spent his life in pursuit of self-gratification and personal betterment. From an early age, he viewed other people as a means to an end and decided they were better used as tools. People, he reasoned, were unreliable and stupid, and were only useful when he was guiding them directly. He'd always been alone, never knowing the joy and warmth of a loving home.

Ying Qi was born a twin to parents who already had a child, something illegal in China at the time. A compassionate doctor helped hide the pregnancy, and so it was blind luck that brought the future emperor into the world. To keep from rousing suspicion, the doctor took each of the twins to separate places, forging their birth certificates so that their parents would be protected. Ying Qi was taken to the orphanage where the doctor himself had been raised.

The problems began when Ying Qi grew into a toddler. An orphan's life was never easy, but this home was a good place to be by any standards. But he never spoke and had trouble playing with the other children. His awkwardness and isolation later led to him being bullied by his peers, but strangely, the bullying never lasted long. For the most part, the other children avoided him.

When Ying Qi turned six, the children started having nightmares. At first, it seemed incidental and random. One or two children would wake up screaming from an indescribable dream. It wasn't long, though, before everyone started to have the terrifying dreams, or more accurately, the same terrifying dream. And while none of them could recall the details, they all knew Ying Qi was the cause. Weeks of sleepless nights turned into months, and everyone in the home was on edge. The caregivers, normally a gentle and sympathetic group, were driven to the brink of madness by the lack of sleep. And because of their superstition, they began to fear Ying Qi was cursed. When a plot among the staff to murder the young boy was uncovered, something had to be done.

Fearing for Ying Qi's safety, and everyone else's sanity, the beleaguered Administrator took him to a monastery in Tibet that specialized in helping troubled youth. He couldn't have known it at the time, but this was the worst possible place for the tormented young boy. It would become a feeding ground for his psychopathy and would lay the foundation for the doom of a nation.

The monks, for their part, were more than happy to help. They paid little heed to what they saw as the childish fears of an irrational mind. When the Administrator returned to the orphanage, he hoped things would go back to normal. Instead, he locked everyone in their rooms, barred the windows, and burned the building down with everyone inside, including himself. The monks never knew, and Ying Qi settled into his new life.

The monastery offered an organized regimen that perfectly suited the young telepath's need for peace and structure. Early on, the monks discovered that Ying Qi had a talent for learning and understanding new languages. It was another manifestation of his powers, like the projection of his nightmares. From their perspective, he was a prodigy. From his, they were feeble-minded and easy to manipulate. The reality was simple; he was reaching into the minds of his teachers and accessing their knowledge.

By the time Ying Qi was a teenager, his talents were becoming well-known in philological circles. The monastery was flooded with requests from churches, universities, and collectors from all over the world, each looking to decipher the previously undecipherable. The Lama of the monastery, a traditional monk named Jangchup, allowed this unusual contact on the condition that Ying Qi work alone and without meeting those who made the requests. He understood the importance of keeping his young student separated from the outsiders.

This arrangement went on for years, and the Lama allowed himself to believe that Ying Qi and his abilities could be used to help people. Those thoughts ended abruptly the night an old Catholic priest arrived unannounced and unexpected. It was like a scene from an old B-horror movie; as soon as he arrived in the courtyard, wheezing and coughing from the arduous climb, he handed over an ancient manuscript, then died on the spot with a look of utter relief etched on his wizened face. Without the dead courier to tell them, they had no idea what the manuscript was, who sent it, or why.

The item in question was a scroll, written on a strange sort of vellum unlike anything any of them had ever seen. Instead of being written *on* the surface, the script appeared to be *part* of the vellum itself. And while obviously ancient, the words hadn't faded at all. Jangchup might not have known what secrets the scroll concealed, but he knew that it made him feel ill in the pit of his stomach just to be near it. And that was reason enough to keep it away from Ying Qi. Some things were best lost to antiquity, he reasoned.

Jangchup's desire that Ying Qi might use his skills for the betterment of his fellow man was a fool's dream. He didn't understand Ying Qi's abilities, but did recognize the danger his student posed to those around him. He worried that one day soon, he wouldn't be able to stop Ying Qi from turning into the monster he feared he could become. Little did Jangchup know that time had already passed. Besides, nothing the old monk could do would have prevented what happened next.

Ying Qi knew about the scroll's arrival before Jangchup. It took little effort to mentally manipulate one of his fellow students into bringing it to him. He knew at once what it was—a summoning ritual. He knew it would take time for him to gather the knowledge needed to decipher the text fully, but the format was clear. He'd seen it hundreds of times. The script was familiar, but he could only make out a single word that appeared over and over in the text. At first, he thought it was a name, but after some reflection, he realized it was an epithet. The word was *Nadach*, and it meant *Outcast*.

Ying Qi reached out and scoured minds looking for people who might have the knowledge he needed. He didn't care who they were, only what they knew. When he was young, he discovered there was more in people's minds than they could recall, and they often experienced more than they realized. Still, it took months of searching before he found the knowledge necessary to begin translating the scroll. For the young monk, it was time well spent.

Ying Qi learned that the *Nadach* was part of a brotherhood of powerful, extra-Planar creatures that called themselves *Be'elohim*—Children of the Creator. The *Nadach* was apparently cast out of their order for standing opposed to his brethren. In casting him out, they re-ordered the universe in order to condemn their brother to an eternity in isolation. Ying Qi concluded that the ritual contained in the scroll was meant to end that incarceration. He just needed to learn the *Nadach's* true name. Without it, the scroll was useless.

Thus began Ying Qi's obsessive search for a name no one knew; a name so powerful and deplorable, it was utterly erased from the collective human memory. Not one to be deterred, Ying Qi combed through every aged manuscript he could get his hands on. He found nothing, so he began sifting through minds. He ached to discover anything that might lead him to the name of this creature. He reasoned that if all creation was changed just to keep it imprisoned, it must be one of the most powerful in the universe. He also assumed that such a being would be grateful for its release. He just needed to find that elusive name.

Ying Qi relentlessly worked toward his goal. But he didn't sleep enough, and it was catching up to him. It was late, he was tired, and he was careless with the knife he was using to cut a pear. It wasn't a bad cut, but it bled profusely and directly onto the irreplaceable manuscript. Panicked, Ying Qi tried to clean the blood with his sleeve, but it only smeared all over the leathery sheet. He reached over to a pitcher on the nearby table, but when he turned back to the desk, he noticed something happened to the scroll. The blood was illuminating previously invisible script in the margins of the page; script he could easily read.

He dripped more blood around the edges of the scroll, then spread it carefully with his fingers. Whether it was luck, fate, or a conspiracy of the universe, Ying Qi was once again the beneficiary. The notes were written in cuneiform, and the author was kind enough to sign his work; he was an Arab Zoroastrian named Ibrahim ibn Harun al-Rashid. Based on the grammar and syntax of the writings, Ying Qi believed the notes were written in the 17th century, and that the combination of language and script were chosen to limit the number of possible readers.

The notes confirmed Ying Qi's conclusions about the nature of the scroll as a set of specific summoning rituals. They also held other collected observations from long lost scholars whose writings hadn't been available for centuries. The document had changed hands dozens of times, been lost and rediscovered just as many, and was at least three and a half thousand years old. This scroll was never meant to be found, and yet through a series of chance events, all of which needed to happen when they happened,

Ying Qi was holding the most dangerous collection of words ever written.

As the young monk studied further, he learned that Ibrahim himself was trying to summon the *Nadach*. The scholar noted though, that without the true name, any attempt would be doomed to catastrophic failure and kill the summoner. Ibrahim himself never tried because he lacked confidence in the names he'd uncovered. Throughout the margins, names like Ahriman and Iblis were written often, but Ying Qi knew those weren't correct. The *Nadach* was feared, and the name would be treated with reverence.

Ying Qi spent weeks reading over the notes and comparing them against other texts. He poured all of his attention and focus into his work. After months of restless nights, he started to feel that he would never find what he was looking for. Perhaps the true name was lost forever. He lay on his bed and began to meditate. Every word was memorized as was their placement on the scroll. As he rested, his thoughts kept landing on a specific word. "Man" appeared an inordinate number of times, and in an unusual arrangement. At first it didn't seem all that strange, but the more he thought about it, the odder it seemed.

Then an astonishing realization hit Ying Qi. What if the placement of the words meant more than the words themselves? He jumped up and went to the desk, replicating on a nearby piece of parchment the words and their placement so he could see them alone. In Akkadian Cuneiform, the word "man" looked like an arrow, and with the arrangement on the scroll, they all pointed to a specific space in the center. Ying Qi looked back to the document and noticed a deformity on the page where the arrows crossed. Reaching for his knife, he scraped at the vellum until an edge appeared, then used the knife to remove a piece of the scroll. It was a patch that had had been added so long ago, it could no longer be distinguished from the rest of the piece.

Under the patch was something different than the other writing. Letters, branded into the flesh of whatever creature sacrificed its hide for the vellum. Ying Qi let out a laugh that chilled to the bone. In that moment, he knew what it was all for. This scroll wasn't created to summon a creature of immense power. It was created so he could fulfill his destiny.

After his discovery, Ying Qi no longer felt the need to subdue his power or hide what he was. As he asserted his will over the others, first the students, then the older monks, Jangchup's rules became irrelevant. The Lama gathered the oldest and most skilled monks and together they shielded themselves from Ying Qi's mental attacks. They wouldn't, however, be able to fend off the enthralled monks indefinitely. Eventually they were captured and imprisoned but kept alive. The remaining monks recognized Ying Qi as their Lama now, and his will was absolute. This was the unseen beginning of the Silent Monk's rise to power; the dark secret no one knew.

That's when the nightmares began again.

This time, the shared dreams were more intense. Ying Qi's control over his fellow monks was more of a two-way door than he cared to admit, and he could never control who saw his nightmares. They seemed to plague anyone whose mind he touched, even if he wasn't controlling them. As such, Jangchup was the only one not afflicted in the monastery.

As the weeks turned to months, which turned to years, Ying Qi found that fear was as powerful a motivator as telepathy, and that nudging a person down the path he wanted was less taxing than controlling them outright. He hoped that not being directly attached to the others' minds would prevent the nightmares from spreading. He hated the vulnerability that the dreams represented. The monks didn't understand what the nightmares were, nor did they care. They just wanted them to end.

The nightmares had been a mystery to Ying Qi his whole life. Even when he wasn't having them, he always felt them pulling at the corners of his psyche. It felt like he was being led somewhere. Even when he wasn't plagued with the nightmares, they haunted him, and he always knew they would return. They made him feel…incomplete. Like he was missing a piece of himself. He used the monks to begin searching for answers.

Without Jangchup's cooperation, the process took significantly longer than Ying Qi wanted. After considerable effort, the monks discovered the circumstances of Ying Qi's birth, his time at the orphanage, and the fact that he had a twin brother. His name was Li Fong, and he lived in Kowloon in Hong Kong, working for a powerful Tong. Despite that, it was easier than expected to get Li Fong to the monastery for a proper reunion. And with that meeting, the nightmares ended for a time.

By now the monastery was no longer a place of peace and serenity. It was filled with fear, anger, and resentment. It worked for Ying Qi's goals, though, so he fostered the negativity and allowed it to flourish. For more than twenty-five years, he ruled from the monastery, using the isolation to master his abilities, grow his power, and of course, perform the rites on the scroll.

Each morning, Ying Qi kneeled in the pre-dawn darkness, facing east as he meditated and waited for the first rays of the sun to warm his face. Since he assumed the throne, the morning meditations were necessary in order for him to keep control of his subjects. It was a testament to his strength and power that he was able to do this with a minimum of effort. And those he couldn't control he terrorized into submission.

The garden where he performed his morning ritual was always empty. He required solitude and the monks learned to avoid the space altogether. It was well-known that the emperor didn't suffer interruptions, and they should only approach when bidden.

Once, while he was meditating, one of the youngest students came in to tend the garden. He never uttered a word and went about his work as quietly as a church mouse. If it had been anyone else there, he would have gone unnoticed. But Ying Qi noticed. When he was done with his morning meditations, he walked over to the boy, smiled, and ruffled his hair before sending him on his way. That night, the boy's mentor took a knife from the kitchen, gutted his student, then used the same knife to remove every inch of his own skin. He never uttered so much as a whimper, though his eyes were swollen shut from crying. Now, no one enters without permission. Ever. Not even Li Fong.

Such is the power of the *Wànsuìyé*.

Chapter 9

On the side opposite where Ying Qi waited for the morning sun was the entrance to the garden. Next to the wood and stone *páifāng* gate a youthful man fidgeted. Ying Qi didn't need to look to know he was there; he could feel the monk's anxiety at being summoned. It exhilarated him knowing he inspired that level of fear in another person. He could almost smell it and imagined it had the sickly-sweet scent of rancid meat.

Ying Qi's meditation was long over, but he liked letting the tension build. It was the smallest form of manipulation, but it gave him a chance to exercise his authority without exerting himself. He knew the monk wouldn't enter until called; it was the manifestation of years of forced compliance. He wasn't controlling the young man. The monk was just terrified of him. Making them wait was an excellent way to test their obedience.

"Come in, Wu Fan."

The acolyte scrambled into the garden as soon as he was called, keeping his eyes down and looking at the ground. He made his way along the stone path that wound through the garden, taking care not to step off the stones. Deviating from the path was frowned upon and punished severely. Wu Fan stopped about twenty paces from his emperor, fell to his knees, prostrated himself, and waited for permission to speak.

"Good morning, little brother. I understand you requested an audience with your Emperor. Is that correct?" Ying Qi asked without turning away from his eastward vigil.

"*Wànsuìyé*," he paused, the words catching in his throat. Ying Qi grinned slightly at the quiver in Wu Fan's voice. He gave a small mental prod for the monk to continue.

"I come before you, *Wànsuìyé*, as your humble servant. I need to tell you about the disquiet among the *distant* brothers," Wu Fan said as he trembled. He spoke of the monks who still resisted Ying Qi's influence. By this time, Ying Qi knew about the concept of the Concealed, but he didn't know how they came to be, or why so many were at the monastery. They had been a persistent thorn in his side.

Another prod and Wu Fan continued, "They say because you still bless us with your dreams, *Wànsuìyé*, despite us having found Master Li Fong…," Wu Fan paused again, fearful of continuing. This time, though, he restarted without prompting, "they say you have lied to us and are leading us to ruin. They tell us we will never be able to reach enlightenment within the walls of this monastery while…." Wu Fan struggled to finish the sentence, "…while you continue to plague us with your curse. Their words, *Wànsuìyé*, not mine."

The young monk visibly quaked, fearful that being the bearer of this news would end poorly for him. He bit his lip until it bled before he summoned the strength to continue.

"There is talk, *Wànsuìyé*, of them taking the L…," Wu Fan stopped to correct himself, "taking Brother Jangchup from this place to commune with the Dalai Lama in India." Before he could say more, Ying Qi stopped him with a raised hand. He still hadn't bothered to face the frightened monk groveling at his feet. Instead, he turned his attention to a large rosebush at his side. He made Wu Fan wait in his prostrate position before he addressed the concerns the monk raised.

"Thank you for bringing this to my attention, little brother. I know this must have been an exceedingly difficult decision for you," he added. This was a test; he was waiting for the proper response.

"No, my Lord. My life for the *Wànsuìyé*," Wu Fan replied emphatically. This was precisely what he needed to say.

"I'm glad to hear that, Wu Fan," Ying Qi replied with a smile, the test passed. "You have always been loyal to me, and I value loyalty more than anything else. I'm glad to see their disruptive influence hasn't tainted you. The world outside our little temple is quite dangerous, so I'm afraid I can't allow anyone to leave. Especially our beloved Jangchup. You are all my charges, my wards, and I must protect you from the evils that exist in the world. I must keep you all safe." He added in a fatherly tone. "You are my responsibility. *All* of you."

Ying Qi stared at a bee that busied itself around the rosebush. He reached out with his mind to look through the bee's eyes, an indulgence he relished. Bees viewed the world in bits and pieces, each lens capturing a tiny piece which the bee's brain pieced together like a puzzle. And the colors were unimaginably beautiful combinations of greens, blues, violets, and colors there are no names for. Experiencing the world this way was a calming experience, and it was the way he'd honed his skills as a telepath.

After what felt like an eternity to the frightened Wu Fan, the emperor finally looked down at the prone form of the young monk. Ying Qi smiled at Wu Fan softly, though it was a cold, empty smile that chilled the air and hurt the soul. But Wu Fan couldn't see it.

"Someone will need to convince them to stay, of course," Ying Qi noted casually. "You'll do this for me, won't you, little brother?" The question was more rhetorical than it sounded.

Even without looking up, Wu Fan could feel his emperor's eyes upon him. The gaze was powerful and uncomfortable, and it made his skin crawl. He dared not show that discomfort, however. Instead, he focused his attention on the stones directly in front of him.

"*Wànsuìyé*, I don't understand. I am only Wu Fan. I am not great or powerful, like you, my Lord, and I do not possess the skills of Master Li Fong. I would not be able to stop them, and they will not listen to me. Perhaps your American friend would be a wiser choice?" Wu Fan offered hopefully.

Ying Qi furrowed his brow in disappointment as he looked back at the rose with the bee on it. Reaching out gently, he plucked the rose from the bush, then knelt in front of Wu Fan. He addressed the monk but kept his attention on the insect.

"Bees are such fantastic creatures, aren't they, little brother?" Ying Qi asked reverently. Wu Fan knew not to answer. "Did you know the queen of the swarm has complete control over everything that happens in her hive? She knows where all her children are, where they are going, what they are doing. I admire that very much."

"Bees are very efficient, despite their short lives," he continued, still looking at the rose. "They live for their queen and her hive, so they must be. Everything they do, they do for their whole community. When under attack, even the lowliest of them becomes a warrior. And not just to protect their food, or their young; they do it to protect their queen. Do you understand what I'm saying, Wu Fan?"

Ying Qi reached down and lifted Wu Fan's chin with a single finger so that their eyes would meet. When their gazes locked, the young monk felt all his worries and concerns melt away into the recessed of his mind. Nothing mattered but serving Ying Qi's will. A wide smile slid across the young man's face and his quivering ceased.

As Ying Qi rose to his feet, he pulled Wu Fan along as well. A look of sheer elation shone on the younger man's face; he'd never been allowed to stand face-to-face with his emperor. He knew of no other monks who had. It was an honor reserved only for the highest ranking of the inner circle. Deep in Wu Fan's mind, a tiny piece of his psyche revolted at the breach of etiquette and the thought of betraying his brothers. But the euphoria quickly pushed it to the side to be forgotten. Wu Fan had never been so happy.

"You have faith in me, don't you Wu Fan? You know I'm leading us down the correct path, don't you?" Ying Qi asked expectantly.

Wu Fan said nothing; he just nodded fervently. He didn't even realize he wanted to nod. It happened entirely by reflex.

"So, little brother, what would you to do protect me, to protect my vision, to protect our hive? Would you lay down your life, just as this bee would for its queen?" Ying Qi asked hypnotically, a calm force behind his words.

Wu Fan knew that he shouldn't want this, but every contrary thought was immediately pushed out of the way by feelings of loyalty. A tiny voice was telling him to refuse, to run away. It wouldn't have mattered, though, his muscles would have refused to obey. He just nodded and absently bobbed his head like a marionette. Wu Fan was no more. His will was gone, his own desires and sense of self drowned by an unyielding need to obey.

"Good. I'm glad you feel that way, Wu Fan," Ying Qi said, turning his attention back to his new pet. His hold on Wu Fan was absolute and no longer required effort. "I knew I could count on you, little brother. I saw the inner strength in you that you couldn't. Now, you need to make sure the others don't leave the safety of the temple grounds. I provide for them, and they are perfectly safe here. Post yourself in the pass that leads into the valley. I am relying on you to ensure that no one ventures too far from our walls. You may go now."

Wu Fan prostrated himself again, then stood up, kept his head bowed, and walked backward to the gate. He never turned his back to Ying Qi. Once he was in the main courtyard, he turned and broke into a full sprint, heading for the monk's quarters. In his haste, he nearly bowled over Li Fong, who was rounding the corner on his way from the kitchen. The young monk muttered a hurried apology and offered a series of quick bows before he bolted again. Sensing his brother's hand at work, Li Fong allowed the frantic monk to go on his way.

Li Fong was the more physically intimidating of the twins, his life having required the development of his body over his mind. He was more disciplined than his brother; his condition required it. He was as blind as a stone, the result of a ruthless teacher's anger and a lack of timely medical attention. It was that event, though, that Awakened Li Fong and allowed him to discover and hone his own talents.

While Ying Qi could experience the world through the eyes of other creatures, including people, Li Fong could experience the world in a way sighted people, including his brother, couldn't. He could *feel* colors, *smell* shapes, and *taste* emotions. Because of these unique skills, he was perfectly capable of navigating the world without aid. His enhanced senses allowed him to notice things other people couldn't, even his brother.

Beyond those differences, the two were otherwise quite alike and of a mind. They shared a special connection, enhanced by their Awakening. What one felt, the other experienced as if it were happening to him; what one learned, heard, or saw, the other knew as well. Separately these men were a force on their own, but together they were powerful enough to assassinate a heavily guarded foreign government asset on their home soil with utter impunity. This made them beyond dangerous.

Ying Qi was still focused on the bee when Li Fong came to the gateway at the edge of the garden. He stopped, as Wu Fan had, just short of the stones that marked the beginning of the garden path. His brother looked over at him with a smile and bade him enter.

"Good morning, Li Fong," Ying Qi said quietly, trying not to startle his new insect friend. "You were right to send Wu Fan to me. He's always been meek, so the others won't think twice about confronting him in their haste to flee. They need to be taught a lesson in obedience. I need them all here; I need them to complete my task. Especially Jangchup," he added with a grave severity.

Li Fong bowed his head slightly before he replied, "As always, I am at your service, *Huangdi.*" It was taboo to address the Chinese sovereign by his given name, or even by a family honorific. So, Li Fong just called his brother *Emperor.* "I noticed that he left in a hurry. I can still hear him panting in his room. You must have been quite inspirational. Are you certain he can prevent the others from leaving on his own?" Li Fong wasn't questioning his brother's judgement as much as Wu Fan's physical ability. They both knew that Wu Fan wasn't a match for most of the other monks if it came to a fight.

Ying Qi didn't answer right away, instead concentrating his focus on the insect. The bee's movements were becoming less frenetic as it started to walk purposefully from the flower onto

Ying Qi's finger. He dropped the rose and repositioned his hand so that the bee could settle comfortably in his palm.

"Wu Fan will serve his purpose," he finally replied, "as must we all. I am certain that when those errant fools encounter him, they will understand that my will is supreme."

Li Fong could feel his brother's slight frown even if he couldn't see it. He didn't understand why the monks were so important to him, though he knew better than to ask.

"*Huangdi*, surely we could bring people from the province, or one of the larger cities to fill your needs; people who would be more willing to serve you without question. I worry that you expend too much energy trying to break Jangchup and those loyal to him," Li Fong lamented, placing a worried hand on his brother's shoulder, something only he was allowed to do.

Li Fong was the more tactical and pragmatic thinker. While Ying Qi might deliberate on a decision for ages, his actions were often rooted in emotion, which skewed his insight on which solutions were best. Li Fong was a strategic genius, and his thought processes were built on logic and observation, not irrational feelings. His intuition was rarely wrong.

Ying Qi grinned smugly and placed his hand on his brother's. He closed his other hand slowly over the immobile and passive bee, squeezing as tightly as he could until nothing was left. The ill-fated insect didn't even try to move or sting the hand closing around it.

That was all the answer Li Fong needed.

> Real vision demands that we make tough choices.
> Real vision is responsible, and it is paid for.
> *- Michael F. Easley*

Chapter 10

"Good morning, Beta 4. It's zero-six-thirty, and it's time for you to get up."

Tim tried to ignore the voice in his head. After all, he felt like a man his age could rouse himself in the morning without help. He was still in bed because he was exhausted from the previous day's exercises. While he wasn't physically capable of being sore, that didn't prevent him from imagining a familiar ache in his muscles or being mentally worn out. Besides, regardless of his lengthy career in the military, he'd never been a morning person.

"Come on, Beta 4! It's time to rise and shine!" the voice persisted.

Tim continued to feign sleep, though now it was more on principle than anything else. All he wanted was an extra minute or two of rest and he felt he deserved it. It's not as if he could ignore the wake-up call anyway. Someone in a control room somewhere was sending a signal directly into his aural nerve. He could no more ignore it than he could ignore a tack in his shoe. But he wasn't about to let a disembodied voice get the better of him. After all, rank had its privileges, and he was still a colonel, no matter what they said.

"I know you can hear me, Beta 4. I'm afraid if you don't get up, I have orders to appropriately motivate you. That would be unpleasant for us both," the voice prodded with an apologetic tone.

Tim rolled onto his back, opened his eyes, and replied sleepily, "Yeah, yeah, I hear you." He said the words aloud, though he didn't need to. Being able to communicate with only a thought had its drawbacks, and more than once, Tim had let his guard down and inadvertently given his handler an earful. This morning was one of those times.

"Was that really necessary, Beta 4?" came an unexpected and curt reply.

Tim sat up and moved to the edge of his bed, composing himself before he said anything else. "I'm sorry. Listen, I know you don't give a shit, and I don't care what anyone says. I'm still an officer, and I would appreciate being afforded the respect I am due. Especially before I've had my damned coffee. You could at least *try* addressing me by my rank," he gruffly added.

It wasn't the first time he'd said that last part, and he knew it wouldn't be the last. Each time, the result was the same. Tim counted to ten slowly, knowing how long it would take this handler to reply.

"I'm sorry, Beta 4, but you know how the Secretary feels about that. We are only allowed to address you by your callsign, nothing else, regardless of how you, *or we*, feel about it," the handler replied firmly, stressing their own discomfort at the arrangements. "I hate to hassle you, Beta 4, but the Secretary wants the final trials to finish ahead of schedule. Today, if possible. I hope you had a good rest, Beta 4; it's going to be a long day."

"They're all long days," Tim replied, deciding not the press the issue. It wouldn't change anything. The handler's comments weren't lost on him, and he knew they weren't to blame for how things were. He was all too familiar with how Secretary Samuels felt about the Beta Project and his place in it. Feeling a bit guilty for being an ass, Tim added, "I appreciate your concern. I'll be fine. Now, if you don't mind, I'd like some privacy while I shower."

"Of course, Beta 4."

Now that he was alone with his own thoughts, Tim walked over to a glossy black panel on the wall and pressed his hand on it, causing it to flicker to life. "Coffee, sweet, 500 cc's, 65 degrees Celsius.," he said with a practiced familiarity. In just a few moments, there was an electronic beep and a door next to the panel opened, revealing a steaming cup of Tim's morning requirement. Disregarding the temperature, he downed the whole cup in a gulp before heading to the shower.

Tim didn't need to rinse off; he didn't sweat anymore, and without sweat, there was no body odor. His body had its own way of handling any detritus or dirt that might stick to him, but Tim preferred doing things the old-fashioned way. He wanted to hang on to those tiny bits of his humanity, and he was encouraged to do so. Besides, showering was the only time he was alone, something Tim missed a great deal.

After drying off, Tim outfitted himself in his workout fatigues. Standing in front of the mirror, he regarded himself with a critical eye. Tim no longer recognized the man who looked back at him, and he was told he probably never would. He was shown pictures of himself from before the accident, and he knew the person in the mirror was him. But it still felt like he was looking at a stranger through a window. The rehabilitation team promised that he'd eventually get used to it, but he wasn't sure he wanted to. He didn't need to recognize himself in a picture or reflection to know who he was.

The real casualty of the recovery process was his patience, what little he had to begin with. It had never been his strongest suit. He understood that by *any* standard, even the most conservative, his recovery had been nothing short of miraculous. But Tim would never be satisfied with the results, despite having literally come back from the grave. He longed for the life he couldn't have back.

Worse still, his memory had never fully recovered, and he resented that more than anything else. He no longer had the large gaps in his recall. Instead, he would often remember two or more versions of the same event, and he never knew which to believe. Matthew Young, the doctor in charge of this phase of his rehabilitation, tried to help, but Tim had difficulty trusting someone that wouldn't call him by his name.

The nightmares didn't help either. The fact he could dream at all was a surprise to Dr. Young and his team. They were concerned it was a side-effect of his brain trying to make sense of the conflicting memories. The first time he mentioned dreams, the rehab team tried a series of therapies to stop them, but none of them worked. More extreme measures, like shock treatments and memory grafts were horrendous for Tim, and similarly ineffective. The whole experience would have broken a lesser man, and Tim was at his limit. So, he didn't tell them about the nightmares anymore, even though they happened every night.

Tim didn't always remember the details of the dream, but he knew they were always the same. What he typically recalled was seeing a man he recognized but didn't know, and a woman with silver eyes speaking, but he couldn't make out the words. And always there was a dark, faceless figure watching it all. Privately, Tim kept a journal of the dreams, hoping that if he could figure out what they meant, he could stop them. Since he didn't trust anyone at the facility, he kept the journal in a lockbox by his bed, one only he could open.

Tim was tired of being full of distrust and paranoia, so he did his best to stay positive. He was alive, after all, and the trials today would mark the end of an exceptionally long recovery process. Finally. He knew he should be grateful, but at the same time he felt *grateful* was too strong a word. He sometimes felt as if he'd sold his soul to the Devil, but he thought doing that would have been easier, more lucrative, hurt less, and been a great deal less bothersome.

Tim frowned at his reflection as he tugged down the hem of his fatigue coat. Being as satisfied as he could be with his appearance, he sighed and walked out of his quarters. He noticed right away that the hall was far more empty than usual. Even at this early hour, the facility was typically quite busy. Today though, it was almost desolate. It was a bit unnerving, but Tim didn't mind the solitude. He didn't want to deal with more people than needed today.

What Tim wanted was for things to go back to normal. This was supposed to be his final journey down this hallway. With his recovery and the confirmation trials complete, he was going to return to Active Duty. He wasn't naïve enough to think things would be *exactly* as they were before, but he needed there to be some semblance of his previous life. He was ready to wear a real uniform again, not the stripped-down replica he wore now. More than anything else, though, he was ready to be called by his name. He was tired of living life as a ghost.

Tim walked silently down toward the Cytotechnics bay; it was just muscle memory at this point. He walked down this hall so many times he could have walked it blindfolded and backward. He was so lost in his thoughts that he almost steamrolled over one of the technicians. Running into Tim was like running into a wall, so when he bumped into the other person, the smaller man bounced off an dropped everything he was carrying. Tim, his reflexes on point, reached out, caught the technician by the arm, and steadied him before offering an apology. The tech gathered up his things quickly and offered an apology of his own before running off down the hall. Tim's reputation for being less-than-amicable was well known, so the technician's reaction wasn't all that surprising.

As he neared the lab, Tim realized how much he hated this place. Notwithstanding the few rare individuals who genuinely cared about his well-being, he felt like someone's science fair project. The technicians, doctors, and therapists, by and large, seemed less concerned with how Tim felt than how he performed. It was a dehumanizing feeling made worse by the fact that they would only call him Beta 4. He loathed it.

Tim stepped through the sliding glass doors that led into the lab entrance. Since the Cytotechnics Bay was a clean room, everyone had to be decontaminated. At the same time, there was a biometric scan that ensured that only those authorized entered; a precaution to prevent a repeat of what happened in Arlington. He stepped into the entryway and onto the grey pad at the center of the chamber, then waited patiently for the process to be finished.

Once Tim was verified and thoroughly cleaned the doors on the opposite side of the chamber opened and he walked into the lab. He still found the clinical smell of the place a bit unsettling; it smelled like a mix of rubbing alcohol, antiseptic, petroleum, and electricity. To a casual observer, it might have been mistaken for Frankenstein's laboratory, which wasn't far from the truth. Tim wasn't going to miss this place even a little. He was tired of playing the monster in someone else's story.

Chapter 11

Tim stepped through the heavy PVC strip door and into the main room of the lab. He was immediately lambasted with hearty cheers and a rousing rendition of *For He's a Jolly Good Fellow* sung in no fewer than seven different keys. The irony wasn't lost on any of them; Tim might have been called a few choice things, but a 'jolly good fellow' wasn't likely to be on the list.

Tim put on his best smile and began to passively scan over the faces of those present. As he moved from face to face, he could recall not only the personal details he was given, or had heard, but also information from their personnel files. He didn't care to know any of these people, though. From his point of view, they were his tormentors and a roadblock preventing him from getting the eagles back on his shoulders.

Once the singing was done, each of them gave Tim their congratulations and either left the lab or went about their assigned duties. Tim forced himself to be gracious. Regardless of how he felt, he didn't want to be the one to spoil the mood. The last person who remained was Dr. Young, who had been the only one who took the time to get to know Tim on a personal level. He was the mind behind Cytotechnics, and the second-in-command of the Beta project. Tim had a lot of respect for Matthew, but he wasn't going to miss him either. If Tim was the Monster, Dr. Young was Frankenstein, and it was *his* science project Tim was trapped in.

"It's an exciting day, Beta 4!" Matthew exclaimed in an annoyingly cheery tone. "I hope you got plenty of rest. I'm sure you're looking forward to today even more than we are," he added happily, a broad smile on his face. Tim's only reply was a half-hearted smile and nod.

Matthew was a small man, even compared to the other technical staff. Next to Tim, he looked positively adolescent. He was also younger than most of the technicians, having been a prodigy and graduating college at fifteen. That's probably why he never showed any sign of being intimidated by Tim, or anyone else, including Samuels. He knew he was smarter than all of them, but he never acted like it. That was something Tim could admire. If anything, Tim was intimidated by him.

Tim gently navigated his way through the people milling about the room to step into the glass-walled chamber in the center. Once inside, the din of socialization came to a quick end and the work began. He knew he would be subjected to testing for the rest of his life, but he hoped the frequency would decrease, and that it would be done elsewhere. He would forever associate this room, and the people in it, with pain and misery. Deep down, he knew it wasn't fair to hold these people accountable for what happened to him. They were just doing their jobs, and they all played a part in making him whole again. But he couldn't reconcile that reasoning with the emotions he felt.

He didn't remember much about his time in Arlington. All he knew was that they moved him to this facility just before the accident that killed everyone. The only person he remembered there was Major Marcum, and he had asked if she would be joining him in Phase 4. He respected her a great deal, and he hoped she would continue his physical therapy. It was explained to him that after the Arlington event, she resigned and walked away. No one was sure where she went. It was a shame, he thought. She was good at what she did.

He was less than half a man when he came into Matthew's care. While he was different than he was before the accident, he was, to coin a phrase, better, stronger, and faster by a mile. Tim's body had been damaged beyond what modern medicine could repair. In Arlington, they used cybernetic implants to bring Tim back; those being Samuels' area of expertise. But traditional implants and prosthetics weren't enough, and over time it was clear they needed to pursue another course. That's where Matthew's work in Cytotechnics came in. It was beyond cutting edge, and Tim's existence put all those theories into practice.

Every step of the way, Tim outperformed Matthew's predicted results. It wasn't because the brilliant scientist underestimated the potential of his life's work, either. It was because Tim didn't know how to give less than one hundred percent to whatever he did. Failure wasn't a choice, especially now. Matthew was aware that if anyone else been the subject of his work the project may not have succeeded. He made sure Tim knew it, too.

After ten hours of testing, scanning, and performance exercises, the bulk of the technicians and scientists said their goodbyes to Tim and left the lab. He had set a very high bar for the future of Cytotechnics, and many of them were starting work on new projects. Tim barely noticed them leaving. None of them were particularly important to him.

The people who worked in that room, Tim included, created an entirely new category of being: Augmented Humans. The term *cyborg*, a word borrowed from science fiction, felt too cliché and inappropriate. It implied a distinct separation between man and machine which didn't exist in Cytotechnics. Tim embodied the union of the biological and the synthetic. He was the first and only of his kind.

Tim sat on a bench in the corner of the training room, mentally decompressing after the grueling trials. He used a wet towel to wipe off some of the dirt from the obstacle course as he waited to be released back to his room. Matthew was in the lab office, reviewing the results with excitement. To his left, a small holographic display flickered to life. He barely glanced at it as he continued working. He'd been expecting the call; it was Samuels.

"Good afternoon, Matthew. Since I haven't heard from you today, I thought I'd give you a call to make sure everything went as planned. Did Beta 4 perform as expected?" Samuels asked, his face dark and grim even as a projection of light. The question was rhetorical; he already knew the answer. He always knew.

Matthew finished what he was writing before he turned to reply. "Of course, Mr. Secretary. Actually, he far exceeded our adjusted benchmarks and outperformed his own previously established limits. Hell, he left a three-foot-wide crater in the exercise yard after his long jump. He's never displayed that kind of raw power before. I estimate that after our last adjustments, he's performing nearly 450% better than any earlier Beta iteration, 600% better than the Alfa cyborgs, and almost 1,000% beyond peak human performance. What's more impressive," Matthew continued, pushing his glasses up the bridge of his nose as he turned to face Samuel's image, "is how quickly he's learned to finely control the Cytotechnics down to the cellular level. The man's a beast. We couldn't have succeeded without him."

Matthew folded his hands and looked down, clearly nervous about what he was going to say next. "We haven't, uh…," he paused, clearing his throat, "we haven't needed to use the override in weeks. I really think he's ready. And you'll have my final report saying just that within the hour. He deserves to go home," he added directly with as stern a look as he could muster. "He deserves to get his life back."

Matthew was as assertive and confident someone in his position could be. Usually, it was more than enough, but with Samuels, it was always a gamble. He didn't know why Tim was so important to Samuels, but he had his ideas. He should have asked more questions before getting involved in the project, and there were plenty he could have. Such as why the Secretary of Cultural Preservation was heading a project which clearly should have been headed by the War Department, or Veterans Affairs. Samuels got

Matthew the funding he needed, so he accepted the offer at face value and got to work.

Samuels was a demanding partner, and he required perfection from everyone involved. Up to that point, he was pleased and today should have been no different. Matthew always felt some resentment from Samuels. Cytotechnics would make the cybernetic prosthetics Samuels invented obsolete. Not to mention, his phase of the Beta project was more stable and powerful than anything Samuels accomplished in his earlier augmentation projects. But he'd never said so, and Matthew didn't think he ever would.

"I'm glad to hear that, Matthew. The main reason I was calling, though, was to inform you that there's been a change of plans. You're to wipe Beta 4 and place it back in stasis for transport. You're to send it to the Groom Lake facility where we'll build a new profile for it and deploy it from there," Samuels instructed flatly. "I will be managing the project myself from now on."

Matthew felt his pulse quicken with an anger that must have shown on his face. "I don't understand. It'll take weeks to tear all of this down and relocate to Groom Lake. My team and I need time to make arrangements for our homes and families…"

Samuels cut him off, "I'm sorry, Matthew, I wasn't clear. You won't be needed at Groom Lake."

Matthew's brow furrowed as he continued furiously, "Are you cutting us out? This is *my* project. I don't care if you paid for it, without me, you have nothing. And honestly, Stephen, we were already prepared to track Beta 4's active duty service and set up wherever he was so that we could monitor and service him as stipulated in our contract. We need that data if we're going to produce this technology for widespread use. And why are you wiping him? It took months to build a stable profile that didn't collapse after a couple weeks."

Samuels' deep frown brought Matthew to a stammering halt. If his smile could chill a room, his frown could frighten the dead. "You and the rest of your team have done an admirable job, Matthew. Or should I say *my* team? Yes, my team because *I* pay them. And *my* team has already duplicated your setup at Groom Lake. I'm not cutting them out, I'm cutting *you* out," Samuels added smugly. "Frankly, I don't need you anymore. Am I to understand that you have a problem with this arrangement?"

Matthew didn't have the words for a reply yet, but the deep red color of his face was visible even through the blue light of the hologram. He always knew Cytotechnics could easily be developed into a formidable weapons platform, but he was assured from the beginning that Tim would never see service as a front-line soldier, nor would this technology be used to that end. It was the main reason he agreed in the first place.

"Actually, Mr. Secretary, I do," Matthew replied after he calmed himself. "I worked hard to gain Colonel Andrews' respect, if not his trust, something I daresay you haven't bothered with. He deserves his life back, or at least something resembling a normal life. And we told him to expect that. He's more than ready. *None* of this would have happened without me, and I can make certain none of it continues without me either," he spat angrily.

Samuels cut in sharply, all traces of his former politeness gone. "I see. You seem to think you have some leverage here, Matthew. You do not. And while I can understand why you think you get some say as it relates to Beta 4, again, *you do not*. It is, and always has been, *my* project. Because of that, I will decide what will or won't happen—with Beta 4 and with *you*."

Samuel's scowled more viciously, if that were possible, and his voice lowered to an almost growl-like state. "I don't care what *it* thought was going to happen after today. *It* doesn't get a say. I shouldn't have to remind you, Matthew, that Colonel Andrews died seven years ago and will remain dead. He is no more. And while Beta 4 is a magnificent piece of engineering and technology, and something to be proud of, *it* is a piece of government property. *It* is no more real than that computer wife of yours…"

Matthew winced noticeably at the mention of YVE, the AI he created to help with the creation of Cytotechnics. Without YVE, the project would have taken years, maybe decades. And without Samuels' deep pockets, YVE would not exist. Both ideas would still be on the drawing board. Matthew took great pains to keep YVE's creation a secret, but it was a fool's hope to think that she would escape Samuels' ever-present eye.

Samuels grinned wickedly, knowing he had the upper hand. "That's right, Matthew. I know about your little side project, *and* how you paid for it. I went over the project documents, and I couldn't find anything in them about appropriations for an advanced computer system. Now, unless you'd like me to call the Attorney General and tell him about your misappropriation of millions in Federal funds, you may want to rethink your position. Just imagine what would happen if we had to disassemble your toy," Samuels added with self-satisfaction. He knew he'd won. He always won.

Matthew sighed and looked down, defeated. How did he miss Samuels poaching his entire team? Why didn't anyone tell him? He knew the answers to both questions; it was ending the way it was always going to end. Samuels had lived up to his reputation of being a man of few scruples and fewer ethics. Matthew was angry at himself for falling into the trap.

"All right, Mr. Secretary. You win. I'll have Colonel...," Samuels cleared his throat, correcting Matthew before he continued. "...Beta 4 wiped, prepped, and placed in stasis at once. He'll be ready to transport to Groom Lake in the morning."

"It's good to know you can still see reason, Matthew," Samuels replied, smiling in his creepy way. "This is really what's best for everyone. The Beta project will be in the best possible hands...mine...and we'll be certain Beta 4 will continue to serve our country. I'll be stopping by Nellis on my way to Groom Lake. I expect you to be gone by the time I arrive. Don't bother packing, we'll ship your things to you. We have your address."

With that final and definitive word, the hologram flickered and went dark. Matthew stifled his tears and composed himself before he stood. His own haste and impatience led him to trust someone who should never be trusted. YVE warned him that their work would never go unnoticed, and he dismissed her concerns. He looked over his shoulder into the room where Tim was waiting.

He dried his eyes, straightened his coat, and walked out of his office with the best smile he could muster.

"Ahh, there you are Beta 4!" he exclaimed with manufactured elation. "I just got off a call with Secretary Samuels, and he asked me to congratulate you on all your success and hard work…," Matthew paused, clearing his throat. "You'll have your orders in the morning. Congratulations."

It was Tim's turn to frown. He'd known Samuels for too long to believe he would ever congratulate him for anything. After all, you didn't compliment the ATM for giving you money, or your car for getting you to work on time. That's how Samuels saw Tim, as a machine performing the task it was created for. Out of concern, he scanned Matthew and noticed his pulse was racing, his voice was stressed, his temperature was slightly elevated, and his eyes were bloodshot and swollen. Something was very wrong.

Tim looked around the room. He could sense the trap, but he couldn't see the danger. The mood darkened considerably. The few technicians who remained avoided eye contact or scurried away when Tim worriedly looked around the room. No more good-byes or well-wishes; no more singing.

"As I was saying, we'll have your orders and new identity drawn up soon. You can't be 'Tim Andrews' anymore, of course," Matthew added softly. He started to choke up and struggled to hold back his tears. He wiped his nose and eyes and tried to continue but couldn't.

Tim was on edge now, every fiber of his being on high alert. His normally stoic and spartan demeanor replaced with one of agitation and vigilance. Glancing toward the only entrance to the training room, then back at Matthew, he asked, "That's great, Doc, but uh, why don't you tell me what's really going on?"

Matthew straightened up, cleared his throat again, and replied anxiously, "I don't know what you mean, Colonel."

Tim's eyes widened in alarm. The use of his rank was a tremendous red flag. No one had mentioned it even once since he'd arrived. Not one time. He grabbed Matthew's shoulder, leaned in, and whispered, "Come on Doc. You know I know you're lying. Let me help you."

Matthew pulled away and stood tall, offering his hand to Tim, who regarded it cautiously before grasping it firmly.

"It's been an honor and a privilege to give your life back, Colonel Andrews. I know it wasn't always pleasant. Hell, it wasn't pleasant for any of us. We pushed you to your limits and you showed us that we had no idea what your limits are. You embodied my dream and brought it to life. Without you, Cytotechnics wouldn't exist. From the bottom of my heart, thank you."

Tim wasn't sure how to respond. He was never a man to use ten words when two would do, but he wasn't often left speechless. It was the first time in years someone treated him like a human being. A rare smile made its way onto his face, only to be quickly replaced by a look of worry. He assumed he would still be working with Matthew and his team. Tim turned to run for the door.

In that moment, he heard YVE's soft voice in his head. "I'm so sorry, Colonel." Then the world went dark.

Behold, I am going to send an angel before you
to guard you along the way
and to bring you to the place which I have prepared.

- Exodus 23:20

Chapter 12

Drake peered out the window of the small trailer he'd lived in for the past six weeks. Based on his first observations, he only planned on being there a few days, and it frustrated him to no end that he was starting to feel at home in his shack-on-wheels. The plain and simple conditions suited him, but he missed his bed. He missed Merlin even more.

What really irked him, however, was that he was six weeks into this incident, and he had not yet summoned the courage to explain what was happening. Not that anyone would understand. They were right to consult with him on the Code Grey. It was an obviously supernatural and dangerous weather anomaly, and it was getting worse.

No one else understood what it was, let alone why it might worsen. It was assumed by all involved that a newly Awakened person was responsible, but Drake quickly dismissed the idea. He had his own theories, but none of them ended happily, so he stayed tight-lipped until he could be certain of the cause. This was always how he operated.

Drake had been sure for about three weeks, but he knew what he presented wouldn't be accepted and he hated being viewed as wrong more than he hated being seen as slow. There were some exceptions, but for the most part, this is what made Drake pensive and apprehensive; a fear of not being taken seriously and those he wanted to help paying the price for their ignorance. He needed to present his findings the right way. And he would. He just needed time to figure out how.

Drake was incredibly good at what he did, and his apparent hubris was more than justified. But sometimes even the best, the most experienced, can come across something new and unknown, as rare as it might be. Even for someone as old as Drake, there were things that hadn't happened in so long, he forgot how to recognize them for what they were, or he himself had never seen them. Even when he eventually did, he didn't always know what to do. And when it happened, each time he did the same thing, he sipped his tea and watched the sky.

Since his arrival in Kansas, the skies above were uncharacteristically clear, particularly for this time of year. There wasn't so much as a wisp of cloud, though the surrounding areas were continually overcast. This was how the anomaly was discovered in the first place. The National Weather Service noticed an odd, circular void in their radar they couldn't explain. When they investigated further, they noticed weather patterns avoided the area entirely, as if it were solid. At least they had the good sense not to go public.

Once the anomaly was reported, every effort was made to keep its existence hidden. People would panic, even if a realistic explanation was given, because people were, by and large, stupid and panicky. So, a suitable cover story was created, but after a month and a half it was wearing thin. No one knew it would take this long, and Drake felt responsible for the delay. Because he was. Regardless, it was vital the public be kept away, if only because of the physical danger of the anomaly. The area inside was bitterly cold, and they feared someone would be hurt, or worse.

Drake peered out the window into the subdued sunlight, an effect of the anomaly. The thermometer outside read a bone-numbing -43.2° C, as it had every day since it had been installed. He didn't want to trust the digital readout, but Capt. Heighton insisted and told him there was no other choice. She explained that coil spring thermometers were highly unreliable past ten below, and mercury freezes solid at -39° C. Drake didn't know any better, so he accepted her at her word. Had he not experienced the cold himself, he would have assumed the thing was broken.

Frustration at the site wasn't limited to Drake. Tensions at the main complex had grown difficult to control. Even on the best days, the bickering among the collected experts was worse than a session of Parliament, even without Drake there. He knew none of them were correct in their assessments, but he also knew adding his own opinion to the mix would only create more arguments. Besides, they respected him less than he respected them, and that was saying something. Most of the others viewed him as a charlatan or worse, a joke. Green was a terrible color, he often quipped.

Drake also assumed the others kept him out of the loop on their more important observations. But it didn't matter; Capt. Heighton made sure he had all the relevant data. He was positive the answer lay firmly in the realm of the paranormal. They knew it too. Most of them resented Drake because since the Awakening, people were looking to him for answers, not them. More people Awakened each year, and Drake thought he knew why, though he knew better than to tell anyone. The impact would have been catastrophic.

The Awakening was already a terrifying event, and it was still ongoing. People turned on their closest friends and family; parents turned on their children, siblings turned on each other, lifelong friends said forever goodbyes as their loved ones manifested powers beyond rational explanation. There were other events too, the Codes, which affected how the public viewed the Awakened.

Three years earlier, there was an incident on the DC beltway during which an animal that could only be described as a unicorn charged a vehicle and began to attack the occupants. It took four police officers with high-powered rifles to stop the assault. Drake was called in because no one trusted the evidence of their own eyes. He confirmed it was indeed a unicorn, and the 'odd' behavior was because it was probably starving.

He didn't have the heart to tell them the behavior wasn't odd at all, and it attacked a car full of children because unicorns could only gain nourishment from eating pre-pubescent animals. He never wanted to destroy a person's childhood whimsy if he could avoid it. When it was over, Drake politely requested the skull be delivered to him with the horn intact. It was on his mantle in Durham. He called it Bob.

"Something's wrong with the world, Merlin" Drake noted at the time. "It feels like it's regressing to an earlier age. It's all very wrong."

Drake moved back to the table where he did his work. The small kitchenette and dining space in the trailer was making do as an office, though he missed his desk and fireplace. Boy did he miss his fireplace. It wasn't necessarily the warmth; there was something about staring into the flames that quieted his mind. He sighed and sat at the table, setting down his cup of tea. It was past time he faced the truth. He wasn't searching for an answer anymore, he was battling to find a way to present it. He also knew his hosts would look to him for a solution, but there wasn't one.

Drake reviewed the contents of the table he had avoided for days. Capt. Heighton was true to her word and made sure he'd been given access to every resource he needed. She even went as far as to have a number of books shipped in from his library at home. It was part test and part delay tactic; he could have retrieved what he needed on his own, but she didn't need to know that.

Early on, it had been suggested the internet might be more useful, but Drake scoffed and commented that most of what was in his library couldn't be found anywhere else, especially online. He made certain of it. Once Capt. Heighton saw the books, she didn't doubt it. She'd never heard of most of them, and many were handwritten. She didn't even want to guess the value of such a collection. Besides, she was pretty sure he didn't know how to use the Internet.

The downside to the delay was Capt. Heighton had become Drake's near-constant shadow, though he didn't mind her company. Despite their earlier difficulties, or maybe because of them, the pair grew quite friendly. He had a sneaking suspicion that she was asked to keep tabs on him. He didn't begrudge her doing her job, and he knew how to keep his secrets hidden. Since he began consulting with the government, he never expected or needed them to trust him. She did, though, and that mattered to him.

Drake set down his tea and finally began to rifle through the imposing mountain of notes on the table. He took notes incessantly, and it was rare to find him without a notebook or pen. He didn't *need* to take the notes it was just easier for reference and a matter of habit. Besides, he'd learned long ago that it was best to prioritize what he kept in his memory. Those things he considered minutiae he wrote down. It also helped keep him from *misremembering* things, something he did far too often for his liking.

"Ah, there you are," he said with satisfaction as he held up the notepad he was looking for. Taking one last gulp of tea, he set the cup down and began flipping through the pages. He looked over everything repeatedly, looking desperately for another cause behind this event. One last chance to find another answer. He wanted more than anything to be wrong.

He rationalized his deceit the whole time, repeating to himself that no one would believe him anyway. At least not until it was too late. That's how it always happened. The adage "seeing is believing" was almost never true, at least not anymore. People preferred to cling to their own ideas and beliefs, even when presented with irrefutable evidence to the contrary. Truth, after all, was subjective, and it was easier to fool someone than to convince them they'd been fooled.

There! He finally found it; the page he needed:

> *Lebanon, Kansas - August 19*
> It was 37° C when we arrived at the Operations Center. They briefed us about the anomaly the locals called The Chill, and I've never seen the like. We were warned about the extreme drop in temperature as we approached. We're going through a chamber to acclimate us, so we don't go through thermal shock when we enter.

He had the right book, now to find the right part. He scanned further down the page:

> *The Chill originally measured 250 meters across, but today it's measuring at nearly a kilometer. Capt. Heighton <Sarah - Keep an eye on her, she's special> mentioned that the rate of growth appears constant. When concerns were raised about populated areas, she mentioned that the only city of note was some distance away, and that there was an evacuation plan in place should it be needed.*
> *She also noted, in passing, that the locals are wary and mistrustful of the government,*

so they were staying away on their own…for now. However, there is an adequate cover story should anyone get curious.

Side note: The Chill appeared after the first earthquake of significant magnitude in the area since 1867.

None of this was what he was looking for, but he was sure he had made the notation he needed on the first day. He flipped a few pages and continued reading:

Inside The Chill, it is terrifyingly cold, so much that it made my old bones ache. The acclimation did little to help, at least in how I felt. I'm sure there are valid reasons for it. That's not my department. Immediately upon entering, I noted that my breath was not visible, and my glasses didn't fog, despite the cold. Also, my lips dried up almost at once and I couldn't keep them wet.

It was explained that the anomaly has an apparent negative ambient humidity, a term they had to invent because it had never happened before and shouldn't be possible. It is so extreme, we are told, that any source of water brought in quickly evaporates, even before it can freeze.

A caged mouse was brought along with us for demonstration purposes, and it was already dead – poor sod. Someone claiming to be a biologist performed a cursory exam and explained that the mouse was still warm, but

*it almost appeared mummified. The effect on
humans, we were assured, would be far less
profound, but to protect everyone, exposure
to The Chill was limited to 30 minutes.*

*I will need to be inside for considerably
longer than that.*

Drake grumbled and continued scouring through the pages of the notebook, frustrated that it was taking so long to find what he wanted:

*I have successfully lobbied to have living
quarters arranged inside the anomaly. I think
the others were taking bets on how long it
would be before I ended up like the mouse.*

*I need to be inside to confirm my initial
observations unhindered by the idiocy in the
main complex. Those are as follows:*

<u>First</u> *– Plants inside the anomaly, while
obviously parched, are not frozen or
otherwise affected by the extreme cold.*

<u>Second</u> *– Inside the anomaly, the sky has a
reddish tinge, and the brightness of sunlight
is greatly diminished. One would liken it to
the effect of an eclipse.*

<u>Third</u> *– There is never any weather inside
the anomaly, and weather patterns outside
move around it – presumably because of the
water-dissipating effect.*

<u>Finally</u> *– As the sun is setting, I've
noticed that the moon is similarly diminished*

while inside the anomaly, along with it having a deep red coloration.
This is all too terribly familiar.
Why am I the only one to have noticed this?

Even on that first day, Drake knew something incredible and terrible was happening. He knew, but he was afraid to come to terms with the observable truth. Some called it the Apocalypse, others Armageddon, others still Ragnarök; it didn't matter what it was called, it all meant the same thing. The end of everything.

It was all was happening just as had been written two millennia earlier, by someone who didn't understand what the visions showed. People had become too far removed from their past and forgotten, or ignored, messages sent to them by their ancestors. Prophecy was no longer taken seriously, and most people felt it was just nonsense, or wasn't meant for them. Even those that did believe assumed the signs would be unmistakable and seen on a global scale. Like everyone would hear the trumpets sounding. Drake knew it didn't work that way. Prophecy never did.

Drake understood that the revelations given to the anonymous author known only as "John" were true, but he hadn't expected them to be literal. He assumed the visions were part of some drug-induced fervor, like those of the oracles of Greece, holding only the seed of truth. The reality of it was simpler; the author did their best to translate what they saw into the wholly inadequate written word. There was never any mention of the signs being visible to all, or them being grandiose in scale, despite the vivid presentation.

Taking the Book of Revelation as fact, the state of the sky meant six of the seven seals had been broken. Time was short.

Drake was angry at himself for missing the earlier signs. He was angry at himself for ignoring Claire. She always knew what was coming, and she tried to tell him more than once. Setting his notebook aside, he reached over to a yellowed envelope dated in his peculiar style for the day before. It had been squirreled away in one of the books he had brought to him, and he never saw it until then. That was the point. Inside was a letter, written in colored pencil, dated on the same day in 1971. It wasn't signed, but he knew who had written it and how it got into his book. The letter had only three sentences:

"Someone terrible is coming, Mister Doctor, but someone who can help is coming first. They'll know what to do. Make sure you listen and don't be so grumpy."

Claire was never wrong, even if she was too clever for her own good. Any previous doubts scattered when he found the letter. Someone was coming, all right. Someone who knew how to make an entrance. It wouldn't be the last time he wished Claire was still with him. She always knew what to do.

Drake was so lost in thought he didn't hear the knock at his door. Chiding himself for not paying attention, he scrambled to his feet to check who it was. Peeking through the curtain, he looked around but didn't see who knocked. Puzzled, he wrapped himself up in his heavy robe and opened the door just enough to see what was going on.

Just as the latch cleared the frame, Merlin burst through the door, nearly knocking Drake off his feet. Merlin plopped down in front of the space heater with a growl, as if to say, "It's about time, you old coot!" The dog shook off the cold and looked at Drake expectantly.

"Oh yes, of course," Drake said, grabbing a large bowl from the cupboard and filling it with water. He placed in front of Merlin who slurped it down greedily. Drake knelt and patted his old friend on the back.

"Now, what in the bloody blazes are you doing here?" Drake asked gruffly. "I didn't send for you for a reason, you damned fool. It's dangerous here, and…," his admonition trailed off, "Wait. How the hell did you get here? Just walking to here from the outer edge should have killed you."

Merlin just huffed and continued drinking the water until it was gone. He didn't care much for being underestimated.

Drake hugged his friend around the neck and rose to close the door before he let out any more heat. Turning, he was stopped dead in his tracks by a stunning figure, the likes of which he'd never seen and hoped he never would. Out of reflex, he blurted something out in his native language, something he *never* did.

"Sancta Maria, mater Dei…," Drake muttered, his jaw agape.

"…ora pro nobis, peccatoribus, nunc et in hora mortis nostrae," came the reply without hesitation in a voice as magnificent as the dawn. Drake was forced to avert his eyes from the glory before him. He wept involuntarily, partly from reverence and partly from fear at what this arrival meant. It was an angel; the help Claire mentioned in the letter she wrote as a child. The one he'd hoped to prove wasn't there.

The creature moved with feline grace toward him, then placed a gentle hand on his cheek. Drake didn't realize it, but he'd fallen to his knees. He looked up when he felt the angel's warm touch.

"Rise and be recognized, Primus Cassius Longinus, as a child of the Creator. I have come bearing hope in the face of grim tidings! Come, let us rejoice!"

Chapter 13

Two weeks had passed since Ying Qi sent Wu Fan to relentlessly guard the passage to and from the monastery. The young monk followed his emperor's instructions without question, even at the expense of himself. He violently and rabidly attacked anyone who was not authorized. In all his time there, he didn't sleep or eat and left his post only for brief moments to drink from a nearby stream.

The Concealed monks made their attempts, as expected, and found themselves unable to deal with Wu Fan's ferocity. They tried to wait him out, but he was machine-like in his vigilance. Jangchup begged them to give up their plans, but the restless monks decided they would make one final push. They assumed after 16 days, he would be delirious from hunger or dead from exhaustion. Unfortunately, they were mistaken. When the dust settled, fifteen monks were dead, including poor Wu Fan. Jangchup put an end to any other thoughts of leaving.

What they couldn't have known was that Wu Fan wasn't alone in his vigil. Ying Qi knew the doomed monk's body might give out before the Concealed monks gave up in their efforts. To prevent this, he made sure someone else was there too, unseen and unheard, backing up Wu Fan in his task. He was the leader of the

Èmèng shouwèi and enforced Ying Qi's will outside of the temple. The people of China feared this man as much as they feared their emperor, and he didn't even speak their language. To look upon him was to look upon death, so they called him *Sǐshén*, which meant God of the Dead. His given name was Gino Lorenza, but he called himself Leapstryke.

Gino was a dangerous psychopath with a talent for killing that defied conventional description. Efficient and ruthless, he lacked the conscience that kept even wicked men from doing the unthinkable. Gino crossed the line many years earlier, and he never bothered looking back. He was never known for his humanity, which was fine now that he wasn't human. He was at the Cincinnati Incident, and the explosion which claimed Tim's body took his as well. This allowed him to take his skills to a new level. He was death personified.

Gino knew Ying Qi before Cincinnati, though. The CIA recruited Gino at a young age, and despite his tendency for free thinking and resentment of authority, he was one of their more dependable agents. This is why he was assigned to infiltrate China more than a decade earlier. He was only in the country a few days before he started to see the advantage in playing for both teams. He made his way to the monastery and into the garden before even Li Fong knew he was there. Ying Qi knew, though; he could feel the anarchy of Gino's mind miles away. He also knew that accepting Gino's proposition would be advantageous.

Gino's mind was too chaotic for Ying Qi to touch for extended periods, and his influence never lasted beyond that connection. So, he was delighted to discover, early on, that it wasn't needed. As long as Gino felt he was being adequately compensated and was given the freedom to get the job done any way he saw fit, he could be relied upon. Relied upon but not trusted.

Claire Thibodeaux had been an issue that needed resolved, and Gino was the key. Ying Qi's plan required him to have access to someone close to Claire so that he could track her movements. Gino was that someone and he passed on that information along with other vital intelligence. Once Gino was cleared to return to service after his 'escape' from China, it only took him a few weeks to get placed on the right details with the right people.

Gino was as deep as a mole could possibly be, and he was an invaluable resource for Ying Qi. He was impressed at the sheer number of people the emperor was able to influence, even halfway around the world. With Gino's help, Ying Qi's plans became unstoppable. Even when it became clear there was a leak, Gino was able to continue unhindered. He was checked and double-checked; fooling the psych evaluations and polygraphs was easy, he'd been doing that for years anyway. When they started using telepaths, none of them wanted to stay connected to his mind long enough to dig as deeply as was needed.

In Cincinnati, they achieved the impossible. What no one foresaw, what they couldn't know, was what would happen when Claire was killed. In the end, she and her special forces protectors were all taken out of play, but Gino was critically injured and his body spirited away with Tim's. Gino became the basis for the Alfa project, Samuels' first attempt to join a human nervous system to a mechanical body. Ying Qi could no longer see Gino, and so assumed, like everyone else, he was dead.

With Gino as the subject, the Alfa project was doomed to fail. It ended abruptly when Gino ignored a recall order and never returned. That's why the Beta project included the development of an override. No one knew what happened to Gino and the first attempt to find him ended when the recovery team was sent back in pieces over the course of a week.

Gino did all his damaged mind would allow. He returned to the last place he could remember clearly…the monastery. Ying Qi gladly accepted his new form with open arms. The Americans' state-of-the-art technology was a gift not to be dismissed. Gino's cybernetic body became the basis for the horrors to come later.

An unexpected development was that whatever happened in Cincinnati made Gino into one of the Concealed. While Gino's mind had always been too anarchic for Ying Qi to connect with, he had previously always been able to sense Gino's presence. Li Fong speculated that the American being more machine now than man might account for the change. Ying Qi agreed, though he hated it.

Li Fong didn't just hate it, though. It would have been different if Gino was just a man, but he was so much more now. He knew Gino could, on a whim, kill everyone in the monastery and not break a sweat. Ying Qi, however, assured his brother than he had things well in hand, and that their American friend would pose no problem. Besides, he concluded, Gino's value as an asset far outweighed any perceived risk. To keep Gino placated, the emperor made sure he got whatever he wanted.

Gino was asleep, if it could be called sleep, when a firm knock rapped at his door. He knew it wasn't one of the monks; the monks wouldn't come anywhere near him, he mused tiredly. They didn't come into his section of the complex. It was as if there was an invisible barrier around his sleeping quarters. He preferred it that way. He felt like they were trying to push their 'unrealistic metaphysical bullshit' on him, and he made sure they knew it. It wasn't a recent development. He'd always felt that way.

"What do you want, Li Fong?" Gino called out through the door. He didn't bother looking through the door with his one augmented eye. The twins were the only ones with balls enough to come to his room, and Ying Qi wouldn't have lowered himself to knocking. He didn't need superpowers to know people.

"Your Emperor requests the honor of your presence, Grand Commandant. Immediately," came Li Fong's insistent reply in heavily accented English. Gino knew Mandarin once, long ago, but the same event that allowed him to have his marvelous mechanical body also damaged his brain. There were lots of things he didn't remember, but nothing he believed important. He might have been able to learn again, but he didn't have the patience. Even if he knew it, he'd have refused to speak it on principle.

"What does his Royal Pain-in-the-ass-ness want now?" Gino asked curtly. "I've only been in standby for about three hours. I was delayed in Japan, and I had 15 monks to kill when I arrived.

Do you have any idea how hard it is to get into and out of Japan without being noticed when you look the way I do?"

Li Fong was aware this wasn't an exaggeration, but he seethed at the freeness of Gino's tongue and the disrespect aimed at his brother. Tradition was important to him, and under other circumstances, he would have been forced to defend the honor of his brother and Emperor. Now, though, any physical confrontation they had would heavily favor Gino. Despite his confidence he could kill Gino, if necessary, he had no desire to test the hypothesis.

Li Fong sighed quietly and replied as passively as he could. "He is aware of your status, Commandant, and he assures you that this is an urgent matter. He asks you to come to his garden as soon as you are dressed," Li Fong added in a saccharine tone.

Gino stretched his arms and back and began bringing himself out of standby mode. He no longer needed sleep in the conventional sense, but he did require time to rest; it was a lesson he learned the hard way early on. Every three or four days, he shut down for 10 hours or so. The lower body Gino had to use in the monastery didn't look particularly different than anyone else's, aside from being obviously artificial. The one he used when he worked was more animalistic, but his body wasn't what terrified people. It was the plain, white, featureless mask he wore that fueled people's nightmares.

Once he was dressed in the uniform Ying Qi required him to wear when summoned, Gino made his way to the garden. Li Fong was already there, waiting with his brother when he arrived, unarmed and without his usual accoutrements. He didn't need them in the monastery, though he was rarely without them. He also knew it was less a safety precaution and more a power play. Ying Qi was endlessly confident, but not so much it made him stupid. He didn't wait at the gate the way the others did, he just strode in smugly. He had his own power plays.

Immediately, Gino noticed the smell of sulfur and wood smoke, and he wrinkled his nose as he walked the garden's stone path. Beneath those scents, barely discernable, was another smell. It reminded him of the smell of burnt meat. Someone less familiar with the goings-on at the monastery might have assumed the odor was wafting from the nearby kitchens, but he knew the smell of death too well. It was a familiar smell in this place.

Ying Qi noticed Gino's self-assured entrance but didn't react. Every interaction between the two men was a carefully played game of chess. The whole point of calling Gino to the garden, requiring him to wear the uniform, and keeping him unarmed were all to remind him who held the power. Gino for his part assumed all the posturing was to keep him from paying attention to what was happening at the monastery. The irony, he mused, was that he didn't care, but Ying Qi didn't need to know it. Gino knew all he needed; whatever Ying Qi had going on was costing him a lot of monks.

In his past life, Gino lived by a single fundamental ideal: knowledge is power. He enjoyed making men who *thought* they were powerful squirm when they realized he knew all their secrets. Normally, he wouldn't have gotten involved with someone without knowing *something* compromising. It was the best insurance. With the emperor, though, there was a lot of mystery and Gino found he enjoyed the challenge.

"Thank you for coming so quickly, Commandant," Ying Qi said casually as he tended to the flowers in the garden, snipping off dried leaves and dead buds. "We need to speak about the Thibodeaux woman."

Gino stopped in his tracks and looked at Ying Qi with a mix of confusion and contempt. He didn't talk about what happened in Cincinnati, not that he remembered much. Never. What memories he did have were painful…literally. Mostly, he recalled the pain of having a building fall on him before it exploded. Just thinking about it was enough to make him sick to his stomach, which was a real feat considering he didn't have a stomach.

"What's to say?" Gino said through gritted teeth. "The bitch is dead. What else could you possibly need to know that you don't already? It was seven years ago. Besides," he added resentfully nodding toward Li Fong, "I know you saw what happened." Gino tipped his hand a bit, showing that he knew Li Fong took the kill shot, and that the brothers communicate telepathically, something they kept a closely guarded secret.

Li Fong clenched his fists, but Ying Qi stayed calm, replying softly, "Of course, my old friend, I know what happened back then. Right now, however, I'm interested in your knowledge of the woman herself." Ying Qi looked up from his pruning for the first time, walking toward Gino slowly but deliberately. "I have reason to believe something important was overlooked."

Ying Qi set down his tools, clasped his hands behind his back and started to walk around Gino slowly. "I know you can't understand the pressures I experience as the supreme leader of an entire people, and that you don't feel the same urgency to end my nightmares as the others here," he continued coolly. "Unfortunately for you, I am out of patience and time. I had it on unimpeachable authority that killing the woman would end my nightmares and allow me to continue my plans unhindered. If the woman is dead, as you say, then why do the dreams plague me still?" Ying Qi stopped walking to accentuate the point, then continued after a deep breath. "There must be something you haven't told me. How certain are you she didn't survive?"

Gino wasn't intimidated by Ying Qi's circling, or his raised voice. In fact, he found nothing about the man frightening at all. He regarded the theatrics as amateurish, at least compared to his own. Aside from that, he was insulted at the implication he didn't know a dead woman when he saw one or, worse, that he was lying. Gino was many things, but he wasn't a liar.

"Listen, Your Highnessness, I've answered every question you've ever had. I handed you Claire Thibodeaux on a silver fucking platter, and I did so without you jumping in my head to pull the strings!" Gino retorted angrily. "Man, you've got balls of solid rock to call *me* a liar, you two-bit side show ringmaster! Tell you what, why don't you poke around in my head and see what you can see? Oh! That's right… YOU CAN'T! I guess my word will have to be good enough, won't it?"

Gino was incensed. He had more than half a mind to show the twins who was really in charge. In fact, now would be the perfect time. He moved his right arm with lightning quickness to grab the emperor by his thin neck, but a split second before his mechanical hand contacted Ying Qi's flesh, he collapsed into a heap on the ground. It was like a giant weight had been dropped on him, but nothing was there. Nothing worked. His cybernetic body wasn't responding to his commands. He was, for the first time since he was a small child, completely vulnerable.

"Well, this fucking sucks," he thought.

*For cunningly of old was the celebrated saying revealed:
evil sometimes seems good to a man
whose mind a god leads to destruction.*
- Sophocles

Chapter 14

Gino was as helpless as a person could be. He was completely immobilized as Ying Qi continued to stalk around him, addressing him through clenched teeth. "You impudent piece of filth! I am no one's fool, and in this place," he motioned, waving his arms around his head furiously, "I have absolute power. I am the hunter, *not* the hunted. If you were less valuable to me, you'd already be dead. But I still have need of your talents, so I will let you keep your life, such as it is." Ying Qi stopped in front of Gino, looking down at his powerless form. "But not yet."

The emperor walked back to the flowers and picked up his clippers while Gino lay on the ground unmoving. An unsettling quiet, broken only by a subtle hum, descended on the garden before Ying Qi spoke again. "As you so indelicately pointed out, I cannot reach into your mind. But, as you just learned, I *can* control your metal body. Right about now, you are realizing your clockwork heart is not beating. I wonder how long it will be before you lose consciousness; I wonder how long it will take before what's left of you dies," he added with a slight smirk.

Gino's mostly artificial frame was completely inert, but he was totally aware of what was happening. His heart had stopped, just the way Ying Qi mentioned, and he started to feel lightheaded. Gino's brain still needed oxygen, even if it didn't come from blood anymore. He had made a serious miscalculation and was paying the price for it now. This could *never* happen again. Gino was moving past lightheadedness as the darkness began to creep in, the red-black mist that meant death was coming. It was something with which he was all too familiar. He struggled to focus as Ying Qi continued.

"You are a tool; you are *my* tool to be precise. It's time you learned your place," the emperor commented flatly without even looking away from his pruning. Gino couldn't respond, even if he'd wanted to. He wasn't one to panic—he'd been dead before—but he hated every second of this. It wasn't the threat of death which was problematic, but rather the helplessness. The world was fading into a red-grey darkness and Ying Qi's words were becoming difficult to hear and understand. The last thing he could see was Ying Qi's sickening grin over him.

All at once, in a warm rush, everything started coming back. The darkness receded. Gino could feel his heart ticking away, and he began to try to rise. But just as quickly, it started over; the weight, the blackness, the dizziness. Again and again, Ying Qi took Gino to the brink of death and brought him back. Gino lost count of how many times he blacked out from the lack of oxygen. He was desperate for it to stop. After two hours, his head was pounding, and he was starting to ache in places he didn't even have anymore.

Something happened while Ying Qi pushed Gino to the brink of death, though. He heard a voice calling out to him from the darkness. Or maybe it was from the large round building on the other side of the garden. Either way, the voice was telling him to be patient, and that everything would be clear soon. The voice chilled Gino to the bone, but excited him, nonetheless. Abruptly, Ying Qi ended the cycle of torment. Gino struggled to his feet as the emperor turned to address him.

"Are you ready to discuss the Thibodeaux woman now?" Ying Qi asked directly. Gino knew saying the wrong thing would just start the torture over again, so he replied with a quiet nod.

"Good! See, brother? I told you he could be reasonable," Ying Qi called out happily to Li Fong, who was still standing at the edge of the garden grimacing. He looked back to Gino, who was struggling to recover, and added with a smirk, "My brother keeps asking for permission to kill you. He didn't think you would be able to set aside your ego long enough to help us. I assured him that you would…with proper motivation."

Gino glanced over at Li Fong, whose scarred, sightless eyes stared daggers back at him. If looks could kill, the garden would have been a bloodbath. Gino pointed an accusing finger at Li Fong, retorting, "I don't know why you don't believe me. He was there! He pulled the god damned trigger! Claire Thibodeaux is dead and buried."

Ying Qi ignored Gino's elevating tone but looked over to his brother. "Is it possible we were all mistaken? Could she have survived the way he did?" he questioned.

Li Fong didn't answer, and Gino shook his head with growing frustration. "I told you, the bullet went in the front, and her brains came out the back, just like anyone else's would have. You don't come back from that." Gino winced internally at the recollection of his final memory before dying. It wasn't a pleasant experience and being forced to continually relive it, both physically and mentally, was almost more than he could stand.

"Why are you asking me for answers you already have?" Gino asked, exasperated.

Ying Qi didn't answer right away. He was staring at the ground muttering something unintelligible under his breath. Neither Gino, nor Li Fong, had seen the emperor so disquiet. He was fidgeting with the clippers anxiously as he paced. Gino could tell it was making Li Fong nervous.

That's when the dark voice's words became clear; Ying Qi wasn't the one in charge. Someone else was pulling the strings; someone hidden and immensely powerful. Probably the owner of the voice. The most powerful man in the world had inadvertently exposed his greatest secret to the most dangerous man in the world. He was glad his thoughts couldn't be read.

The emperor put down the tool and sat on the bench where he did his morning meditation. Sighing, he placed his hands on his thighs and tried to center himself to focus.

"I know what you saw, what we *all* saw," Ying Qi said slowly, his eyes closed tightly. He breathed deeply before continuing, "She has to still be alive. It's the only answer that makes sense. All my plans hinge on her being out of the picture. And now, it's all in jeopardy. We must discover what went wrong."

Gino's head was still aching. Only Ying Qi could torture someone, then expect their help five minutes later. "I don't know what to tell you. If you don't believe me, why don't you scan the minds of the other people who were there. You have the list. Can't you see into the minds of people either of you have seen?" Gino asked, motioning at Li Fong. "You should start with her daughter. I bet you'd dig up some painful memories you could enjoy."

Ying Qi looked up sharply and raised his hand to keep Gino from saying anything else. Gino braced, preparing for another torture session. "Daughter? What do you mean daughter?" he asked frantically.

Gino looked back at Ying Qi with confusion. "Yeah, daughter. As in female offspring. She was always around, but she was just a normal kid. She didn't matter, so I never thought…"

Ying Qi's face turned red with fury as he jumped to his feet. "You never THOUGHT?" he yelled, loudly enough to startle Gino and Li Fong both. "I did not bring you here to THINK! You are a weapon; you are a bludgeon. You are an instrument of my wrath. You exist to inflict pain on my enemies. Why didn't you tell us about her sooner? Now I have to deal with the consequences of your carelessness…"

Li Fong walked slowly toward his brother as he ranted then gently reached out and grasped him by the shoulder to get his attention. "*Huangdi*, he *did* tell us about the girl numerous times," he said, offering an unexpected defense for Gino, "though I expect she's a woman now. What sorcery exists that not only shielded her from your mind, but made you forget of her existence?"

Ying Qi looked over his shoulder at his brother, the blind rage subsiding. He had been ready to kill them both, which was troubling enough to keep to himself. He touched his brother's mind to find the image of the girl they mentioned, but he couldn't focus on her, no matter how hard he tried. Every image of her was little more than a shadow, and once he let go, he immediately lost the perception of her altogether. It was like knowing her and forgetting her at the same time. This never happened before, even with the Concealed.

Finding a normal person shouldn't be beyond his power, Ying Qi thought to himself as his frustration grew. He always expected to discover limitations to his power and was delighted at how few there were. The Concealed, up to a point, were a problem he could control with the Nightmare Guard. But this was something new. He'd never encountered someone so completely shielded from his mind's eye, and not just that, impossible for him to even know. This changed everything.

"It is clear to me now that our combined destinies cannot be realized until this is resolved. There can be no more mistakes," Ying Qi said resolutely, looking first at Gino, then his brother. "Since I am already forgetting who this woman is, brother, you will ensure my will is done," he said as Li Fong nodded. "Commandant, you will go to America, find her, and bring her back here to me. She will die by my own hand. Am I understood?"

Even if he wanted to argue, Gino didn't have the strength. He'd not seen Ying Qi this angry or vulnerable, and he was still processing what he saw. He was disconcerted that the emperor found a way to make him helpless and he'd not even suspected it was possible. So, he just replied with a terse, "Yes."

Ying Qi looked at Gino with eyes that would wither an ancient oak.

"Yes, *what?*" he asked pointedly.

Gino frowned slightly before correcting himself, bowing his head ever so slightly, "Yes, *Wànsuìyé.*"

"You may leave, Commandant, I'm through with you," Ying Qi said dismissively, waving Gino away with a hand. "We will expect a report soon."

Gino collected himself and made his way back through the gate and away from the garden. He felt sluggish and achy from whatever Ying Qi used against him. Gino promised himself in that moment that he would do everything in his power to ensure it never happened again. *Helpless* wasn't a word Gino was comfortable with.

As he walked slowly back to his room on the far side of the complex, he started thinking about all the ways he could kill the brothers: slowly, deliciously, agonizingly, and horrifyingly painful ways. Even as dark as Ying Qi was, Gino was decidedly darker. The emperor just didn't know it. Ying Qi, despite falling squarely into the Dark Triad of narcissism, Machiavellianism, and psychopathy, was still governed by recognizable goals and desires. Gino, on the other hand, was defined by the Dark Tetrad, which includes sadism, and he was the personification of chaos. He often did things just to know he could do them, something Ying Qi had never done. Gino was unpredictable and had no restraint, and that gave him an edge.

Before he shut down to rest again, Gino pulled out a transponder that was watched by his handler in the CIA. He hadn't used it in years, and he knew it would raise more than a few eyebrows. But he expected it would be the easiest way to get Stateside. He needed to find someone, and he needed their resources to help him. It wasn't Claire's daughter, though, at least not yet. He needed to find someone to help him overcome Ying Qi's new power over him. And he knew just the right person to help. The dark voice led the way.

Chapter 15

Drake fought to regain his composure when he was hit with a startling realization. He was regularly watched and someone at the compound might have seen his guests arrive. He still struggled to explain a unicorn skull to people and that happened three years ago. He had no idea how to explain that his dog and a naked giant made it through The Chill to his trailer unscathed and undetected. Even if no one saw them, Capt. Heighton would be arriving soon for their morning chat, and there was no way to adequately hide his guests in the cramped quarters.

Drake's mind raced. He had been so caught up in stalling he didn't consider how to deal with the reality of the situation, a reality now standing in his trailer. He hadn't exactly lied to anyone, but he wasn't forthcoming with details either. Despite knowing what he knew, he never imagined he'd stand face-to-face with an angel. At least not while he was alive.

Now, he didn't just need to explain that the Apocalypse of John was true. He also had to convince everyone angels were real and could walk among us. Not to mention explaining how his dog made it all the way from Durham, through top-grade military security, and a metaphysical anomaly that dehydrated everything smaller than a person in less than a minute. He was fairly positive nothing he said would be adequate. This was what happened when he was rushed; things were overlooked, and he ended up in a tight spot.

Drake moved past his guest, opened the door and peered around to make sure the coast was clear. Thankfully, no one was nearby, so maybe no one was aware. He slammed the door shut and locked it, just to be safe. Then, turning around, he took off his robe, averted his eyes, and handed it to his unclothed guest.

"Oh, for heaven's sake," Drake said waving the robe with his outstretched hand, "put this on before you blind everyone in the state. Couldn't you have manifested as something less…shiny?"

The large creature cocked their head to the side before taking the robe and draping it over their shoulders and cinching it at the waist. It was still quite a bit too short, but it covered all the right places and diminished their radiance enough. Content that he didn't have a spotlight shining out his trailer windows, Drake slumped back into his seat at the table, breathed a sigh of relief, and placed his head in his hands.

He'd been lying to himself for a long time. As he thought back, the signs were all there, and they were obvious. He saw them all, and he chose not to recognize them for what they were. Sometimes consciously, sometimes not. At some point, he convinced himself that the end would never come, and he was OK with that. Over all those years, he wanted portents and signs and messages, and now he had been sitting in one for weeks. He didn't want to face his failure. Looking up, Drake realized that his visitor was still standing awkwardly in the middle of the room and was regarding him with concern.

"Sit, sit, sit, sit," he said excitedly, motioning for them to sit across the table from him, "you're making me nervous. You're just standing there all regal and brilliant and…angelic. Why do you have to be so bloody perfect?" he asked rhetorically. The angel didn't answer, instead moving to sit as Drake asked.

The daunting figure squeezed into the booth-like seat, their knees bumping into the underside of the table. The mountain of papers collapsed, falling partially onto the angel's lap. Drake mumbled an apology and leaned over to collect the assorted notes and books. Once everything was settled, the pair sat across from one another in uncomfortable silence.

Drake stared at his guest—his eyes were getting used to the brilliance—unsure of what to say. "So, umm, do you have a name or something, or am I to just go about calling you, 'that angel over there,' or 'hey you?'" he asked, his tone dripping with impatience.

The angel just smiled softly. "You know my name Primus, son of Longinus. I am the one with many names. The Persians called me *Mithras*. The Egyptians called me *Akhnoohk*. The sons of Ishmael call me *Idris*. My names among the children of Isaac are too many to name here. Most of you call me *Metatron*. My mother, however, called me Enoch," the angel said nostalgically, "though that name no longer feels right. I suppose it would be most proper for you to call me Bathael."

Drake scoffed and replied cynically, "*You're* the messenger? The *Vox Dei*? The *Bat Qol*? I'm not sure if I believe that. One expects the Voice of God to be louder and to arrive with more fanfare and less freezing cold." Drake was intentionally rude, and he knew it. He was angry with himself, and he had nowhere productive to direct it.

"Well, *Bathael*," Drake continued, emphasizing the name, "before we go any further, I think we need to get some things cleared up. First and foremost, and this is very important: you need to address me by my current name. I haven't used *Primus* in two dozen lifetimes. If you are who you say you are, you should already know that," he added scornfully.

"Yes, of course. You are Drake Sullivan, Dean of the College of Paranormal Arts and Sciences, and you hold doctorates in…" the angel replied matter-of-factly.

Drake shook his head, "You can stop, you made your point. I don't need you to recite my CV to me. Next, am I to assume that you being here means all the Seals are broken? Is that why you're here?"

Bathael looked grave but shook their head slowly. "No, Drake Sullivan, the final Seal is still intact. I am *not* here as the harbinger that was foretold. I am here of my own accord, against the wishes of my brethren. But know this: the Seal will be broken soon, and once it happens, nothing in all Creation can stop what happens next."

Drake furrowed his brow with concern and asked, "If you aren't the harbinger, then why are you here?"

Bathael's tone darkened, and their look was grave. "None of this was destined to happen, Drake Sullivan. These events are not in the Plan. Despite what humans have thought for centuries, the Seals were never meant to be broken. They are not tangible things, they are metaphysical constructs that hold the Planes in place, forever keeping them separate," they explained. "Or at least long enough for humans to ascend."

"But something has changed, Drake Sullivan. I fear the *Nadach* is not content to wait for the natural progression of the Plan. I am not sure how, but the first Seal was broken and created what you call the Awakening," Bathael said gravely. "Now the Planes have begun to collide, allowing the *Nadach* access to the creatures of the other Planes. I suspect they have conspired with other powerful beings to change the Plan. My brethren in the Aetherium do not feel the Plan *can* be changed, but you and I know differently," Bathael said bluntly. "Take me to the *Bachar'im*. Together we will tell them what must be done."

Drake couldn't help but wince at the mention. He hadn't tracked the locations of the *Bachar'im* for centuries. He gave up long before he should have. It was time to own his mistakes and face the reality of the situation.

"The Chosen?" Drake asked as he stalled for time to think up an adequate excuse. "Well, to be frank, the world has grown too rapidly for me to keep track of all the blood lines."

Drake was lying, something he usually did with ease, despite not doing it often. He found, however, that lying to an angel was something else entirely. It made his skin crawl.

"I doubt any survive," he continued uneasily. "No, my large, shiny friend, you're stuck with this very grumpy old man, and his even grumpier old dog, in your attempt to save the known universe."

Bathael's expression went from quietly determined to devastatingly disappointed in an instant. It's impossible to describe how it felt to be the target of such a look, as Drake was in that moment. "I did not take you for a man who would need to be reminded of your responsibilities. You were supposed to be educating and training them in the duties of their ancient bloodlines."

Drake knew Bathael was right. He'd gotten complacent and cynical over the centuries. He'd grown tired of watching friends die and having his warnings dismissed in the name of hubris. He was old, and very, very tired. That was the true reason for his failing. He was tired of losing everything again and again and having to start over so many times. He placed his head in his hands and started to weep softly.

Bathael reached over and placed their hand lightly on Drake's head. "Oh child, take heart. You were given a task which would have tested the resolve of the greatest men. Your Creator is proud of you and blesses you. You are blameless. I should have intervened sooner. Know this though, Drake Sullivan; your redemption is within reach!"

Drake involuntarily leaned into the warmth of Bathael's touch. As bad as he felt under the angel's admonishing gaze mere moments earlier, now he felt relieved and loved. The words were comforting in a way he'd never felt, though as the weight of them sank in, he became confused.

"Wait," he said, sitting up and pulling away from Bathael's hand, "what do you mean my redemption is within reach?"

"Two of the *Bachar'im* yet remain, Drake Sullivan, and both are connected to you. They are being drawn to you, though they may not know it. Even if it is not part of the Plan, Drake Sullivan, I have foreseen it. You still have a chance to fulfill your greater purpose," the angel added with a smile.

Drake stood up from the table and started to pace. "I've had enough of plans and prophecies. I'm just a man, an *old* man, and there's nothing special about me, despite the 'gift' of my endless life, and the time it granted me to learn and develop the talents I have. You say the Chosen are near, and I say since you know where they are, you can find them and teach them yourself," he cried out in frustration. "I no longer have the will or the desire to lead more children to their deaths for a cause they cannot understand and wouldn't believe in, for creatures who don't care about them."

Bathael continued to smile softly at Drake and replied, "You will do it because it is what you are meant to do. I would have thought your time with the Seer would have taught you that some things cannot be avoided. She understood this, better than most humans, and she tried to pass this knowledge on to you."

Drake looked down at the mention of his relationship with Claire. He still felt the pain of her loss on a visceral level. He blamed himself for Claire's death; he always felt there was more he could have done. She tried, many times, to get Drake to acknowledge that some of the things she saw were absolute and couldn't be prevented or changed, and that the specifics of her death were among them. He never accepted that, so she hid the details of her impending demise from him until it was too late. He didn't understand why she was resigned to her fate. Because of this, as much as he never forgave himself, he'd never forgiven her either.

"She knew I don't care for absolutes. I am not *Be'elohim*," he said angrily. "I care even less for being a pawn in someone else's game. Even if they are omnipotent beings from another plane. I have served the Creator as well as I could from the moment...," Drake struggled to find the words. Some things were too painful to talk about, even after millennia. "I have served the Creator for a very long time. I gave up everything without even knowing the cause. But I did *not* sign up to raise an army. Have you lost so much of your humanity that you must see the prophecy to the bitter end?"

Bathael stood up and moved toward Drake, placed a gentle hand on his shoulder to stop his pacing, and spoke in a soft, calming voice. "Now, which of us is more like the *Be'elohim*? Yes, they believe that prophecy is law, so much so that they are moved to inaction and allow things to continue which should not. I have a secret to share with you, Drake Sullivan," Bathael said more solemnly; "the Aetherium have not communed with the Creator since the Shattering of the Planes. They are rudderless and refuse to act for fear it will be against the Plan."

Drake's jaw was agape at this revelation, but he didn't have time to absorb it before Bathael continued. "I can assure you, Drake Sullivan, others will not be so reserved. They *will* act, even if you do not, and they will act to the detriment of all Creation. I always hoped the Outcast could be saved and brought home. But it was my own arrogance speaking. I forgot that to be forgiven, one must *seek* forgiveness. The *Nadach* has no desire to be brought back into the fold, only to remake Creation in their own image. And without the Creator, the Aetherium will do nothing to stop it. You know what the means, do you not?" Bathael asked softly.

"The end of everything," Drake replied with a resigned sigh.

"That is correct. And could you carry on into the end of days knowing that you may have been able to do something about it and did not?" Bathael prodded.

Drake shot the angel a look that would have cause a normal person to wither into nothing, but before he could answer, there was a loud knock on the door.

"I'm busy! Go away!" he shouted, loudly enough to be heard in the main complex.

"Dr. Sullivan, we need you back at the Command Post immediately," came the reply in Capt. Heighton's familiar voice. "The Chill...," she started before Drake cut her off.

"...will be there tomorrow, Captain!"

"No, Dr. Sullivan. The Chill is *gone!*" she retorted sharpy. "Now, open the door right now, or I'll shoot the hinges off!"

Drake marveled at how inconvenient and complicating angels were and suddenly understood why everyone was afraid of them.

> He that has eyes to see and ears to hear
> may convince himself that no mortal can keep a secret.
> *- Sigmund Freud*

Chapter 16

Tim had been undercover for about five weeks. Even though his trials were successful far beyond anyone's expectations, Samuels was always overly cautious. Everything, all the time, had to be perfect – down to the millisecond and micron. He accepted no excuses for any mistakes, or issues that may arise due to unforeseen circumstances. That was why, it was explained to Tim, the override protocol had been tested beyond necessity. It was the first mission he was leading, and he felt more than ready. It was hardly his first rodeo, after all.

Tim slowly sipped on his fifth cup of coffee of the morning. He casually flipped through that morning's *Washington Post*, or at least that's the way it appeared. The paper and coffee afforded him the cover he needed to properly surveil his target. The coffee shop was in the right location and his engineered eyes looked through the newsprint. He was following a former Pentagon employee who was allegedly selling secrets to a company who did business with Mexico. The same man was also supposed to be the leader of a grassroots anti-government organization which had been making threats against specific agencies and leaders. Homegrown terror was the worst kind, in Tim's mind, and far too often the victims of terror attacks were innocent bystanders.

Tim was uniquely suited for this kind of work, especially now, but he wasn't comfortable operating on American soil. Something felt off about it. It was one of the last remaining policies that kept America from sliding into authoritarianism; the military didn't police civilians. And those rules mattered to him. Since a former member of the military was involved, and a number of Federal Judges had been threatened, Samuels wanted to skirt Posse Comitatus. Tim's requirement for doing so was that he first be deputized by the U.S. Marshals. Samuels, in a rare show of acquiescence, agreed. Once everything was above board to Tim's satisfaction, he got to work.

The Agents and Marshals Tim worked with all complained that he had an unfair advantage over them, not that they minded the help. They tried to get detailed information on the target's activities for some time, but Tim had done more in a couple of weeks than they had in over a year. For his part, Tim remembered doing some surveillance work in the past, but it was never this easy. Previously, losing focus on a target might mean losing track of them for weeks. Now, he didn't even need to pay attention to track everyone and everything going on around him.

With his new body and abilities, Tim easily blended into the local color, becoming effectively invisible. He also had access to petabytes of information on languages, customs, history, and current events, so he could have an intelligent conversation with anyone in the world, in their language, at any given moment. He could even emulate regional accents. This gave him an unprecedented ability to monitor and even interact with targets without their knowledge.

Across the street from the small coffee shop where Tim sat, an intensely nervous man paced along the crowded sidewalk. The man clutched a well-worn brown leather satchel that seemed vaguely familiar to Tim. Maybe he had one like it once? The man clutched the case like it held the nuclear codes, and it might as well have, as far as the FBI was concerned.

Tim focused his attention on the man, still holding up the paper so as not to be noticed. It took him half a second to confirm that the unwashed, unshaven face was that of his intended target, Nate Lange. Tim could smell him from across the street; being on the run didn't leave much time for hygiene, it seemed. Once his objective was marked, Tim was able to go back to reading a fascinating article about honeybees.

Nate was a shadow of the man he was, though Tim didn't know that. As far as he was concerned, he didn't know this man at all, or at least outside of what he'd read in his personnel file and the FBI dossier. Nate and his briefcase reminded Tim of something, but he could never put his finger on what. So, he shrugged it off. The file said they went to the same school as kids, so that was probably it. If a fraction of what they'd gathered on Nate were true, Tim didn't *want* to know him.

There was an innate curiosity about what was in the satchel, though. While it looked, and smelled, like Nate hadn't seen in the inside of a shower for some time, the way he clutched the bag made Tim think he would have taken it in with him. Tim had his suspicions about what the satchel contained, but he didn't dwell on it. Nate was the mission, not the bag, though Tim wasn't naïve enough to think the two weren't connected.

The idea that the real mission was the bag occurred to Tim more than once. That would explain why all involved were so willing to jump into the legally grey area with so little hesitation. If Nate *was* stealing secrets, they were likely in the bag, and if not, the means to access them was. That meant no matter what went down, the case would be important. Whatever was inside was probably a serious threat to national security. That was obvious. It seemed odd, then, that retrieval of the case wasn't part of Tim's objective.

Nate walked back and forth over the same stretch of pavement long enough for people to avoid him. He was obviously paranoid, muttering to himself as he paced. If he wasn't completely insane, he was playing the role well. He kept looking back and forth down the street, as if he was waiting for someone, at least that was what Tim hoped. They held off on arresting Nate so they could also grab his co-conspirators. Up to this point, it was all speculation, but the evidence pointed to the meeting happening sometime soon. Tim watched people enough to tell the difference between anxiety and anticipation. Someone was definitely coming, and they were late.

Still, Tim's gut told him something was off about the whole operation, but he kept those feelings quietly in check. He trusted his instincts, and he certainly knew better than to trust Samuels or anyone on his team. To keep things on the level, and his intuition in check, he dug up his own information, used his own sources, and followed his own leads. He played along with the other agencies, and with Samuels, but he wasn't going to act until he was certain what the end result would be. His primary concern at this point was making sure no bystanders were hurt, something no one else seemed particularly concerned about.

Tim quickly gulped down the rest of his coffee and continued pretending to read the paper while still tracking Nate passively. If he stayed at the table much longer, he'd become as conspicuous as Nate. So, he folded up the paper, left a tip in the jar on the counter, and walked toward the door of the coffee shop. Just then, a nondescript grey car sped around the corner near him, causing pedestrians in the crosswalk to scramble like mice in the pantry. It happened so quickly, he missed getting a look at the driver, but he had the plates and that was all he needed.

Tim tossed the paper in a nearby trash bin as he walked through the doors, waving to the baristas as he left casually. Meanwhile, Nate scrambled feverishly to get into the car. In contrast, Tim walked deliberately to his motorcycle that was parked on the street around the corner. The sound of squealing tires alerted Tim that his target was now on the move.

"Beta 4, Overlord," Tim heard in his head. "Was that your target speeding away in a car without so much as a peep from the man on the ground? Please tell me you aren't letting him get away," the voice added with an annoyed tone.

"Overlord, Beta 4," Tim replied nonchalantly, "you need to relax before you give yourself an ulcer. I have a lock on the vehicle. It's a rental: grey, late model four-door sedan, Virginia plates, zulu-alpha-quebec-one-one-seven-five. I have the VIN from Motor Vehicles, GPS appears to be disabled, but I have them on traffic cams locally. I'll be Oscar Mike in thirty seconds."

"Beta 4, Overlord: copy on Oscar Mike," the handler noted. "Your orders have been updated. Apprehend Commander Lange by any means necessary, alive, and as undamaged as possible. All other concerns are secondary. We believe his briefcase has information on dozens of classified operations and projects and including how to access specific military satellites and network hardpoints. The contents are classified TS-SCI, and you do *not* — repeat you do *not* need to confirm contents. The bag is to be attained, sealed, and marked for retrieval by Federal agents."

"Overlord, how the hell do you know what's in that bag?" Tim asked directly. "I've been watching this asshole for weeks. I've followed everything, listened to every conversation. Hell, I can tell you how many times he took a shit, and I have no idea what's in that bag," Tim added sharply. "Is there a second team in play? God damn it, I've told you people you have to tell me if there are other friendlies in theater," he added with heightened frustration.

"Beta 4, this is Overlord Actual," came the terse reply in Samuels' dark tone. "This mission is Priority Alpha. You have your orders and you've been told everything you need. Now, acknowledge, or we shut you down and send in the secondary team."

Samuels had a method of getting right to the point in a way Tim would have admired if he didn't hate it. "Overlord Actual, Beta 4: orders acknowledged. Beta 4 out," he replied curtly.

Tim turned his jacket inside out and put on a pair of dark sunglasses. Reflexively, he shifted his facial appearance again, this time to its native state. It wasn't 'normal' to him still, but it was the face he wore when he wasn't trying to look like someone else; the one he slept in. That was normal enough for now. The changes in his appearance were silent, but Tim always imagined snapping and popping noises, which made it hard for him to watch in a mirror. Most people would. After a few seconds, he looked like a completely different person from the one who sat at the coffee shop.

No one watching would know Tim was in pursuit of a dangerous and wanted man. He casually straddled the motorcycle, started it, and tapped into the traffic monitoring system for the city. Since the War and the Awakening, the widespread paranoia allowed the government to take rather extreme measures. It's how people like Samuels came to have so much influence. Fear is a powerful motivator. Every car now had a government-monitored GPS locator, and there were cameras everywhere.

Even without the GPS, Tim would have no trouble following the mystery sedan. He started into traffic and followed at a respectable distance. Since he was linked to the traffic system, he already worked out the best path to get to the fleeing car without worrying about lights. He didn't even need to follow them. Nate's car was about three quarters of a mile ahead and Tim could cut it off easily if he wanted. But he thought it would be better to get them out of the city and away from more heavily populated areas.

As Tim watched the progress of the grey sedan on the cameras, he noted that it was expertly moving at breakneck speed through the crowded city streets. Whoever was behind the wheel was a highly skilled driver. If he didn't know better, he would have thought they were trying to evade someone, though they shouldn't know that they were being pursued. The driving was too frenetic to just be an escape. That convinced him there was indeed a second team in play and that they were spotted by the driver of the getaway car. It was time to close the gap.

Just as Tim cranked the accelerator, the traffic system went dark. Every camera in a 20-mile radius stopped sending data. That cinched it; they knew they were being followed, and they were well prepared. It was a good thing he also didn't need the cameras to follow the car. When he'd scanned for the license plate, he subconsciously made note of the unique chemical composition of the exhaust. Slight differences in cars made it possible for someone augmented like Tim to tell one car from another, and even to track it up to 30 minutes after it passed. He made his way to the planned interception point and was relieved to pick up the trail there.

Tim was able to dart through the remaining city traffic with ease, following the trail of the speeding car ahead. After a few miles, he could see the sedan in the distance, but it was deceptively fast, and he was struggling to keep up. At this point, he was content to keep them visible since they would have to stop eventually. Once they were out of the city, the mystery sedan slowed a bit. Perhaps the driver thought they were in the clear. Tim followed suit and relaxed a little. He was impressed at the lengths Nate and his accomplice had gone through to escape. He wasn't sure if he wanted to shake their hands or punch them in the face.

"Overlord, Beta 4: I'm continuing pursuit of the target out of the city. It's my opinion that following them to their destination might give us Lange's contacts or co-conspirators, as well as the buyers, or least valuable intel on them," Tim proffered. Waiting for a reply, he added, "Please advise."

"Beta 4, Overlord," came the quick response. "Mission change approved. Proceed as recommended. Update objectives upon arrival."

Tim grinned as he answered, "Acknowledged, Overlord. Continuing pursuit of target. Will advise of new parameters upon arrival. Beta 4 out."

The drive went on for hours, deep into the foothills and mountains of northern Virginia. It was easy enough for Tim to follow Nate's car and stay out of sight. He figured they would need to stop for gas soon, and he checked every turn off to see if his quarry pulled off the highway. Tim noticed a sign ahead – it read "McDowell – population 425." Where the hell were they going? Tim looked it up and there was nothing worthy of note nearby. He realized, though, it could be a great place to go unnoticed if you were on the run.

Just as he was ready to report in, his handler's voice chimed in, "Beta 4, this is Overlord: We have additional information that is pertinent to your pursuit, and an update to your objective."

Tim didn't like how this mission kept changing, but he knew better than to mention it. "Go head for Beta 4, Overlord. Maybe you can tell me what I'm doing ten miles west of nowhere."

"Beta 4," the operator continued, ignoring Tim's comment, "we were able to confirm with the rental company that the driver of the car paid in cash and used a fake ID to secure the car. Since they don't keep much cash on hand, we were able to get the serial numbers from the bills."

"Overlord, please tell me there's a point in there somewhere," Tim interrupted.

"I was coming to that, Beta 4," the operator continued. "The money was traced to a trust account held by Emma Thibodeaux."

There was a flash of silver eyes in Tim's mind that vanished as soon as he saw them. It happened from time to time, but he'd learned to ignore them. Besides, he didn't have time to ponder them now. "Overlord, is it possible that Nate Lange had access to that account, or that someone other than her withdrew that money?"

"Negative, Beta 4," came the grim reply. "The account can only be accessed by her and requires biometric confirmation for changes or withdrawals. We circled back to the rental company with a driver's license photo and the agent confirmed that she was the person who paid in cash. We have Miss Thibodeaux on security footage and a warrant for her arrest."

While Tim was listening, he followed the exhaust trail off the main highway and into the mountains. Before he could acknowledge, something started to go terribly wrong. As he traveled further away from the main highway, he noticed that his connection to the satellites and radio systems started to waver. He tried connecting to GPS and found he could not. This was a communication failure that shouldn't have been possible.

On cue, his handlers radioed in, "Beta 4,… lord Actu… we can no longer… BZZZZZZ… stop purs… immediately. Repeat… BZZZZZZZ… Beta 4, ackn…"

"Overlord Actual, Beta 4: Can you read? Last transmission was one by one. Retransmit, over."

The only reply was garbled static. Tim knew it was a recall order, but he knew how important Nate Lange was, and he didn't want to be responsible for losing track of a terrorist. He also knew what would happen if he returned empty handed, but that was the least of his concerns. He was emotionally invested now and wanted to know what was going on. First the driver, then the cameras, now a communications blackout; who was helping Nate Lange escape and how did they have access to all these systems? He needed to get to the bottom of it all *before* Samuels, or anyone else, got involved.

Tim pressed on, making his way along the winding road, following the trail left by the grey sedan. He had the nagging feeling in his gut again, and he needed to sort it out. The operator said Emma's name as if he should know who she was, but he didn't. He knew Nate Lange inside out, every contact, every person he'd ever known. But Emma Thibodeaux never came up, not once. And there was that troublesome familiarity he felt for Lange, and nothing for Emma. He felt like he *should* know her, but where she should be was just an empty place. It was like he simultaneously knew she existed but didn't. And then to see the eyes again after so many weeks of not seeing them. It all had to be connected. It was too much.

That's when the world went sideways…quite literally. Just as he was heading into a bend in the road, an all-too-familiar feeling crept into his limbs. The override protocol was being executed, and there wasn't anything he could do to stop it.

"Oh, for Christ's sake, not now," Tim lamented as he tried desperately to slow down the speeding motorcycle. But it was too late; he could no longer control his limbs. He could only experience the full speed horror of his bike hurtling headlong into the approaching guardrail. The darkness was closing in rapidly as he hit the barrier and careened into the valley below.

"This is going to leave a mark," Tim thought to himself as he slipped out of consciousness.

For the human soul is virtually indestructible,
and its ability to rise from the ashes remains
as long as the body draws breath.
- Alice Miller

Chapter 17

"He's over here!"

Emma looked back over her shoulder toward the voice which called out. She couldn't see him, but Nate was at the bottom of the ridge, on the banks of a shallow creek. She couldn't help but be a little sad each time she looked at him. He was a shell of the man she'd known all those years ago, haggard and unshaven, a month's growth covering the deep lines in his cheeks. He was too skinny, she thought, and his clothes, which probably once fit well, were baggy and loose. His eyes told her that he hadn't laughed in ages and rarely slept.

Choosing her footing down the slope carefully, Emma made her way in the direction of Nate's voice. Loose rocks skittered and clattered down the hill and landed with a splash in the water below. After some careful stepping, and more than a few expletives, she finally reached the bottom. There, next to the water, lay the crumpled form of the man they were looking for.

Emma gasped audibly when she was able to see him clearly. One of his arms was positioned awkwardly over his head, the other bent in at an impossible angle. His legs, too, appeared obviously broken by the fall. She looked up the wall of the ravine toward the road; Tim hadn't *just* fallen, he was thrown and ended up rolling and sliding more than 100 yards away from the edge of the road. They might not have found him were it not for the path the motorcycle cleared on its way down.

"Are you sure he's alive?" she asked, her face filled with concern. "I mean, look at him. Did you check for a pulse or something?" They were reasonable questions given Tim's condition.

"No, but I'm not sure he has one," Nate replied. "Anyway, I didn't want to risk, I don't know, hurting him more than he already is? Matt said he could survive anything up to a tactical nuclear strike, but he looks so…," Nate didn't want to say out loud what they were both thinking.

"Broken," Emma finished for him with a profound sadness.

After gathering the courage Nate couldn't, Emma knelt next to Tim's mangled body and began to shift him. She adjusted his limbs into a more recognizable position, then turned him face up. They both winced, almost in unison, as Tim's bloodied face rolled into view. As she tenderly cleared the blood-caked dirt and leaves from his face, her look of concern was replaced with one of confusion.

"Are you sure this is Colonel Andrews?" she asked, looking back over her shoulder at Nate. "I know you said he might look different, but this," she paused, motioning at Tim's face, "he doesn't look anything like the way I remember him. Not even close."

Nate was gathering up whatever he could find of Tim's belongings and putting them into Tim's bag, which he found nearby. He looked back at Emma and replied, "I'm positive. He's been tailing me all day, so it has to be him. He can change his face, his eyes, his skin color, everything. But I'd know him anywhere. He still walks and carries himself the same way. When I saw him two years ago, he looked totally different. They've made him invisible, so the people who loved him wouldn't know what they've done to him. He doesn't look the same but," Nate paused, looking down at his old friend with a mix of grief and pity, "I know it's him. I can't explain it better than that. Besides, Matt told us this is the guy, and he'd know."

Emma stood up and walked over to Nate to embrace him. Tears had been welling up for both of them since they'd found Tim on the ground, and now she could no longer contain hers. Emma had said horrible things about Tim in the weeks that followed her mother's death. She was young, and she blamed Claire's 'so-called protectors' for not saving her. Tim would have borne the brunt of it, but he was dead, so she was able to move on quickly. Emma understood now there was nothing that could have been done that wasn't, and that Claire's death was inevitable. She made sure of it.

Emma wanted to go to Cincinnati with them, but Claire had made it clear that she didn't want Emma in harm's way if it could be avoided. Tim supported this decision wholeheartedly; there was a credible threat, and keeping Emma away made security easier. He said, more than once, that he couldn't protect both of them effectively enough for his own satisfaction. Tim's father had a cabin in Virginia which would be a perfect place to meet once the seminar in Cincinnati was over. So, Emma stayed with the second team, led by his protégé, Lieutenant Sarah Heighton, in a cozy cabin as her mother waited for her own death. It was a cabin Tim had forgotten about; a cabin that was nearby. Tim's decision saved her life that day.

There was her savior, lying in the water next to her. All those feelings rushed into her mind, all the anger and hate, and all the love and happiness as well. It all came back as she looked down at his motionless and broken body.

"What are we going to do, Nate? Mom's letter was pretty clear on this. We need him. He's crucial to everything, and if he's," she stopped herself from choking on the word, "if he's dead, what then?"

"Who's...dead?" came the weak response from behind Emma. She nearly jumped out of her skin, then covered her mouth with both hands. She wanted to scream, but she stifled herself. Instead, she just hugged Nate and sobbed in relief. Nate and Emma pulled Tim out of the mud and muck and struggled their way up the side of the ravine. He was heavier than he should have been, and the trip exhausted all three of them, but they made it back to the cabin safely.

It was hours before Tim groggily opened his eyes. Something wasn't right, though. His vision was blurred and shaky, like looking at an old television that wasn't tuned in all the way. He ached, if that was the right word for it, and as he attempted to sit up, a stiffness in his back halted the motion halfway up. He settled for propping himself up on his elbows, but they hurt too. His head and neck were sore, so he rolled his head around trying to loosen up a bit. He hadn't hurt this way in a long time. One of his trials put him up against a prototype M75 tank, which was awful. This was worse.

Looking down the length of his body, Tim could see that his shirt and pants were shredded and covered in blood. The stiffness and aches told him that his systems were busy repairing some serious damage, which also meant the blood was his. He tried to remember what happened, or how he got in the bed. He looked around, and there was the irritatingly vague familiarity again.

Where *was* he? Laying back, he tried to start a diagnostic, but he got an error showing he was offline. He didn't know it was possible to be offline if he was awake and trying to self-diagnose. Was he awake? He wasn't sure he could tell anymore. Then the light bulb went off and he realized what happened.

"Damn it, Samuels, you can't keep your finger off that button, can you?" Tim complained aloud, thinking he was alone.

"He's never been big on self-restraint," came an unexpected reply.

Tim would have shot up in the bed, had he been able. But since he couldn't, he simply propped himself up on one side. He narrowed his eyes as he tried to focus on the figure on the far side of the room. "Who's there?"

"It's Matthew Young, Colonel Andrews. I'm not sure if you'll remember me, considering how the Secretary likes to do things," he commented with a disgusted tone. "Now, lay down. You've been through a lot, and it's going to take time for you to repair all the damage from the fall."

"How did I get here? I was chasing someone… it was Nate Lange. Are you his contact? You've set up some kind of dampening zone here, haven't you? Is that why I can't contact base; why I can't do a diagnostic?" Tim demanded, his mind milling with dozens of questions.

"I wish we had time for all that, Colonel. I really do. However, it's a near certainty that once he lost contact, Stephen sent a team to locate you," Dr. Young said grimly. "So, we must make the best use of what little time we have. I made a mistake, a horrible one, and I intend to make it right," he concluded with resolve.

Tim grew concerned now, and tried to sit up, finding he still couldn't. "Mistake? I don't know what you're talking about. The only mistake I know of was thinking you'd get away with any of this!" Tim said as he struggled to lift himself. He found, though, that there was too much damage, and his limbs were still useless.

Matthew put his hand on Tim's chest and gently, but firmly, urged him to lie still. "Colonel there really isn't time for this. I'll tell you what I can, but you must listen. I wasn't part of the Alfa or Beta projects at the start, but I do know what happened in them. And why Stephen insisted there be a way to shut down any project devices—people like you—if you didn't follow commands. You weren't his first test subject, you see. The last time, it went very poorly. He lost control of his toy soldier, and people died. You know Stephen; he despises failure, especially his own."

Matthew was moving around the table as Tim listened. The twinges of remembrance were there again, and he felt like he'd seen all of this before. "He was never satisfied with how the override worked, though. Once he took over my team, he put them to work upgrading his original designs for the platform. They created a system that didn't just shut you down, it allowed another person to take control," Dr. Young said grimly. "If you've blacked out, it's because someone else was driving."

Tim wasn't sure how to react to this information. The whole idea seemed ridiculous, but he wouldn't have put it past Samuels. He'd been on half a dozen or so missions since being cleared for service. The blackouts were somewhat common, but he just assumed it was Samuels' way of reinforcing the pecking order. The idea that Samuels was actually controlling his actions; it was a bridge too far. Sure, Samuels was an asshole, but what Dr. Young was suggesting went beyond that.

"That can't be true. You're lying to protect Lange!" Tim yelled. "I know who you are now. You're the guy they fired for embezzling money out of the project. Is this some sort of revenge? Were you teaming up with Lange to sell me to the Chinese?" Tim was frantic and tried to get up but found that he couldn't.

"It's a compression field, Colonel. Something I cooked up long before I met Stephen," Matthew said dryly, removing his glasses to rub his eyes. They were sunken and dark from days with little to no sleep.

"I've got no reason to lie to you Colonel, and Mexico has nothing to do with this, but I think you know that. Neither do Nate or Emma, really. I asked for their help, and they offered this place. They told me it was once yours. Fitting, really," he said as he glanced around.

"Now, I want you to think back on all those times you lost consciousness; it always seems to happen at critical moments, right? Maybe when you questioned an order in your head, or perhaps you decide to do something off plan, like today? Tell me the last thing you remember," Matt asked with purpose.

"Why should I help you?" Tim spat.

"You aren't. I'm helping you," Matthew replied calmly.

Tim hated to admit it, but Matthew was right. The blackouts always happened at the least convenient times. He tried to focus on those moments before he lost consciousness, but he couldn't. His memory was unreliable, even on the best days. Everything was cloudy and unfocused. Instead, he tried to focus on the chase and the crash. Maybe being more recent, it would be easier to remember.

"Ok, I'll play along. The last thing I remember," Tim replied uncertainly, "was following a grey sedan carrying Nate Lange driven by an unknown person. Then," he hesitated, working to recall the events, "I lost contact with everything, like I was in some sort of massive dead zone. Ops told me to pull off, but I didn't. I didn't want to lose…," Tim's voice trailed off with the realization that just as he made the decision to ignore the recall order, he lost control of his body. Dr. Young was telling the truth. Matthew was sitting on a nearby stool, staying quiet and waiting for Tim to draw his own conclusions.

"Let's say I believe you," Tim finally said quietly. "Why didn't they get control this time?"

Matthew stood up and walked over to the table where Tim was lying. "Simple. I didn't want them to. As I said, I asked Commander Lange for help, and he offered this place. He and I worked together to prepare it and draw you here. I meant everything I said earlier. I did you a terrible disservice for the most selfish of reasons. I need to make it right."

Matthew moved to the end of the table as he continued explaining. "Stephen wasn't the only one who knew how to find hidden things. I wrote the programs that allow you to communicate, so it was easy to create a system that blocked the signals. In order for me to correct my mistake, I needed to know they wouldn't use you to kill me," he added matter-of-factly.

Tim looked down at Matthew who was still standing at the foot of the table. "So, what's the plan?"

"I'm going to remove your memory blocks, remove the hardware for the Override Protocol, and connect you to an independent, secure mainframe that will take Stephen a dozen lifetimes to find and decrypt. You'll be no different functionally, aside from being completely autonomous. However," Young added with a smile, "the decision is yours. I won't make any changes unless you want me to. I am not him."

Tim didn't even blink before answering, "What the hell are you waiting for?"

We are immortal until our work on Earth is done.
- George Whitefield

Chapter 18

Drake knew enough about the assertive young officer to know she was more than capable of forcing her way into the trailer if she felt she needed to. He didn't think this was one of those times, but he wasn't sure he wanted to find out. Raising a finger to his lips, he motioned for Bathael to quietly move to the rear of the trailer. Once the angel was in the back, he closed the curtain that separated the sleeping area from the rest of the space. He moved to the door, took a deep breath, and opened it just enough to peek out.

"Gone you say? Are you certain? It still seems a bit nippy out there," he said, feigning a shiver. Capt. Heighton was not amused, so he smiled a bit and continued, "Just having a laugh, Captain. I suspect you're here to tell me I'll be leaving in the morning. Well then, consider me informed and check me off your list. I'll start packing right away. Good morning!" he exclaimed before trying to shut the door.

Sarah's reflexes were quicker than Drake's, though, and she reached out to keep the door from closing. "I have no idea how people deal with you every day; you're the most infuriating man I've ever known. I have orders to bring you back to the Command Post. Immediately. As in, *now*," she added for effect. "I would prefer you to be dressed and walk under your own power, but the idea of knocking you out and carrying you over my shoulder is more appealing than… it… should be…," Sarah's words trailed off as her eyes drifted over Drake's shoulder.

Drake was so focused on dealing with his unexpected visitor that he didn't notice Bathael move directly behind him. When she stammered, Drake looked over his shoulder and made a disapproving noise. However, he sensed an opportunity to take control of the situation, so he grabbed her by the hand, pulled her into the trailer, and slammed the door shut behind her.

The noise snapped Sarah out of her daze, and she exclaimed, "Sweet Mother Mary!"

"Not quite," Drake joked, "but not as far off as you might think."

Drake guided Sarah into the booth-like bench seat at his kitchenette table. He quickly moved to the cabinet, pushing Bathael out of the way gently, grabbed a cup, and filled it with hot tea. He handed the cup to Sarah who accepted it with a half-hearted smile. She quivered so much, though, she nearly dropped it. To say she was in shock would have been a massive understatement. Coming face-to-face with a supernatural being was more than most people could take. He thought she was doing well.

Drake let Sarah collect herself, but he noticed that she still retreated at the sight of the angel. A natural response, he noted, to any being of great power. Sarah's instincts were overpowering her reason, so Drake pulled her attention back to him. At this point, he felt he owed her more than a few explanations.

"I'm sure you have a great many questions, Capt. Heighton," he began as he chose his words carefully. She was staring into her cup, half listening, but mostly lost in thought. "I should begin by explaining that most of what you think is true, isn't; I'm speaking even of those things about which you are certain. I'm going to ask that you set aside those firmly-held beliefs and preconceived notions and assume that everything I'm about to tell you is the absolute, indisputable truth. Can you do that?" Drake asked solemnly.

Sarah glanced up and nodded slightly, still taking care not to look at the angel standing behind Drake.

"Good. First, and this one will be difficult to hear, my name is *not* Drake Sullivan; at least, that's not the name my mother and father gave me. My father wanted a large family, so when I was born first, I was named Primus. My father was a Roman Legionnaire named Marcus Cassius Longinus," Drake said dramatically before he paused and waited for a reaction that never came. Sarah just raised her eyebrows expectantly, waiting for Drake to continue.

"You've never heard of the Legend of Longinus?" Drake inquired, aghast.

Sarah shook her head. "No. Should I have?"

Drake sat back in the seat, his jaw slack. "Spear of Destiny?"

Sarah shook her head again before answering in excitement, "Wait, I think I've heard of that one. Wasn't it a video game?"

Drake hung his head in defeat. "What do they even teach people these days?" he pondered rhetorically. "Surely, you're familiar with the Biblical account of the crucifixion."

Sarah didn't reply this time and only nodded.

"Good. Now, as you know, at the moment of death, Jesus was stabbed with a *pilum*—a type of long spear—by a Roman soldier. That man was my father, and my life has been spent serving the penance he could not. It's been 2,000 years since I took on his burden, waiting for the signs," Drake said, a look of exhaustion settling on his face.

Sarah nearly choked as she sipped her tea. "Wait, are you saying what I think you're saying?"

"If you think I'm saying that I'm over 2,000 years old, then indeed I am," Drake replied flatly. "As hard as that may be to believe."

"Not as hard as you might think," Sarah countered. "What were the signs? Was this one of them?" she motioned as she looked all around, referring to the Chill.

Drake cleared his throat before continuing, "Somewhat, but I'll get to that in a moment. They weren't the signs people would expect, mainly because they were written as allegory. The most important was to be the emergence of the *Bachar'im*, descendants of those who shared the final meal with Jesus. You, young lady...excuse me...you, Captain, are one of the only two remaining," Drake added gravely.

Sarah sat back in the seat. Her hands weren't shaking anymore, and she regarded Drake skeptically. If there wasn't a supernatural creature hovering behind Drake, she wouldn't have believed any of it. The whole thing was preposterous, and she was sure he was having a joke at her expense.

"I think I've seen this movie before, Dr. Sullivan," she said with no small amount of snark. "You're talking about the Holy Grail. Wouldn't those people be immortal like you? Wait! Is that why you're immortal? Am I immortal? Do you have it here? Did you meet Galahad? What was he like?" Sarah stopped when Drake held up his hand, a stern look etched into his face.

"Please, this is serious," he snapped. "I told you before, you have to forget what you think you know about those legends. They *are* real, but not as you know them to be. You think the Grail matters because you read a story that told you so; a story *I* wrote. Well, helped to write," he corrected himself. "I didn't want people knowing the truth because that knowledge could be dangerous. Wars were fought over the Grail, and it didn't even matter. It was never the Grail that granted immortality. It was the Spear."

Sarah sipped the tea and held her disbelief in check as she listened to Drake intently. "As Christianity spread throughout Europe and the Near East, political leaders discovered that so-called Holy Relics could increase their influence and power with the early Church and its followers. Young men were sent to their deaths daily in search of relics that didn't exist, or to claim lands that couldn't be used or cultivated. I couldn't risk the Spear being lost or stolen, nor allow people to be sacrificed to test false spears," he explained. Sarah nodded in understanding.

"Fraud and counterfeiting were real issues back then," Drake added looking down a bit. "Every king from Constantinople to Oslo had a piece of the True Cross or a shred of the Veil of Veronica. Everyone had something they claimed belonged to or was touched by or bled on by the Christ. So, I created the Grail Legend, because no one was going to bleed to death drinking water from a cup," Drake remarked sadly. "If I couldn't stop them fighting over nonsense, I could at least protect them from themselves. Arthur was just another mark, albeit a well-known one," Drake said chuckling a bit. "Pleasant chap, for the most part, but not too bright."

Sarah's brow furrowed in confusion as she asked, "But I thought Merlin...,"

Drake held up his hand again to stop her. "After a 1,000 years of wandering, and over 400 years in Wales, I was going by the name Sieffre o Fynwy; or more more commonly in English, Geoffrey of Monmouth. I told stories about the long-past days of Arthur when I had met my oldest and dearest friend, Myrddin Wyllt. You know the name better as Merlin," he added.

"It belongs to an ancient creature bound to me by a life debt he's repaid a hundred times or more," Drake said as he smiled and looked over to his shaggy companion as he rested nearby. "I borrowed his name in those early days because, at the time, it was unknown and mysterious. I needed to go about my work unnoticed, and taking a new name gave me the anonymity and berth I needed to do just that. As Merlin the Wild, Merlin the Mage, I was scary and strange, and people avoided me," he said before continuing, "I guess I really *haven't* changed all that much." Sarah chuckled a bit.

"Anyway," Drake continued, "His name wasn't his only gift to me. In return for saving his life, and a place at my dinner table, he taught me the secrets of the Planes and how to channel and manipulate planar energy, what you'd call magic, in a way that wasn't possible for most people. I was only able because of the effects of the Spear, and I had the time necessary to master the skills." He added with a cheeky grin, "Most people only have one lifetime to learn in."

On cue, Merlin got up from his corner and plodded over to where Sarah sat and placed his large woolly head on her lap. He whimpered a bit and nudged her hand expectantly. Sarah looked down, unsure of what she might see, but it was only Merlin's shaggy face looking back. She reached down and scratched behind his ear, a gesture he enthusiastically accepted. She looked back up at Drake skeptically.

"Honestly, Dr. Sullivan, you had me right up to the point that you told me your dog taught you how to do magic. Has anyone ever fallen for this?" she asked, her tone dripping with sarcasm and cynicism.

"You're only the second person I've told, but yes, the last one believed me," Drake answered with a hint of sadness before carrying on. "And he's not a dog. Not really. Though he's been a dog for so long he's probably forgotten how to be anything else. He's a creature ancient beyond reckoning, and powerful beyond measure." Merlin approved of this description with a soft bark before laying back down. "These days, he mostly just sleeps and is generally harmless. Can we move on?"

Drake stood up, he knees and back popping as if to accentuate his newly revealed age. He walked over to the tea pot, then frowned when he saw that it was empty. "I have much more to tell you," he said as he started making another pot.

"Sure," Sarah said glibly. "I figure this all has to be a dream anyway. I'm probably still asleep in my rack. That's the last time I have *Papaw Peanut's Five Alarm Jerky* before bed. Or maybe it was the chiles rellenos Master Sergeant Arroyo shared with the team. Either way, this isn't really happening, so please, carry on," she concluded with a sarcastic smile.

Drake regarded Sarah with a slight frown and sighed. He never understood why people were so eager to deny the truth, usually when it was staring them in the face. They always, *always*, preferred the lie. Even he did when he was a young man, so he recognized it as a universal truth. Rare was the person who went against that grain.

It took him decades to come to terms with the penance he was serving for his father's sin. It began as he watched the woman he loved fade slowly into old age and death when he grew no older. Even now, he used magical means to conceal his apparent youth. Behind the façade of the grumpy old man, Drake would have appeared to be in his late-20's; he looked fit, vibrant, and youthful. But he didn't wear that face anymore.

After the coffee started, Drake walked over to the small closet near his bed and pulled open the accordion door. On the floor was a long wooden case with ornate carvings and brass fittings. He lifted it up and carried it to the table with a care normally reserved for handling babies or volatile chemicals. Setting it on the table, he sat back down across from Sarah, then opened the latches carefully. Inside was an object wrapped in leather which Drake reverently untied so he could unfurl the trappings.

"This is my father's *pilum*, or what's left it. The wood shaft rotted away centuries ago, but this is as it was when it was forged by a Roman Blacksmith in Judea at the beginning of the first century," Drake explained, carefully handling the relic.

"It has been called many things: *Vivificantern* – the Life Giver, the Spear of Destiny, the Lance of Longinus, but it doesn't really have a name. Naming weapons is ridiculous. As you can see, it still carries its edge, even after two millennia," Drake said, beaming with no small amount of pride.

Sarah leaned in to have a closer look, expecting something pitted, rusted, and misshapen, like a piece from a museum. Instead, Drake held up a remarkably well-preserved spear head. It might as well have been forged yesterday from what Sarah could tell. It was the dark color of soft iron, and it looked as if it were stained with blood, though it was polished and clean. The metal almost shone with its own radiance, even in the dimness of the trailer's lighting. It was glorious to behold; a true relic.

"It looks…perfect," Sarah whispered in awe.

Drake smiled at the compliment. "I've taken good care of it, but I can't accept credit for its condition. Honestly, I've done little more than dust it and keep it out of the way. That day in Jerusalem, it became something more; it will no longer tarnish or age, nor will it lose its sharpness. Save for the shaft, it looks exactly as it did when my father carried it all those lifetimes ago."

"He never forgave himself for what he'd done, or for his complicity in killing an innocent man. He condemned himself. So, when I was made aware that he was not at peace, I offered to pay penance on his behalf. And so, here we are," Drake said, his smile fading as he spoke.

"The penance wasn't specifically to live forever, of course," Drake continued, still looking at the spear. "I have a job to do. I was told how things were supposed to unfold, and I am here to make certain they do. With some help, I have been able to ensure things happen the way they needed to. Most of it was really quite easy and happened almost immediately; I only made small changes, but they had massive impact later. Most of it had to do with the *Bachar'im*. But two thousand years might as well have been eternity. I saw nations rise and fall, and I lost track of people I should not have. I fear I'd given up hope," Drake lamented, hanging his head in shame.

Sarah reached across the table and put her hand on Drake's in a rare show of intimacy. "You don't strike me at the type to give up Dr. Sullivan," she offered with a smile, "and your story is very compelling. But you haven't told me what any of this has to do with me. Beyond what one of my ancestors did, which is pretty cool by the way. Do I really matter?" Sarah asked, not sure what to believe, but still wanting to make sense of everything.

"I already told you; you are *Bachar'im*. This has *everything* to do with you," Drake replied in exasperation. He stood, pulled his hand away from Sarah's, and paced the trailer.

"You say that like it's a real explanation, but it isn't," Sarah chided. "Why does being this 'bacha-whatever' mean something? I'm just a normal woman."

Drake stood and stared out the window, trying to formulate a response. "When civilization was young, there was a prophet named Enoch. When it was his time he wandered into the desert, but he didn't die. He was so beloved, so special to the Creator, that he was taken to the Aether to sit by their side. Before that happened, he spoke one last prophecy. It was about an Outcast, the *Nadach*, and how they would try to remake Creation after their own design…"

Sarah held up her hand this time, motioning for Drake to stop. "Wait, you keep saying things you seem to think are real words, but I don't understand. Aether? Nadach? Speak plainly, or we're leaving now."

Drake growled in frustration. He often took his knowledge for granted, forgetting that most people's ideas about these concepts were formed by their personal theology and not fact. After calming himself for a moment, he remembered that he was talking about things no human should know. At least not one that people considered sane.

"Yes, of course. Let's see, the Aether is the name for the Plane of Light, and it's the place that inspired ancient concepts of an afterlife. Places like the Elysian Fields, Jannah, Valhalla, and

Nirvana are all human renditions of the Aethereal Plane. It's more or less what you think of as Heaven, and it's governed by a council of powerful beings—you'd call them Seraphim—called the Aetherium," Drake explained hurriedly. "What else? Oh yes, Nadach is their word for outcast, so using more common parlance…"

"Wait, are you talking about the Devil?" Sarah interrupted inquisitively.

"That's just one of many names," Drake confirmed, "though I would say that's more of a description than a name. All of them are, actually. Satan, Beelzebub, Devil; all of these are epithets. I don't think *they* know what their true name is anymore. But the Aetherium, and all the other angels, call them the *Nadach*. After they and their followers were cast out, the Aetherium pooled its power and did the unthinkable. They separated the Planes; Aethereal, Nethereal…,"

"Hell?" Sarah interjected again.

"Yes, yes; more or less," Drake replied impatiently before continuing. "Where was I?"

"The planes," Sarah offered helpfully.

"Oh yes, there are many, but the ones that matter right now are the Aethereal, Nethereal, and the Material; that's where we are. Now that the Planes are split, the residents in them are trapped, as travel between the Planes is now exceedingly difficult. But that's a whole other issue," Drake added quickly as he saw Sarah grow confused. "What's important is that Enoch's prophecy pairs with another prophecy. One that you know. You see, in order to leave the Nether, the *Nadach* needs the help of someone here, on this Plane. That's what the second prophecy is about—how that all happens—and it *is* happening now," Drake said emphatically.

"You're talking about the Apocalypse, aren't you?" Sarah asked quietly.

"You're a quick study, Captain," Drake replied solemnly. "Yes, I am."

There is no chance, no destiny, no fate
that can circumvent or hinder or control
the firm resolve of a determined soul.
- *Ella Wheeler Wilcox*

Chapter 19

Sarah was mentally processing the very heavy information she was just given, and she started to feel overly warm. She wasn't sure if it was the tea, or that Drake's heater was still unnecessarily on, but she was getting uncomfortable. Of course, it might have been the conversation, or the seven-foot tall, mildly-radiant supernatural being. In any event, she needed time to wrap her head around everything she was just told.

"All right, I'll bite," Sarah offered after a few moments of uneasy silence. "Let's say I believe you. If this prophecy is so important and dangerous, and the *Nadach* is that much of a threat, why don't the, uh…" she paused, trying to recall the correct name, "what are they called again?"

"The Aetherium," Drake replied.

"Right, the Aetherium" Sarah noted. "Why don't they just put an end to him? You know, permanently? Why go through all this trouble just to change the locks?" she asked frankly. "That's what they're doing, right? Making sure he can't escape?"

Drake chuckled, "You're really quite bright, Captain. I asked almost the exact same thing when all of this was revealed to me. It's not an unreasonable question. After all, from our perspective, the *Nadach* is clearly evil and must be dealt with. But in reality, good and evil are subjective, and an angel's view of the concepts is rather more complex," Drake explained. "They don't see the *Nadach* as evil, despite the danger they pose. No, this is about punishing the *Nadach* for going against the Plan, not for being nefarious or acting as an agent of chaos against humanity."

"Besides that," Drake continued, pouring another cup of tea for himself, "the *Nadach* is a creature of the Aether, and the rules of the other Planes are different than ours. They could no more hurt or kill one of their own than you can stop the world spinning. The same is true on all the other Planes. The Material is the exception. Only the Creator knows why. That's why they were cast out, it was all the Aetherium could do."

"You still haven't explained what this has to do with *me*," Sarah said in an exasperated tone.

Drake set the cup down and hung his head in sorrow. "It's my fault you don't know these things, Captain. I should have found you and told you long ago. Maybe things would have been different." He sighed, drank all the tea in his cup in a single gulp, then continued.

"You need to listen now, no more questions. When universe came to be, it was ordered into a single Plane composed of six distinct parts: Aethereal, Nethereal, Pyreal, Gaeal, Aereal, and Ydrael. Each represented a major element of creation: light, dark, fire, earth, air, and water. When they formed together, they created the Material Plane; the one everything you think is real exists in.

"Each element had creatures that were born from its energies alone and each had an opposite: light and dark, earth and air, fire and water. Ancient people knew of these creatures, and regarded them as gods, loa, and nature spirits," Drake explained. "And they understood these creatures weren't good or evil the way we think of them, though they were all to be feared and respected," he added solemnly.

"Creatures of the same ilk cannot harm one another," he continued. "It would be like trying to stop a flood by pouring water into it. And there is always a balance between opposing forces. When Michael and the Aetherium decided to break the Planes, they knew that to do so would destroy Creation, so they created the Seals. They allow the Planes to remain connected, thus preserving the Material Plane and all of Creation with it. But they also prevent beings from passing easily from one Plane to another. At least not without help," Drake added. "Do you understand?"

Sarah nodded and sipped her tea; having let it grow cold in the cup. "Good," Drake said resolutely. "Now, I told you about Enoch, but it's important to know he's from a time far older than you might have been taught. He was born into a world that was filled with magic and mystery, nothing like our world today. That's why we see all those old stories as myth; we can't comprehend a world like that. Enoch was a true prophet, gifted with the Aethereal ability to see the future in a way no others could. In his lifetime, he made hundreds, maybe thousands of prophecies. All of them came true. Every last one," Drake noted, looking over to Bathael. "There's just one prophecy left."

Sarah looked like she was about to ask another question, so Drake continued quickly. "That's not the only reason why Enoch is important. He was the last human to speak to the Creator. As you might expect, the Creator didn't often directly address *any* creatures, so it speaks to Enoch's importance that he was singled out this way.

"Enoch was different, Awakened at a time when everyone had access to magic and monsters walked the Earth. The Awakened are connected to the other Planes in ways even I don't fully understand. Enoch himself was particularly in tune with the Aether, as are all Mentalists, and that might explain why he walked out into the desert one day and never returned. He was assumed into the Aether by the Creator and transformed into one of the *Be'elohim*. That one over there, to be precise," Drake explained, motioning at Bathael.

Bathael, still standing behind where Drake was sitting, smiled, and bowed toward Sarah slightly. Sarah, still unsure of the towering creature, just smiled tentatively and waved in reply. This was a lot to take in, even for her, but she stayed quiet. She looked back at Drake, and he continued.

"That single action created a rift within the angels, and it started a war that never ended. The *Nadach,* whose true name has been hidden from us, felt threatened by the elevation of a mortal being to sit at the head of the Aetherium, a seat they previously filled. Those feelings were only worsened when this new angel was named *Bat Qol* – the Voice of the Creator, a role all of the Aetherium previously shared. The *Nadach* refused to accept this, and you know the rest. The Planes were sundered and all of

Creation suffered for it," Drake lamented before looking up from his mug at Sarah. "I know you have a question, so ask it."

"If it took all of the Aetherium together to break the Planes and put the Seals in place, why are they so afraid of one? Was he that much more powerful than the rest?" Sarah asked inquisitively.

"I knew you were smart, and you'd know which questions to ask," Drake said with a delighted smile. "The Creator gifted each of the members of the Aetherium with the power of Creation itself, each of them being tied to one of the Planes. The power was forged into artifacts called *kohyetz'briah* which they wore on their heads. You'd call them halos," Drake explained, moving his hands around his head.

"The *Nadach* was given a halo which was tied to the Material Plane, which meant his had the power of all the others. To sunder the Planes, they cleaved his *kohyetz'briah* into two, and in doing so, destroyed all the others. Both pieces were lost, but at that point, the Aetherium didn't care. Their belief was that the halos could not be reforged by anyone other than the Creator, and that without them, the Seals could never be broken."

There was a long silence. Since Drake had already mentioned that the Seals were breaking, that implied that the Aetherium had been wrong about the halos. It also meant that if the *Nadach* were successful, theirs would be the only one left. It would give them a decided advantage over the other *Be'elohim*, and they were already the most powerful. This was worse than Drake let on, Sarah thought to herself.

"That's what the Outcast is looking for, isn't it?" Sarah asked, almost rhetorically. "Since that halo was tied to this Plane, it would make sense that the missing piece is here. What I don't understand is how could it be here and still be unknown? Has it been found? Is that one of the signs?" Sarah jumped up and started frantically pacing, her mind going a million miles an hour at the possibilities. Then all at once, she realized it may already be too late.

"This is all *your* fault!" Sarah screamed, storming at Bathael. "You knew this was all going to happen, and you did nothing to stop it! You're in charge now – why can't you just FIX IT?"

Drake jumped to his feet quickly and placed himself between the agitated captain and the powerful angel. "As I said, Capt. Heighton, it's not that simple. Everything has happened the way it had to happen. You're right about the halo, and you aren't the first to come to that conclusion. Since the beginning, the acolytes of the *Nadach* have tried to make their way to this Plane. Few have succeeded. It isn't easy."

Sarah was visibly upset as she pointed at the angel exclaiming, "Then how the hell do you explain THAT?"

Bathael stood tall and let the robe slip off, showing their full glory, and illuminating the inside of the trailer. "Cease your unrest, Sarah Heighton, daughter of Debra, of the line of Yohanan ben Zavdi. You speak when you should listen. You question that which is known."

Sarah stumbled back in shock at the display, and the booming voice of the angel. She sat down and shrunk in the seat as Bathael continued. "Have you not been paying attention to Drake

Sullivan? Six of the Seals are broken. The barriers between the realms are falling. So, it is much easier to travel between the Planes now than it might have been. However, it is still beyond difficult. In order to exist in this place, an extra-planar creature must either create a new body, as I did, or we must displace the planes-connected aspect of another living creature already on that plane," Bathael said with authority.

Sarah looked over to Drake, who just translated, "Souls, Captain. They're talking about displacing a soul and possessing the body." Sarah nodded with understanding.

"There are many disadvantages to existing in this place that most of my kind prefer to avoid. Because I chose this path, I am trapped here until I recover the *kohyetz'briah* or the Planes are once again merged. In this place, all things can die. While I may not age or get ill, I can be destroyed, and if I am, I will cease to be. The same would be true for any creature so bound to this Plane."

Sarah's eyes widened at the revelation. "That's why you need me, why you need the *Bachar'im*. Even here, you can't kill him, but if he's here, we can."

"I would prefer the Nadach not be killed, as I expect would the Creator, but you are correct, Sarah Heighton," Bathael said gravely. "If there is to be a confrontation, it must be handled by one of the Chosen. The *Nadach* can hold no power over you, though it is unlikely they would try. They will use their acolytes and minions to do that work for them. You must be vigilant, Sarah Heighton of the line of Yohanan. You are needed," Bathael concluded.

Sarah's face was expressionless as she absorbed what was said. It was a lot to take in. Bathael had said in moments what Drake had been struggling to explain for the last fifteen minutes. Drake looked over to Bathael with a frown, but before he could say anything, Sarah broke the awkward silence.

"All right then, what do we need to do to get started?" she said resolutely. "I may not understand what's happening, but I'm a quick study, and I'm no one's fool. But I warn you: I take my career seriously, and I won't act against my country. I swore an Oath to protect the Constitution, not the Aetherium or the Creator, or whatever. Am I clear?"

Drake stopped Bathael saying anything else and smiled wide. No matter how often he felt humanity was beyond redemption, he found someone who rose to the occasion. Last time, it was Claire. The depth of the human spirit always amazed him, even after 2,000 years.

"You have no need to fear Captain, your work with me will be sanctioned; I'll see to that. I still have good friends in the right places," Drake said. "Now, go back to the Command Post and tell them I'll be arriving in short order, then go pack your things. You'll be leaving with me. Tell everyone else there's nothing left here to see, and I'll explain when I come in. And uh…," Drake added, almost forgetting, "please don't mention our glowing friend. They wouldn't understand."

"Of course," Sarah said with a wink and a grin. "No one would believe me anyway. I'll be ready by the time you get to the main building." And with that, she sped out the door and started running toward the compound.

Drake stood in the door and watched her speed off, making sure she was well into the distance before he let his smile fade. He felt Bathael's warm touch on his shoulder. "You are afraid for this young mortal, aren't you Drake Sullivan?"

Drake just nodded slightly and replied, "I am afraid for us all. You still have your gift, don't you? Does she survive this?"

Bathael turned away, picking up the robe that was on the floor. "You know I cannot burden you with that knowledge, Drake Sullivan. You would work against destiny and endanger all Creation to save her life if you knew she must die. I can say, however, that her chances of survival will greatly increase if you find the other *Bachar'im*."

"That's good to know. I know *who* he is, but I thought he was dead, so I don't know *where* he is. You've told me he isn't, so I suppose we'll have to locate him the old-fashioned way," Drake said with a sigh. This wasn't going to be easy, even with Sarah's help.

Chapter 20

It had been sixty-eight hours since Tim had chased Nate and Emma into the heavily forested mountains of Virginia. It had been fifty-five since he was given the truth about the current circumstances of his existence. It had been forty-nine since the recovery teams failed to return to Groom Lake. Matthew's dampening fields had done their work, but the young doctor knew they weren't out of danger yet.

Matthew hadn't slept more than a few minutes in three days, and he'd been working non-stop since Tim agreed to have the Override removed. Time was of the essence, so he felt he couldn't stop until the job was done. With YVE's help, he didn't need to, though the exhaustion was catching up with him.

The work was slower than he planned. Despite Samuels poaching the brightest minds from Matthew's former team, their work was sloppy compared to his. Samuels' fingerprints were all over it, and the hardware looked the same as what Matthew saw in the Alfa Project documents. Most of his work was cleaning up their mess.

Matthew always struggled with his mistakes, and working with Samuels was among the worst. He reckoned that helping Tim regain some semblance of a normal life would help set things right. Not everything maybe, but enough that he could sleep again. He was never an 'ends justify the means' type, but he did things he wasn't proud of to get this project off the ground. His work could change the nature of human existence forever: disfiguring diseases, amputations, paralysis, and congenital deformities would all be things of the past. But right now, there was only one person that mattered.

"You're working too hard."

Matthew barely looked in the direction of the voice. "We're short on time. We were lucky Samuels sent his B-Team after the Colonel. But he won't give up, and next time you *know* he'll send more capable people. We may not be able to hold them off, and I'm still working on the damned memory inhibitor. It's like none of these people even read up on my work," Matthew lamented.

"So, you've already removed the failsafe and the override module?" the genteel feminine voice replied.

"Yeah, it was the first thing I did," he said, pointing to a mess of wires and circuitry on the tray next to the table. "It's been patched and re-patched a dozen times or more, and they swapped to an older memory inhibitor to make it work. It's all completely incompatible with the Cytotechnic systems. I'm surprised it functioned at all. I suppose the old team deserves that credit, but damn them all for selling us out," Matthew added as he focused on his work.

Samuels' designs were cutting edge ten years earlier, but Matthew's research was as far ahead of it as space travel was the horse and buggy. Samuels married machine and man together in magnificent ways, ways that had never been done before. Matthew, on the other hand, rebuilt an entire human being out of nano-biomachines.

Matthew discovered the reason for Tim's never-ending issues. Since every cell in Tim's body acted as part of the immune system, they were constantly attacking the foreign cybernetics. It was clear that they'd repeatedly damaged the override module, which made the inhibitor less effective, and forced the use of the older systems. Tim's memory never stabilized because his body was trying to reject the implants. He understood now that his team at Nellis had never been his. They'd been working for Samuels the whole time.

Matthew wished he'd told Tim everything from the start. He knew the Colonel to be a man of honor, even after he lost his sense of identity. YVE urged him to include Tim in his plans, but Matthew didn't trust him enough. He had to protect YVE; she was the reason for all of this.

Yvette was already sick when Matthew met her, but she kept it from him. ALS slowly stole her body in bits and pieces, and she wanted him to enjoy their time together as best he could without the cloud of worry constantly hanging over him. When she couldn't hide it anymore, she confessed that she hid it out of fear that he'd leave. Matthew just laughed and told her that he had fallen in love with her brain and her eyes, so the rest didn't matter anyway. It was in that moment that Matthew resolved to build her a new body; one that would last forever.

"You shouldn't be so hard on yourself, my love," the voice said in a comforting tone. "You're not responsible for their decisions, or the quality of their work. They chose the shortcut, not you. Honestly, I shudder to think what the poor Colonel went through before he came into your care."

Matthew allowed himself to smile as he turned toward the holographic display situated behind him. There, in the flickering light, was the face of his beloved Yvette. "You know, we should really be grateful to Stephen. Without him, you wouldn't be here," he said mischievously.

Matthew thought back on the conversation he and Samuels had on the evening he was removed from the Beta Project. The next morning, Samuels sent him copies of all the information he'd gathered: an accounting of all the money he'd funneled into this AI research, how he fraudulently reported how the money was being spent, and a video of Matthew booting YVE up for the first time. It was a reminder that he could destroy Matthew with a phone call or email.

For Matthew, though, it was a bit of a relief. It showed him Samuels didn't understand what YVE was, which meant they were safer than he'd feared. As far as anyone else knew, YVE was an advanced artificial intelligence which used Cytotechnic cells to create a synthetic neural net. That wasn't even in the same ballpark as the truth.

Matthew's first breakthrough was the creation of synthetic neurons using human DNA as a starting point. He discovered straightway that the brain wave patterns of the computer processing he put in place closely resembled those of a normal human. As he tested on himself, he found he could copy portions of his memory and knowledge into a rudimentary copy that could access and display information requested on demand. He could back up a human brain. This was all before he met Samuels.

When Yvette's body deteriorated to the point that she was bedridden on a respirator, Matthew used his knowledge, and a great deal of Samuels' money, to copy her neural patterns into a Cytotechnic brain. He used her DNA for the synthetic cells, so the move was seamless. He made sure she could still see and hear the world around her, and that every memory and every emotion was captured and stored perfectly. No one else knew. Yvette became YVE – Young's Virtual Entity.

YVE, for her part, was perfectly happy with her new existence, though were she not, she'd never admit it to Matthew. He gave her a new lease on life, and she would never take it for granted. Matthew, though, wasn't satisfied. He wanted to hold his wife again, to kiss her, so using YVE's expanded abilities, and Samuels' bottomless pockets, he expanded his research. This is how he ended up on the Beta Project.

Cytotechnics used a patient's DNA as a blueprint for creating nano-biomachines out of organic materials. This would allow doctors to create prosthetics and replacement organs that integrated seamlessly into the body and worked just as well or better than the originals. The Cytotechnic implants didn't have any of the issues associated with transplant organs or cybernetic replacements; there was no pain and no possibility of rejection.

And it would have been a revolution in medical science had Matthew not placed it squarely in Samuels' lap.

Tim was the first successful application of Cytotechnics, on a whole-body scale. Matthew was brought in to resolve the issues with Tim's cybernetic implants as part of the third phase of the Beta Project. When they moved to Phase 4, Matthew was tasked with creating an entirely new body for Tim. His mind was struggling to deal with so many replacements, and it was setting the project back to the point Samuels feared a repeat of the Alfa failure. It was a chance for Matthew to prove he could create an entire body and move a living human consciousness into it. If it worked on Tim, it would work for Yvette.

Matthew hand crafted every cell in Tim's body; at least the first of each different kind. Saying he built Tim's body wasn't entirely correct. It was better to say it was grown. It was an impressive physical specimen by any standard, and it would serve as the vehicle for Matthew's dreams. Tim would bleed, he could be burnt, he could feel pain, but all of that could be controlled at the smallest level. He could turn off pain receptors, stop bleeding, and repair damage much faster than a normal human. His cells could be reconfigured to make him immensely strong or allow him to breathe underwater, which is why Samuels wanted access to this technology. Matthew just wanted to bring his wife back.

Now he lost that chance because he was reckless and foolish. He'd struggled to come to terms with his decisions over the past two years, but he wasn't about to let someone else suffer for them. Samuels was a leach, and he took everything he could from someone until there was nothing left. Tim had already given everything before Samuels got his dirty mitts on him, and yet he found ways to take more. This is why Samuels had little use for men of principle, like Tim and Matthew, and why he had no problem removing those who stood between him and what he wanted.

Matthew was finishing up his work on Tim when a klaxon sounded inside the cabin. Emma jumped and nearly fell out of the chair she'd been sleeping in. Nate, who wasn't caught so off guard, quickly walked over to the security panel on the wall to silence the alarm. Then, he started cycling through the security camera feeds, looking for whatever had tripped the security.

"There's been a perimeter breech to the southwest," he called out. "I'll pull up the monitors on the big screen."

Matthew rushed into the room and looked at the large monitor on the wall flicker to life to display all of the camera feeds they set up. When they decided to use Tim's cabin, they spent two weeks setting up cameras and laser trip alarms, so they'd know of any unwanted visitors.

"Wait, the southwest you said?" Emma asked with confusion. "That's the side where we found Colonel Andrews down in the creek. It's probably a hundred, hundred and fifty foot drop on that side. Pull up those cameras," she asked.

"I've been trying," Nate replied frantically, typing commands into the panel. "The first two were offline, so I'm bringing up the one on the other side of the gorge."

The monitor switched views and they could see the back of the cabin facing the ravine they were in earlier. The drop off was clear, which made Tim's survival and recovery all the more miraculous when put in that perspective.

"There!" Nate exclaimed, pointing up at the image on the screen before typing in a command to zoom in. "Right there! What the hell *is* that?"

What they saw was nothing less than astonishing. It appeared to be a man leaping his way through the trees up the side of the gorge. At least as far as they could tell it was a man, but he was doing impossible things at unimaginable speed; things Nate and Emma had never seen. But Matthew had, and he instantly knew who it was. All the color drained from his face as he struggled to speak.

"Mother's mercy," he muttered, almost to himself. "You both need to get out of here right now. It's no longer safe here."

"But the Colonel...," Emma tried to interject.

"No arguments!" Matthew shouted. "I'll take care of him. GO!"

Emma and Nate never saw this kind of behavior from Matthew before, though neither had known him long. Up until then, though, he'd been quiet, reserved, and agreeable, even if he was a bit paranoid. He was positively panicked now, and it put them both on edge.

Emma looked over to Matthew and then back to the screen, scrutinizing the image as the camera tracked the intruder. "Do you know what that...thing...is?"

Matthew stared at the image intently, following it with his eyes as the camera struggled to keep up with the frenzied motion. There was no denying what he was seeing. He'd been worried about Samuels so much he'd not even considered any alternatives. There, heading toward them was the failed Alfa Project unit. Leapstryke had come.

"There's no time! You must leave. NOW!" Matthew yelled desperately.

Emma was confused, but Nate understood the fear he heard in Matthew's voice. When they set up the dampening field and cameras, they discussed that it was inevitable that someone would come to retrieve Tim. Nate was hoping they'd have more time, but he was used to being on the run. He didn't know who or what was coming, but he knew firsthand what kind of person Samuels was. So, Nate grabbed Emma by the arm and pulled her away. Looking over his shoulder as they moved toward the door, he yelled, "I'll come back for you."

Matthew said nothing in reply. He knew that he'd be gone or dead by the time Nate returned. He heard the door slam and the tell-tale sound of gravel flying as the car sped away from the cabin. He assumed Leapstryke wasn't there for them, but he wasn't willing to risk their lives on it. Matthew headed back into the room where Tim was still shut down and sat at the computer.

"Well, my dearest," he said as he typed, "that just leaves you."

"Don't you think we should be introduced first? I mean you're not really my type," came the sarcastic reply from another room.

Matthew's heart nearly stopped. He only knew Gino, and his alter-ego Leapstryke, by reputation and from reading the files from the Alfa Project. He hadn't been part of the project directly, though he'd been given access to those files as they related to the work done on Tim in earlier phases of Beta. Gino's capacity for cruelty was well-documented as was his contempt for intellectuals. Matthew composed himself and slowly pressed the ENTER key to complete the command he was typing. Just then, Matthew felt the cold sharpness of hardened steel sliding simultaneously under his fingers and along his chin.

"Ah, ah, ah, Doctor Young. No more tippy-tappy or you'll need someone else to do your typing for you," Gino said with a treacly sweetness.

Matthew slowly lifted his hands away from the keyboard and turned in his chair to face his visitor. Without warning, Leapstryke swung the chair around roughly, then started spinning it continually, making Matthew dizzy and nauseous. Without warning, he grabbed the back of the chair, causing it to lurch to an immediate stop, nearly throwing Matthew to the floor.

Matthew straightened his glasses, sat back in the chair, and closed his eyes, trying to calm his stomach. When he opened them again, he gasped audibly at the mechanical monstrosity he saw. What appeared before him was nothing like what he read about in the project files. While Samuels' work was definitely about function over form, it was clear further changes had been made to Gino by someone who wanted to instill fear in people.

Everything about Gino's form was terrifying. His muscular legs had high, thin ankles—something like a large cat's—and he walked on taloned toes. His fingers, all of them, were stretched out into long, slender blades that looked razor sharp and deadly. He had no waist to speak of, and his spine was visible and obviously cybernetic, so he could spin all the way around on his hips in an unnatural way. Everything about him was unnerving and wrong. Especially the stark white, featureless mask. This was the man the Chinese people feared, their Death God.

For once in his life, Matthew didn't know what to do. He didn't plan an escape, and now he regretted it. He always assumed Samuels would eventually kill him for what he knew. It never occurred to him that Leapstryke would be the one to do it, though. He was supposed to be gone. Now Matthew worried about his final keystroke. Did he complete the command? Tim should have been awake by now, but there was no movement. He looked nervously at the table, and Gino picked up on his anxiety.

"Oh, what's this?" he asked giddily, moving over to the table. "Is this who I think it is? Is this the fabled Beta 4; my old friend, Colonel Andrews?" Gino asked rhetorically, spitting out Tim's name with no small amount of disgust. "And it's not even my birthday!" Gino joked, walking around the table, examining Tim's prone form. He moved his bladed fingers over and through the white cotton sheet that was covering Tim after the procedure. By this time, all the damage from the fall into the ravine was repaired, and Tim looked like any other person, albeit an incredibly fit, strong, and physically perfect person.

Gino was quiet as he looked Tim over. Only one of his eyes was cybernetic, and while it afforded some expanded vision into infrared and ultraviolet, it didn't scan things the way Tim's eyes could. But he didn't need special vision to know bleeding edge tech when he saw it. Gino hated the idea that Tim was better than him in any way. The two had a long history of competing and the rivalry was a bitter one. At least from Gino's perspective.

Looking over to Matthew, frowning behind the mask, he commented angrily, "So this is what Pappy Sammy spent his money on? I heard you were good, man, but this," Gino commented, poking into Tim's body with a sharp finger, "this is some top-grade shit. Pappy's got to be *pissed* that you broke his new toy. This is perfect."

Matthew furrowed his brow at the revelation. He never believed Gino had gone rogue. He assumed that it was a ploy; a way to keep Gino's activities off the books at a time when Samuels' actions were being highly scrutinized. Matthew had no idea what to expect now, and the insight painted itself on his face.

"I see you're just realizing that I'm not here for Whiteboard," Gino smirked. "I read that you were a smart one. I didn't even have to give you a hint. I saw Cornbread take out a team earlier," Gino commented, referring to Nate, "and Sammy did send some more people, but they didn't make the cut," he joked, wiggling his bladed fingers. "He thinks I'm still in China, and I was until yesterday. Some things have changed, and I decided it was time for some much-needed upgrades. I stay in the loop, and I have to say that I've been impressed by the work you've done on Whiteboard here."

Gino ran his hand along Tim's torso, applying enough pressure to cut him deeply. The bleeding started at once but so did the healing, much to Gino's disgust and dismay. He continued cutting patterns into Tim's flesh, some of them vulgar, just to see if he could slow down or overload the healing process. After a few moments, Tim was covered in blood but had no wounds. Matthew could only watch on in horror.

"Just tell me what you want," Matthew pleaded.

Gino ignored Matthew and continued slicing off large pieces of Tim's flesh. As he tossed it to the side, the chunks of bloody skin just melted into nothing, leaving little trace where they'd been. The healing continued though, no matter what Gino did.

"Honestly, I thought he'd be harder to maim. I mean, sure the damage doesn't amount to anything after a minute or two, but I can still do this," Gino, to accentuate his point, slid a blade into Tim's cheek and out the other side. "I take it back. I like it on him; he's just a man. But me; I'm a god. I need something…more. Now," Gino said, turning away from Tim to address Matthew directly, "why didn't I get invited to the upgrade party?"

Matthew knew he was being baited and refused to bite. It was clear that Gino didn't have the whole picture about Tim's current state and was fishing for more information. At least now he knew Tim would survive this encounter, and that's all that mattered now. It might also make Gino's demands easier to accommodate, whatever they were.

"I did what I was told, Mr. Lorenza, just like everyone else. You know I wasn't calling the shots, and you know who was. If you have an issue with the hand you were dealt, take it up with Stephen. Besides, didn't you run off?" Matthew retorted, walking a line he knew was dangerous. "How could I have included you in something when you were off making nice with the Chinese? It looks like they already gave you some upgrades," Matthew noted, doing his best to deflect. With the mask, though, it was impossible for him to know if he was getting under Gino's skin.

Gino cocked his head to the side a little and chuckled. "You don't seem to understand, Doc. I don't care about what you did or who you did it for or who you were fucking while you did it. What I want is a body like his, and you're going to give it to me. I am…," Gino paused, carefully calculating his words, "I am restrained by what's left of my humanity, and weakened by this old, metal machinery. You," Gino added, pointing a long, bloody finger right at Matthew's left eye, "are going to help. I need to be better than HIM!"

Matthew was terrified beyond all reason, so he did his best to hide it by scoffing. "I can't just 'build you a body,' Mr. Lorenza. What's lying on that table is literally my life's work. It took years to develop, and months to…"

Gino slammed his fist into the metal table, leaving a sizable dent and causing Matthew to nearly jump out of his skin. He walked over to Matthew, growling, then stopped, took a number of deep breaths, and composed himself.

"I've been reading up on breathing as a means of stress relief. I highly recommend it." Gino stood up and composed himself before continuing. "You're lucky I need you alive, or I'd leave you here to die with Whiteboard the Oversized Action Figure. Is that what you really want, Doc? I'll give you thirty seconds to decide."

Gino started tapping out the seconds against the frame of the nearby door. Matthew was frantically trying to think of a way out; not so much for him, but for Tim and YVE. He knew that Gino would have cut the land lines before he came in, so YVE was trapped in the cabin. He also knew Gino wasn't going to let him carry anything out of the cabin, so his only real hope was that Nate and Emma would come back.

"Time's up!" Gino proclaimed, leaping across the room, and grabbing Matthew in one arm before crashing through the windows on the back wall. Just as they passed through the shattered glass, Matthew felt something searing hot behind him as a concussive blast knocked the breath out of him. In the half second before he lost consciousness, Matthew looked back to see his entire life explode in a massive ball of flame.

七転び八起き
Fall down seven times, get up eight.
- Japanese Proverb

Chapter 21

"Colonel…"

Tim heard the voice, but it sounded very far away. He wasn't sure they were speaking to him. Wasn't he a colonel? Maybe they *were* talking to him. Were they, though? He didn't get called Colonel anymore.

"Colonel Andrews, you need to wake up right now." The voice was more insistent.

Tim's head was heavy, and he had trouble opening his eyes. He couldn't remember the last time he felt so rough. He barely remembered driving over the edge of a ravine. Where was he now and why was this person being so insistent? He could smell a wood fire, maybe someone was cooking. Definitely cooking. He smelled bacon and sausage, and that made him hungry enough to want to open his eyes. But they were too heavy, and he couldn't seem to manage it.

"Don't wake me up until the coffee's ready," he mumbled.

"I'm really sorry to do this, Colonel, but we have no more time to waste."

In a flash, every nerve in Tim's body woke at once. His head throbbed from all the work Matthew had done, and he was sore from some of the deeper lacerations Leapstryke made. He was also keenly aware that he was on fire. Tim tried to roll off the table, but he couldn't; he was pinned under a large burning timber.

"What the hell is going on?" Tim cried out as he started to come fully to his senses. With little effort he lifted the flaming chuck of cabin laying on his chest. Despite all he was now, he was still human in his mind, and being on fire instilled a sense of panic in him. He moved off the table and made his way to where he could stand up straight, then patted himself wherever he felt burning.

"Please try to remain calm, Colonel," the voice said gently, but firmly, "you aren't as flammable as you seem to think, and there are more pressing concerns. I suggest that we make our exit before the propane tank outside explodes? You are durable, but not invulnerable," the voice said pointedly.

"Roger that," Tim replied tersely. He looked feverishly around the wreckage of the room looking for the person speaking to him. He was familiar with the voice, but he couldn't place it. It sounded near enough, though, that they had to be in the same room as he was. "I can't leave without you. Where are you?"

"Oh, you still haven't recovered from the implant removal," YVE lamented. "That's going to complicate things. There's too much to explain, but I'll try. Matthew feared that this place would be discovered, so he gave me instructions on what to do if…"

Tim cut off YVE sharply, "The short version!"

"I'm in your head, Colonel," she said plainly.

Tim didn't take time to absorb what he was told. He scanned what was left of the cabin and noted there were thirteen places where the structure was compromised and failure was imminent.

He had no more than thirty seconds before the floor gave way. To his left, he saw the bag he'd had on the motorcycle, and in it the change of clothes he was going to need. The bag was sitting next to a doorway that was now blocked, but he noticed the wall behind the bag was significantly weakened. He knew exactly what to do.

"Time to go to work," Tim muttered under his breath as he sprang into action. He leapt forward at the bag, but the force of pushing off caused the floor to crumble and lessened the power of his stride. A burst of flame and embers caused by the collapsing timbers provided an unnecessary reminder that the cabin was burning but ensured that he moved with a quickness. He grabbed the bag, wrapped the strap around his hand, ducked his head, and plowed through the wall in a shower of wood, plaster, embers, and dust.

Just as Tim smashed through, the rest of the floor fell out from under him, right on schedule, just as he knew it would. Tim already had a plan as he fell to the level below. He knew the room opened onto a patio, and that he would be facing the glass doors when he dropped. He tucked his legs and prepared to bound forward when he landed.

When Tim's feet touched, he sprang forward, crashing out onto the patio; something that would have been difficult to do even if the house wasn't falling down around him. He didn't bother looking back as he leaped down into the ravine, ignoring the cabin as it collapsed into a roar of hungry flames. He just kept running.

Once Tim reached the creek, he waded into a deeper part, dousing the few hot spots that remained on his body and washing off the grime and ash. Now that he had the chance to reconnoiter, he realized he was naked and wounded in the middle of nowhere. He wasn't bleeding, and his burns were healing, but he was still badly scorched and was sore from Gino's recent attention. He looked around to take stock of his surroundings and see what he had at his disposal.

"What the hell happened to me? What's going on?" Tim asked, deeply confused. It was as if he woke from a very long, deep sleep.

"Colonel, I'd love to give you a full account," YVE replied, "but we really should continue on. While this location is remote, I find it unlikely that the fire will remain unnoticed," she added with a note of concern.

Tim looked back at the plume of greyish-black smoke that came from the ruins of the cabin. It was then he realized that he knew this place: the cabin, the road, the creek. This was where his father grew up, and the cabin was their getaway when Tim was young. He hadn't been there since before…he couldn't remember when. Things were still fuzzy but becoming clearer by the minute.

"There wasn't anyone else in there, right?" Tim asked remorsefully. He had a vague memory of other people in the house, but he wasn't sure how recent it was.

"No, Colonel, there weren't," YVE replied. "It was just the four of you there. Emma Thibodeaux and Nate Lange left moments before the attack…,"

Tim interrupted, "Wait, a minute. I was following Nate Lange from Washington. That's how I ended up here. He's wanted for espionage, and his contact…was Emma Thibodeaux? She was the one driving?" Tim's eyes opened wide with sudden realization. "Sunshine was his contact? Wait…why did I call her that? I *just* remembered that I knew her, but I didn't when I was chasing them. What the hell does she have to do with any of this? And why do I think Nate Lange is a terrorist?" Tim asked confused.

"Colonel, you've been through a lot today. You've been under the influence of a memory inhibitor, so I expect things to be confusing for a bit while your brain sorts it all out. Matthew was helping…," YVE paused pensively, "oh, poor Matthew"

"I don't mean to be insensitive, but weren't you just concerned about people finding us?" Tim interjected while dressing. "Stay focused. What's going on?"

"Yes, of course, Colonel, I'm sorry," YVE replied. "Matthew removed foreign hardware from your body. It was an override module that Stephen used to control you. A side effect of that removal is that your memories will return; all of them, both since your conversion and from your life before. While your memories are no longer being erased or altered, it may be some time before they return to normal. Stephen has done his damage, I'm afraid," YVE added spitefully.

"Ok, so that explains why my head is spinning. What about Nate and Sunshine…I mean Emma?" Tim asked as he looked through the bag, taking stock of his supplies.

"Miss Thibodeaux and Mister Lange arrived and left together in a rented car. It's the one you followed earlier today. I believe Matthew's Jeep is still parked down the road from where the cabin was. Provided it's undamaged, we could use it to get away before any prying eyes arrive. Once we do, we might be able to catch up with them," YVE offered helpfully.

Tim didn't need to hear any more. He finished getting dressed in his cover clothes from the bag and started back up the side of the ravine. He didn't want to double all the way back, but he figured Dr. Young would have parked close enough to the house to walk, but far enough for the vehicle not to be noticed. He jumped over boulders and dodged trees with inhuman speed.

While Tim made his way back to the road on the ridge, his mind milled with questions, some he didn't expect. Who attacked the cabin and why? Was Samuels behind it? If so, why wasn't there a whole team of people? That would have been the smart move and the SOP. Where was Dr. Young and why was he working with Nate Lange? Why was Emma involved? Too many questions, and no one to answer them all. He was getting a headache, or at least one he imagined.

Once at the top of the ridge, Tim looked down the road at the raging fire that consumed the cabin. Down the road to his right, maybe 30 yards away, sat an aging Jeep Wagoneer, parked on the berm. It looked familiar, but he didn't remember seeing it before. Maybe it was in the recon photos of Nate. No, it was something deeper, but he wasn't sure which memories to trust now. Instead of focusing on that, he waited in the scrub by the side of the road, scanning both the cabin and Jeep for new arrivals.

"Why have you stopped, Colonel?" YVE pressed urgently. "It is imperative that we leave before the authorities, or anyone else, arrive."

Tim held fast. "I agree, but I'm not going anywhere until you answer some questions. Like who attacked the cabin. I was watching Nate Lange because he sold secrets to the Mexicans, so why would Matt Young be working with him? Then Doc Young tells me I have this… thing… in my head and he needs to take it out, and then I wake up on fire. I'm missing a lot of context here, and it's making me uncomfortable," Tim said matter-of-factly.

"There will be more than enough time for questions later, Colonel Andrews," YVE replied with an almost frantic tone. "I promise I'll answer any questions you ask, but right now, we need to leave. We need your help. *I* need your help."

Tim started to connect the voice in his head to YVE, the AI that worked with him on the Beta Project. He had never heard YVE sound so emotional and, for lack of a better word, human. YVE's tone was usually quite antiseptic, robotic, and cold. This sudden revelation of a more human-like persona made Tim understand that there was a great deal at stake, and accentuated that he needed a debrief sooner rather than later. He didn't bother replying, he simply ran toward the Jeep.

Just then, a large explosion came from the ruins of the cabin as the propane tank YVE warned about finally succumbed to the flames. The shock wave nearly took Tim off his feet. It was followed by the loud whoosh of a large object moving through the air which made Tim look to his left just in time to doge the smoldering husk of the tank as it landed with a crash. Tim blinked, stood still for a moment, waiting to see if something else was going to happen. When it didn't, he reached for the handle and tugged, but to no avail.

"Shit, it's locked!" Tim exclaimed. "I hope the keys weren't in the house," he said as he looked back at the smoldering ruins.

"Allow me," YVE said. Suddenly the doors unlocked, and the engine roared to life. Tim, not wasting any more time, pulled the door open and jumped into the driver's seat. He didn't bother with the seat belt, instead grabbing the wheel and shifter. But before he could make any motions, the shifter moved on its own. The car spun around in the gravel and began speeding away from the billowing smoke.

"I know you're more than proficient, Colonel, but you should let me drive," YVE said directly then added, "You should get some rest."

Tim didn't see the point in arguing.

Chapter 22

Sarah processed everything she saw and heard as she walked back to the operations complex. With the anomaly gone, the normal late-summer temperatures had returned, making the early morning unbearably warm and muggy. She wasn't wearing her parka, but she was wearing winter fatigues. It was only about half a mile from Drake's trailer to the rest of the compound, but in this heat, it might as well be in the next state.

As Sarah approached the main building, she slowed her pace. There should have been lots of activity, but it was disconcertingly quiet. Maybe everyone was inside escaping the heat, but she didn't see anyone at all, which struck her as odd. People were probably packing up, she thought. That made sense, given how little anyone wanted to be there in the first place. Without the Chill, there wasn't a reason for them to remain, though they would all need debriefed. Any further analysis, which shouldn't be much, could be done later and by other people.

Sarah went into the main building and headed toward the Operations Center. After she put in the code, the door opened, and she was hit in the face with a blast of frigid air. As she relished the coolness, she began to think her earlier misgivings might have been a combination of the heat and the outrageous conversation.

But as the cold air caressed her sweat-damp skin, she realized the only noise was the rush from the vent. It was otherwise deathly quiet in a place that should never be.

Convinced that she was paranoid, Sarah wiped the sweat from her forehead, walked through the building and checked all the open doorways. There should have been more people, even if there was a debrief. She was nearly panicked as she made her way to the Command Post. She tapped in another code, but this time, she opened the door slowly before peeking in. She was beyond relieved when this room wasn't empty too. As she walked in, one of the Airmen looked up.

"Oh, it's you Captain. I'm glad you're back," the young man said with a smile. "We received a call from the Department of Cultural Preservation for you while you were out. They asked that you call back as soon as possible."

"Why am I just finding this out now?" Sarah asked angrily.

"I'm sorry, ma'am," The Airman replied apologetically, "but you left in such a hurry, and you neglected to take a handheld or your cell phone." To accentuate his point, he held up her phone.

"Damn. Of course I did," she said sheepishly, looking at the phone. "Wait you meant the War Department, right? I report to Secretary Blake."

"No ma'am," the young man replied. "It was definitely Secretary Samuels. If I can speak freely; the man gives me the chills. You can't speak to him and not know it. He called on the hotline and said you can reach him back on that same line. He sounded...impatient. Irritated maybe? With him, it's hard to tell the difference. I'd call right away, ma'am," he added before he returned to his work.

Sarah took several deep breaths before moving to the console where the hotline was connected. Things were getting stranger by the minute. She was more upset about the call than learning the world was ending. The hotline was supposed to go to Blake's office. Something was wrong, something she felt in the pit of her stomach. Her first commanding officer taught her to always trust her gut, and it was screaming to run away. That's when she noticed the odor; something faint, like the combined smell of burning wood, rotted meat, and spoiled eggs. It was barely there, but definitely noticeable.

"Airman, do you smell that?" she asked, crinkling up her nose.

The young man looked up from his console and sniffed the air as well. "I'm sorry, Captain, I don't smell anything. I mean, nothing out of the ordinary."

It was getting worse. So much so that Sarah assumed that either the Airman was lying, or she was having a stroke. Neither of those prospects was particularly comforting, so she focused on making her call instead. She had only spoken to Secretary Samuels once, and it wasn't an enjoyable experience. He wasn't a pleasant person by any standard; he wasn't popular, and on social media, many compared him to Oliver Cromwell. There was a belief that he was putting himself in a position to take over the American government by proxy, since the Constitution prevented him from being President. Even those in his own Department called him 'Puppet Master' among themselves.

The smell was starting to unsettle Sarah's stomach. She tried to center herself and started inhaling through her mouth to subdue her nausea. She took one last deep breath before picking up the handset and waiting for the hotline to connect.

"This is Samuels," came the immediate reply as his voice assaulted her ear. It was so forceful that Sarah reflexively pulled the handset away from her face before putting it back and speaking.

"Mr. Secretary?" she asked tentatively. "This is Capt. Heighton calling from the Command Post at the Lebanon Site. The Airman-on-Duty informed me that you requested I call, sir," she explained as she worked hard to keep her voice from trembling.

"Ah yes," Samuels replied, taking on a more pleasant tone. "I'm looking forward to finally meeting you face-to-face. I've heard very good things about you from my colleagues in the War Department. I have some things to finish up here in Washington, but I should be enroute in the next hour or so. I'll want a full briefing when I arrive, and individual meetings with all of the consultants. In fact," he added, darkening the mood, "I've already sent orders that they be sequestered. I don't want contrived or coordinated answers from them. I also understand that you were speaking with Dr. Sullivan; he'll need to be brought into the operations complex, of course. Right away."

Samuels continued rattling off instructions, but it was difficult for Sarah to focus past the smell of burnt rotten meat that assaulted her nostrils. She was writing everything down, mostly out of reflex, but she had zoned out of the conversation.

"I said, am I clear, Captain?" Samuels asked impatiently.

"Yes, of course, Mr. Secretary," she replied, though she really had no idea what he'd been saying. She could deal with that later.

"Good, I look forward to working with you," he replied coldly. Sarah doubted his sincerity.

"If I may ask a question before you go, sir?" Sarah inquired, not waiting for an answer before continuing. "Does Secretary Blake know about this? Normally I would have gotten this information from him since I report to his office directly."

There wasn't an immediate reply, and Sarah swore she could hear Samuels frown. "This is no longer a concern of the War Department, Captain, nor will future Coded Incidents. I have convinced President Bushnell that these should fall under *my* purview. You will no longer communicate with his office without my permission," Samuels said flatly, barely hiding his contempt for the War Secretary. "If you're unhappy with the change, I'm certain we can arrange a transfer once you're done there."

"Yes, sir. Of course, sir," Sarah replied softly. The two exchanged niceties and she hung up the phone. She wasn't prepared for these changes. She worked hard to get her position; this change would take it from her, and she hated it. She collapsed in a nearby chair as a wave of nausea overtook her. The smell combined with the overwhelming wrongness she felt was too much to handle at once. None of this followed established protocol, and that was the larger concern for her. After having worked on a number of Coded Incidents, she'd grown to appreciate Secretary Blake's leadership style, and they had developed a strong rapport. He would have called to warn her.

"Shit," she thought out loud, "Dr. Sullivan's not going to like this at all."

Back in the trailer, Drake couldn't be less aware of what was happening if he'd been trying. He was packing his things in a way only he could. Items were swirling about the room of their own accord, finding their way into boxes that shouldn't have been large enough to hold them. No one ever came to his trailer but Sarah, and he was fairly certain that wouldn't change even with The Chill gone. None of them asked how he fit so much into so few boxes, and a question never asked never had to be answered.

Bathael swung open the curtain that separated the bedroom from the rest of the space. They were draped in a dingy white top sheet that had been cinched at the waist with an electrical cord. Being without gender or sex, angels had no need for modesty, but Drake insisted that they cover up, if only to dim the brightness some. Drake looked over to the angel, then just closed his eyes and shook his head.

"No, no, no, that won't do at all," he said frowning. "You look like a Greek statue, and we need to be less…conspicuous."

Drake went over to the table and rifled through an aged leather bag. "Here it is!" he said happily when he produced a medium-sized bottle filled with a sparkling yellow-brown substance. Tossing the bag aside, he walked over to Bathael and pulled out the stopper, tapping some of the contents on the angel's high shoulders. As the golden flakes touched the cloth, they flashed to life, cascading down the length of the ill-fitting sheet, transforming it along the way. When the last glittering flake fell spent on the floor, Bathael stood clothed in something more fitting and modern, though still white.

"There," Drake said, satisfied with the outcome, "that's far better. Much more proper, and far less eye-catching. You were going to stop traffic looking the way you did, and no one has time for that."

Bathael looked in the mirror and regarded the new clothing skeptically. The sheet was gone, in its place a linen pantsuit with a suitable shirt and tie, all tailored to fit. Eventually nodding their approval, Bathael turned back toward Drake. "I am unfamiliar with this substance, Drake Sullivan. What is it?"

"What, this?" Drake asked, wiggling the bottle in his fingers before placing it back in the satchel. "It's a helpful concoction of my own design. I call it Combobulation Powder."

Noticing that the angel was looking for more information, he continued. "Cross-planar events create a syrup-like substance that has many names. It's the stuff of which the universe is made. I expect there would be a large puddle of it where you…formed…or appeared or whatever. Anyway, whenever I have time, I take what I've gathered, spread it over a piece of hazel wood and let it dry. I scrape it off the wood and grind it into the powder you just saw. Some people would call it magic, but I call it practical."

"I see," Bathael replied, "How ingenious. Do you use it often?"

"Not as much as I used to," Drake said with a certain sadness as he secured the bottle in the bag. "Since the Awakening, the results have been less predictable. I guess I know why, now. But really, people are just too skeptical these days. Like all magic, it requires a certain amount of open-mindedness for it to work properly," he said with a slight frown. "People today wouldn't know a miracle if it came up and offered them a coffee."

Bathael cocked their head to the side slightly. "I suppose that makes sense. Did your companion teach you how to do this?" they asked, motioning toward Merlin, who was sleeping near the door.

Drake looked down at his ever-present friend, but before he could answer, Merlin perked his head up and looked toward the door with a low grumbling growl. Perplexed by Merlin's behavior, Drake walked over to the door and pulled the curtain aside so he could look out the window. He was surprised to see Sarah making her way back across the field toward them. He looked back to Merlin who was no longer lying down and was growling more aggressively.

"Come now, you know Captain Heighton. She was just here, you old codger!" Drake scolded.

Merlin stopped growling just long enough to look at Drake and bark forcefully. Something wasn't right, and he needed Drake to know it. Drake furrowed his brow and looked out the window again and focused into the distance. There, behind Sarah quite a bit, he noticed a pair of dark figures following her. Faintly, he noticed the smell of burning wood, rotted meat, and sulfur, and his heart sank. Now he knew why Merlin was on edge.

I have learned over the years
that when one's mind is made up, this diminishes fear;
knowing what must be done does away with fear.
- Rosa Parks

Chapter 23

Drake opened the door, waved his arm and called out to Sarah. "Captain, you must hurry!" Sarah started jogging as he continued to wave his arm to urge her faster. When she arrived, he pulled her into the trailer, then looked off into the distance before slamming the door shut and locking it.

Bathael, quiet up to this point, cried out in alarm, "Drake Sullivan, there is danger! There are *mashl'khim* approaching, and I fear they mean to do harm to you and Sarah Heighton. Prepare yourself!"

Drake was helping Sarah sit down and replied with a scoff, "That would have been helpful two minutes ago!"

Sarah was still catching her breath when she asked, "What the hell is a masha... whatever?"

"*Mashl'khim*," Drake replied sourly, looking out the window. The two figures were closer now, much closer than they should have been. They were faster than he remembered.

"They are nightmares made real, and they have too many names to remember them all. Things like shadow people, ghosts, wraiths, or even demons. They are creatures of the Nether, and they are the reason humans fear the dark," he added grimly, checking the window again.

"Their name means 'harmers' and it is more apt than you can know," he continued, not giving Sarah a chance to ask more questions. "They aren't real the way you think of things as being real. Because of the Sundering, they cannot exist here in their true form. So, like other extra-planar creatures, they have to possess a human body. They attack us from the dark corners and shadows, weakening us and making us fearful and despondent. Then they attach to us and devour all that we are."

Drake looked back to Sarah who was having difficulty processing what he'd said. "They eat souls," she surmised, and he nodded in confirmation.

A sudden wave of fear washed over Sarah, causing her heart to race and her body to shiver. It was a feeling she wasn't familiar with, and she hated it. "What's going on?" she asked frantically. "I can't move. I can't breathe!"

Drake leaned down and touched her cheek and answered calmly. "It's them, this is what they do. They project an aura of fear at their quarry, meaning to panic them into submission. It does seem though," he continued, looking back tentatively at the door, "that they've turned it up to eleven."

Drake did his best to subdue the tremble in his own voice. He wasn't nearly as susceptible as Sarah. He'd been alive too long to be afraid of much, and the *Mashl'khim's* power was more profound on the unsuspecting. But he was not immune the way Merlin and Bathael were. He should have been, though, if he had prepared the way he ought to have. He was sorely out of practice. It had been centuries since he met a Harmer anywhere near as powerful as the ones approaching.

He could feel them getting closer, so he quickly opened his bag to grab the Combobulation Powder again. As he did, Sarah noticed that a small crossbow floated out of one of the nearby boxes of its own accord and settled on the counter behind Drake. He opened the bottle, then motioned for Bathael and Sarah to stand together. Once they had, he tapped the contents of the bottle in a circle around them and warned them to stay inside. Bathael placed their hands reassuringly on Sarah's shoulders and nodded silently for both of them. As the circle was completed, it glowed for a brief moment as the flakes appeared to drift up toward the ceiling – shrouding the pair from prying eyes. Satisfied that his guests would be safe, he took a moment to breathe.

The uneasy silence was shattered with a resounding knock at the door. It was violent enough to shake the whole trailer and interrupt the short meditation Drake was using to settle down. He looked over to the crossbow, which readied itself and aimed at the door which he opened just enough to peek out.

"Yes, Captain, I'm quite busy…Oh! I'm sorry, I was expecting Capt. Heighton. Is she with you?" Drake queried as cheerfully as he could, poking his head out slightly and pretending to look around.

A man and a woman in black suits and sunglasses stood motionless outside the door. Their expressionless faces were pale, and they each wore a small earwig headset in their right ears. This was a Secret Service detail, but he couldn't remember seeing any of them on site before now. Something had changed, and he wondered why they were here.

"We're sorry for disturbing you, Dr. Sullivan," the woman spoke in a congenial tone that didn't match her visage. "I'm Senior Special Agent Holly Tingal, this is Special Agent Mark Alvord. We saw Captain Heighton coming this way a few moments ago. There's been an incident in the compound and we're here to escort you both back to the Command Post. We have orders to detain you both," she added flatly, "for your own protection, of course.

Drake's mind raced. Very little of this made sense. Now, on top of everything else, he was concerned that Harmers had possessed people with access to government officials. Things were worse than he thought. He was worried for his friend, Xavier Blake, the former student, and current War Secretary that brought him in as a consultant all those years ago. He wondered to himself if Stephen Samuels had something to do with all of this, and he shuddered at the thought of these creatures being involved with so dark a person. He needed to get Sarah and Bathael as far from here as possible, but first, he needed to deal with these two.

"Well Agents, as you can see, the good captain isn't here, and honestly, I'm far too busy to entertain right now. So, if you don't mind, please give everyone my warmest regards, and let them know my report will be available tomorrow morning. Good day!" Drake was hoping that his abruptness would throw them off footing enough for him to slam the door and get the four of them out of there before the Harmers could break in. He was never a lucky man.

As Drake moved to slam the door, Agent Alvord grabbed the edge and held it fast with an unnatural strength. "I'm sorry, sir, but we were told to escort you and Capt. Heighton back to the complex, under protest if needed," he said in an emotionless voice. "My associate will search your accommodations for Capt. Heighton while you come with me back to the Command Post. We have reason to believe you are both involved in a plot to steal classified information. Now please, come with me quietly. I will use force, if necessary," Agent Alvord concluded, his expression never changing. Drake wasn't looking at his face, though. He was looking at the agent's shadow.

Anyone else would miss it. Even someone trained to see these monsters for what they were, though there hadn't been any of those in centuries. Harmers were skilled at hiding in plain sight, even in broad daylight. He had to be doubly certain. These people, after all, might just be devoted agents performing their assigned duty. Sometimes to their detriment, people could be blindly loyal.

There it was, just barely noticeable. The shadow of the man holding the door moved of its own accord. Twice, Drake watched the shadow move out of sync with the man who was casting it. Once he saw that, Drake glanced over to the shadow of Agent Tingal, and it was not angled correctly compared to the position of the sun and appeared to be moving ever-so-slowly toward the door. Drake had all the proof he needed; it was time to act.

"You really should remove your hand, young man, before I remove it for you," Drake said threateningly, his tone as grave as death. The agents looked at each other, then back to Drake in unison. In the first sign of emotion since they appeared, the agent holding the door smirked.

"Dr. Sullivan, I really don't want to have to hurt you…,"

Before the man had opened his mouth to speak, Drake was already muttering silent words of power. Without warning, the small crossbow by the door released its readied bolt, which passed through the wall of the trailer like it was made of tin foil. The speeding projectile hit the agent holding the door squarely in the eye and shattered his sunglasses explosively. At the same time, in a swift motion, a sword flew out of the sleeve of Drake's jacket and into his waiting hand. He brought the sword up quickly, separating the man's hand from the rest of his body, causing him to fall back onto the ground.

"Not even on your best day, lad. Don't be daft," Drake said confidently as he pointed the sword at Agent Alvord. The sound that came from the wounded agent was inhuman. He writhed on the ground grasping at what should have been a bleeding stump, but there was no blood to be seen. The hand, which still gripped the door, was connected to the agent by barely visible whisps of shadow. The female agent let out a blood curdling scream followed by a loud hiss.

"You don't know who you're dealing with, old man," she screeched in an unnatural voice that was clearly not Holly Tingal's. "You're in over your head. If you put down the sword, I promise to kill you first, so you don't have to hear the woman scream"

They didn't know about Bathael, Drake surmised. That was a good thing. He swung the point of the sword at Agent Tingal and stepped forward deliberately. "I know you for what you are, *Mashl'khim*. Do you not recognize that which I hold in my hand? You should. It has slain more of your kind than I can remember; most by my own hand," Drake added resolutely.

"As you can see, it is *you* who is in over *your* head. Your master has been remiss in preparing you to deal with the likes of me. I will draw you from that stolen flesh as I would draw poison from a wound, creature of the Nether," Drake threatened boldly.

Agent Tingal, or rather the creature pretending to be her, said nothing. Instead, it just snarled and growled at Drake while backing away cautiously. In an instant, the creature turned and bolted away at an inhumanly fast pace. Drake held out his open hand toward the door, calling the crossbow to him and firing a bolt at the ground behind the running creature. Another screech told him he'd hit his mark. The creature's shadow was pinned by the bolt, and the possessed Agent Tingal was unable to touch or remove it.

Drake tossed the crossbow aside and walked casually up to the writhing creature who was now begging for mercy. Without a word, he stabbed the shadow's head, drawing the darkness into the blade and causing the agent to collapse dead. She had been dead for days, it appeared. Frowning, he walked back toward the trailer and did the same to the other creature, who had been looking on in horror.

"You can come out now," Drake called out as he wiped the dirt, and some remaining black ichor from the blade. Sarah stepped into the doorway and watched as what remained of Agent Alvord decayed rapidly into oblivion. Stepping past the disembodied hand, she bent down to pick up the crossbow where Drake dropped it. He was busy cleaning the sword and sliding it back up his sleeve.

"I see I have a lot to learn about things," she said seriously, looking over the well-crafted weapon she held, admiring the handiwork. "Where'd you get the sword?"

"Oh, this old thing?" Drake replied, waving the arm where he'd moments earlier produced a long sword. "Had it for ages. I've used it to settle more than one dispute and crown more than a few kings. I even had this whole elaborate setup where I'd send them to this lake and have this vision of a woman appear…," Drake's voice trailed off. "That's not important. What I need now is to know what happened at the main building. Anything out of the ordinary? What did you see?" Drake asked urgently.

"Nothing," Sarah replied.

"What do you mean, 'Nothing?'" he replied curtly.

"Just that," she said. "There was nothing there. The place was practically abandoned. There were just the airmen…," Sarah stopped and gasped. "Oh, God, do you think that they…?" She couldn't bring herself to finish the thought. Drake shook his head solemnly.

"Oh…" She paused for a moment, sorry at the thought of what may have happened to the young men. "Well, it was just me and them, I didn't see anyone else. I had a call with Secretary Samuels and that's it. And then there was this awful smell," she added, crinkling her nose again in reflex.

"The smell of burning wood and something rotten?" Drake asked.

"Yeah, how did you know?" Sarah replied curiously.

"That smell is the Harmers," Drake replied with a frown. "Not many can detect it, and it's usually faint. The stronger the smell, the closer and stronger they are. I'm such a fool," Drake added cursing himself. "We need to prepare, and we can't do that here. I expect there's no one here left to save, and you and I are going to be blamed for it. It's best we make ourselves scarce for the time being. Perhaps we can…"

A sudden hissing screech interrupted Drake, causing both he and Sarah to look toward the noise. Suddenly, the hand that grasped the door, flew off and toward them. Without hesitation, Sarah lifted the crossbow and pulled back the string, which magically generated a bolt. Half a second later, the hand was pinned to the side of the trailer, twitching as the last remnants of life oozed out the bottom in shadowy tendrils.

Drake just stood agape, while Bathael examined what was left of the hand. "Well, I think we can skip that part of the training," he quipped as he started back into the trailer. "No more delays; we have work to do."

When you look in the mirror, what do you see?
Do you see the real you, or what you have been conditioned to see?
The two are so, so different.
- David Icke

Chapter 24

They weren't driving long before the column of smoke disappeared behind them. Tim heard the sirens in the distance, right on time, but he wasn't concerned about them now. As far as the authorities would know, the house had been abandoned for years and was destroyed in an accidental gas explosion, probably caused by a corroded tank. No one would be notified, and it wouldn't be in the papers.

Now that they had some miles behind them, Tim took over driving and slowed the pace. He didn't want to attract any undue attention. He drove on for hours before he felt it was safe to stop. They were somewhere in eastern Tennessee, off the beaten path, when Tim stopped at a motel. It was late and he needed time to figure out what to do next. He didn't need to shut down as often as Leapstryke, but he still needed rest.

After checking in to room 113, he locked the door behind him, then turned on the television. Sitting in a chair by the window, he stared at the TV while listening to what little traffic there was outside. He sat there for two more hours before he felt assured no one was following them. He'd been replaying the events of the past weeks over and over. Then he went further back, trying to recall

all the missions he'd been on until his head ached, which wasn't supposed to be possible anymore.

Satisfied no one was coming, Tim stood up and headed toward the small bathroom. He took a long look at himself in the mirror; he was a wreck. His bounding through the underbrush shredded his clothes and his face was still covered in dried blood from Gino's attack. Nate would have said he looked like he'd been 'rode hard and put away wet,' and remembering that made him smile a little. Why was he just remembering that? Tim had been battling with his memory for a long time and now, finally, the haze was lifting. YVE has said by morning, he would remember everything normally. Whatever that meant.

"All right, YVE," Tim spoke out loud, "I need to know what the hell is going on, and I need it plain." He began undressing to prepare for a shower.

"Of course, Colonel, and I agree. You should have been told all of this before, but it wasn't our decision," YVE lamented. "Matthew knew that Stephen's leash on you was a tight one, but he hadn't counted on there being other people involved. This may take a while."

Tim undressed and showered while YVE filled him in on all the important events of the last seven years. Everything from the Cincinnati Incident to the time he woke up on fire in the cabin. Well, nearly everything. YVE was concerned that some things would be too much, so he didn't get too many details unless he asked a question. She made sure, though, that Tim knew where his loyalty should lie.

"I always knew Stephen was driven. He was a leader in the field of cybernetics, so Matthew followed his work closely," YVE continued explaining. "It isn't always obvious, but Stephen sees other people as things to be used. That is their only value to him; they are tools he uses to carry out his plans. And it's so much worse now that he has real power. You, Colonel," she continued, "are the embodiment of those goals. Despite the amount of work Matthew put into helping you, you wouldn't be here if not for Stephen Samuels' personal ambitions."

YVE paused to let Tim absorb everything before continuing. "You didn't know Yvette Young, Colonel. She was only 24 when she was diagnosed with Amyotrophic Lateral Sclerosis. ALS steals your body, and Matthew couldn't stand watching her wither away. They tried everything: gene therapy, pharmaceuticals, endoskeletal implants, even cybernetics. They even went to an Awakened healer. None of it worked. Matthew was running out of options, and that's when Stephen contacted him.

"When Stephen approached Matthew," YVE continued in a somber tone, "he offered the world. When Matthew realized that he'd have access to nearly limitless funding, he started expanding on his initial breakthroughs. He created a system of synthetic neurons and transferred Yvette's consciousness into them before she died. You were Matthew's proof-of-concept for building her a new body. To do that, he was funneling money from the Beta Project and Stephen found out. We didn't think he knew about it, but…," YVE paused, preparing the revelation. "Colonel, I'm not just an AI. I'm not Young's Virtual Entity – I am Yvette Young."

Tim sat back in the chair with his workout clothes on. It's all he had left in the bag he brought. He could remember times when he felt uncomfortable at YVE's aloof nature and recent change of tone. He knew now that her detachment and sterile presentation had been a ruse to protect both her and Matthew. They were fortunate Samuels didn't know the whole truth.

"It was a massive risk getting involved with Samuels. I don't even want to know what he'd do with this kind of technology. Surely the Doc could have found another investor. He could have offered immortality to the world. This sort of thing would have set the both of you for life; financially, I mean. Literally too, I guess.," Tim said matter-of-factly.

"That's not what mattered to him, Colonel," YVE replied with a sad tone. "He just wanted us to be whole again. He would say it over and over. He knew Stephen would have dismantled my main storage unit had he found out. That's why he kept the unit portable. Then he could focus on finishing his life's work, you, without having to worry about me. You were his greatest achievement, Colonel, and a necessary step before he could finish his work."

"All right, fair enough. But that still doesn't explain what happened in the cabin," Tim said directly, "or why my memories are still jumbled." He was remembering things he'd not known he forgot, and all the explanations were confusing him even more.

While it made sense that Samuels would prefer to have an agent without a past or family that would come calling, Tim never got the impression he was so devious that he would create an entire false life for someone else just to keep them under his control. He didn't like Samuels, but he respected him. Or at least he thought he did. Or had he been manipulated to feel that way? It was starting to feel like he had, and he didn't like that one bit.

"OK, let's say I believe all of this," Tim finally chimed in after a long silence, "I don't understand why the Doc stuck his neck out to fix me, and what it had to do with Nate Lange. I had credible intelligence in my hands that Nate Lange was a threat to National Security. And now that I see that the Doc was working with him, I'm inclined to think he can't be trusted," Tim added resolutely. "Maybe you can't be either, now that I know you're capable of lying."

"What does your gut say?" YVE asked.

The question took Tim by surprise. Even after everything YVE had just told him, he didn't expect that sort of insight from someone who he thought was just an advanced computer. But it was a good question. What *was* his gut saying?

"That none of this feels right," Tim admitted.

"That's because none of it *is* right, Colonel," YVE said in a reassuring tone. "Don't you see? You didn't see any intelligence, and you didn't spend weeks surveilling anyone. You hadn't seen him before yesterday morning. Everything else you remember was planted by Stephen using that horrific implant. They needed you to distrust your best friend, and the best way to do it was to take advantage of your sense of duty. We expect the plan was for you to find him so that Stephen could kill him, and anyone helping him, using you as the weapon. You wouldn't have even known it happened," YVE said angrily.

Tim wasn't sure how to respond. He remembered much more about Nate Lange in the hours since they escaped the cabin. In fact, most of his thoughts during the drive were about Nate and Emma. He knew Nate was his best friend, and that they'd served together, honorably, in the war and after. That's what was making the *other* memories feel so wrong. He remembered them just as if they'd happened to him, but somehow, deep down, he knew they weren't right.

"How do you know?" Tim asked with a frown. "How do you know that I wasn't there watching Nate Lange every day for a month?"

"Because he was with us," YVE replied directly, "setting up the equipment in the cabin. You couldn't see him in Washington when he was in Virginia. You weren't even in Washington until yesterday morning; you were at Groom Lake. We still have friends on Stephen's team, and they told us when you were on the way. We gathered the rest from a letter mailed by Ms. Thibodeaux, Emma's mother, to Matthew. It had everything we needed in it, including the address of the cabin and the place where you'd be watching. She was quite informative. I would have liked to have met her," YVE added solemnly before continuing.

"The rest was me. I may be a human consciousness, but I am also an advanced machine intelligence. Government firewalls are designed to stop human attackers and AI-written programs, not anything like me. It wasn't long before I'd found Stephen's private server and the schematics for the implant. That's when we discovered its true purpose. Our original plan was to try to convince you that you'd been lied to, but with this information, we could be sure that you'd be free of him forever," she said proudly.

"But what does that have to do with Nate? Why would Samuels want to kill him?" Tim asked. He was pacing the room now, his mind flooded with images from YVE's memories now, not just his own.

"We weren't sure," YVE continued. "But we think it had something to do with an incident that happened in Arlington two years ago. Nate broke into the Beta Project facility there and spoke with you, or what was left of you."

"I am Orion. You are Argus…," Tim whispered to himself as he remembered a chilling night in a hospital room. How could he have forgotten?

"It's also possible that Nate found out the identity of the Alfa Subject; Stephen always jealously guarded those secrets. It doesn't really matter, though, Nate was definitely in danger. Emma insisted on helping after she delivered the letter, and without her, we wouldn't have succeeded."

Tim sat in the chair again, leaning forward with his elbows on his knees. This was a lot to absorb. He could accept that Samuels was malevolent and secretive enough to kill anyone who he viewed as a threat, but that didn't explain what happened in the cabin. If Samuels wasn't behind it, then who?

"There's something you aren't telling me," Tim surmised, sitting up and waiting for YVE to confess.

After a short silence, YVE spoke again. "Yes, that's true. Your body, like my mind, isn't limited by your DNA. You are a biomechanical miracle, Colonel, and even when you're not awake, your body is gathering data and recording it. Without Stephen's implant holding you back, you'll be able to access that information the way you would any other memory," YVE explained.

"Which means I can see what happened in the cabin while I was unconscious," Tim added. "All right then, let's see what there is to see."

Tim leaned back in the chair and closed his eyes, focusing on the last thing he recalled before waking up on fire. He had just given Dr. Young permission to work on him, and then he laid back and shut down. It wasn't much effort for him to switch to the sensor view, but it was an off-putting experience and didn't feel natural. He wasn't viewing the room as he had when he'd been awake but rather experienced the room from a third-person view. It was disconcerting and amazing all at the same time.

Tim could see himself on the table, and across the room, Dr. Young was preparing. He watched the entire process, even noticed Emma sleeping in the chair in the far corner of the other room, and Nate sorting through supplies and reading something at the table in the next room. He couldn't tell what was on the paper, though. This was going to open whole new worlds for him. He scanned ahead until he saw a flurry of activity that made him slow down. It was about ten minutes before he woke up.

He saw the panic, saw the escape, and he saw the reason. Just as Nate and Emma left, a new person entered the room. Tim had never seen a cyborg like this one; a featureless white mask, monstrous legs and bladed hands. He matched a description he remembered about a monster people feared in China. But then the cyborg spoke, and Tim's heart sank. Gino's voice was unforgettable.

Tim started putting the pieces together as he accessed memories farther back. Gino was the missing Alfa project cyborg, Alfa 2. Everything was starting to make sense; nearly a decade's worth of questions getting answered. It was almost overwhelming, but Tim pushed through the discomfort. Gino and he had been teammates *after* the Cincinnati Incident. The Alfa Project was started first because Gino's body was in far worse shape than Tim's. By the time Tim became Beta 1, Gino was already Alfa 2. Their methods were wildly different, and Tim usually ended up paying for Gino's rashness. Tim was in his third iteration as Beta 3 when Samuels designed the implants meant to control them. Gino found out and went rogue. Tim was sent after him and returned to Samuels' office in a box, barely alive. That had been roughly a week before Nate found him in the Arlington facility. It had been a test, and Tim failed, and that's what sent Samuels to Dr. Young.

"I know what he wants," Tim realized in a flash, "and I know what we need to do next."

"Are we going to find Matthew?" YVE asked hopefully.

"Yes. And we need to get you back in your own head," Tim replied. "But there's one more thing we need to do before we go."

"What's that, Colonel?" YVE asked.

Tim didn't answer. Instead, he moved over to the mirror and closed his eyes. As he settled his mind and sorted out the garbage memories from those that were truly his, he began to feel the familiar sensation of his skin, bone, and muscles moving into a new position. When it was over, he opened his eyes and greeted the familiar face staring back at him. He was finally himself.

Chapter 25

It had been some weeks since Ying Qi ordered Gino to bring Emma Thibodeaux to him, and still there was no word. That wasn't particularly unusual, in and of itself; it wasn't uncommon for Gino to forego communication until his tasks were complete. Ying Qi was just impatient to continue with his plans. Having apparently killed the wrong woman set him back considerably. Despite his brother's misgivings, he also knew Gino worked best when left to his own devices. He was always reliable even if he wasn't timely.

Ying Qi expected Gino's disrespect. He understood the undeniable truth that they were similar in many ways, and he believed he would act the same way in Gino's position. That didn't make it less unacceptable. However, Ying Qi didn't needlessly destroy useful things, even if they were bothersome. Gino would eventually outlive his value. The brothers took for granted that the American would eventually betray them; it was in his nature to be duplicitous. Li Fong already had a plan for Gino's demise. Li Fong had plans for everything.

The emperor walked across the garden to the round building in the far corner. He finished his morning meditation and let the sunrise and crisp morning air calm his anxious mind. The peace that he once found in those rituals was getting more elusive, and that was concerning. He needed a clear mind to keep control of his subjects. It was a well-guarded secret that the reason Ying Qi kept the monks was that he was leaning on their mental discipline to supplement his own. In the past, he didn't need to. Now, they were barely enough.

That's why the nightmares never went away, despite Li Fong's presence. He was constantly connected to their minds. Now, he'd lost too many of them in the escape attempt, and his control was slipping. When Li Fong was away, like he had been for the past week, the nightmares were so powerful they affected people living in the nearby village. His impatience was being fueled by his own weaknesses. He needed Gino and Li Fong to return soon.

The night after Li Fong left the monastery, twenty people in the surrounding area died from terror caused by the nightmares. If he waited any longer to go ahead with the ritual, the next deaths might be in the monastery. He couldn't afford that. He sent the *Èmèng shouwèi* to pick up what he needed: a male child, no older than eight, no deformities or diseases, and he could not be an orphan. It needed to be someone who would be missed, someone who was loved and would be mourned. The combination of perfection, purity, and love were potent. The kind of power one would need to summon a mighty extra-planar creature against its will.

Ying Qi knew that the universe didn't care about good and evil. Good and evil were subjective, and like light and dark, couldn't exist without one other. What mattered was power, and subjugating this creature was his first step toward controlling the Planes themselves. He would control everything. And then he would undo all that had been done so he could remake it as he saw fit.

Since Ying Qi discovered the nature of the ancient scroll so many years ago, he had opened a portal to communicate with the creature it summons two hundred and fifteen times. Today, he would open the portal for the two hundred and sixteenth; an auspicious number, six times six times six. He pondered the days coming events as he meditated, noting the importance and trying to keep himself from being too excited. Today would have special significance, but the scroll hadn't hinted at what it might be. He had his guesses, but he feared none of them. Fear was for lesser men.

Ying Qi was waiting at the entrance of the building as he heard his guard approaching. The Nightmares were more machine than men, but he could still feel their presence. They stopped at the entrance, just like everyone else, awaiting his acknowledgement. These were not people he needed to control; they were utterly devoted to him and his causes, and they followed his commands without question. That's what made them so dangerous and why they were feared.

The emperor motioned for them to enter as he opened the door of the summoning chamber. One of the guards was carrying a small boy, still sleeping soundly from the sedative he'd been given. He motioned for them to carry the boy into the room and to set him on a small altar in the center. They hesitated, but only momentarily. Everyone in the monastery, including Li Fong, avoided this building like it would eat them alive if they entered. Not because they feared Ying Qi; they feared the building and the room within. Or, more correctly, they feared what happened in it.

Ying Qi gently examined the boy laying asleep in front of him. He checked him over for any flaws or marks, not because he didn't trust his guards, but because they didn't have his discerning eye. There could be no mistakes. Once he was satisfied that the boy would fit his needs, he began to mentally prepare for the ritual. This time, he wasn't only going to communicate with the creature; it was time to bring it forth onto this plane. The boy would be a vessel for the powerful creature. The scroll had been very specific about the kind of individual that would be needed, but not their age. Ying Qi chose a child because he would be easier to physically control.

Ying Qi knelt next to the altar and whispered words of thanks into the boy's ear before he kissed him gently on the forehead. He made sure that the child's mind was at ease and that he was sleeping soundly before continuing. That calm was necessary; panic during the ceremony would kill an adult, let alone a child, and would put the emperor himself at risk of being possessed by the summoned creature. That could not be allowed.

Moving to the outer edge of the chamber, Ying Qi opened an ornate box carved from Lebanese Cedar. Inside was the scroll he was never supposed to read. He discovered quite early that the words weren't inked onto the vellum as the others believed but rather tattooed onto a living subject that was then flayed alive. The skin was then taken, painstakingly preserved, and made into the scroll he now held. The process was agonizing for the poor soul who was selected for the honor, but that was part of the process. The pain, suffering, and blood helped give the words their power.

He read the scroll every day since he stole it, even though he'd memorized its contents long ago. He began performing the prescribed rituals once he took over the monastery, waiting for the required conditions before starting. Each of the twelve incantations had to be completed eighteen times on each of the 216 days in order to complete the summoning. But those days had to be specific days, when certain stars and planets were in certain places in the sky. It had been two decades of waiting and wanting to get to this point. Today was the day he would begin his ascension to his destiny. He would need to be cautious. No, he would need to be perfect.

Muttering words from a long-forgotten language, Ying Qi removed his robes and placed them in the cedar box. The portals created were essentially whirlwinds of smoke, brimstone, and fire, and while the flames wouldn't hurt the emperor, they would destroy his robes. He wouldn't mind that so much, but he'd discovered quickly that the burning robes *could* hurt him. They would remain safe and unscorched in the box.

Once he was unrobed, he settled onto a small mat situated in front of the altar, still chanting. He gently unfurled the scroll and settled into his knees. He began to recite the contents of the scroll from memory, but he always stared at the words intently while he rocked back and forth. The candles all around the perimeter of the room lit of their own accord in unison, then began to flicker wildly, causing frenetic shadows to dance on the walls. After a few moments, the flames began to spew forth an acrid yellow smoke, quickly filling the room. The sulfuric fumes would have overcome anyone else, but Ying Qi was already deep in his trance state.

The raging flames of the candles turned blue as they ignited the sulfur in the smoke. Ying Qi's chanting increased in intensity as the blueish-orange flames began to swirl around him and the boy on the altar. The heat was becoming oppressive, and the shadows seemed to be dancing in rhythm with the chant. The entire room was filled with a vortex of smoke and flame, building in intensity. All at once, Ying Qi's rocking stopped as he finished the incantation. Then he screamed out the final words, which echoed around the wood and stone chamber.

"*Aismi lak SHAKRA'EL!*" he cried out as loudly as he could, evoking the name of the creature he was summoning.

"Shakra'el, Destroyer of Lies, Creator of the New Universe, most powerful of all beings, heed my call. Answer to your name!" Ying Qi yelled. The smoke, already thick and choking, turned black and tightened into a funnel with the altar at its center.

"Take this offering of flesh, bone and blood as your own vessel. Use this form to enter this Plane. Do it now as you are bidden!" Ying Qi commanded. The cyclone moved about wildly, as if it were seeking something. It settled once it found the boy's mouth, which opened in a silent scream as the flame and smoke and ash flowed in, causing his body to convulse wildly.

"Shakra'el the Many Named, Defeater of the Great Deceit, mightiest of all creations—by your name I bid you OBEY ME!" Ying Qi shouted, his face red from the effort. "By the power of your True Name, I compel you to answer my call. I bind you to this vessel and to my will!"

Ying Qi's words could no longer be heard over the noise in the chamber. It was a terrifying combination of howling wind and disembodied screams. He couldn't even hear himself think in the noise. He squeezed his eyes closed, not daring to look at the violence taking place on the altar, still screaming the final words over and over. And then, as quickly as it began, it was over.

The emperor opened his eyes slowly, just in time to watch the last of the smoke drift into the boy's still-open mouth. The wind was gone, and the air cleared of the foul-smelling smoke and ash. The candles, which had just moments before blazed intensely, now danced normally, and the shadows calmed to the normal flickering of candlelight. Everything was calm and back to normal, though the smell of death and brimstone was heavier than before.

Ying Qi took a deep breath of the pungent air and rose to his feet. He moved to the altar to examine his handiwork. There, on the stone slab, lay the lifeless body of the boy with his eyes wide open and face fixed with a look of contorted horror. Then, without warning, the child arched his back and let out an unearthly screech; a scream that could, and likely did, rouse the dead. Blood trickled from the corners of his eyes, ears and nose as he shot up and looked around the room frantically. Grinning like a lunatic, Ying

Qi helped the boy off the altar, admiring the culmination of his life's work.

"Tell me," Ying Qi asked in the boy's native dialect, "what is your name?"

The room darkened noticeably as the candle flames lowered to near nothing. Ying Qi could hear whispers coming from the shadowed recesses of the room, from places that never saw light. This wasn't what he expected, and he was ill at ease. He looked around the chamber with an uncharacteristic anxiety. The voices and whispers were everywhere and nowhere, all at once.

"Wǒ shì jūntuán, yīnwèi wǒ hěnduō," answered a seductive whisper in Ying Qi's ear in his native Mandarin.

"'Ana faylaq li'anani kthyr," came a second reply, this time in Arabic and from the far side of the altar.

"Legio quia ego sum multis," answered a wicked sounding third voice, this time just over Ying Qi's shoulder, causing him to flinch. There was no other word for how he felt than afraid; the whole experience was exhilarating. But his reflex was to back away from the boy slowly. The child's response was to contort their face into a maniacal grin.

"I am Legion," he said in a harsh whisper that sounded like many whispers at once, "for I am many." He laughed in an unnatural way as he moved toward Ying Qi with halting, lurching steps. It was like watching a poorly puppeteered marionette. Whatever was residing inside the boy's body wasn't used to having a physical form to control. It looked down at itself with clear disgust. Ying Qi, sensing that the danger was only imagined, stepped forward, smiling like a fool.

"I see you're very proud of yourself, little monk," the creature scowled with the boy's face in an unnatural way. "I put up with your clumsy attempts at conjuring me to this plane for counsel because it amused me. I enjoyed watching you sow chaos on your insignificant world. But now…" it paused, growling slightly, "now you have trapped me in this *ridiculous* form. What insolence, what arrogance! Who do you think…"

Ying Qi, having had time to recover from the ritual, stood tall, his face red with anger. He snapped angrily, "I am QIN TIAN ZI! I am the Lord of Ten Thousand Years! The Son of Heaven! The…"

This time, it was Ying Qi who was cut off as the creature launched itself violently at the emperor, gripping his throat tightly. "You bastard son of a witless whore! How DARE you call yourself the lord of anything! You are worthless! You. Are. NOTHING; nothing compared to…," the body screamed with countless voices before he lost his voice.

Suddenly, the boy's hands peeled off Ying Qi's throat as if pulled by the fingers, and the body flew away and against the far wall of the chamber. The emperor, free from the boy's grasp, picked the scroll up off the floor and rolled it up reverently, walking over to the cedar box to swap it for his clothes. The creature stood shaking his head to clear the cobwebs, but before it could attack again, it found its body held fast and firm to the wall.

Ying Qi smirked as he put his robes back on, buttoning up to the collar before turning to regard his guest. "Compared to what, I wonder? To you, the mighty Shakra'el: the *Nadach*, Beast of the Pit, Prince of Darkness, and Great Satan? And why shouldn't I? I discovered your true name and brought you to this plane and sealed you in that vessel. You are bound to that mortal shell now, and I can destroy you at my will, Shakra'el the Weak and Powerless," Ying Qi spat the name as if it tasted bad. He walked over to the trapped entity, towering over the boy's slight frame, giddy as a schoolgirl.

The wives' tale was true: if you spoke of the Devil, he would appear.

Chapter 26

Sarah dropped to her knees and vomited violently. A mere second earlier, she, Drake, Merlin, and Bathael were in a trailer in Kansas. Now they were surrounded by the rich hardwood and leather of Drake's study. She tried to stand, but the room was still spinning, which caused her to retch again. Waving a hand, Drake summoned a chair over from the corner, moving it behind Sarah so that she could sit. He looked over at the nearby hall closet and whistled loudly, summoning a clattering mop and bucket. He pointed to the mess and the cleaning supplies set to work, moving of their own accord.

"Shit, I'm so sorry," Sarah stammered. "I don't know what came over me. I didn't even get sick in the centrifuge. Why won't the room stop spinning?"

Drake patted her shoulder reassuringly and replied, "Think nothing of it, Captain. It happens to everyone on their first trip. Some even after that. Astral travel is never easy." To accentuate the point, he found a nearby chair and sat down himself.

Once the floor was cleaned, the clattering cleaning supplies made their way back into the closet and the room was quiet. Drake got up from his seat and busied himself looking over the contents of the study, making sure that everything he'd sent back was in the correct place. It was no small feat moving them *and* all his things at once, but he couldn't risk Harmers getting their hands on any part of his collection. The trailer in Kansas was now completely empty, save for some bedding and dishes that were already there when Drake moved in. Once he was satisfied, he slumped back into the chair.

Drake just leaned his head into his hand and rubbed his forehead. It had been a hell of a morning. After some rest and a drink of water Drake conjured, Sarah was able to stand up without the room turning around on her. She walked over to where Drake sat and asked, almost rhetorically, "Does 'travelling astrally' mean what I think it means?"

"If you think it means we teleported, then in a way yes, Captain, it does," Drake replied tiredly. "However, it would be more correct to say I transported our planar essences across time and space and our bodies came along for the ride. Some people call it 'projecting,' but I always thought that sounded too pretentious. The books and things, those I teleported. You can't teleport living things. They always arrive on the other side dead," he added matter-of-factly. "Now, if you don't mind, the whole affair was rather draining, and I need a few moments' rest."

Drake didn't often travel this way because the exertion was monumental, never mind the danger of leaving their bodies vulnerable for the handful of seconds the process took. Besides, with projections, you could never know what was on the other side. It's very easy to go from the frying pan into the fire. He had only trusted one other person enough to teach them the technique, and he regretted it deeply.

Sarah wandered around the study and looked at all of Drake's collected books and objects. Some of them were familiar: original copies of Breakfast of Champions, The Catcher in the Rye, Great Expectations, and War and Peace, what looked like a Doughboy helmet from WWI, and other weapons and armor from various ages from all around the world. Then there were things she'd never seen: books in languages she didn't know, a skull that could only be described as a unicorn's but with carnivore teeth, and a large doll house that was beautifully intricate and seemed to have its own lights.

Sarah was drawn to a wide, tall glass case that sat against the wall opposite the windows. Inside, held up invisibly, were large pieces of what she assumed was papyrus, vellum, paper, and cloth, each with writing, most of it illegible to Sarah. On the far left was a clay tablet, remarkably well-preserved, which had markings that looked like an odd mix of pictographs and scratches. Whatever it was, it was ancient.

"The language is that of the denizens of the Aether," Bathael chimed in as they noticed Sarah looking at the writings. "It is called the *Nash'shal Tzrah*. It is the language from which all other languages come, as difficult as it may seem to believe. The other writings are all translations of that original text."

"But what does it say?" Sarah asked without looking back at the angel.

Bathael stared at the stone for a moment before they replied, "What you see before you are various copies of the prophecy to which Drake Sullivan earlier referred. Those are the last thoughts I committed to posterity as a human well over 8,500 years ago. I remember none of my life as a human, but I remember writing those words. It is as if they were etched into my being by the Creator."

Sarah turned and looked at the angel now, their radiance dimmed considerably since their arrival. Or maybe Sarah was getting used to it. Even still, it was almost too much, too glorious. Sarah was raised Catholic, so she had an ingrained deference for what Bathael represented, even if it didn't exactly align with what she was taught. There were some preconceived notions that weren't met: wings, a harp, flowing robes, maybe a trumpet, the typical trappings represented in all the imagery. Bathael didn't present with any of those things. They were just a creature of brilliance and perfection, and so much more than Sarah could have imagined.

When she was around Bathael, everything felt right in the world. Even with everything they were just through, she felt calm and at ease, despite thinking she shouldn't be. She mentioned it to Drake right before they left the trailer, and he said something about how the part of her soul connected to the Aether was affecting how she felt. It was based on how that creature would want to be perceived and how that person reacted instinctively. Some illicit fear, some anxiety, some calm; it depended on the creature and the plane.

Drake then added a comment that someone who wasn't Christian might feel quite differently in Bathael's presence. The same was true of the Harmers. All Sarah knew is that when Bathael smiled, it felt like the whole world was smiling. That made her wonder what it meant when they cried.

"Why are you crying?" Sarah asked with a comforting tone as a pearlescent tear formed at the inside of Bathael's eye and started to trickle slowly down their cheek.

Drake's eyes opened wide, and he jumped from his seat. He practically ran over two where the two were standing, asking Sarah frantically, "Did you say *crying?*"

"Yeah, I said crying," Sarah replied plainly. "I mean I guess I could be wrong. I've never met an angel before, but that certainly looks like a tear to me," she added, pointing to Bathael's cheek and the tear trailing toward their chin.

"Quickly!" Drake shouted. "Don't let it fall!"

Before either of them had time to react, the tear dripped off the angel's chin and dropped unbelievably fast to the floor with a deafening impact. Sarah was thrown against the magically reinforced glass case. Drake, however, was tossed halfway across the room, then slid the rest of the way, stopping in front of his chair. The whole of Drake's house shuddered and creaked from the force of the blast, and windows shattered throughout. Merlin barked his annoyance from the upstairs bedroom before pulling the door shut to go back to sleep.

After everything settled, Drake moaned and rose to his feet, slowly walking back to where the angel stood. Reaching into his pocket, he produced a silk handkerchief and handed it to Bathael. "For the sake of my home and my old bones, please use this."

Bathael still staring at the tablet, took the cloth from Drake and dabbed another tear that was forming in their other eye. Off on the far wall, the doors to the doll house spang open and two small figures on glittering wings flitted into the study as the books and other assorted contents of the room started to sort themselves back into position. Sarah almost didn't notice until one of the small creatures came up and smacked her harshly on the cheek with a force larger than the diminutive frame should have been able to produce.

"What the hell is going on and who the hell are you?" The tiny creature demanded, buzzing intently in front of Sarah's face.

The other winged creature, slightly larger, though still very small, rushed over to apologize. "You'll have to pardon my pixie friend; she's never taken well to strangers."

"Who asked you?" the other retorted sharply before Drake interrupted.

"That's quite enough out of you. Captain Heighton, this is Jelly and that is Whimsy. Jelly is a Pixie, Whimsy is a Fairy, and they live here with me. They were trapped when the planes were disjoined, and they were causing trouble. So, I built a pocket dimension for them; it's inside the doll house," he motioned at the replica of his own home on the far wall that Sarah admired earlier.

"And that's where they're supposed to stay," he added, motioning for them to go back into the house.

"Yes of course, Merlin," Whimsy replied, curtseying in the air before dragging Jelly by the arm with her.

"Mother fu…" Jelly started to spit out before the door closed, cutting her off again.

Sarah stood dumbfounded at the entire exchange. She looked over at Drake, who was rubbing his forehead again. "My dear Captain," he said as he slumped back into his favorite chair, "we have witnessed something no other creatures in all of creation have ever seen. Something powerful and terrible."

"Oh, I don't know, Dr. Sullivan," Sarah replied with a grin, "Jelly wasn't any saltier than my TI in basic training. It's not like I haven't said those words myself."

Drake furrowed his brow and frowned. "I wasn't talking about the Pixie," he said with disdain. "I was talking about the tear. From time immemorial, from the very beginning of all things, none of the *Be'elohim* has ever cried. They can't, really. I don't even know if they're familiar with the concept," he added as an afterthought.

"But then, how…?" Sarah stammered, motioning to the moderately sized divot in the wood floor where the tear had fallen.

"Don't look at me," Drake replied curtly. "I don't have *all* the answers. I'm old, not omniscient." Sarah put her hands on her hips and scowled at the old man as he leaned his head back against the chair. Sensing something was off because he didn't receive the reply he expected, he looked up and noticed Sarah's sour look.

"I'm sorry, that was unnecessarily harsh," he apologized sincerely. "Look, they are beings from another plane, one where the physical laws are different than ours. In their home plane, angels wouldn't have bodies the way we think of them. Crying is a biological response, and biology is something that only really exists in the Material Plane," he explained. "Even when they Incorporate and make their own bodies, they are incomplete: no sexual organs, no glands, no stomachs, and so forth. While they may appear male or female based on their self-image or needs, they are neither."

"I live in the 21st century, Dr. Sullivan," Sarah chided. "I understand all about sex, gender, and biology. You haven't explained anything."

"Use your head, girl," Drake snapped again, his head throbbing, "They don't have the plumbing to make or shed tears. Even if they did, they don't understand the emotions behind crying, or have the biological processes needed to create tears as a reflex. At least they shouldn't. That one over there," he added in frustration, "is unique in the universe."

"I understand that!" Sarah yelled. "But that doesn't explain what just happened. You're shit at explanations! I can't understand how you ever taught anyone anything!"

Bathael turned toward the arguing pair, walked over, and placed a hand on Sarah's shoulder. "Calm yourself, Sarah Heighton. I am different because I was once human. I know what it means to shed tears, though I did not know I still could." To accentuate the point, Bathael wiped another tear into Drake's handkerchief.

"You can't cry!" Drake exclaimed! "I don't care what we just saw, it *cannot* happen!"

"But why can't it happen?" Sarah asked in frustration. "Clearly it can. The bruises on my back prove it."

"You don't understand," Drake shouted. "Angels don't cry because they can't. That's the Plan. Angels don't cry and humans…can't become…," Drake's voice trailed off as he was hit with a massive realization.

"There's no Plan," Drake said as he got up and started pacing the room. "There hasn't been a plan since…," Drake looked over to Bathael urgently. "What was it you said to me when we met? Something about the Creator."

"The Creator has not communed with the Aetherium since the Shattering of the Planes," Bathael answered.

Drake cursed in Latin, and began muttering to himself, something Sarah instinctively knew was a bad sign. She had a hard time swallowing all of Drake's stories and explanations, but she could accept that she was standing in a room with an angel. None of it, until then, scared her. What was she supposed to think when an immortal man who's done and seen unimaginable things says something isn't possible and looks as worried as he did?

"All right, so angels can't cry, but this one did," Sarah mused, looking to be helpful. "I suppose the *real* question is – what could make a creature that can't cry, cry?"

Drake looked up with eyes that shone with pride, despite the sad look on his face. "There she goes, asking the right questions. What indeed? But I think I already know."

Bathael nodding knowingly and turned back to regard the ancient clay tablet, then began to recite from it. "Creation will be sundered, and the exiled will be trapped among those they hate. The Deceiver will spill the blood of innocents the number of times

Shabbatai and *Tzedeq* will meet between the great cataclysms. The exiled seeks power, and Creations seeks to be whole, but not as it was. The Deceiver becomes the deceived and Creation will begin anew, a dark reflection." When Bathael finished, they wiped another errant tear from their cheek.

"Umm, what are *Shabbatai* and *Tzedeq*," Sarah asked, puzzled at the reference.

"Saturn and Jupiter," Drake replied with a deepening frown. "Enoch was referring to the Great Conjunction, one of the more important astrological events…"

Sarah cut him off quickly. "I know what the Great Conjunction is. It was all over the local news. It's tonight." Checking her watch, she quickly added, "Actually, it's happening right now!"

Drake scrambled over to his desk and scribbled something down. "The Great Conjunction happens every twenty years or so. Since I only know of one great cataclysm, and when it occurred, it would seem that…," he completed his calculations before continuing, "we're due for another. Today is the 216th Conjunction since the Shattering."

"And that's important, why?" Sarah asked flatly.

"Two hundred sixteen is six times six times six," Drake said quietly.

"Wait, you mean like the Demon?" Sarah asked, trying to suppress a growing pang of fear.

"Yes. There is no Plan, and no way to know what's next except for the words on that Clay tablet," Drake lamented, pointing to the case.

Bathael began to speak, but Drake interrupted. "We don't need to hear it. I'd rather focus on how to stop it. The Devil walks among us, and I fear Hell comes with them."

There is no terror in the bang,
only in the anticipation of it.
- Alfred Hitchcock

Chapter 27

Gino despised having to interact and blend in with normal people. He'd never fit in with them, even when he tried. They were beneath them, and from a young age, he only ever saw other people as fodder, sheep to be slaughtered, prey to be played with. He didn't just think he was better than they were, he knew it, and he didn't need the mechanical parts for it to be true. He always despised weakness, and it's all he saw in the people around him.

Despite this, Gino hated easy kills. He learned early on that weak people weren't good sport. There was no challenge in killing them, and he needed that challenge now. That didn't stop him, of course. A person needed to earn life, to deserve to continue living, and that meant fighting for it. Weak people couldn't do that, so he didn't get any satisfaction from those kills. That meant whenever he had a chance, he made sure they felt every second of what life they had left before he took it from them. That day, though, he was in a hurry. He needed some things, and those people were slowing him down. It was their fault.

Gino unlocked the door to the large warehouse. Despite everything he was, he still had a sentimental streak, and he had a hard time letting his past go. His lifestyle didn't lend itself to settling in one place, so he arranged to have his possessions stored in the only thing his father ever gave him; a large empty building on the docks in San Francisco. As the large roll-up door lifted, the bright light of midday pushed its way into the darkness of the cavernous space. The only shadows that remained were those behind the boxes and crates and in the corners near the front.

Gino deeply inhaled the musty, sea-salted air. He smiled a bit as he walked into the building and slid on his mask. He wasn't his true self until he wore that white, emotionless face. He walked over to the large electrical box, opened it, and clicked on a series of large breaker switches. He didn't need the lights, but it had always been a habit to turn them on. He hated weakness, but he loved his humanity, and he refused to let it go. Besides, his guest would need to be able to see.

As the sodium-vapor lights warmed up, Gino pulled down the front door with a loud rattle and crash. From the far side of the room, Gino heard the distinctive clanking of a massive chain. As the orange-yellow lights brightened, the source of the noise came into view. There, chained to a large steel loop on the floor, was Matthew Young.

The chain looped up from the floor to a thick metal collar that cut into Matthew's neck and shoulders. The whole arrangement was so heavy, he couldn't stand up fully while wearing it. His hair was matted, and his dirty face was covered with a patchy beard. Even with the overgrowth of facial hair, his face was noticeably gaunt and drawn from a lack of eating. Gino hadn't fed him since they left the cabin five days earlier.

"Hey there, Doc," Gino greeted him with an insincere warmth, putting a sarcastic emphasis on *Doc*, and setting down the large paper bag he was carrying. "I trust you slept well."

"Oh yeah," Matthew replied softly, but curtly, "the concrete floor and steel collar are deceptively comfortable. Did wonders for my back. And those hunger pangs put me right to sleep. I've gotten rid of my pesky love handles too. I should have been kidnapped by a psychopath years ago."

"Oh, that's cute," Gino retorted, "very cute. I guess you must not be hungry, then," he added sarcastically, dumping the contents of the bag all over the floor. A cascade of wrapped sandwiches scattered everywhere, just out of Matthew's reach. Gino was only a little disappointed that Matthew didn't lunge for the food. It meant Matthew wasn't weak and that was good.

Gino walked over to the large steel loop and unhooked the chain that connected Matthew to the floor. "Go on, eat. You have a lot of work to do, and I don't need you passing out from hunger on your first night working."

Matthew watched Gino with an understandably skeptical eye, and he didn't move to the food right away. He knew Gino too well at this point to assume he'd be given something for nothing. It wasn't long, though, before his hunger overcame his caution, and he dove into the pile of food. He was shoving food into his mouth so greedily that he almost didn't bother removing the wrappers. While he gorged himself, he wasn't paying attention to what Gino was doing with the other items around them.

Before he brought Matthew to the warehouse, Gino had already spent time gathering some of the equipment and items needed for the job to come. Matthew had no idea what was under the large tarps, or what Gino knew about his work. He hadn't been asked what he would need, so he wasn't sure what to expect. As he slowed down the pace of his eating, he started to look over the equipment being uncovered and recognized some of it as having come from the lab at Nellis, where he'd worked on Tim. Other pieces, though, were newer, and Matthew didn't recognize them at all.

"You really want to go through with this?" Matthew asked with a mouthful of food. "I've told you; it took over a year to build a body for Colonel Andrews, and nearly half again as long for him to learn how to control it." Gino had explained to Matthew why he'd been taken, and Matthew had tried, in vain, to explain it was impossible.

In a flash, Gino jumped across the room and had his hand around the back of Matthew's neck. He slammed Matthew's face against the concrete, causing half-chewed food to fly everywhere. Matthew struggled to breathe as Gino pressed a knee into his back. He was in no condition to fight back, not that he would ever have been a match for Gino.

"You know what, shit dick," Gino said through gritted teeth behind his featureless mask, "I didn't bring you here for your opinions. I'm tired of everyone else deciding what I can and can't do. You, Whiteboard, Pappy Sammy, that asshole in China; you can all go screw yourselves. I have things to do, and to do them, I *need* to be like *HIM!*" Gino stressed, referring to Tim.

"But you're going to make me *better* than him, and you will do it now. I read everything about Phase Four, and I gathered all the tools you'll need. And if it's not here, I'll get it. If you're lucky, you might get out of this alive. But you will do it," Gino added in a tone that could melt steel, "or you'll end up like your pretty little wife."

Matthew laid still. He didn't want to die. No one did. But he knew Gino wasn't going to let him out of this alive, whether he helped or not. He'd been pushing Gino's buttons since he was taken, hoping to drive him beyond the breaking point. Gino wasn't the only one who knew how to read a file. YVE was safe and that's what mattered. That's all that ever mattered. He wished she were here now. She would know what to do.

"I get the point. I'll do as you say," Matthew conceded. He was concerned that if he didn't, Gino would try to kidnap one of the others from his team, and they wouldn't be able to sabotage the work the way he could. He was already dead. There was no sense in letting someone else die too.

"Good," Gino said with satisfaction. "You're done eating. Get off your ass and set all of this up. Time's a-wastin'!" Gino added with simulated enthusiasm.

Matthew worked in silence while Gino sat on a crate eating and watching him work. He made sure all the equipment was in working order, but had Matthew test it to be sure. There was more than enough power in the old warehouse to run everything; he'd made sure of that. When Matthew was nearly finished, he sat back and wiped his dirty brow.

"Where did you get all of this?" Matthew asked, his curiosity finally getting the better of him.

"I swiped a set of keys from Area 51 on my way out the door," Gino replied sardonically. "Let's just say I know where Pappy keeps his trash. I'm up to speed on Phases Three and Four, and his plans for Five—oh you probably don't know about Phase Five—I know all his dirty secrets."

Matthew was concerned. He had never worked with Gino, but he did look over most of Samuels' notes about him from the original Phase One and Phase Two projects. He knew why Gino and Tim were picked, and that Gino, as Alfa 2, was impossible to control. At least that's how it was made to look. Matthew's heart sank as he realized how Gino was able to access this equipment and information. He wasn't back on the farm, but he was definitely working for—or at least with—Samuels. Or at least Samuels thought so. Matthew knew it was in his best interests to keep this epiphany to himself, though.

"I was thinking," Matthew spoke up, trying to delay as long as he could, "If you want me to create an Cytotechnic body for you, I'm going to need your stem cells. You didn't happen to…"

Gino pointed to a refrigeration unit against the far wall. "Over there, Doc. Now, clock's ticking, so you should get to work right away. I'm expected back in China in, oh I don't know, let's say a week. And I need to be ready. I need to be…perfect," Gino added, clicking his bladed fingers together for emphasis.

Matthew's mouth jaw went slack. "You can't be serious. You're giving me one week?" Matthew yelled feebly. "If I had a full staff working around the clock, and the best facilities money could buy, it would still take me three months at a minimum. But in this place…it can't be done."

Gino jumped off the crates where he'd been sitting and landed directly in front of Matthew. "So short sighted and such a bad liar, Doctor Young," Gino spat out angrily. "I know what you are capable of; I know everything. I know that you did most of the work on Phase Four by yourself, and that you can do the work of ten people when properly motivated. I'll help you, when necessary, until it's time for me to take up residence in my new body. But you *will* move me into a new body, and you *will* do it in the next seven days. Because if you don't," Gino leaned in and spoke quietly, "it will take you seven weeks to die from what I do to you, and you will feel every second of it. Now get to work."

Matthew shrank back from his captor. He knew from Gino's file that the Phase One work damaged him emotionally. He never accepted that his body was gone and that he was 'a human head and spine attached to an erector set,' as Gino put it. Making matters worse, Gino's sociopathy was hidden from the Phase One team by Samuels, a decision he later paid for.

The control implant—Samuels' precursor to the override module—was poorly designed, and Matthew believed that it exacerbated Gino's psychosis. And he didn't even know how much of a psychopath Gino had been *before* the Alfa Project. Gino was the living embodiment of why it was dangerous to create a cyborg out of a psychotic. He might have been able to handle the Gino Lorenza from the file. But this wasn't Gino; Gino was a face he wore when it was convenient or necessary. No, this was Leapstryke, and Matthew knew he was in real danger.

Matthew started to back away, but Gino stepped forward slowly, moving slightly closer with each movement. Matthew was painfully aware of the collar and chain still attached to his neck as he contemplated if he could escape. Without realizing it, he'd backed himself into a wall of crates, but he was close to the side door. It had a panic bar, and he might be able to get out that way, even wearing the chain. If he could get outside, maybe someone could help.

"You see, Doc," Gino continued, oblivious to Matthew's scheming, "I already got everything started. You just need to work your magic. I even did all the hard work for you. All that's left for you is to put the pieces together. But I need to be better than Whiteboard," Gino spat. "I need to be unstoppable. Make me into a god, Doc. And if you do, I promise I won't kill you," Gino added as he menacingly held up and waved his pointed fingers.

Matthew shook from fear. He was never going to get out of this alive, but he also couldn't allow this to happen to anyone else. Gino was asking for the impossible. There just wasn't enough time, and he panicked. Making a break for the door, Matthew ran as fast as his malnourished body could carry him dragging that massive chain. He didn't get very far before everything faded to black in an instant.

Matthew awoke some hours later, sitting in a chair at one of the desks. He opened his eyes slowly and realized that the chain and collar had been removed. He tried to get up, but found he was held fast to the chair. There was a stinging pain in his back and Matthew wondered what sort of tranquilizer was used on him. Looking over to the side sleepily, he noticed that Gino was moving a large covered object nearby.

"There's the sleepy head. Did you have a good rest? You know, Doc," Gino mused, "I'm really not an unreasonable man, but you are starting to test my patience. You tried to run away, and after I went to all the trouble of bringing you a present," he scolded as he pulled the tarp off to expose the tank underneath. In it was a humanoid form, connected to wires and suspended in some sort of liquid. When the fog lifted from his eyes, and Matthew could see what it was, he gasped.

It was the body he'd been making for YVE. The body no one was supposed to know about. Matthew was speechless, but Gino wasn't. "Look what I found! You don't have to start from scratch now; you can just use this body for me. I bet you didn't think Pappy knew everything about your side gig; he even knew where you hid this. What, were you going to turn that girly computer into a sex bot or something?" Gino asked mockingly before getting serious.

"Now," Gino continued, turning to face Matthew, "You'll do what you've been told or next time, I'll take more than your legs. Capisce?"

Matthew was still dazed and preoccupied with the discovery of YVE's body to fully comprehend what had just been said. "Fine, untie me then. I'll do as you ask," Matthew offered, defeated.

Gino laughed in response. "You aren't tied up, Doc."

The words finally sunk in; Gino just told him that he'd taken his legs. Matthew looked down and saw that he was indeed not tied to the chair, but he couldn't move his legs at all. He could see them, but it was like they weren't his legs. There was no feeling, no movement, no life in them at all. That's when he noticed he was in a wheelchair.

"What have you done to me, you monster?" Matthew sobbed.

Gino walked over, uncharacteristically lifting his mask so that Matthew could see him smirk. "I knew you'd try to run, and you couldn't work with that chain around your neck. I needed to make sure you didn't renege on our deal. That chair there," Gino motioned, "has one of those electric dog collar fence things on it. If you leave the building…" Gino didn't say anything else, he just made an explosion noise and motion with his hands to illustrate his point. "You should probably get to work, you know, before I decide you need some air or something."

Matthew hung his head and quietly cried while Gino walked away laughing as he put back on his mask.

> Religion is regarded by the common people as true,
> the wise as false, and by the rulers as useful
> *- Lucius Annaeus Seneca*

Chapter 28

Drake had always been a homebody. Even as a younger man, he preferred the trappings of a home to life on the road. Perhaps it was precisely because he spent so many decades traveling that he found settling down so much easier these days. Even still, no place felt like home anymore; not in quite a long time. And while he hadn't been alone in centuries, he needed other humans. Merlin was a wonderful companion, but not prone to conversation, and he rarely saw Jelly or Whimsy. It was nice having Sarah to talk to, even when she was being cross with him.

It had been five days since they fled the Harmers and left an empty trailer and a mountain of unanswered questions in Kansas. He knew they'd be safe in his home, but he also knew that whoever or whatever sent the Harmers wouldn't give up easily. Drake and Sarah were both people who would be missed, and if the ringing phone was any sign, they were already. It required Drake to take extreme measures.

From the outside, the house appeared dormant and empty. Not abandoned; that would rouse suspicion. But to the casual passerby, it just looked like no one was home. The grass and hedges were kept, and the mail and papers were collected. Of course, Drake used magical means to make those things happen, and the look of the house was a carefully crafted illusion. Drake was aware of the people who came by, and if he needed a visitor to know they were there, they would.

It was draining, though, keeping an illusion like that up for so long, and it meant he had less time to teach Sarah the things she would need to know. So, when Drake was resting, Sarah would spend the time reading some of the more obscure pieces in Drake's library. He gave her a pair of glasses he stole while visiting the Library of Alexandria as a young man. With them she was able to translate all but the most obscure languages. She also spoke at length with Bathael about the nature of the Aether and the other Planes and what it meant that she was *Bachar'im*. Eventually, she couldn't prevent herself from asking what everyone else would have asked right out of the gate.

"So, umm, how do you do it?" Sarah asked tentatively.

Drake didn't bother opening his eyes to answer. "How do I do what?"

"All of it," she replied. "Hiding us in the house, making sure no one can see we're here, no one knowing we're gone, transporting us across half a continent… all of it."

Drake opened a single eye and peered over to where Sarah was perched on a stool. "Oh, they know we're gone," he corrected. "I expect they're saying I kidnapped you, or you kidnapped me, or that we've both been kidnapped by nefarious agents of the evil Chinese Empire, or that we've just gone AWOL or UA or whatever it is you call it. Since we've been here, about 30 people have come 'round. But they didn't really think we were here, so they didn't find us. That's how illusions work," he added wryly.

"You make it all sound so easy," she said with a sigh. "Like it's something everyone should know."

"I suppose I take some things for granted," Drake conceded, "but none of it's easy, Captain. An enchantment powerful enough to work on everyone must also be concealed, lest it act as its own sort of beacon. We're not just dealing with people anymore. Extra-planar creatures like our angelic friend and the Harmers aren't easily fooled and would be drawn to the energy used to create the illusion. I had to add a second enchantment to hide it, and all of this draws on *my* energy as fuel. It's all very exhausting," he said, adding a yawn to drive his point home.

Drake was impressed with the way Sarah handled the whole situation. She was, in fact, dealing with it far better than he was. Drake had grown complacent in his old age, and he could see that now. Since their return to North Carolina, he'd been chiding himself for being caught off-guard by the Harmers in the first place, and for not keeping a closer eye on Samuels. He found the man unsettling at a fundamental level.

After Sarah told Drake about the change in Coded Incidents, he began to wonder if Samuels was connected to the Harmers' attack. It would make sense; the Secretary's colleagues and employees had a habit of disappearing or dying off. But he wasn't aware of any human able to control or influence the Harmers, even someone Awakened. That only led to more troubling questions.

For her part, Sarah had a healthy sense of skepticism, but didn't disregard the evidence of her own eyes, even if she didn't understand it. It was difficult to ignore the more fantastic elements of Drake's life while an angel was standing in the room.

The idea of the Harmers, though, was more disturbing and difficult to accept. So was the idea that they'd 'consumed' some of her colleagues at the site in Kansas. It worried her even more that Harmers may be influencing decision makers at higher levels, like Samuels, Blake, or even President Bushnell. She was trained to deal with anything, but high-ranking government officials under the influence of supernatural beings wasn't on the syllabus.

Despite her discomfort and initial cynicism, Sarah didn't regret any of her decisions to that point. Oddly enough, it all felt quite natural, as if it were what she was meant to do. When she was with the SPARTAN unit, her CO taught her to follow her instincts and training, and that advice hadn't let her down yet. She wasn't sure she believed in destiny, but she did think things happened for a reason.

She hadn't told Drake, but she volunteered to be his liaison. He had a well-earned reputation for being difficult and condescending and Sarah had seen it more than once. But Secretary Blake had often referred to Drake as his mentor, and she respected Blake nearly as much as that first CO.

Sarah accepted Drake's answer and went back to her research. Over the course of her time there, she discovered several references to her mother's maiden name, *Christoforos*. Drake reminded her of her grandpa a bit, both in his wisdom and his love of history, so she was delighted that Drake might have been watching him from afar.

Her grandpa told her stories about how her ancestors were part of the earliest church in Ephesus, and how they proudly changed their name and refused to live in fear of the oppressive Roman persecution. Then her mother would chime in and scold him for putting nonsense in Sarah's head. She never believed the stories and now seemed all the more naïve for it. Sarah's grandfather was right; they were special. She was special.

Looking up from the book where she was reading her family history, Sarah cleared her throat to get Drake's attention. When that didn't work, she did it again, more obviously.

"Yes, yes, what is it now?" Drake asked with an annoyed tone.

Sarah frowned and barked back, "Don't get short with me old man. Since I met you, you've been not much more than a condescending elitist asshole. I've listened to everything you've said, done everything you've asked, and seen things I can barely understand. It's been days and you still haven't told me anything I *really* need to know. If I didn't know better, I'd think you were avoiding telling me," she spat out. "You were the one who said we were running out of time! To do what? Wait?" she added accusatorily.

Drake sat up and pulled his glasses down from his forehead. He turned to Sarah with a solemn look, then motioned for Bathael to come over to where they were sitting.

"You're right, of course. You usually are," he said flatly, garnering a look of surprise from Sarah, "which is a tad annoying, but useful. I *haven't* told you everything. But there was a reason. I needed to make sure we were safe. Yes, we are short on time, but safety first! Always safety first, my good Captain. I also needed to be sure that this one," he said, pointing to Bathael, "was correct about who you are. They aren't infallible, despite their accuracy at prophecy."

"And who am I supposed to be?" Sarah demanded indignantly.

"You are Sarah Heighton, daughter of Debra of the line of…," Bathael chimed in before Drake stopped them and motioned for the angel to sit.

"That's not what she means. Here, hand me that book and I'll explain." Sarah brought the book, and her stool, over to Drake's chair and handed him the hefty tome. He opened it back up to the place Sarah had been reading, as if the binding were already used to the place being held.

"I told you before that you and the other *Bachar'im* were descended from the people who attended the 'Last Supper' of the man you call Jesus. In your case," he illustrated, pointing to the page, "you have direct lineage back to, let's see here…," he scanned the page looking for the correct entry. "There it is – Yohanan ben Zavdi."

"Who is that?" Sarah asked incredulously. "I thought you said it was an apostle."

Drake scowled a bit. "He *is* an apostle. Don't they teach you anything in Catechism anymore? John, son of Zebedee, youngest of the Apostles, brother of James the Greater… is any of this ringing bells?" Drake asked impatiently.

Sarah threw Drake a look that could fell a stag, so he just continued. "John died in Ephesus sometime near the start of the second century, surrounded by his children, grandchildren, and great-grandchildren. He was actually quite…prolific," Drake said, impressed. Before Sarah could interject, he went on, "Never mind what you've been taught. They all had children or the *Bachar'im* wouldn't exist, right?"

Sarah just nodded in agreement and Drake continued. "Now that we have that settled, it's time for you to learn the rest. We already talked about how the Grail wasn't what mattered. That doesn't mean that what happened at that gathering wasn't, though. There's a reason the Catholic Mass recreated that specific event and no others, but it wasn't quite the way it's described in scripture."

"What do you mean?" Sarah asked.

"The person you call Jesus was an Incorporated being; he was like Bathael here," Drake explained. "His disciples knew that if they told everyone *everything*, they'd be stoned as liars, heretics, and heathens. So, they took some liberties. But for the most part, the story is true and accurate."

"Are you telling me that he really did change wine into…," Sarah paused, her eyes widening with the revelation, "they drank his blood?"

"If you want to call it that, yes, yes they did," Drake offered, patting her on the shoulder. "But it's not what you think. He was Aethereal, which means…," Drake paused making a rolling motion with his hand, urging Sarah to draw the conclusion on her own.

"It means that he didn't have blood like you or I, or even understand what blood really was, just like with the tears," she answered.

"Exactly!" Drake exclaimed. "It probably looked like blood, I'm sure, but my understanding is that it tasted more like watered-down honey. They all dutifully drank what was offered, marking and protecting their progeny for all time. See, the Grail…the cup itself…didn't matter. You think of it as this golden, jeweled treasure. But it was just a ceramic cup. They left it at the table when they finished, and it was lost to antiquity before anyone even knew what it was," Drake explained.

"But the scripture also says that John, my ancestor, I guess, took the cup to the crucifixion," Sarah offered.

"No, he didn't," Drake replied flatly. "I was there; I was young man, but I recall the event as vividly as I do our first meeting. John and Mary were indeed there, but because that crucifixion was a political statement as much as it was an execution, the men being killed were guarded until they died. No, that bit about catching the blood was added later for dramatic effect, I expect. It worked out, though because it made it easier for me to shift focus away from the Spear in later years when people hunted the relics of the early church," Drake added, frowning a bit.

"Which brings us back to the Spear," Sarah surmised. "But before we get to that, I have another question. If there's a prophecy, and the angels think it can't be stopped, and nothing is the way we think it is, why was Jesus here? And don't give me a line about salvation because based on everything I've seen and heard, I'm pretty sure that's bullshit," she said matter-of-factly.

Drake sat back in his chair with a wide smile. "I told you she'd be a quick study," he said to Bathael, motioning at Sarah. "They were afraid you wouldn't understand, but I knew you were insightful," he added, clearly proud of himself. "You're right, it had nothing to do with humans, at least not at first. After the Shattering of the Planes, the Creator wanted to ensure that the beings on the Material Plane survived…"

"Not the Creator, Drake Sullivan, the Aetherium," Bathael interjected.

"What you mean, *the Aetherium*," he asked with mock seriousness. "I was very clearly told the Creator sent the *M'Shyha* to…"

This time Bathael held up a hand to stop Drake, "You were misinformed, Drake Sullivan. Misled, even. The Aetherium sent the *M'Shyha* because they could no longer commune with the Creator after the Shattering. They feared they had destroyed Creation and angered the Creator. Once Incorporated, the *M'Shyha* acted on my behalf to set the stage for the *Bachar'im*. They and I are…of a shared mind," Bathael added, smiling at Drake and Sarah.

"What does…?" Sarah started to ask.

"Investigator," Drake replied. "Though the humans misunderstood, so to them it meant Savior."

Bathael continued, "Yes, and we were worried that the *Nadach* would first attempt to strike against the humans since they were still connected to the other planes. The *M'Shyha* set about to protect as many as possible, but the humans were stubborn and only a few were marked. It's unfortunate that fewer still survive. We had hoped your numbers would be legion."

"Protect them from what?" Sarah asked, her confusion growing.

"I think it's time we opened her eyes," Drake said with a sigh. He motioned for Sarah to stand as he himself stood and extended his right arm again. Just as at the trailer, Sarah watched Drake produce the long, pristine blade from his sleeve. Drake held the sword reverently, and as he approached Sarah, he looked over her shoulder and nodded at Bathael. The angel grabbed Sarah by her arms, holding her fast as Drake leveled the point at her heart.

"Wait! What are you doing?" Sarah asked with a nervous chuckle, thinking the situation was obviously a prank. Drake pressed the point against Sarah's chest and placed his other palm on the pommel of the sword.

"No! STOP!" she screamed as Drake leaned into the sword, pressing the blade into her chest. She gasped for breath, waiting for the searing pain and darkness that never came. Looking down, in disbelief, she saw the blade lodged firmly in her chest. She felt some mild discomfort, but otherwise she wouldn't have known she was run through. She reached up and grabbed the blade, mostly to confirm it was real. The blade didn't cut her, though it sliced through her clothing easily enough. With a sudden surge of anger, she yanked the blade out of her chest and pushed Drake away.

"For fuck's sake!" she exclaimed furiously. "Was that really necessary? I could have been killed!"

"Oh, stop being so dramatic," Drake said, waving his hand dismissively at Sarah. "You were never in any real danger. That's the point; as *Bachar'im* you cannot be affected by creatures or objects," he waved the sword for emphasis, "that are native to the Aethereal Plane."

"For the love of all that's holy, man, SPEAK PLAINLY!" Sarah yelled, frustrated that her shirt now how a hole in it.

"The *Nadach* and his fallen brothers can't harm you. Neither can I," Bathael chimed in. "It took all my strength just to hold you in place. You and your ancestors were marked with the blood of the *Be'elohim*. You are as I," Bathael said with a smile.

"And it also means that you and the other Chosen are distinctly suited for stopping whatever the *Nadach* has planned…" Sarah stopped Drake cold with a hard slap, nearly knocking him over.

"You arrogant heartless bastard! People aren't born knowing what you know, and that they won't die when stabbed with swords—magical or otherwise!" she screamed before stomping across the room to look in the mirror.

Drake rubbed his stinging cheek and winced a bit as he did. "I suppose I deserved that. I've never been very good at people," he added looking over at a picture on his desk. He stood up, put the sword back up his sleeve and walked over behind Sarah, being sure to keep his distance.

"I'm sorry, Sarah," Drake said quietly. "I'm old, and I've been alone a very long time. You're right, I take my knowledge for granted. I remember things that humanity doesn't remember forgetting, and because of that, I've lost my patience with people in a way I should not have."

Sarah largely ignored Drake, but she did look him in the eye through the mirror when he apologized. "Apology accepted, old man," she said flatly. "Now, I know who I am, what I am, who you are, who they are," she nodded at Bathael, "and about 25% of what's going on. Oh, and I need to stop the bad guy from destroying the universe, but we need to find the other Chosen. Who is it and do you know where they are?"

"I've been struggling with that one a bit. I know who it is, but I'm having a difficult time divining his location for some reason. What about you?" Drake asked Bathael.

"I cannot see Timothy Andrews, son of Lena, of the line of Shimon bar Yonah. I know that he lives only because I know that he is not dead. But I cannot sense him the way I can Sarah Heighton. I do not know why," Bathael said with a frown. "I fear we may be too late."

"Wait did you say Andrews?" Sarah asked, turning quickly toward the angel.

"Yes, Timothy Andrews, son of…," Bathael repeated.

"Lena, yeah, I know," Sarah interrupted. "*He* was my first CO. He's the one who taught me everything I know. He died in Cincinnati seven years ago," Sarah added sadly.

"I thought so as well," Drake added with a frown, glancing back to the picture on his desk. "You don't know this, but I was also there. But our angelic friend here is convinced that the Colonel survived, and I'm inclined to believe them. They tend to know these things."

"All right then," Sarah said, straightening up. "Looking for my dead boss is far from the weirdest thing I've done this month. Do we have a plan?"

"Not exactly," Drake replied sheepishly, "But I know someone who did, and she was kind enough to write it all down for us. We just need to go get it."

Sarah frowned again in disappointment. "I really expected you to be more prepared. Do you at least know where we're heading?"

"Do you at least know where we're heading," Drake repeated mockingly. "Of course, I do. Now go pack your things. We're heading to San Francisco. We just need to make one stop first."

"Good, I always wanted to see Fisherman's Wharf," Sarah smiled as she moved to leave the room. She stopped, turned and called back, "Oh and Dr. Sullivan—you owe me new workout gear," she said, accentuating the hole in her top.

*Deep into that darkness peering, long I stood there,
wondering, fearing, doubting, dreaming dreams
no mortal ever dared to dream before.*
- Edgar Allen Poe

Chapter 29

Ying Qi no longer found solace in his morning meditation. He could feel his control slipping, little by little, and he was forced to use his Nightmare Guards to intimidate or cull those he could no longer influence directly. At first, there were only a few people in remote villages. But as the weeks drew on, the problems grew larger. With Li Fong still gone from the monastery, the emperor was left to deal with things on his own.

The issue wasn't weakness or a lack of capability; Ying Qi's power was as potent as ever. Maybe even more so. He was dangerously distracted. He found that keeping his 'guest' under control took quite a bit more effort than he originally thought. It wasn't enough to know the creature's name, it seemed Ying Qi also needed to ward off its corrupting influence. He couldn't let his guard down even for a moment. But he felt it was worth the added effort. He held one of the most powerful beings in the universe at his beck and call.

With that in mind, Ying Qi headed toward the round building in his garden. He kept the creature there mostly for convenience, but the truth was that he feared the effect his guest would have on the remaining monks. There was no denying that the creature's dark presence was pervasive. Three nights after the summoning, one of the monks brought Ying Qi his dinner and then tried to stab him with the chopsticks. He understood the gravity of the situation when he heard the innumerable voices laughing from inside the round building. Since then, Ying Qi took his meals away from the garden.

Ying Qi centered himself and walked to the summoning chamber carrying a bowl of noodles. He opened the door and stepped carefully over the wards he placed to keep the oppressive darkness in check. He left the door open to let the morning sunshine flow into the room. With a screech, the possessed boy scrambled into the shadows behind the altar.

"Come and eat," Ying Qi said as he placed the bowl down.

"The truth is revealed," the boy growled in an unnatural voice. "You summoned me to destroy me with bland food I don't need to eat. You've kept me here for some time, mortal. What is it you want from me?"

"Nothing less than your total obedience," Ying Qi said plainly as he sat on a bench bathed in sunlight. "I feel you testing me constantly, fighting my control, which is absolute. I know your true name, I know the words to bind you, and I could kill that pitiful form with a thought and end you eternally."

The boy looked up in disgust from the bowl, mouth filled with noodles. "I've always given you everything you asked for, monk," he spat, shooting half-chewed food across the altar. "It's not my fault you lack the conviction to follow through on the information I provided."

"I lack nothing!" Ying Qi exclaimed, slamming his fist down on the bench.

"You didn't kill the woman I told you to," the boy corrected, nonchalantly slurping more the noodles into his mouth.

"You misled me!" Ying Qi yelled, his face turning red with anger. "You should have told me her full name!"

"You didn't ask," the creature looked up with a smirk. "Haven't you learned yet, monk, that it's not *how* you ask, it's *what* you ask."

Ying Qi jumped to his feet and started pacing about the room. "Keep your riddles to yourself, parasite. You asked what I want; I want you to speak plainly," the emperor ranted. "I would see my destiny fulfilled and you play games. The Thibodeaux girl will die in this room by my hand, and then you will…"

The boy was laughing quietly, interrupting Ying Qi's rant. The raged emperor leapt across the altar and grabbed the creature's young body by the throat and threw it across the room like a doll. The boy just continued to laugh and stood back up, ignoring the abuse. Ying Qi grabbed him again by the throat, this time lifting him high into the air.

"I tire of your insolence, slave," Ying Qi spat in disgust. "I should rid myself of your presence now and seek my destiny without you and your useless aid." He squeezed the boy's throat tight, causing the laughter to turn into a gasping choke.

"Forgive me, *Wànsuìyé*," came the croaking reply.

Ying Qi frowned and held on a few seconds longer before finally releasing Shakra'el and the boy who held them. He walked back toward the bench and sat down again, trying to calm himself.

The warmth of the morning sun did little to soothe him. He was quicker to lose his temper than he had been. He wasn't at peace, and he struggled to focus. His mind was filled with thoughts of his brother, and he missed Li Fong's presence sorely. His brother should be here to see him ascend.

"We had a bargain," Ying Qi said once he calmed down. "I would release you from your mortal prison, and you would teach me the secrets of ascension. I spent most of my life working on the rituals that freed you from the depths of Hell, and here you are…not in Hell. Once you hold up your end, you will be freed from that body, as promised." Ying Qi looked over at the possessed boy with a gaze that would melt steel. "I did not sell my soul. You sold yours."

There was silence in the room for what seemed like an eternity. Ying Qi sat cross-legged on the bench while it was Shakra'el's turn to pace. But this movement was different. Ying Qi paced out of frustration; Shakra'el paced like a caged animal waiting to pounce on its captor. At that moment, Ying Qi held the cards.

The rituals on the scroll were specific. Many of them were protection spells that kept the creature contained in the boundaries of the Summoning Room. Others protected Ying Qi from anything the creature might do to harm him. The final steps had been clear; make a deal with the Devil, but make it specific, and make it conditional. Ying Qi had done this. Shakra'el was bound to him until their deal was done. And once Ying Qi ascended, Shakra'el would no longer be a threat.

"I am a creature of limitless power, *Wànsuìyé*," came voices from around the room. "Surely you didn't expect me to just hand you ascension on a platter. It is not a gift I can bestow, but an achievement which must be earned. It has happened only once in all the history of Creation. I must know you are worthy, or I must lead you to worthiness."

Ying Qi took a deep breath before he answered. It was taking all his strength to remain composed. "I expect you to remain true to our bargain," he said between deep breaths. "I expect you to obey."

"What is your command, *Wànsuìyé?*" the voices asked in unison.

"Tell me why I can no longer feel my brother's presence. I know he lives, but I can't see his thoughts the way I should," Ying Qi said in a worried but firm tone. He couldn't afford to show weakness now, but he needed to know why his brother was being hidden from him.

The boy just smiled as voices echoed around the room. "You already know the answer, *Wànsuìyé*," the voices said in a myriad of languages from all the dark recesses of the room. "Do you need me to spell it out for you?" the boy added, smirking.

"What are you saying?" Ying Qi asked, looking at the boy sharply.

"He has closed his mind to you. He learned to do it years ago. He didn't want you scrutinizing his every decision. I can't say that I blame him," Shakra'el said dryly.

"Impossible!" Ying Qi said in a raised voice. He was losing his temper again. "I would know. Our connection is still in place, I know where he is and that he's alive. I just can't hear his thoughts. I can't see through his eyes. Someone must be interfering. He must be in greater danger than I feared. I should go to him," the emperor declared. Why did he say that? He can't leave the monastery now, and he certainly couldn't travel to the US.

"Don't ask questions if you don't want the answers," the boy scoffed before adding a hasty, "*Wànsuìyé*," under the emperor's steely gaze.

Ying Qi fought back the darkness at the corners of his thoughts. He reached out with his consciousness, as he had countless times, following the glowing path that led to his brother's mind. As he did, his unease grew. The path was there, it led to Li Fong, but at the end there was an empty void. Li Fong was somewhere on the west coast of the US, presumably following Gino, but every attempt to connect to him or communicate with him was met with darkness and silence.

"He's betrayed you," came the whispers from all around him. "He's working with your enemies. He seeks to usurp you. He will never bring you what you need. He is plotting with the Thibodeaux woman to destroy you." The whispers continued, scratching at the edges of his sanity, seeping into his very soul.

"ENOUGH!" Ying Qi yelled forcefully.

"Are you well, *Wànsuìyé*?" Shakra'el asked mockingly. "You seem unsettled. Is everything all right?"

The room was spinning around him. He needed to get out. He stood up, walked toward the door slowly. As he moved, he felt his feet dragging, as if the very floor was turning into mud and he was sinking into it. The shadows grew and the lights dimmed. How long was he there? Was it already night? Each step was a fight, every movement a sojourn as he fought his way closer to the door. Was the door moving farther away, or was he being pulled back?

"You really need some rest, *Wànsuìyé*," the voices repeated over and over. He felt like he was being pulled to the ground.

"No!" Ying Qi yelled. "I BIND THEE, SHAKRA'EL! I COMMAND THEE TO RETREAT TO THE DARKNESS!"

With that proclamation, the heaviness stopped, and the darkness retreated. Ying Qi walked to the open door and saw that the sun was still low in the East. Satisfied he won his battle with the creature, he looked over his shoulder and called out. "I don't know how you are keeping me from my brother, but I will break through eventually, deceiver. I will be back tomorrow."

Ying Qi walked into the garden and closed the door of the Summoning Chamber behind him. He could feel the creature's eyes following him through the walls. He dared not to touch its mind; it was far too powerful for that, but he would continue to weaken it by defeating its illusions. He was worried about Li Fong, though. It wasn't like him to be so distant and out of touch, and he'd never felt him cut off their connection before. He was convinced that Shakra'el was behind it, but he hadn't risen to rule a quarter of the world's population without thinking of all the possibilities.

He called for his guards who were just outside the garden gate. As they approached and kneeled, he gave them instructions. They were to locate his brother in America, and the easiest way to do that would be to locate Leapstryke. He had a tracking device in his skull that should still work, and Li Fong should be near him. Once they found him, they were to tell him to return at once.

Together they could do anything. But only one of them could ascend.

Chapter 30

It took Tim longer than he'd hoped to clear the fog from his brain. YVE was trying to help, but he wasn't sure how much he trusted someone whose entire existence was a lie. Besides, she spent most of the time complaining about 'Samuels' butchery' and not doing anything helpful. If he was being honest, he felt like YVE was changing. It was subtle, but he knew that they needed to get her in her own device and out of his brain sooner rather than later.

That's why he was spending most of his time trying to find where Gino took Matthew. Without access to the considerable resources he once had, he was falling back on rusty skills from before the incident in Cincinnati. All his old contacts thought he was dead, but he had a talent for imitation now and he was using it. He made some calls and had some equipment delivered to the motel. Armed with a computer and high-speed internet, he was able to weasel his way into several poorly protected systems. From there, he could find what he needed easily.

Like he did in his pursuit of Nate, Tim connected to local law enforcement and traffic control cameras using a backdoor built for the NSA. He knew it would be impossible for Gino to avoid being seen entirely. However, based on what little Tim was able to find, he was rather good at it. Just three images came up: one in Kentucky, another in Colorado, and the last in California. The last image was Gino carrying a large paper bag and trying very hard to conceal his cyborg nature. That was in the Bay Area in California, and it was the only image that didn't also include Matthew. That had to be it. But where? The Bay area covered nine counties and 7,000 square miles. He needed more.

Tim didn't understand the concept of giving up. It just wasn't in his DNA. But after days searching, Tim was no closer to narrowing down his search options out West. He was able to get Gino's personnel file from the CIA, which was no small feat. From it, he gleaned that Gino was a man singularly equipped at evading detection. While he didn't have Tim's ability to hide in plain sight, he was able to remotely hack into wireless camera systems to obscure or remove his presence. That's why there were only three pictures of him. YVE had commented that she was surprised there wasn't a trail of bodies to follow, but Tim scoffed. Gino didn't get where he was by being careless.

Tim remembered Gino, but what he remembered most was the tension his presence created on an otherwise well-oiled team. He and Nate hand-picked everyone in the SPARTAN unit; everyone except Gino. He didn't realize it before, but his actions in following Nate very closely mirrored the protection detail for Claire.

Tim and his team were deputized, and members of the FBI, CIA, U.S. Marshals, and Secret Service were added to his team. Of those, Gino was the only one who qualified for the ground team.

Tim didn't want *any* of the new people in his unit, but he was outranked and overruled at the command level. Tim almost resigned over it.

Gino's background in the CIA meant he was an expert in infiltration and intelligence gathering, which explained how he so easily discovered the cabin. He was also highly skilled at hand-to-hand combat, regularly besting Tim and Nate both in sparring matches. And while he could be irreverent to the point of being disrespectful, when it was time to work, he always got the job done. When he was on the clock, he was calm, cool, and collected in a way that was almost disconcerting. Tim had pegged him as a high-functioning sociopath, but he reckoned anyone working in the field for the CIA had to be. Gino proved to be a valuable asset, just not Tim's asset.

Something troubled Tim in the back of his mind, though. Grabbing Mathhew seemed to indicate that he was either looking for insight into how to defeat Tim, or that wanted access to the technology for his own purposes. What Tim didn't understand is why Gino needed Matthew for either of those things.

If he was still working for Samuels, even off the books, he should have access to everything he needed. So, why was he in California and not closer to Groom Lake? That was the weird part for Tim. Gino could have taken him anywhere and started work quicker without traveling all the way across the country by car. What was in California? Then a light came on.

"YVE," Tim said out loud. He found it more comfortable to speak with her as if she were in the room rather than in his head. "What was the backup plan?"

"What do you mean, Colonel?" she asked.

"Nate would have had a backup plan in case you were discovered before I arrived. Where was the fallback point?" he asked seriously.

Tim might have been the leader, but Nate was the tactical genius of the unit. That's why his callsign was Argus; he saw everything. He wouldn't have started an op without having Plan B if something went wrong. Especially with Emma and Matthew involved.

"If there was one, I am unaware of it," YVE said. "I'm sorry."

"Do you know where they were heading when they left?" Tim asked.

"I do not," YVE replied. "I believe they intended to return once it was safe, but I find that unlikely given the state in which things were left. Commander Lange and Miss Thibodeaux provided no clues as to their next steps, only that we needed you."

"Yeah, they had one of those letters," Tim recalled. "Those things are dangerous. Claire should have known better."

Just then, there was loud knock at the door. Tim's head shot up and he instinctively reached for a gun he did not have. Looking around, he grabbed the only thing in reach, a pillow, and headed to the door. A quick scan showed a group of people and a dog, though he was having trouble focusing on the largest member of the group. That made him even more uneasy since the largest person was usually the greatest threat.

Tim stood to the side of the door and called out in an altered voice, "Who is it?"

"Umm, we're looking for Colonel Tim Andrews," came the tentative reply in a woman's voice. "Is he there with you? I'm an old friend and it's important that we find him right away."

The voice had a ring of familiarity to Tim, but he was so mixed up he wasn't sure he could trust himself. "Should I recognize that voice?" he asked YVE silently.

"I don't have an answer for you, Colonel," YVE replied. "I don't have access to voice print records, and neither do you, or you wouldn't be asking. It isn't anyone I know."

"Who are you?" Tim called out in the same voice.

This time a man replied, "Listen, my good man. We're friends of the colonel's and we were hoping to catch up. If he's not here, can you just let us know where he is so we can be on our way?" the stranger asked insistently.

There was the nagging recognition again. He knew these people, but he didn't trust that the memories were real. It wasn't beneath Samuels to send people he knew from his time in the Beta Project to bring him back. If there was any person more stubborn than Tim, it was Samuels. He couldn't let his guard down now.

"If you're his friends, then you know what his unit's motto was," Tim offered. Only a handful of people would know the right answer. It wasn't official, so each member of the team had it sewn in special thread over the approved motto on their patches. It was only visible in infrared light.

"Well, umm," the man stammered to reply before the woman with him stepped in.

"E tan e epi tas," the woman answered in Greek without hesitation, adding, "With it or on it. Our patch was a lambda shield on a field of red."

Tim was flummoxed, but he had no reason not to trust his instincts now. It was clear that this was a person from his past, so he unlocked the door and opened it. There in front of him was the most ragamuffin group of people he'd ever seen. They looked like they hadn't slept much, and the woman had a greenish tinge as she seemed to be holding back from vomiting. He didn't recognize the old man or the massive person behind him, but he recognized the woman instantly.

"Athena? Lieutenant Heighton?" Tim asked, unsure if he should believe his eyes. He'd not seen her since she left with Emma for the safe house, the cabin in Virginia, seven years earlier.

Sarah's eyes widened with misbelief. She leaped over the threshold and hugged a startled Tim around his neck, tears streaming down her face. Almost as quickly, she composed herself, stood at attention in front of him, and saluted. It took Tim a moment to return the salute, though. No one had given him the honor since he'd been in the Beta Project.

"It's so good to see you, sir," Sarah blubbered out, trying to stop her crying. "I didn't believe them when they said you were still alive. I was at your...," she cleared her throat and dried her eyes before continuing. "I was at your funeral. We all were. So much has happened since then. And Commander Lange…,"

The older gentleman who arrived with Sarah put his hand on her shoulder to calm her. "There's plenty of time for that, Captain. I'm sure you both have plenty to share. But first, may we come in? It's starting to rain."

Tim nodded and stepped aside, motioning for the group to enter. First Sarah, then the older gentleman, then a shaggy dog that barked his sincere thanks before jumping on the bed and falling asleep, then a large, bright figure Tim had a hard time looking at. After everyone filed in, Tim checked outside, then closed and locked the door.

"All right, I need some explanations, and I need them now. First, who the hell are you?" Tim asked frantically, pointing to the man and the figure. He did have the same feeling of familiarity with the man's voice, though he couldn't place it no matter how hard he tried.

"Fair enough," the man said holding up his hands. "I don't think we've ever met, but I certainly know you, sir. My name is Drake Sullivan, and I was friends with Claire Thibodeaux. You didn't see me, but I was there in Cincinnati. My large friend here," Drake paused, pondering the best explanation before giving up. "We'll come back to them. The shaggy one is Merlin. You know the Captain. We're here because we need your help, Colonel."

Tim began to recall things Claire had told him about Drake. She kept a picture of him on her mantle, and he looked exactly the same now, though that picture had to be nearly 20 years old. Tim kept this observation to himself and started to wonder about the large person Drake avoided explaining. But he had another question first.

"How did you find me?" Tim wondered. "I know how not to leave a digital footprint, and anyone who knew where I was is either hunting me or missing."

"Ah yes," Drake said with a slight smile. If it makes you feel better, you weren't easy to find. And my friend over there is particularly talented in that department. No, I had one of these," Drake said as he pulled something from his pocket. As he unfolded it, he saw that it was a picture of Claire and her haunting grey eyes. Drake regarded the picture with a sad look before turning it over to reveal the writing. "It simply said that I should be here at this time and day. I noticed it when I had to replace the frame a couple days ago. She knew that would happen, and I knew that it would be you I'd find here. She always found a way to give me what I needed, even when I didn't know I needed it."

Tim frowned and looked at the note. It was her handwriting, and she looked to be in her twenties in the photo. Handing the photo back to Drake he added a mournful, "Yeah, she had a way of doing that."

Looking back up at Drake, then to Sarah he continued. "Those damned letters are nuisance. Every time I see one, people get hurt. How did you get involved in this, Lieutenant?"

"Actually, it's Captain now," Sarah corrected him gently.

"Oh. Of course. It's been plenty long enough. Hell, you're probably getting close to Major now," Tim said with a smile.

"I'll be eligible next year, sir," she replied. "Since I was reassigned, I've been working with Secretary Blake at Defense. He was a fan of yours and he wanted to make sure that I was put to good use. Since I wasn't in Cincinnati when everything went to hell, I got a pass. He's the one who made sure you got honors at your funeral," she added, looking at the floor.

"Remind me to thank him next time I die," Tim said sarcastically. "So, who's the other one?" he asked, pointing to the unintroduced figure. "And why do they look all fuzzy?"

"That's a bit difficult to explain," Sarah offered. "It's probably better if they explain themselves."

The massive figure stood up to their full height. Tim looked, but he couldn't focus on whomever, or whatever, it was. It was more than just a blur, it was like seeing hundreds of the same image, but all of them askew slightly, and all of them phasing in and out of existence. They were bright beyond belief, and when they spoke, it was like sitting under Niagara Falls. Tim squeezed his eyes and held up his hand to stop them from speaking further.

"What do you mean, 'Why are we here?'," Sarah asked the figure. "That's Colonel Andrews. You know, Timothy Andrews, son of Lena, of the line of Shimon bar Yonah, et cetera, et cetera." The roaring began again, and Tim covered his ears with his hands. It didn't hurt as much as it was overwhelming.

Drake stood up and stood between Tim and the figure. "You don't see the man standing right behind me?" After a short pause, Drake turned to Tim with a frown. "Colonel, can you tell me what you see when you look at my friend?"

"I can't see anything, really. I know something is there, but I can't describe it. It's like something moving side-to-side really fast. And there's this noise, like sitting in a room full of speakers listening to static on full blast," Tim described.

"Dog bollocks!" Drake exclaimed sourly. "That's going to make this a great deal harder. Plug your ears." He turned to look at his companion, asking, "Well, what now? You're the one with all the answers."

Bathael looked at Drake solemnly, saying, "Drake Sullivan, there is no other living human in this room. I cannot feel the presence of Timothy Andrews. I take your word that the being behind you is him. However, he is not as he once was, and I do not know if he can still be called *Bachar'im*. You would need to test him. If what Sarah Heighton has said is true, then it is likely this person has had their connection to the Aether severed. I will be silent until this can be resolved."

Drake looked at Tim with a furrowed brow, motioning for him to unplug his ears. "Colonel, I don't have time to explain everything right now," Drake said gravely. "I don't need a test to know who and what you are. If you cannot see the angel standing behind me, then you cannot be harmed by it. You are Concealed, Colonel, and that means you can be of use. We need your help."

Life is always a matter of waiting
for the right moment to act.
- Paulo Coelho

Chapter 31

Drake was having considerable trouble convincing Tim to help them. He had to explain what it meant that he was Concealed and Tim, at YVE's request, didn't discuss Cytotechnics, or YVE's presence. What finally moved Tim to action was the disclosure of their intended destination: Emma Thibodeaux's home in San Francisco.

Sarah was able to rent an SUV, but they assumed that her transactions would be watched. Tim didn't need to sleep, but he didn't want everyone to know that, so he split driving duties with Sarah. They made sure to stay off any highways that might have cameras or tracking equipment. He also made sure that the GPS was recording false information, in case it was being tracked.

When he wasn't driving, Tim tried to use the time to his advantage. He worked to fine tune his sight and hearing so that he could better perceive Bathael's presence without being overcome. What he'd figured out, with YVE's help, was that Bathael was trying to appear in a way Tim could best understand, cycling through millions of possible images and sounds. YVE speculated that Drake and Sarah likely saw Bathael differently, a hypothesis Tim promised her that he would test later. Eventually, he was able to make Bathael's presence bearable.

What was important now was getting in touch with Emma. Drake was convinced that she was either in possession of, or knew the location of, something that would help them stop some sort of world-shattering catastrophe. Tim was having a hard time digesting all of it, though, and he wasn't sure he believed any of it.

Even when presented with the irrefutability of Claire's gift, Tim remained skeptical of it. He was even less sure of the nonsense Drake had been throwing at him, but he knew an opportunity when he saw it. Tim needed to find Gino, and Matthew may have had a contingency Nate would know about. Finding Nate and Emma seemed a logical plan. Tim didn't need all the other junk, but he was happy to play along for now.

Once the five of them arrived, Merlin included, they set up in an empty apartment across from the building where Emma lived. Her apartment was above a jazz club and restaurant called the Fuzzy Apricot. Since they served lunch, the foot traffic made it hard to track who was coming and going. Tim kept watching over the place, looking for either Emma or Nate to appear, but as of yet, he'd had no luck. But it had only been a few hours.

"I told you already, Sullivan," Tim said in a frustrated tone, "I'm not interested in your crusade. Even if I believed half of what you're saying, and I don't, what good can two people do against an all-powerful creature from…," Tim paused, "where was it again?"

"The Nether," Drake snapped back, clearly annoyed.

"Yeah, that place," Tim continued. "Listen, I've spent my whole career putting my life on the line for other people, and what do I have to show for it? Nothing! I lost EVERYTHING! My wife, my kid, my life; everything. And now that I have some of it back, you want me to hand it over to you. No thanks."

Before Drake could reply, Sarah placed a hand on his shoulder and motioned for him to step aside. Drake frowned but complied, and Sarah sat down while Tim continued monitoring the street below. She sat silently with him, watching the people come and go from the building across the street, waiting to speak.

"You know," she started tentatively, "It took a long time for me to understand why you didn't let me come with you and the others to Cincinnati. I was so angry at you that day," she explained, looking down as he continued. "I would have followed you into hell, and you knew that. But you also knew something was wrong and you wanted to protect me."

She stood up and leaned on the balcony railing next to Tim, who was seemingly ignoring her, still watching the street outside and chewing on a piece of *Papaw Peanut's* jerky. It had always been his favorite, so she made sure she brought some for their trip.

"I resented you *so* much. You sent me to babysit, and I could have helped. I tortured myself thinking that maybe if I'd have been there, you'd have lived. So, finding out you didn't die was a *real* kick in the teeth," Sarah expressed angrily.

Tim finally looked up from his vigil. "Oh, I died," he retorted emotionlessly. "I died more than once. I've died so much that I don't even know if I'm me anymore!" Tim exclaimed. "Yeah, I was trying to protect you. You don't get to be in the position I was in without knowing things, and nothing about that op was above board. Nate knew it too. So, we sent you on a milk run. Sue me,"

Tim added sarcastically before looking back to the doors of the club again.

Sarah sat back down and let out an exasperated sigh. "I stopped being mad about it five years ago. Once I started leading people, I got it. Later on, I realized how much trust you placed in me. You put someone precious to you in my care, because you knew I'd keep her safe," she surmised. Tim just looked at Sarah without moving his head.

"Do you still trust me that way?" Sarah asked sincerely.

Tim turned away from his surveillance. "What are you talking about?"

"Do you trust me?" she asked again. "Come on, it's not a difficult question."

"It's a stupid one," Tim scoffed. "If I didn't trust you, I wouldn't be here." Then he looked back toward the bar across the street before adding, "And you aren't stupid. What're you getting at?"

"So, you know I'm not stupid, and you trust me," Sarah confirmed, "but you won't listen to Dr. Sullivan, someone I have trusted with my life. I've seen stuff, Colonel. Stuff I can't explain, stuff that will haunt me. Dr. Sullivan knows things no one else knows. He needs us and I need you. Please don't make me do this alone."

Tim looked down, wringing his hands. "I'm not here for him, or for you. I'm here to fulfill a promise."

Sarah leaned forward in her chair, crossing her arms. "A promise? What are you talking about? Promise to whom?"

It was Tim's turn to sigh as he leaned back and looked up at the sky. "To me," he said quietly. "It was a promise to me. Did you know I was in the room with her? I was standing…," Tim paused, collecting himself before continuing, "I was behind her when it happened. The thing we were supposed to stop. And he was there too; that bastard CIA spook they forced on our team. He put some sort of beacon in the window, right in front of her. And she just let him do it. Before I could pull her out of the way, I was covered in her blood while he laughed. HE LAUGHED! Poor Whiteboard, he said. And that's last thing I heard before everything ended."

Tim wiped his eyes, even though there were no tears. It was a reflex at this point. "In that half a moment before my world ended, I promised myself that if we survived, that son of a bitch would find justice by my hand. Now, I don't know if I believe in God, or a Creator, or whatever nonsense that old man has filled your head with, but here I am alive, and that monster is out there breathing my air, walking my streets, mocking me. He dies and then, maybe, I'll listen. But not until he's dead."

Sarah took a moment to absorb what she'd just been told. She didn't even realize that she was crying. She remembered the way Gino looked at her; not like a dirty old man watches a sorority girl, more like the way a wolf watches sheep. She never liked him, never trusted him, and certainly didn't mourn him. Finding out that he was at least partly responsible for what happened in Cincinnati was shocking, and there was more there to process, but there would be time for that later.

"All right," she said, slapping her knees. "I'm in."

"Wait…, what?" a confused Tim replied. "That wasn't an invitation, Athe…"

Sarah held her hand up to cut him off. "With all due respect, sir, I wasn't asking permission. You're dead. You're not really a Colonel in the Air Force anymore, which means you don't get to give me orders. Yeah, I'm in. The way I see it, he's still a threat to Miss Thibodeaux, and I'm sure Commander Lange would probably be on board too. You're getting help, you're going to like it, so can I get a, 'Yes, ma'am,' Airman?" She concluded rising to her feet.

Tim was shocked at first, he looked to the side over to Drake, who just shrugged, and then back to Sarah with a slight smile. "Yes, ma'am," he replied directly.

"Oh, I like her," YVE said to Tim with more than a little admiration.

"So do I," Tim replied silently. "She was my best and brightest student. I'm glad to see that she's flourished in my absence. What do you think of all this stuff Drake's been spewing? Do you believe any of it?"

"Honestly, Colonel," YVE replied cautiously, "I don't know if it's important whether or not *I* believe it. You and I are both examples of the previously impossible and borderline miraculous. If we had been described to even the most open-minded scientist two decades ago, they would have denied we could exist, yet here we are. Who are we to say what is or isn't possible?"

YVE was right, and his instincts were telling him that Drake was right too. He just needed to take care of Gino first, and he needed to talk to Emma…Sunshine…it had been so long. Would he be able to face her? He was still mentally bracing himself for their eventual reunion. He surely deserved whatever she would say or do.

Tim stood up and walked over to the others. "How certain is your… friend… that this is where Emma and Nate are? There are apartments above the club, but I haven't seen either of them, and I'm patched into the street cameras on all sides of the building."

Bathael was by a window on the other side of the room, stroking a cat which had come up the fire escape. "I am certain, Timothy Andrews. Gaylord has confirmed that Emma Thibodeaux and Nathanael Lange are in the building across from us."

Tim squinted and replied skeptically, "Who the hell is Gaylord?"

Bathael motioned at the cat. It was a blue-point Siamese with shocking blue eyes. "Gaylord had told me a great many things. He is quite fond of them, though he does not own them. His human is two buildings down at street level. He just thought Emma Thibodeaux needed help. Quite an intuitive and honorable creature."

The entire group looked at Bathael with slacked jaws while the angel continued to stroke the feline on the windowsill. Sarah leaned over to Tim and whispered, "This isn't even the weirdest thing they've done."

Tim looked over to the angel and asked, somewhat mockingly, "So does, *Gaylord* think it's safe for us to go over?"

Bathael was either ignoring Tim's snark or didn't understand it. "No, Timothy Andrews, it is not yet time. But soon. Until then, you should rest. You will need your strength for the trials to come."

Tim looked over to Drake who just shrugged again and then went over to his seat by the other window. He was tired of waiting. He needed resolution and closure. He felt like he'd been waiting for an eternity, though a week ago, he didn't even know Gino was alive. For that matter, he didn't even know who *he* was, let alone who Gino was. He made a mental note to pay Samuels a visit when this was all over.

"I guess I'm taking orders from a cat now," he said as he slumped back. "It could be worse, I suppose; it could have been a cockroach."

> There are some wounds that one can heal only
> by deepening them and making them worse.
> *- Auguste de Villiers de L'Isle-Adam*

Chapter 32

Emma heard the knock on the door in a coded pattern. Nate was returning with food from the restaurant below. It was the only place she could get decent Cajun food in California. She missed her mom's cooking, and this was as close as she could get to it. Claire grew up in Lafayette, Louisianna, and when she was angry, her Cajun accent grew more intense. She would have loved the food at the Fuzzy Apricot, Emma mused.

She had been coming to the bar since her days at Stanford. She and her friends preferred the bars in the Castro; there were fewer leering eyes and grabbing hands and the atmosphere was always more fun. She found the Fuzzy Apricot on a fluke; it was the only place with a kitchen open past midnight. After that she never went anywhere else. She'd even grown to love the jazz. The bar's owner, Ted, managed the bar and played the music, and her wife, Robin, cooked the food. She got to know them, and they warmly offered her the apartment over the club after she graduated. They were as close to family as she had now.

Emma looked through the peep hole and saw the distorted fisheye image of Nate carrying a tray of food. She unlocked the door and opened it, peeking around the edge as Nate carried in the food and set it on the table. He went to the cupboard and pulled out two plates and started unwrapping everything. As he laid out all the food, he heard a loud meowing from the window, which made him look over.

"Don't worry, I didn't forget yours," he said without looking up.

"God, that smells *so* good. What did they send up?" Emma asked after inhaling deeply.

"Umm, let's see. Crab and Shrimp Étouffée, Red Beans and Rice with Andouille, and some corn bread," he said, reading the labels on the lids. "Oh, and a piece of raw salmon for Gaylord," he added before the cat could protest.

Emma brought over Gaylord's dish and placed the salmon in it before carrying it over to the window. As she set it down, Gaylord purred happily and buried his face in the fresh meat. Emma smiled and returned to the table for her own meal.

"How was it down there? Crowded?" she asked.

"Not particularly," he replied while he was getting the flatware. "But it's still early. I did get a charming proposition from an older gentleman in a cowboy hat, and someone very politely placed their number in my back pocket. It's nice to know *someone* still finds me attractive," he added with a smirk.

Emma just laughed as she started eating her meal. She knew she was safe here, and it was the only place she felt at home since her mom died. Claire wouldn't have let her settle somewhere dangerous, but she let Emma find the Fuzzy Apricot on her own. She didn't like the letters any more than Tim did, but she respected her mom's need to write them.

As they ate, the sultry tones from Ted's sax carried up through the vents. The odd acoustics gave the already melancholy melody an even more haunting tone. As they cleaned up, they heard someone walking in the hall outside the door. They stopped what they were doing to listen. Emma was the only person who lived on this floor, and it wasn't usual for Ted or Robin to come up while the bar was open. They heard a sliding noise, and the steps faded and went back down the stairs. Emma went over to the door and saw an envelope on the floor. Picking it up, it read, "Anne Montgomery and Tom Lonchar," and her address down to the floor and door number.

"What is it?" a concerned Nate asked.

Emma handed him the envelope, and his mood soured. The names were the cover names they took on for traveling once they hatched their plan to free Tim from the Beta Project. They hadn't even told them to Matthew, and there was no connection to their real identities digitally. The only person who could have possibly known was Claire.

"Well, it's addressed to both of us this time," Nate commented, looking over to Emma. "Do you want to open it or should I?"

"I hate those things," Emma said with disgust. "They never say anything nice; it's always doom and gloom. Why couldn't she give me the lottery numbers or something? Like, would it have killed the universe to let her see kittens instead of monsters?"

Emma had long since come to terms with her mother's advanced knowledge of her death, and the fact she hadn't been there when Claire was killed, not that she wanted to be. But she resented her mother's power; not her mother for having it, but the power itself. So rarely did Claire see anything wonderful or uplifting. At least if she did, she didn't make as much of a note of it. No, she was cursed to see all the ill in the world and doubly so because she felt the need to fix it all.

Nate patted Emma's shoulder and said with a grin, "Hey, at least she got the band back together, even if it was only for a couple hours. Have faith, kiddo. We'll get through this." She smiled slightly and nodded in agreement.

"All right then, let's see what we have," Nate said as he tore open the end of the envelope. He reached in and pulled out a yellowed piece of paper and unfolded it. Nate instantly recognized it as something Claire wrote as a child. At the top was the date March 20, 1969. The paper had strange markings with words next to them, like a translation matrix or codex of some kind. He scanned the page, turned it over, then handed it to Emma.

"What do you make of this?" he asked with confusion.

Emma took the page and reviewed It carefully. She held it up to the light, looking for some clue as to the meaning, but found nothing. "She was very young when she wrote this; maybe four or five?" Emma noted. "Damn it, why couldn't she just write it out like a normal person? What the hell are these markings? Is this Hebrew? How did she know Hebrew at five when she was Catholic?"

Emma slumped in a chair at the table. Her mother made sure she was well cared for after her death. She was seventeen the last time she saw Claire and started college the following year. She could have gone to Duke, where Drake could help her, but her mother wanted her to experience life away from her old circles and suggested that she apply to a college out west. She earned a full ride to Stanford and majored in History and Computer Science – her two favorite hobbies. She wanted to see the ruins of Mycenae and Tiryns. That is until she got the first letter the day she graduated. That was the letter which sent her to find Nate. With it was the letter Nate used to find Tim. It's what started everything in motion.

Nate sat across from her at the table, looking at her sympathetically. For the past two years, they had been near-constant companions. It took time, and a considerable amount of money and patience, to set everything up. And all of it was driven by Claire's letters. A letter delivered to Matthew Young connected him to Emma and Nate. A letter to the family lawyer freed up the funds necessary to get the tools and gear they needed at the cabin. So many letters, they'd lost count. Claire's whole life must have been spent writing letters.

"So, what next?" Nate asked. For the first time, the letter didn't explicitly tell them what to do.

"I don't know," Emma replied with a sigh. "The last one told us to wait here, I'm guessing so we could get this one. We don't have any way to get in touch with Colonel Andrews now, if he survived. You saw the cabin; there was nothing left. Mom said there were other people that were going to help, but she didn't say who they were. Maybe these are directions? She was really young, and this spy craft bullshit was popular with kids back then. You know, decoder rings and x-ray glasses and all that nonsense. Maybe she made this all up? But it would be weird for her to send it if it weren't important."

Gaylord sat in the open window across the room, cleaning himself after his filling supper. He meowed for attention, but the pair ignored him. Up to this point, all the letters had been specific, even if they were a bit cryptic. They were all easy enough to decode and always pointed in a direction to go. The childlike whimsy in what had to be Claire's first letter was unexpected. Nate only knew Claire as a serious, almost severe woman, driven and motivated by her visions. Even Emma hadn't seen her mother be lighthearted often. She was too haunted by what she saw.

"Hey, what's this bit at the bottom?" Emma asked, breaking the silence.

Nate took the paper back and put on his glasses. It was hell getting old. He noticed at the bottom a very slight stain. The page was slightly more yellow, and it looked deliberate, almost like there were letters, but there wasn't enough visible to tell. He sniffed the paper. It smelled old, and very slightly of lemons.

"I think I know what this is," he said excitedly as he walked over to the nearby lamp. Carefully, he used the heat from the bulb to expose a feathery script. Having seen so many of the letters, he knew it was Claire's writing, probably some decades older than the Claire who wrote the code.

"Here, have a look at this," he said while offering the paper to Emma.

She grabbed the paper and held it under the lamp so that she read the light brown text. "Ask the cat who came to dinner," she read. "What the hell does that even mean?"

As if on cue, Gaylord walked between Emma's legs, rubbing his face against them. For the first time, she noticed that something was attached to Gaylord's collar. She reached down and gingerly untied the string that held a tightly rolled up note. She took the note back over to the table and sat down to unfurl it. There, in the tiniest possible writing, were symbols like those the young Claire had written.

"A riddle wrapped in a mystery inside an enigma," Nate commented. "Where's Athena when we need her?"

"Who?" Emma asked.

"Oh, um, Lieutenant Heighton," Nate replied while looking at the tiny letters. "You remember her, right? She's the one who took you to the cabin when you were a kid. She was always the best code breaker in the group. Even better than Sphinx, and breaking codes was literally his job. She was better than everyone at everything. That's why Tim called her Athena. Give me a little bit to get this sorted."

Nate dove into the decoding. It reminded him of his time with the SPARTAN unit under Tim's command. Things were simpler back then. They knew who the enemies were, and they knew what they had to do. He just wanted his friend back. He didn't want or need to save the world again.

"Ok, it seems to be a very formal greeting," Nate explained. "Let's see, I think it says, 'Emma Thibodeaux daughter of Claire of the line of Carolus Magnus, and Nathanael Lange, son of Roseann of the line of Yngvi Odinson, we bid you tidings from,'…I don't know this word…anyway, 'we bid you tidings. Step onto the metal staircase and welcome us. We would like to have you join us. Speak welcome and we will enter'. Then it has these syllables. I think it's a foreign language – something like Hebrew, but not."

Without thinking, Emma looked at the paper and sounded out the translation, "Val…hobb… ock?"

There was a bright flash of light, which startled Gaylord so much he fell out of the window and onto the fire escape. There was a loud crash as Tim and Drake fell since the chairs on which they were sitting were no longer there. Sarah appeared near the window and did a better job keeping her food down this time. Maybe it's because Bathael's teleport was gentler and less rushed than Drake's. The angel was the first to speak.

"Behold!" Bathael spoke, shaking the room. "I am the *Bat Qol*, the messenger of which you were told. My name is Bathael, and I am the Voice of the Creator. Your time has come, Emma Thibodeaux, and yours as well, Nathanael Lange. The *Bachar'im* have need of your aid."

Nate and Emma looked dumbfounded at their unexpected guests, unsure what to make of what just happened. Tim was hit the hardest, the transition was something his artificial body was having difficulty processing.

"Hey Sunshine," he said weakly. "You got anything to drink?"

Emma bounded over to help Tim to his feet, hugging him tightly for a long time before taking a step back and slapping him hard enough to turn his head. "We thought you were dead! And you've been nearby this whole time? I have a mind to toss you out the window."

Before Tim could say anything, she walked over to Sarah and gave her a tight hug as well. "It's been too long, Sarah," she said with a smile.

"Yeah, it has," Sarah replied with a smile of her own. Then she sniffed the air, adding, "Wait, is that étouffée I smell? I haven't had anything but jerky in two days."

Emma laughed and walked Sarah over to the table, offering what was left of the dinner. Sarah dug in happily, making all sorts of approving noises as she feasted. Once she was satisfied Sarah was taken care of, Emma walked over to the sink, poured a glass of water from the tap and took it to Tim.

"Your drink, sir," she said flatly before turning toward Drake and Bathael. "And you two… I don't know you. But since you're with them," she motioned at Tim and Sarah, "you can stay. Which one of you wants to clue us in on what's going on?"

"You don't know who I am?" a wounded Drake asked.

"No, I don't," Emma replied flatly. "Should I?"

Drake sighed and frowned a bit before replying. "No, I guess not. My name is Drake Sullivan, and I am…," he paused, picking his words carefully. "I knew your mother. We were close once. My shiny friend over there already introduced themselves. And before you ask, they're an angel. Kind of *THE* angel. No, I don't have time to explain everything. We need your help."

Emma crossed her arms and looked over to Nate, who was catching up with Tim. "That's not going to work for me. I've spent the last two years chasing my mother's ghosts without any explanation. Go here and do this, go there and do that; I'm tired of not having control of my own life.

"Listen, child…," Drake began before being cut off.

"I am NOT a child," Emma spat out.

Sarah stepped in, looking at Drake harshly. "Has being a patronizing asshole *ever* worked for you? Seriously, you need to rethink how you talk to women. I'll handle this."

Turning to Emma, she said softly, "Let's go sit on the fire escape and I'll explain everything." Emma nodded in agreement and the two women stepped through the window and out of view.

Nate, who was sitting with Tim away from the others. "Are you sure that's the L-T?" Nate asked in awe.

"She's a Captain now," Tim replied with a grin. "I think she could whip both our asses, if I'm being honest. And I'm a robot. Listen man, I feel like I owe you…,"

Nate reached out and patted Tim on the shoulder to stop him. "You don't owe me anything," he said with a wide smile. "After I found you, I knew they'd probably just make you forget it all again. Do you remember anything we talked about that day?"

"I remember everything, now," Tim said as he put down the empty water glass, "and most of it sucks. I won't lie, I've been struggling. I don't feel like *me* anymore. I know I look the same, and I sound the same, but that's all built from files, not memories. There's nothing left of the man I was."

"The Ship of Theseus," Drake chimed in solemnly from across the room.

"The what of who?" Nate asked.

"The Ship of Theseus," Drake repeated. "Colonel Andrews here is living out of the most well developed and oldest philosophical question man has ever raised. Legend has it that the ship Theseus used to return to Athens was preserved well into the 4th century BCE. They did this by replacing any rotting or damaged planks with new ones. Eventually, there remained no original wood from the time of Theseus, which then led to the question: was it still the Ship of Theseus though Theseus himself touched none of the planks?"

"So, what's the answer," Tim asked, looking up at Drake with sad eyes.

"Well, my good Colonel, I think that's up to you," Drake replied directly. "On one hand our bodies bear the marks of our journey on Earth. On the other hand, our memories and experiences are what define who we are and how we act. But your unique condition explains a lot about why we couldn't find you, and why you have such a hard time with our large friend. But from what I've seen, you are absolutely the same man you've always been."

"What's that even mean," Nate asked. "Does he always talk like this?"

Tim just laughed and replied with a hearty, "Yeah. Speak plainly, Sullivan."

"What it means, gentlemen," an annoyed Drake continued, "is that you're still perfect for our needs, and once we help you find the cyborg assassin, I hope you'll continue to travel with us."

"Cyborg assassin?" Nate asked confused. "Man, what the hell are you into?"

"He's talking about Gino Lorenza," came Emma's voice. She and Sarah were back from their talk outside. "They're going after Gino. He's alive, and he's kidnapped someone important. They're going to need our help, Nate."

"Gino…" Nate just stared at the floor for a minute. "Gino's alive? You're sure it's him? I mean if you survived, I suppose he could have too. But damn it, why? Why him and not Sphinx or Hermes?"

"Yeah, I'm sure," Tim answered gravely. "And let's just say that unless we stop him now, we might never have a chance again. He'll be too powerful."

"You know I followed him once," Nate continued, as if he hadn't heard Tim. "I never trusted him. I know you didn't either. But we couldn't get the brass to listen. So, I thought if I followed him, maybe dug up some dirt, I could get him kicked off the team. I tracked him all the way to the docks here in San Francisco. He met with some Chinese guy. It was everything I needed. I recorded what I could, but you couldn't see them clearly enough, and I was ignored. I didn't have a chance to get it to you before we left for Cincinnati. And then…," his voice trailed off.

"It's not your fault, Nate," Tim comforted his friend. "I've played over that night in my head millions of times, which is easy to do now, and I still blame myself, even though I know there's nothing we could have done."

"Where was this place?" Sarah asked. "Which docks were they?"

"I think it's near the Shipyard," Nate replied. "There are a lot of empty buildings to hide in down there. I'd know it if I saw it again. It was a brick building with rounded window tops. We should send someone to scout it."

"That won't be necessary," Tim chimed in. "While you were talking, I was connecting to the local surveillance network. I found a building like the one you described. There are lights, and the heat signature is off the charts. I think that's our spot."

"All right then," Nate said, slapping his knees and standing up. "Let's go kill that bastard."

I have had dreams, and I have had nightmares,
but I have conquered my nightmares
because of my dreams.
- Jonas Salk

Chapter 33

The first inkling that something was wrong came when the music downstairs stopped and the screaming started. The discord of raised voices and broken glass raised an alarm among the troupe. Drake feared the worst; more Harmers. Nate and Tim assumed a more practical explanation; Samuels had found them, or worse, Leapstryke. At that moment, all were equally possible and equally terrible. They were not prepared for what was coming.

Nate pulled a pair of handguns from the side pocket of his bag, then shoved one into Sarah's hands. "Here, take this, and we'll be right behind you," he said resolutely.

"Hey, you have another one of those?" Emma asked, holding out her hand.

"No," Nate replied flatly.

Tim looked at Nate firmly. "You need to get them all out of here. If it's who we think, none of you will be able to handle what's coming."

Bathael, who until this point had been standing by the window petting Gaylord, suddenly yelled out, "Drake Sullivan, you are in danger!"

"Yes, I know!" Drake replied before turning to face Tim. "You have no idea what you're dealing with Colonel, and I'm far more capable than it may appear. I was slaying monsters before your ancestors started using forks to eat."

Nate looked at Tim with a smile and added, "If he's staying, I'm staying." He chambered a round in his own gun to accentuate his point. "Besides, the last time I left you alone, you forgot who you were for two years. That's not happening again."

Drake nodded at Bathael to gather Emma and Sarah, who were protesting loudly, to escape. In a flash of light, the trio were gone, back across the street where Merlin was still sleeping, unaware that his friends had even left. Drake reached into his sleeve and produced the long, shining blade he'd used back in Kansas while Nate looked on in shock.

"It's a long story," Drake commented, setting himself in a defensive posture facing the door.

Before anyone could comment further, the noise from downstairs quieted. Tim tried to scan the area, but something was interfering with his optics. All he could see was a large ambiguous void. There wasn't enough time for YVE to help him figure it out before the door came crashing in. Drake muttered something unintelligible and the sword in his hand hummed to life. The splintered remains of the door burned away to nothing as they approached.

As the embers cleared, Nate started firing at the massive figure in the door. He'd never seen anything so large. His shots ricocheted off the giant creature's frame, causing him to step back and reconnoiter. "What the hell is it?" he cried out, feeling a sudden dread like he'd never felt before.

The monster answered with a chilling chorus of voices, "We have come for the one called Thibodeaux. Surrender her and your deaths will be painless. Resist us and suffer." The creature took a step into the room, ducking to get through the door. The shape was more-or-less human, but the proportions were wrong. If there was a man inside this monstrosity, there was little left of him.

"It matches the description of the *Èmèng shouwèi*; a group of enforcers in the Chinese Empire," YVE offered while Tim reviewed his options.

"Weaknesses?" Tim asked silently.

"None known," YVE lamented. "Their brains appear organic, but their skulls have been reinforced. I would suggest the eye as a weak point. Can't you see that?"

Before Tim could answer, the robotic creature yelled, "Mercy period has ended! Suffering to commence immediately!" It then backhanded Tim with one of its massive mechanical arms. The blow might have crushed the skull of a normal person, but with Tim, it just knocked him off balance a bit. How was he supposed to fight this thing if he couldn't see it? He needed to know what he was facing.

"Why can't I see this thing?" Tim screamed in frustration, not caring who heard him or answered.

"Please let me drive for a moment, Colonel," YVE offered. Tim accepted, allowing YVE to control his reflex actions while he tried to adjust his sensory inputs. He tried everything; every type of spectrum just led to the same result. His enemy was just a large, vaguely humanoid black spot. The best he could do was to lessen the effect of the blackness by forcing it into the outline of the creature. At least that way he'd be able to see what was coming… kind of.

"This isn't what it appears," Drake shouted, using the sword to parry a blow that still staggered him. "I don't know how, but this is a supernatural creature called a *Mashl'khim*. If it hasn't already, the fear it exudes should be setting in on you soon. I see it's already affected Mr. Lange," Drake explained before adding an urgent, "Watch out!"

Tim didn't move quickly enough to dodge the smashing blow, followed by a massive kick. He could feel his artificial ribs break as he launched backward onto the table, smashing it into pieces. He couldn't fight like this. He didn't have the Zen mentality to fight blind.

"I'm not afraid," Tim spat out, wiping blood from the corner of his mouth. "I'm pissed off."

"Come now, Colonel," Drake retorted while taking a broad swing with the sword. The blow landed but glanced off the heavy armor on the shoulder of the beast. He looked at the sword as if it were defective. "Now is not the time for stoicism. The fear will overtake you if you don't acknowledge it."

The only thing Tim felt in that moment was helpless. "I thought you were driving," Tim yelled internally.

"I am not trained in hand-to-hand combat, Colonel," YVE replied tersely.

"How are you able to see them?" Tim asked her. "You're using the same eyes I am."

"Yes, but I don't use them the same way," YVE replied. "Let me see if I can replace your missing sensory data with mine."

"Hurry!" Tim said aloud, confusing Drake, who nearly missed a parry because of it. As YVE worked, he started to see a wireframe of the massive opponent. He was able to dodge the next punch, but the creature followed through, spun its torso around completely, and connected on the second attempt. The power of the blow sent Tim flying past Nate and through the brick wall. He slumped against the steel rail of the fire escape, catching his breath. It wasn't that it hurt, but physics were working against him fighting this monster. All he could think about was fighting the M75 when he was still learning how to use his Cytotechnic body.

"Data integration complete. You should be able to see the cyborg now," YVE offered.

Tim looked up, but all he saw was the basic wireframe he saw before. It was better than nothing, but it wasn't helpful. "I still can't see shit," an annoyed Tim replied. He dodged the next blow and retaliated with a massive kick to the attacker's midsection. The creature staggered back, and Drake used the chance to bring the sword down on its shoulder. The monster shrieked as its left arm dangled uselessly from a few wires and tubes after Drake's sword destroyed the joint. All that remained were the dark, wispy tendrils that marked Harmer possession. There had been a human inside this machine after all.

The cyborg howled and ripped off the dead arm, swinging it wildly and with such power that Drake was unable to block or parry. The hit sent him flying to the side where he landed unconscious on the couch next to where Nate was hiding, cowering in fear. The cyborg turned its attention back to Tim who was still recovering on the railing. It began to pummel Tim mercilessly with the arm remnant. The creature was able to still control the hand, because of the shadowy connection, and it grabbed Tim by the throat while the other hand pounded into him relentlessly.

Tim was helpless, he tried to defend himself from the blows, but the damage was too much for his system to keep up with. YVE warned him that he was getting close to blacking out, and that he needed to do something soon or they would both die. Tim wasn't ready for that and called out, as loudly as he could while being choked, "Argus…the eye. Shoot the eye. Nate…please…I need you."

But Nate couldn't move. He was overcome with devastating fear and his instinct told him to be as still as possible and maybe, just maybe, the monster would ignore him. Just as the darkness started to close in on Tim, he heard a gunshot, and then a second, then the attack suddenly ended. He turned and looked, and even with his vision blurred and bloody, he could see Sarah standing in the window across the street, holding the handgun Nate had given her earlier. The shots were perfect. Just as Tim was starting to relax a bit, he heard a disquieting noise from behind him. Turning around, he saw the massive figure getting back up. What was it going to take to kill this thing?

Just then Drake, who had recovered from being thrown across the room, stepped behind the cyborg and raised his sword. "Allow me, Colonel."

With that, Drake took the sword and thrust it firmly into the hole created by Sarah's shots. The monstrous cyborg let out a final terrifying wail before erupting in a cloud of shadowy mist which was quickly absorbed into the sword. Using his foot, Drake pushed the creature away, causing the sword to shine with its own light. Once the Harmer was gone, Tim was able to see his assailant for what it was. There, lying in front of him was the remains of one of Ying Qi's Nightmare Guard. Why was it there?

Drake slid the sword back up his sleeve and reached over to Tim to offer him a hand up. Tim waved the offer away and staggered through the hole in the wall, stepping over the cyborg corpse. Without the Harmer's influence, Nate was able to compose himself and come out from behind the arm of the couch. He was suddenly aware that he was unable to help in the fight, and he rushed over to Tim to help him. Tim again refused any help as he made his way over to the kitchen sink to get a drink of water, maybe something stiffer.

"What the hell was that?" Tim strained to ask as his larynx worked to repair itself. "And don't give me any bullshit about Chinese secret robot death squads. I can see what's on the floor. But I couldn't see it when it was kicking my ass."

Tim drank the water quickly and moved to the refrigerator, which was mercifully intact. He opened it, looking for something stronger than water. All he could find was apple juice. He took it, opened the lid, and guzzled it. Once it was empty, he turned to Nate angrily, "And you! Where the hell was my backup? Or have you been behind a desk so long that you don't remember how to cover your teammates?"

Nate was clearly distraught, but before he could answer, Drake motioned for him to sit and rest. "Colonel, I know you've had a lot to absorb in the past few days, but I implore you to set your bias aside and just listen for a moment. Can you do that, please?"

Tim looked at Drake skeptically, then sat on the only undamaged kitchen chair. He then looked up at Drake expectantly. "All right. Tell me the secrets of the universe, Sullivan."

"Now I know how Capt. Heighton was able to deal with me so easily," Drake commented dryly. "You've been quite a puzzle for me. I've not met anyone quite like you before, which I can assure you is saying something. There have always been those unaffected by the planar energies—what you might call magic. I call them Concealed, because they were invisible to powers not of this earth. But I've never understood how they came to be until now. That creature had no effect on you," Drake added pointing to the hulking mass of machine parts.

"Tell that to my broken ribs and crushed larynx," Tim spat out. "I can heal really fast, but I *felt* all of that." Tim didn't think they needed to know he chose to feel it.

"Of course, you did," Drake reasoned, "it was hitting you with giant metal arms."

"You don't say," Tim replied sarcastically. "Get to the point before *I* start hitting *you* with those giant metal arms."

"You weren't afraid," Drake said matter-of-factly. "Humans aren't afraid of the dark because of predators, we fear the dark because of *them*," he explained, motioning at the dead cyborg. "They exude fear the way you exude pheromones. It surrounds them like an aura that they can direct at their will. Even Bathael and I are affected by it, though to a lesser degree. But not you. It also explains why you can't see Bathael very well, and why you didn't stop me from stabbing you in the chest with my sword."

"You didn't...," Tim said as he looked down. There, he could see a tarnished old sword sticking out from his chest. He hadn't felt anything, and he didn't see Drake produce the weapon. He knew there was something there, but he struggled to define it. YVE was panicking, but Tim was completely calm. He'd never felt so calm.

Drake pulled the sword out and slid it back into his sleeve before continuing. "This is a weapon forged in another Plane. It belonged to the Archangel Michael. It can't hurt you, Bathael can't hurt you, and the Harmer that possessed that cybernetic beast couldn't hurt you, at least not in the way it wanted. I expect it didn't know what to make of you. But your friend, Mr. Lange, well, he was the main course. Once you were dead, the Harmer would have feasted on him. That's why he couldn't move. He was too afraid, and there's nothing he could have done."

The room flashed bright white as Bathael, Emma, and Sarah reappeared in the apartment. Emma tried to appraise all the damage, but Drake insisted that the group gather what they needed and leave at once. "The Harmers rarely travel alone. There's likely another one nearby or on the way. We should leave."

Tim digested the information he'd been given while he continued to heal himself. Sarah was prepared to bandage him, but when she saw him healing, she instead watched in awe.

"Well, that's a neat trick," she said as she reached out and touched the area around his left eye, which had previously been completely smashed in. "Can you teach me how to do that?"

"It's really not worth the price of admission," Tim joked, "and the contract they make you sign is a bitch to get out of."

"I need to check on Ted and Robin," Emma said as she bolted for the door.

"No one goes anywhere alone," Drake ordered, motioning for Sarah to follow her. "Stay together and come back here if the hairs on your neck stand up."

As Emma headed out what remained of the door, Nate called out, "I guess visions of kittens aren't all that great either." Emma chuckled a bit as she and Sarah headed toward the stairs.

Across the room, Gaylord sat on the ruins of the window Tim had smashed through. He didn't groom himself; he didn't meow this time. He just watched the events happen. He'd watched everything unfold from the fire escape. If Drake had been paying attention, he'd have noticed the difference in the cat's behavior, but he was preoccupied. Instead, Gaylord just frowned in a way only a cat could, then shook his head and ran off into the night.

Ambition is the last refuge of the failure.
- Oscar Wilde

Chapter 34

Ying Qi severed his connection to the cat quickly, cursing aloud at the failure of his Nightmare Guard. There was still another tracking the group, but the element of surprise was wasted on this attempt. He ordered his other servant to fall back and observe for now, and to report regularly. He ruminated on what he'd seen. He knew who Drake Sullivan was, of course. Even in China his reputation was well-established. And he knew who Nate Lange and Sarah Heighton were because his military intelligence was impeccable. He was more troubled by what he *didn't* see. Or rather *who*. There were three people present that he couldn't see clearly.

Ying Qi started to learn about the Concealed after his experiences with Gino. He couldn't connect to Gino's mind, and he initially wondered if it was because of his conversion into a cyborg. He later discovered that wasn't the case. Gino was different; he had died. That was the secret, and Drake confirmed it in front of the cat. Somehow, people who had survived death were impervious to his mental abilities. That didn't explain everything, though.

He had not known Tim was still alive before that day. Gino had never spoken of him, though he did know that Gino wasn't the only cybernetic soldier created by the Americans. Since Gino's return, he'd not been able to get the answers he needed from the American, so he assumed that Tim was dead along with Claire Thibodeaux. He hated being wrong, but he saw this as fortuitous. The fight in the apartment turned out to be the perfect test. He learned from that encounter, so he would be better prepared to deal with both Tim Andrews and eventually Gino.

The Nightmares were aptly named. One of the earliest rituals he mastered was one that called forth *Mashl'khim* to serve him. He offered up his personal guard, seeing the advantage of having them supernaturally frightening. That's why they were called the Nightmare Guard. Even *he* felt a bit of disquiet in their presence, and Li Fong did his best to avoid them. When he transformed them into cyborgs, they only became more powerful. But there were always people who weren't afraid. The ones who escaped and told the stories that informed his enemies.

The second missing figure had to be Claire's daughter. Did she have a daughter? Yes, of course she did, but he couldn't remember her name. So instead, he focused on the other figure. He found that one more concerning. He hated surprises more than he hated being wrong, and this was a surprise. And while this being hadn't taken part in the combat, that didn't mean they weren't dangerous. Based on how the others reacted, he assumed the creature was extra-planar. He knew who to ask. He was already walking to the Summoning Room without even realizing.

Ying Qi opened the door, walked in, then closed it behind him, something he did not usually do. The room was dimly lit with candles, candles that no longer needed replenished, and no longer went out. Sitting on the altar was the decaying form of the boy-turned-prison, though he wasn't *on* the altar, he was about six inches above it. He was picking the wings off a bee that had come through one of the tiny windows that ran all along the upper part of the wall. Ying Qi frowned at the affront, but he ignored it for now.

"Shakra'el, I have need of you," Ying Qi demanded. "I need to know the nature of a creature who was aiding the Thibodeaux girl."

The boy didn't answer, but instead looked over to Ying Qi expectantly, waiting for the images to be given over in his mind. Ying Qi suddenly felt no reservation connecting to the mind of his imprisoned guest as he once had. Once the boy was able to see everything, he broke out in maniacal laughter that chilled the emperor to the bone. The furious emperor cut off their connection and stormed over to the altar and grabbed what was left of the boy's ragged shirt.

"What is funny about what you've seen, Deceiver?" He yelled furiously. Any attempts to subdue his rage were now met with abject failure. The monks no longer went anywhere near the garden for fear of the emperor's wrath.

"What's funny," the cacophonous voices said in unison, "is that you don't even know what's funny." With that, the creature started laughing again, this time louder and more intentionally.

Ying Qi threw the boy off the altar, but he landed on his feet. He was more comfortable in his prison-body now and wasn't quite so easily abused while in it. "You don't understand anything, and yet you think you are all knowing and all powerful. That creature spells your doom and you're too stupid to know it."

"Then enlighten me, you cretin! Explain how I am so stupid and unfortunate!" There was no hiding the anger and hate coming from the emperor now. His mind was unrested, and he was on the edge of losing control. His captive just smirked.

"Your mind is so small, *Wànsuìyé*," the echoing voices mocked, "you can't see the obvious. You missed your chance at destiny. The woman you must kill is protected by a member of the Aetherium. Its most powerful member, in fact. You now face the very Voice of the Creator." The boy's unearthly cackling could likely be heard all the way in the village. Not that many were left to hear it anymore.

Ying Qi's mind erupted with more anger and vitriol. He expected that summoning a powerful being from the Nether would challenge him and his powers. He hadn't expected his influence over the beast to be so limited. He'd gone over the rituals and incantations in his mind over and over, hoping he might find some explanation for his lack of control. He assumed it was related to his inability to meditate effectively since its arrival. He was impatient for his brother to return. He needed support even if he couldn't ask for it aloud.

Ying Qi sat in front of the altar and started to turn his mind's eye inward. He read every religious text ever written, and he had no idea what the Aetherium was, though he did correctly surmise that the creature was from another plane. The light it gave off was blinding to him, even through the eyes of the cat, and he felt oddly calm in their presence. He longed for that feeling again, as the tranquility of meditation continued to elude him. What did his captive mean, 'the Voice of the Creator?'

The emperor scrolled through the texts stored in his mind, but he found concentrating on them difficult. He could feel Shakra'el's hateful eyes staring into his very soul, but he focused on the task. Assuming the Voice of the Creator was a powerful angelic creature, then it would need to be attacked with something from the Nether; something *truly* of the Nether. And his bound servant would be of no help because he had fallen from the Aether. He needed a weapon, or better yet, an army.

Opening his eyes, he looked over to the boy who was indeed staring at him intently. Ying Qi's ego wouldn't allow him to be disconcerted, but he was struggling to hold the feeling off. He focused on the calmness he felt while he was watching the angel, and he pushed back against the darkness that threatened to consume his mind. He needed his brother. Where was Li Fong?

"He's abandoned you," Shakra'el taunted, whispering in Ying Qi's ear. "You know it to be true. Even now, he plots with your enemies against you. He would steal your destiny as his own."

"That's…not…TRUE!" Ying Qi screamed, veins popping out of his neck and head. "My brother would sooner die than betray me! You are a liar and deceiver, and you sow malcontent. I know your mind, Shakra'el!" Ying Qi screamed as he invoked the creature's name in an effort to subdue it. It didn't work.

"Of course, you don't believe me. Why would you? I am the Prince of Lies, the Lord of Deception, the Great Satan; only a fool would take me at my word. And you're no fool, are you, *Wànsuìyé?*" the dissonant voices whispered in his ear. "Allow me to show you the truth of the world."

Ying Qi was fighting with his whole being. Shakra'el's words were clawing at the corners of his mind, and it was difficult keeping the monster at bay. It felt like he was trying to bail out a leaking boat with a teaspoon. It was a battle he knew he would eventually lose. His thoughts invariably strayed to his brother, and that was the crack in his armor the nefarious Shakra'el needed.

The emperor's mind flooded with images of Li Fong on his trip to ensure Gino's success. The way he had when Claire was killed. And he was going to kill Gino when it was over. He saw Li Fong's journey to America, his covert activities in the enemy country, and him following Gino on his journey. But things weren't going as planned. Li Fong was watching Gino, but Gino was off mission. He had kidnapped someone. Someone who wasn't Emma Thibodeaux. And Li Fong allowed it.

None of this was right. They were in the same city he'd seen through the cat's eyes. He could see Li Fong tracking his Guards as they looked for Gino and Emma. He didn't interact with them, in fact, he avoided them. He didn't want to be seen because he knew they would alert Ying Qi. He was there, watching the attack on the other altered human and the old man. He watched it all and did nothing. He was talking to someone too; someone he shouldn't be. He was talking to Stephen Samuels.

Ying Qi's whole world turned red with seething hatred. How could his brother do this? What secrets was he sharing with this

American? How long had they been colluding against him? In that moment, Ying Qi's whole world dissolved into nothing but hate. He no longer had the strength or the will to fight what was coming. It was time for him to become the power he sought.

The emperor opened his eyes and stood slowly. He walked purposefully toward the doors. When he opened them and looked out on the garden, he saw it was filled with people; his Guards and the remaining monks, all but Jangchup, facing him. As he walked through them, they all kept their eyes on him, eyes darker than the deepest night.

He strode through the gateway and into the main courtyard, where there were even more people, hundreds gathered for him, all carrying the mark of the *Mashl'khim*. They were the emperor's army, the army he needed. As he walked toward the entrance gate of the monastery, the throng followed behind him. All that remained was the decaying body of a little boy left lifeless in a circular room in the garden.

Chapter 35

Emma felt much better once she knew her friends downstairs were all right. She told them that she had more than enough money to cover any damages, but they just said, "Honey, this is why insurance is a thing. Don't worry about it. We're just glad you're ok." They agreed to hold onto her things and promised to let her know when the apartment was fixed up. After a round of hugs, even for Sarah, they went back upstairs to gather the last of their things.

When they walked through the doorway, Tim was still sitting in the only intact kitchen chair holding a half-empty gallon milk jug. Emma wasn't sure how old it was, but she was certain it was spoiled. She tried to tell him, and he replied that he knew, but he needed the water and the calories, and it couldn't make him sick. "Besides," he said with a chuckle, "I've had worse.". He mentioned that the others were back across the street waiting, and that he needed about ten more minutes to heal, so he offered to wait for them.

Nate gathered the last of his things from the main room and grabbed Emma's bag from her bedroom and some toiletries from the bathroom. Emma gathered some non-perishables from the cabinets and the last two packs of *Papaw Peanut's* jerky from the counter. She wasn't sure what they'd need, so she just grabbed whatever made sense. She fully expected there to be more letters, no matter where she ended up, but until then, she'd just wing it. It had worked for her so far.

"So, uh, Sunshine," Tim said, finally able to speak without sounding like he'd swallowed a box of nails, "how did you get in touch with Nate? I mean, what made you go looking for him in the first place? I'd have thought you'd do your best not to cross paths with any of us."

Emma stopped what she was doing and looked down at the floor, then over to Tim in the chair. "You know what, Colonel," she began, "you're right. After everything we went through, after losing Mom, I would have been fine never seeing or talking to any of you ever again. But that was seven years ago, and I grew up a lot being on my own. It wasn't easy moving on, but Ted and Robin helped. I surrounded myself with good people, like Mom did."

Emma sighed and continued, "But I got a letter; the first letter she sent me. It sent me directly to Commander Lange. I was halfway through college, and he was just waiting to retire. The letter I received held a separate letter for him, the one that set all of this in motion, I suppose. I think you've seen that one." Tim nodded as she carried on, "Anyway, he got into a lot of trouble after that, and I didn't see him for a few months. Not until graduation. I was slipped a note at the commencement to meet him back in Ohio, and that it was urgent."

Emma took the bag of groceries and set it down next to the entryway, brushing aside debris from the shattered door. She walked over to where Tim was sitting and leaned back on the counter. "The note gave an address for a diner out in the middle of nowhere. When I got there, there was just the waitress, the cook, and some old guy sitting at the counter drinking coffee. Everything seemed so normal, but weirdly off. I felt like everyone was looking at me, and when I'd try to catch them, they'd look away just in time."

"I sat in a booth there for nearly an hour," she continued, "but Commander Lange never showed up. Instead, a package courier from the city rode up on a crotch rocket, threw an envelope at me and left before I could tip him. It was from mom, and when I opened it, it just said, 'Leave now and don't look back!' and I did. I ran to my car. The waitress and the old man chased after me. She'd put something in my last cup of coffee. As soon as I got in the car and locked the doors, I passed out. Lucky for me Nate was just really late and arrived in time to scare them off. I don't know what they were, but they weren't human. Their eyes were black as coal, and they smelled horrible. Anyway, after that, I knew that the letters would be an important part of my life. Even if I hate them."

"How many have you gotten?" Tim asked quietly.

"Forty-two," she answered directly, "counting the one today. And I know she's sent them to other people as well. She knew what would happen and where we'd all be. Even you, I expect. She's probably the only person who knew you survived that building collapsing…," Emma's voice trailed off.

"I did everything I could," a solemn Tim interjected. "I hope you know that. I was right there, but that bastard…he was already in the room. She'd let him in even though she knew…"

Emma reached over and put a hand on Tim's shoulder. "Mom saw everything, not just this stuff. She saw all the possibilities. I don't know how she kept track of it all in her head. But she knew which path was the best; she always knew. I guess that's why I resented her for so long. I felt like she chose to die instead of staying with me. It took me a long time to realize that it wasn't about me. Sounds like you still haven't."

"What's the supposed to mean?" Tim asked indignantly.

Emma knelt down in front of him and put her hands on his. "It means, Colonel, that it was never about what we wanted." She reached over and picked the most recent letter up off the floor. "She wrote this when she was five. *Five*. She always knew what could happen, and she knew which paths led where. I wasn't about what we wanted, or even what she wanted. It was about what was needed. She needed us to live and be safe."

Nate finished packing and came over to where Tim was still sitting. "Listen man, I can't even imagine what you've been through over the past seven years. I only got a glimpse of it back when I found you the first time. And now you have a whole existential crisis going on. But you aren't alone in it anymore," Nate said sincerely, adding, "and you don't have to fight that bastard alone either."

"How are we supposed to fight this supernatural bullshit, though?" Tim asked in frustration. "I still don't even know what the hell I was fighting. I might as well have been fighting my own shadow."

"Maybe when we find Matthew, he can fix that," Nate offered.

"You heard the old man. I'm not even me anymore," Tim lamented. "How am I supposed to…what I mean is what if Lorenza is like that thing over there?"

"What did you used to tell us?" Nate asked Tim sincerely. "You always said you can't plan for hypotheticals; you should only plan around what you know and understand that things can always change. That's why we train."

"That's why we train," Tim echoed half-heartedly. "You're right. I just…I haven't felt so helpless since that night in Cincinnati. I fought a god damn tank and won. But that thing…I was like a rag doll."

"But now you have that experience, and you can plan," Emma said. "Isn't that the point?"

"I think the LT rubbed off on her," Nate joked.

"Don't let Athena hear you say that. She's a Captain now, and don't you forget it," Tim replied with a weak smile.

"So, what's the plan," Emma asked, "the others are waiting for us. Are we going to join them?"

"I don't think we have a choice," Tim said directly. "Claire seemed pretty intent on bringing us all together. I expect if we tried to separate again, she'd just have another letter waiting for us."

"Hopefully, they'll help us with Gino," Nate chimed in.

"Honestly, I've been thinking about that while I've been sitting here, and I think we're all heading to the same place. I just need to ask the old man some questions, and I think it will confirm my conclusions. Besides, I already told them I won't join their crusade until Gino's been dealt with. The angel-person-thing will just have to deal with that."

"Are you able to be moved?" Nate asked, knowing how badly Tim had been injured just a short time earlier.

"One hundred percent," Tim said spryly, standing up and showing that he didn't have so much as a bruise left from the onslaught. I've had harder fights, but not many. When I escaped the cabin, I was on fire. That only took about ten minutes to heal."

"Good," Emma cut in, "you can carry the bags, then."

The trio gathered up their things, and Tim did indeed carry the lion's share. They took the fire escape down into the alley, crossed a less-traveled side-street, and then walked the long way around and entered the other building from the side. Since it was empty, there weren't any peering eyes to avoid. Tim had already hacked the cameras in the area, so they couldn't be tracked by any more augmented enemies.

Once they were on the third floor, they saw the others huddled around a small table. Merlin was on the floor at Drake's feet, sleeping as usual. When Drake noticed them coming in, he rose to greet them all.

"Ah, here they are," he said, smiling. "I trust you're in good health, Colonel? Everything in working order and all that?"

"Yeah, I'm fine," Tim said flatly. "I heal quick."

"Ah yes, of course," Drake said clearing his throat uncomfortably. "Have you made a decision about how we are to proceed?"

"I have," Tim replied before correcting himself. "*We* have. But before we do anything, we need to get some things out in the open. I need to know what you're looking for, and who you really are. I know there are things you're not telling us, Athena included, and if we're going to work together, we will do it as a unit. We didn't keep things from each other in SPARTAN, and we won't start now."

"I suppose that's fair enough," Drake said, offering Tim a seat at the table, shooing Bathael away. "I'll tell you everything, but we'll start with our goal, because time is short. We need to find a book, one that will have a great many answers. It was written by our mutual friend, Claire."

Emma and Nate looked at each other and Tim looked at them before they all looked back to Drake. Emma spoke up first, "What are you even talking about. I don't know anything about a book. I never once saw Mom write anything."

Drake frowned. "That's a shame. I was hoping you had it, and we wouldn't need to use more…unusual methods to find it. I'm concerned that using those will draw more attention to us than we already have. We're obviously of interest to someone with great power."

"I have some ideas on that," Tim offered. "and I may know where the book is. Claire was always right. All these letters always lead us right to where we needed to be. She needed us to be safe, so none of the letters put us in real danger."

"How can you say that?" Sarah interrupted. "You could have died up there."

"Right, but I didn't," Tim continued. "And Claire would have known that. Ask Emma or Drake. She was never, ever wrong. And she hasn't led any of us anywhere she knew would kill us. Sure, it's been dangerous, but not deadly. We're all here, and all unscathed."

"That's not how it works," Drake tried to intercede.

"The hell it doesn't," Tim cut him off. "You know as well as I do, she was way beyond what any of us could understand. Even you. I'm not saying there won't be real risks, or that she saw absolutely everything. What I am saying is that I have faith in her not to get me killed a second time after she put so much effort into saving me."

No one said anything for a long time after that. It made good sense, after all, even for Drake. He had always placed his own knowledge ahead of what Clair's visions showed her. More than once, she'd proven that she had a greater grasp on the world than he did, and he never truly accepted it. It drove a wedge between them that he regretted not repairing before she died.

"Let's say you're right," Drake finally said, breaking the silence. "What does that have to do with the book."

"I know where it is," Tim said plainly. "And Claire knew it would take all of us to get it. This is where she's been leading us."

Bathael stepped forward and placed a hand on Tim's shoulder, though Tim couldn't really feel it. "Timothy Andrews speaks with wisdom. The Oracle had a greater grasp on the ebb and flow of time than even Enoch did. This one has seen what you have not, Drake Sullivan, and you would do well to listen."

"Yes, yes," Drake said impatiently, "The good Colonel here is a smart man, and clearly, he's thought this through. Sarah trusts him and I trust her. So where is the book?" he asked Tim directly.

"In the possession of a psychopathic assassin named Gino Lorenza. He was a member of my unit code named Leapstryke. Nate, you weren't the only one who didn't trust Gino," Tim explained, "and I had done some looking into his past. I was able to connect him to a series of political assassinations all around the globe. I assumed the CIA and our higher ups already knew about it, but I planned to raise my concerns before everything went to hell."

"There was a report," Tim continued, "from a routine inspection of the living quarters. I discovered he had trophies from all his kills on display. It was like his whole room was a sick temple to his own depravity. Since Emma never saw her writing, it's a safe assumption she kept the book with her and wrote when she was alone. He must have taken it. It's the only thing that makes sense. He would have needed it to remind him of the kill."

"But how did he keep hold of it?" Sarah asked. "You were both missing, and there's no way a book would have survived."

"I don't have that answer, but I'm positive he has it," Tim continued. "He's incredibly resourceful. He was brought back before I was, and I know that everything of value from that site was taken by the same people who brought us back. It's not a far stretch that he knew where it was and stole it from them. I don't think he knows what he has."

"Then let's pray he never does," Drake interjected. "I suppose you have a plan, then?"

"I always have a plan," Tim said with a smile.

"They just rarely survive contact with the enemy," Nate and Sarah both said in unison before collapsing into laughter.

Drake didn't get it.

One moment of patience may ward off great disaster.
One moment of impatience may ruin a whole life.
- Chinese Proverb

Chapter 36

It had seven days since Matthew started work on the Cytotechnic body to make it so Gino could use it. Without the use of his legs, he had to take time to learn how to maneuver the wheelchair to get around the makeshift lab. Gino made sure he had everything he needed to get it done on time, and he made sure Matthew wasn't stalling or delaying. Gino didn't know the process, though, and that gave Matthew enough time and freedom to pursue his own goal, destroying Leapstryke forever.

The work had been nothing less than tedious. Gino was helpful, to a degree, but Matthew was forced to do much of the work himself, which was fine with him. It was easier to work when he didn't have to constantly instruct his help. It also made him more comfortable making the alterations he needed. Even if he'd seen them, Gino likely wouldn't understand the differences or why they were important.

Matthew didn't sleep much, mostly because of the pain. He was certain an infection had set in from the wound Gino inflicted to cripple him. While there was no feeling in his legs, he was often left in his own filth, which was why he didn't eat much. Matthew knew he wouldn't survive, but he was going to make sure Gino didn't either. But everything had to be perfect.

Getting Gino's DNA had been the difficult part. The vials Gino provided were too degraded and new samples had to be taken. All that remained of the human he'd been was one eye, and his brain and spinal column. Since his spine had been artificially reinforced, and there wasn't an easy way to get to his brain, Matthew had to get what he needed from Gino's vitreous humor. Matthew warned that the process would be incredibly painful, but Gino refused any anesthetic. He laughed throughout the process and commented later that 'dying by having a bitch explode a building all over him' was worse.

The core of the Cytotechnic system is that it used DNA as a blueprint to create synthetic cells which could replicate the processes of normal living cells. It worked essentially the same way cloning did, but without the ethical quandary of using living creatures for spare parts. With prosthetics, it was imperative that the DNA match the host, or there would be issues with rejection.

But for a whole-body replacement, that wasn't specifically necessary. That much Gino was able to glean from the files he hacked into. That's why he planned on using the prepared body Matthew made for Yvette. Matthew convinced Gino that the body would still need to be updated with his own DNA so that it would align with his brain scan. Otherwise, he explained, Gino would never be able to fully control the body. It was a lie, but one Gino believed.

Gino spent most of the last week away from the warehouse. Matthew didn't really want to know what he was doing, but he often came back with food and sometimes covered in blood. He enjoyed the break from Gino's incessant talking, though. And he was numb to the fact that his respite cost someone else their life. With an infection eating away at his body, and a psychopathic assassin watching his every move, Matthew was understandably short on empathy.

"Today's the day, Wheels!" Gino yelled out loudly as he entered the warehouse from one of his nightly excursions.

"Joy of joys," Matthew said quietly as he prepared the transfer process. He said it loud enough for his captor to hear him, but Gino let it slide, mostly because he still needed Matthew. Under other circumstances, the repartee between the two men would have been comical. As it was though, the retorts were Matthew's feeble attempt at goading Gino into killing him. It never succeeded. For a serial murderer, Gino had an amazing amount of self-control.

"That's not going to work today, Wheels," Gino replied, as if reading Matthew's mind. "When will you be ready? I want to look my best when Whiteboard gets here."

Matthew didn't have any hope left. Gino had been teasing that someone might come to save him, but Matthew didn't believe him. So, he just looked toward the windows. Based on the shadows, it appeared to be early afternoon. He needed more time, but he wasn't going to get it. He'd make do like always. "We'll start at sunset, and you should be awake by midnight."

"Wait," Gino said, suddenly concerned. "You're putting me to sleep? You never said anything about putting me under. You can't put me to sleep!" Gino grabbed the arm rest of the wheelchair and spun Matthew to look at him. Then, sniffing the air he added, "Jesus, you stink. But seriously, I *have* to stay awake."

"I get it, you don't like being unconscious," Matthew sighed in response, "but I'm hardly in any condition to run away at this point. I can barely move enough to do the work I need to."

"Cute, Wheels," Gino replied sharply, "but you aren't who I'm worried about."

"That may be, but I can't do it while you're awake," Matthew reiterated. "You can't exist in two places at once. We tried it and the results were catastrophic. It's apparently a fundamental law of the universe. So, you can go to sleep, or you can stay in the body you have." Matthew wasn't lying this time, but Gino had no way to know for sure. He didn't have Tim's increased intellectual potential but would change soon enough.

"All right, Wheels," Gino said, spinning Matthew around two or three times before stopping him fast. Matthew couldn't get sick because he hadn't eaten in days. "We'll do it your way. And when we're done, we have to do something about that smell," he joked, making a disgusted face.

Matthew ignored the comment, and the associated raucous laughter as he continued his work. Gino would get what was coming to him. Matthew was thankful that Gino was so ignorant about the science behind Cytotechnics. One of the key advantages was the programmability of the cells. They could be a person, but they could also be anything. He could rearrange them on a molecular level and even cut whole groups off from the brain of the driver to act independently.

Early in the testing of Cytotechnics, Matthew wanted to know what the limits of the artificial cells were. Playing around with a cluster on a microscopic level, he accidentally created a powerful explosive. He made sure to document the process, so he didn't inadvertently do it again. Now he was doing it on purpose. He would destroy the body he made for his beloved as a final act of justice and revenge in an explosion that would destroy the entire warehouse. And the beauty of it was that Gino would never know. Once the transfer was complete, the bomb would go off after 10 minutes. Then it would be all over.

Matthew went silently about his work. He struggled these days to stay awake. He was weaker now than ever before, and he had to fight to stay conscious. He had pain in his chest and stomach, and he was nose deaf to the smell of his decaying lower body. He was afraid to look under the blanket now. Death was waiting for him either way. At least this way, it would be on his terms and not Gino's. Hours passed and the sun set. Gino paced impatiently behind Matthew as he typed in the last of the commands.

"All right, put on the leads, and plug this into your connection port," Matthew directed, holding up a fiberoptic cable. Gino hesitated, sighed and plugged in. Once he was connected to everything, he climbed onto the table and closed his eyes.

"You do it fast, Wheels, and I'll do you fast too," Gino promised.

Matthew ignored him and just set up the final processes, sending Gino's control module a command to put him to sleep.

Once the transfer started, he just sat back in his chair and waited. It was going to be a long night.

*We must let go of the life we have planned,
so as to accept the one that is waiting for us.*
- Joseph Campbell

Chapter 37

"Are you sure this is the place?" Nate asked tentatively.

"Are you being serious right now," Tim replied in annoyance. "It's the only building with power in this part of the pier. Besides, I checked it against the County Auditor and the owner of record is 'Vincenzo Lorenza.' What are the odds it's *not* him?"

"OK, OK, I get it," Nate acquiesced, "I'm not connected to the collected knowledge of the entire human race, and you are. Can you see anything?"

"No. It's like there's some sort of covering on all the walls. Everything looks the same temperature," Tim said in disappointment, "but I do occasionally see moving shadows along the edges. Someone's definitely in there."

"Wait, don't you have like X-ray vision or something?" Nate asked with a smile.

"No…maybe…," Tim retorted sharply. "Actually, yes. But those coverings are blocking that too. What you think I'm a Plebe or something?"

The men shared a laugh and continued their surveillance. Emma and Sarah were off to the side, going over everything Sarah had learned at Drake's. Kansas felt like an eternity ago, and each woman had a story to share. They heard Tim and Nate laughing and Emma asked, "Where they always like this?"

Sarah looked over at them, chuckling a little. "Mostly. We're all a bit more…serious now, I guess? We've all been through a lot, and it's made us all a little harder. The Colonel most of all. I suppose that dying changes you."

"How could it not?" Emma added with a slight frown. "I'm glad you're all safe, though. I thought about reaching out, you know. I even found out what unit you were in. I just…I was so shitty the last time I saw you. I was afraid you wouldn't want to hear from me."

Sarah pulled Emma in for a tight hug, saying, "Don't worry about that, it's all in the past. You were young, and you'd just lost your mom. Goodness knows we all could have handled it better. What's important is that we're all together now. At least I know *you* wouldn't have stabbed me," she added with a laugh.

"I still can't believe he did that," Emma exclaimed. "With that ridiculous sword and everything?"

"Yep," Sarah continued. "Didn't even warn me. Made Bathael hold me in place. Who does that?"

Emma laughed out loud, adding, "Oh, I'm sure mom could have told some stories. She never really talked about him, though, and I never met him before now. She said she could see the future but never knew what he was doing."

"He is a man of his own will, for sure," Sarah added laughing along. They both looked at Drake and burst into another fit of laughter, causing him to jolt awake from his impromptu nap and nearly fall out of his chair. Merlin picked his head up at the ruckus, snorted his disproval, and laid his head back down.

Bathael reached over and helped steady Drake, then walked over to the women. "I am pleased to see that you are in good spirits, Sarah Heighton. Positive emotions are the best ward against the *Mashl'khim*. They feed on your fear and despair."

Emma just stared at the angel slack jawed as Sarah replied, "You sure know how to kill a mood, don't you?"

"Have I done something wrong, Sarah Heighton?" Bathael asked sincerely. "I am no longer familiar with human ways."

The women laughed again before Sarah answered, "Not at all, friend, but I think Emma had some questions for you."

Emma stifled her own laughter and chimed in, "That's right, I do. You seem very powerful. Just being near you makes me feel…better. Like everything will be all right. Is that because you're an angel?"

Bathael smiled, answering, "It is…complicated, Emma Thibodeaux. I am different than my cohorts in the Aetherium; different from the other *Be'elohim*, the beings you call angels. Because I was once human, my compassion is somewhat greater than theirs and that is what you feel. They, likewise, have powers I do not. They have powerful relics, forged in the Aether, which allow them to perform great feats. Drake Sullivan carries one, and he can only call a fraction of a fraction of its true power."

"Are you talking about the sword?" Sarah asked.

"I am, in fact," Bathael replied directly. "I believe he claimed it to keep it out safe from more…nefarious owners. It was carried by Michael but was trapped here when the Planes were shattered. I believe Drake Sullivan named it Excalibur, though I know not why."

"Well, that explains a lot," Sarah offered.

"No, it doesn't!" she exclaimed, furrowing her brow. "If you have powers, why didn't you use them? Colonel Andrews was almost killed!"

"As I said, Emma Thibodeaux," Bathael said with a slight smile, "it is much more complicated than that. I did not take part in the battle because I was not needed. Timothy Andrews' insight into the Oracle's methods is correct. Everything happened the way it was supposed to happen. He was in no real danger."

Emma opened her mouth to continue, but Bathael held up a hand to stop her. "Rest easy, Child of the Oracle. I have also seen the coming events, though from a greater distance. I would have stepped in to aid the Colonel had it been needed, though I would not have been much help. The *Mashl'khim* are creatures of the Nether. Should I directly engage one, we would both be annihilated…to devastating effect. Besides, I know that you will protect Timothy Andrews."

"I'm not sure I understand, but I accept what you're saying as true," Emma said quietly. "You don't strike me as the type that could lie well anyway."

"Heads up!" Tim called out to the room. "The sun's down and I'm detecting a power surge in the building. It's time to move."

"We're going in blind?" Drake asked with confusion.

"*You* aren't going anywhere," Tim said flatly, clearly annoyed at the suggestion. "I can't protect all of you and take care of him as well. You'll be a liability. No, you'll stay here with Sunshine, Athena, and…them," he added, pointing to Bathael and Merlin."

"Like hell," Sarah retorted angrily. "You aren't the only one with a score to settle. Do I really need to remind you who saved your ass last night?"

Tim looked over to Nate who just shrugged. "Don't look at me. I'm not her boss anymore either."

"Damn it," Tim acquiesced. "Just stay behind me. And if things go sideways, you get them all the hell out with your Star Trek shit," he said, pointing to Drake and Bathael. They didn't get the reference, and Sarah mouthed the word 'teleport' to Drake who then nodded his understanding.

"All right then, let's move," Tim commanded. The group gathered their small bags and headed outside. They look the long way around the berth, walking at a quick pace, but trying to keep up appearances. Nate pulled up the rear and made sure they weren't being followed. It took them nearly ten minutes to walk all the way around to the large brick warehouse. It was probably the oldest on the wharf and it had *Lorenza Trade and Imports* on a large, tarnished bronze nameplate to the left of the carriage-style doors.

Tim opened one of the doors very slowly, leading with his handgun, hoping that the ancient doors wouldn't creak or groan. It was no use, though, as the aged metal hinges strained under the weight of the heavy wood doors. As the rusted hinges creaked,

Tim stopped and raised his guard. Now that he was inside, he could scan the interior of the building.

There was no movement, and there were two figures at the far end of the open space. The area around the outer walls was stacked with boxes and crates of various sizes. He felt like a cat stepping into someone's garage. It even had the same smell: oil, gasoline, and rather faintly, electricity and antiseptic. He knew those smells all too well.

Tim moved quickly, motioning for the rest to follow at a distance, Sarah took up the rear position now, and Nate followed Tim, his handgun drawn. The pair walked the length of the massive building, checking around the edges of the obstacles, making their way toward the humming and the lights. After a couple of moments, they found the room opened up. The faint light they'd seen was coming from equipment Tim recognized immediately.

"Fuck!" Tim exclaimed as he started moving faster.

Before Nate could ask what was wrong, he saw what made Tim react. At the far end, near the other set of doors, was a setup of machinery and medical equipment. The light came from a series of consoles, and a large tank which had a body floating in it. He didn't know what it was, but he knew it couldn't be good.

"What am I looking at here, partner?" Nate called out.

Tim easily outpaced Nate and was already at the consoles looking over them and muttering, seemingly to himself, about what he was seeing. "It's a Cytotechnic transfer setup. It's how you make someone like me."

"And who is this," Nate kneeled in front of Matthew's wheelchair, waving his hand in front of his face at the smell. "Damn, is he still alive? He smells like death took a shit."

Tim spun around and was suddenly filled with sadness. It wasn't just his sadness that he felt. In his head, he heard YVE's tortured scream at the apparent loss of her beloved. Tim quickly scanned the body and saw that he was still alive. He was comatose from malnutrition, and he was running a high fever, presumably from whatever infection was ravaging his body. But he could still be saved. Gino would be robbed of his last victim.

"I'm going to need you to control yourself," Tim said to YVE aloud, confusing Nate a bit.

"I didn't realize I wasn't," Nate replied.

"I'll explain later," Tim said before turning back to the table. "It's time to go to work."

"Get me up to speed and tell me what I need to do." Tim said internally this time.

"Mr. Lorenza is connected to the transfer system. Right now, 48% of this neural activity has been processed in the Cytotechnic frame. But he's still in both places."

"Will disconnecting kill him, or will it just stop the process?" Tim asked her.

"Unknown," she replied matter-of-factly. "Matthew wasn't willing to risk a human life to find out. If you're asking for a hypothesis, I would say that there is a good chance that even if the original body were killed, that there's enough of his consciousness in the Cytotechnic frame that he could still awaken and control it."

"Shit, I had a feeling you were going to say that," Tim replied in frustration. "Any other ideas?"

"Just one," YVE offered. "You could transfer me into the Cytotechnic frame, and I could take control before he does. I would have an easier time since it was made for me. My original DNA pattern is still stored in the memory, I expect. If you destroy his original body first, he'll have no way to escape."

"I like this plan," Tim admitted aloud.

"Who are you talking to," Nate asked again.

"No time now. I said I'll explain later," Tim answered, again brushing off the question. "I need another one of these cables," he said, holding up the cable that was connecting Gino's body to the transfer device. "See if you can find one."

"Sure thing," Nate said enthusiastically. He then set about scouring the area for another fiberoptic cable. As Nate ran off to search, Tim stood over Gino's motionless form. He could remember their missions together as Alpha and Beta. He remembered how senselessly cruel he could be, but how powerful and intelligent. He always got the job done. That's why Samuels wanted him. But now, he was too dangerous, it was past time to put him down.

"You have to let me do it," YVE implored him.

"We'll do it together," he said empathetically.

Nate returned and saw Tim staring at Gino's body. "You all right, boss?" he asked with concern.

"Yeah, we're fine," Tim answered. He pulled the knife from his belt sheath and stood still for a moment before stabbing Gino through his left eye – his most vulnerable spot. The blade was one he had made to easily pierce through armor plating, and it moved effortlessly though Gino's now-lifeless skull. Warning lights and alarms began to sound, catching them all by surprise.

"Quick! Give me the cable!" Tim shouted at Nate, but before he could pass it to Tim, there was a massive crashing noise as a large section warehouse wall collapsed near them. Tim looked through the cloud of dust and recognized the same black void he'd seen in Emma's apartment, though much smaller and less pronounced this time.

"Of course, there were two of them," he sighed as he reached for his gun.

Light thinks it travels faster than anything, but it is wrong.
No matter how fast light travels, it finds the darkness
has always got there first and is waiting for it.
- Terry Pratchett

Chapter 38

Nate fired out of reflex this time, choosing shots at the head space of the giant cyborg. He was battling a growing dread in his heart, but he was determined not to let it consume him again. The feeling was less profound than the last time, and for that he was thankful. He still hated everything about it, though.

The Nightmare Guard stood and moved into a defensive posture, raising an armored hand to deflect Nate's attack. The monster began shouting in Mandarin in an amplified electronic voice as it moved to engage Tim and Nate. Tim was connected to the transfer device, but before he could start the transfer, one of Nate's deflected bullets smashed through the console.

"Shit!" Tim shouted as he pulled the cable free from the damaged computer and turned to face the attacker. Since he was able to see the cyborgs extremities this time, he was more capable of engaging it directly. As he spun around, he aimed and fired three shots into the Kevlar and steel plated arm, all one on top of the other, creating a channel through the armor and into the beast's head. The cyborg let out a wail and cursed Tim in Mandarin.

"What did it say?" Nate asked, trying to keep his mind off the fear.

"Well, the first bit was a demand that we turn over 'the Thibodeaux girl,'" Tim answered while dodging an arm swung his way. "That last bit was telling us to screw our ancestors to the eighteenth generation or something like that. Maybe it's lost in translation?" Tim said while blocking a kick. "It's really hard to understand with all the screaming it's doing."

To accentuate the point, Tim fired his gun again. He didn't have a great view of the cyborg's head, because of the obscuring void, but he could see the heat coming from the hole he'd made previously. His bullet shot clear through the armored skull and burst through the back, taking with it a large portion of the creature's brain. The monster gurgled a bit, then collapsed in a heap, leaving Tim and Nate to catch their breath.

There was a commotion at the far end of the massive room, and Nate readied his gun again. He lowered it, though, as he saw Bathael's faint radiance through the dark shadows. Sarah came running up, well ahead of the others, her own weapon drawn.

"What the hell was that?" she asked urgently, pushing her way past Nate to see the cyborg's lifeless remains. "Oh. There was another one of those things?"

"Seems that way," Nate answered, "but this one was less problematic."

"Well, that's a relief," Sarah commented as she approached the cyborg and kneeled down next to it, looking it over with a critical eye. "This cybernetic work is so primitive. It's like someone saw what we were doing and tried to copy it from memory. It's functional, but crude."

Sarah was examining the Nightmare Guard as Drake, Bathael, and Emma walked across the open floor to where the others were gathered. Tim and Nate holstered their weapons and started to move back toward the large tank where the Cytotechnic frame was still floating. As they moved closer to Sarah, Bathael cried out in alarm.

"Drake Sullivan!" they shouted in a voice that could move mountains. "*Mashl'khim* are near, and the *Bachar'im* are in peril!"

Drake quickly looked around the room and saw Sarah kneeling next to the remains of the Nightmare Guard. He could sense the malevolence festering in the crumpled frame, waiting to strike. He had to act quickly to get her attention.

"Get away from it, girl!" Drake yelled urgently. Sarah looked back over her shoulder; her brows furrowed in anger at his patronizing tone.

"Who the…," she began as he cut her off with a sharp tone.

"It isn't dead!" he exclaimed. "There's a Harmer inside. Now MOVE!"

Sarah's eyes widened as she started to feel the terror building within her. She turned her head around slowly, just in time to see the hulking metal frame start to show signs of life. She fought back at the growing dread that started to overwhelm her as she stood and backed away from the previously dead cyborg. As the beast rose to its feet, Sarah turned and bolted into a full sprint to get away, the fear finally overwhelming her and forcing her into a mistake.

Drake was looking at Sarah, making motions for her to get on the ground and stop running, but the fear was too much, and she just needed to get away. Drake watched in abject horror as the Nightmare Guard picked up a piece of the broken roof and hurled it like a spear. Half a second later, a jagged piece of steel pierced through the right side of Sarah's chest in a spray of blood. The color drained from her face as her legs gave out and she crumpled to the floor.

"NO!" Drake screamed as he ran to Sarah's side, ignoring the Harmer to tend to her wounds. "Help us, or to hell with you and the Creator!" he called out, aiming his ire at Bathael. "Are you here to protect us or gawk at us?"

"You know I cannot!" Bathael answered emphatically. "The *Mashl'khim* are of the Nether. You do not know what will happen!"

"I know what will happen if you don't! You aren't like the others! You were human! Act like it!" Drake admonished Bathael.

Bathael looked down and felt a gentle nudge at their feet. Merlin just snorted and barked a gruffy but gentle bark. The angel nodded and stepped forward, placed their hands together, then drew them apart. As they did, the room lit up with a bright light emanating from between their open palms. Within the light a long sword appeared, similar to the one Drake carried. Except this one burned with a bluish-white flame.

Bathael leapt through the air, landing between Sarah and the massive Harmer, using the light from the sword to hold the creature at bay. "I am Enoch ben-Yared ben-Mahalalel of the line of Seth! I am the Prophet! I am the *Bat Qol*, appointed Voice of the Creator! I am Their Will made manifest! You have no power here, child of the Nether. Return whence you came!" The Harmer reeled from the burning light, staying out of the sword's reach.

Meanwhile, Drake pulled the vial of Combobulation Powder and began to chant while sprinkling it over the twisted metal sticking out of Sarah's body. As the powder touched the shrapnel, the metal dissolved and melted away into nothing. He tried to pour some on the wound, but it just sizzled and disappeared. Looking at her back, Drake noticed a long smokey tendril connecting her to the Harmer. The creature needed to die, but it was protected by the armor of the cyborg. He was left with few options.

Satisfied that Sarah was out of immediate danger, he rose and pulled his own sword out of the sleeve of his coat. Immediately, the blade lit with its own flame, but unlike the other sword's, this was a dark reddish orange. He stepped forward, bringing the blade down across the billowing tentacle. A resounding CLANG rang out through the warehouse, which caused Nate and Tim to stop their work trying to repair the console.

"Go help them," Tim said directly. "I don't think you can help with this."

Nate turned back toward the center of the room and stopped dead. He hadn't expected to see the massive cyborg back on its feet, especially with a giant hole in its head. For the first time, he saw the writhing black void seeping out of all the joints of the creature. Something was terribly wrong. He heard the telltale metal-on-metal of the swords attacking the Harmer's makeshift armor. As he moved to flank the monster, he noticed Drake and

Bathael attacking fervently with their flaming swords and Sarah lying on the ground.

Where was Emma? He looked around, and he saw Merlin, off to the side growling and barking. something Nate had not yet seen him do. He scanned the perimeter of the well-lit area of the fighting, but he couldn't see her. He didn't want to call attention to her by yelling out, so he raced along the edge of the clear part of the room, zigging and zagging between the crates and boxes.

Emma was nowhere to be seen. Nate was panicking. The sounds of the battle echoed around the warehouse's rafters, making it easy for him to lose his bearing in the darkness. He was still searching when his earwig radio refocused his attention.

"Argus, can I get an update?" Tim's voice asked. "What's going on over there? Am I seeing flaming swords?"

"Orion, yes, you are," Nate answered quickly. "Athena is down, I don't know how bad it is. Right now, I don't have eyes on Sunshine. I'm trying to find her, but this place has too many corners. How about on your end?" Nate asked urgently, out of breath from his quick pace.

"There's no way I'm getting this thing working again," Tim lamented. "I was able to pull up schematics, but it's a quantum computer and I don't think there are any extra parts here. And it's not like I can make a run to the computer store."

"So, do we scrub?" Nate asked with concern. "Can we just leave it for the authorities to clean up?"

"No, we can't leave the body here, and we need to get Dr. Young medical attention immediately," Tim said with concern.

"He has a critical infection, and I think he's going to lose his legs. Based on what I know of Cytotechnics, Lorenza will still be able to take over the body, he just may not know everything he knew before. We need to shut it down the process and destroy that body."

"Well get to it, boss," Nate said urgently. "We need to get the hell out of Dodge."

"I can't," Tim explained. "The tank is armored and shielded, and I can't force it open. It's vacuum sealed and I'm not strong enough to pop it. Without the computer, I can't send the command to shut it down. We just have to wait it out and strike quickly when it opens."

"Let's trade spots," Nate offered. "You'll have an easier time finding Sunshine in the dark. Besides, I think the old man needs help, and you're better equipped to fight that thing than I am."

"Copy that, but I don't know how effective I'll be either," Tim replied. "I shot that thing with three Raptors, and it got back up. Tell you what; you head up front, and I'll flank out your way. On the double."

"Aye aye, Orion. Oscar Mike," Nate confirmed.

Nate continued his path through the clear part of the warehouse room, skirting the wall and staying in front of the crates. He could see Drake and Bathael holding the Harmer cyborg at bay, but barely. As weak as the creature seemed before, now it was frighteningly powerful, easily holding both attackers in check. It seemed even flaming magical swords weren't a match for the adaptive graphene armor.

Nate and Tim passed each other on their routes and just shook heads, indicating that neither had seen Emma. As Nate continued toward the far wall, he pushed back the mounting fear. As he reached the front, he took up a sentinel position and started scanning the perimeter for movement. Once he was satisfied no one else was coming, he went to his bag and started rifling through it. He looked up, watching Tim shoot at the cyborg, trying to weaken the armor for the others' attacks.

Out of the corner of his eye, Nate saw movement to this left. He raised his gun and looked up, and noticed Emma behind one of the crates, cowering to stay out of sight. Nate waved to get her attention, but he needed to call out to her to get her to look his way. He waved her over, but she was too afraid to move at first. He wasn't sure if it was because of the Harmer, or if he was just afraid to get caught in the fight; either way, she wasn't coming to him.

"Orion, I have eyes on Sunshine," Nate said into his radio. "I'm bringing her to the front side with Young. Hurry up and kill that thing."

Emma slowly inched toward Nate. He waved frantically at her to come, and just as she rose to her feet to run, she stopped cold. Her mouth opened as if to scream, but Nate didn't hear her. In fact, he hadn't heard anything at all; he couldn't hear Tim's gunshots, or the sword's ringing against the cyborg. He didn't even hear the Cytotechnic storage unit opening, or the newly animated frame walk up behind him. And he didn't hear the blade enter his chest, or his attacker ask sarcastically, "Miss me, Cornbread?"

Nate's vision was blurring and turning red. He looked down to see something long and thin sticking out of his chest, coated in his blood, just in time to see a second, then a third poke through. He couldn't feel it; he couldn't feel anything anymore. Who would protect Emma? He just found everyone again. It wasn't fair. He shuddered slightly as the blades slid out, followed by his precious life blood.

"You never were good in a stand-up fight," Gino mocked him. "Never aware of your surroundings the way you should have been. This was too easy. There's nothing fun about easy, but this one was personal. See you in hell, Cornbread."

Nate fell to his knees silently as Emma's screech filled the warehouse. Gino walked slowly toward her, trying to get the hang of using this new body. From Emma's perspective, it was a horrifying spectacle of wildly mutating limbs. Gino didn't have full control yet, so the body was trying to form itself to his default self-image. It wasn't designed for a psychopath.

Once he got to her, he placed a single finger on her lips saying, "Shhh, that's enough out of you Lambchop. Whiteboard can't hear you over his own heroism, anyway. Don't worry, he'll try to save you soon enough. But for now," Gino said quietly before whispering into her ear, "Shut the fuck up."

Gino hobbled back over to Nate's body and looked at it with a smile. "Now it's time to see if this new body has all the bells and whistles I was promised."

He reached down, grabbed Nate's lifeless body by the top of his head and lifted him up effortlessly. Grabbing Nate's neck, he pushed down and easily separated his head from his body. Tossing the head in the air and catching it like a ball, Gino just laughed.

"Oh, Daddy likes. Now it's time to get Whiteboard's attention."

Chapter 39

Gino walked over to the wheelchair where Matthew sat unconscious. He placed Nate's head in Matthew's lap in a vulgar position before he looked back toward Emma, feigning a look of shock and disgust. He went about destroying all of the equipment as Emma backed away toward the crates slowly. She never felt so frightened, but it wasn't an overwhelming fear. She just knew that she was in mortal peril, both from the large shadow monster and from Gino. She knew who he was. She would never forget his voice.

Once she knew he was fully occupied with testing his new body by destroying everything in sight, she turned and ran toward the battle, calling out to Tim along the way. She skirted the far sides of the crates, to avoid getting the attention of the Harmer. Once she could see Tim, she called out again.

"I'm a little busy here," Tim shouted as he dodged a wide swung fist. "Argus, I have eyes on Sunshine. Can you get her somewhere safe, please?"

There was no immediate answer, so Tim radioed again.

"Argus, do you read?" Tim asked frantically, ducking behind a large crate.

"I'm sorry, Cornbread isn't available right now," Came the saccharine reply. "I'm afraid he's completely lost his head. Can I take a message, Whiteboard?"

Tim's heart sank. He cut off the radio so he wouldn't have to hear Gino's mocking laughter. He looked over to Drake and shouted, "Hurry up and kill this asshole. Things just got complicated!"

"I'm trying, blast it all," Drake replied in frustration, his blows glancing off the armor again. "I've not seen one this powerful!"

Tim sighed and looked back to Emma. "You stay put. You don't move from there until I come and get you. Am I clear?"

Emma nodded her understanding. Tim nodded back, sprang over the box and ran to the front of the warehouse. He glanced over the whole area quickly, looking for signs of movement or life. As he made it up to the ruined equipment, he stopped short. There, near the table, lay Nate's crumpled body. Tim walked up to his friend's corpse slowly, their entire lives playing out in his head. He knelt down next to Nate and rolled him onto his back, noticing at that moment that his head was gone.

Tim's heart filled with a fiery rage that he could barely hold in. He couldn't cry, but he could scream, and he did. A scream that rent hearts and shattered windows; a scream seven years in the making. He screamed as if he still had his soul, and in that moment, there was no doubt in his mind or any other's that he was the man he remembered being. Not a copy, the genuine article.

"Lorenza!" Tim cried out in pain. "They're never gonna find all of you! You're done killing people I love!"

"Oh, I haven't even begun, Whiteboard," came the smarmy reply. "But Gino's not here anymore. You made sure to take care of that. There's nothing left of poor little Gino Lorenza." As if to accentuate the point, there was a loud crash as the old cybernetic body flew across the room. "Gino is dead. I am Leapstryke! I have scores to settle, Whiteboard, and you're at the top of the list! We have unfinished business, you and I, and it's time to settle up."

"Yes, it is," Tim said quietly as he stood up, facing his nemesis. Before him he saw the Cytotechnic frame that had been dormant in the tank. It had a decidedly feminine form, but the body seemed to be in flux. The features were changing rapidly, and Tim recalled his own experience with his body and how long it took him to understand fully how it worked. He had an advantage, and he needed to press it. It was time to see if his idea would work.

"You said that's your body, right?" Tim asked YVE silently.

"Yes, Colonel," came the quiet response. "That's the frame that…that Matthew was making for me."

"Can I connect directly to it? You know, the way the transfer rig would?" he asked bluntly, ignoring her obvious pain. There would be time to grieve the fallen when the work was done.

"I don't see why not," YVE replied. "You could create a port on your body that worked the same way the one on the…wait, do you really intend to connect yourself to that monster?" YVE asked in shock. "You have no idea what could happen."

"Well, I was hoping you'd be able to upload yourself and take him over," Tim offered optimistically. "Based on what you've said, with you in control of a body that was designed for you, you could push him out and he could eventually just cease to be, right?"

"Theoretically, yes," YVE postulated, "but it's never been tried."

"Well, we won't know until we know," Tim replied silently before he said out loud. "Time to go to work."

Tim started walking toward Leapstryke with purpose, tossing his weapon aside. He wouldn't need it for what he was going to do. He had seven years' worth of aggression, rage, and vengeance built up inside of him that he hadn't allowed himself to feel until that moment. When this was over, one of them would be dead. Tim needed to make sure it wasn't him.

Tim launched himself across the table with a single leap, landing a solid blow right across Leapstryke's jaw. Tim kicked out solidly and sent Leapstryke flying into the far wall. Pinning him there, Tim pummeled his face repeatedly with enhanced blows, causing blood to fly and bones to crack under the force of the attack. He kept on and on until Leapstryke's face was a collapsed and bloody pulp. Breathing hard from the exertion, he stepped back and examined his handiwork.

As Tim did so, he heard an odd noise coming from what remained of his opponent's head. It took him a moment to realize that it was laughing he was hearing. He watched in horror as Leapstryke's face rebuilt itself; in mere moments it looked as if nothing had happened.

"Wow, that's a neat trick," spouted a delighted Leapstryke. "I didn't feel a thing." Then he looked at Tim with a devious glare and asked, "I wonder if you can do it too."

In a flash, Leapstryke tackled Tim to the floor, pinning him and smashing his fists into Tim's face the way Tim had done to him a moment earlier. He screeched with laughter the whole time. Tim took the blows, allowing himself to feel each one as he actively worked to repair himself while Leapstryke was still hitting him. With a thought, he made his skull denser, causing Leapstryke's fingers to smash as the punches continued.

"What's this?" Leapstryke lamented, looking at his damaged hands, then down at Tim's barely damaged face. "Oh, you're just full of surprises, Whiteboard. Well, so am I!" Leapstryke yelled as his hands repaired and turned into sharp blades coming straight for Tim's eyes. Quickly, Tim used the break in the attack to switch the momentum, punching Leapstryke in the midsection with enough force to launch him a dozen feet across the room.

Not wanting to miss a chance to put an end to the fight quickly. He ran over to where Leapstryke landed and started pounding him in the midsection, trying to weaken it enough to break through. Tim made his hands harder, but he wasn't making headway. They were too evenly matched now. Distracted for a moment thinking about what to do next, Tim found himself impaled through the chest and lifted into the air. The pain was searing, but he didn't have time to hurt. Leapstryke was learning how to control his frame too quickly. Tim needed to end the fight.

Just a little longer.

"You know, Whiteboard," Leapstryke commented while holding Tim with a single bladed hand. "You really should have shared this secret sooner. We were supposed to be partners," he said turning his hand to make the blade to cut deeper, causing Tim to grunt. "You always had to be a Boy Scout, though. You told them I was a psychopath…TWICE! You tried to take all of this away from me. But this is all I know. This is all I'm good for!" To accentuate his point, he threw Tim against the far wall with massive force, causing the bricks to give and the building to shudder.

Tim's breath was labored because of his damaged lung, but he needed to feel the pain. He needed it to remind him why Leapstryke had to die. So, he soldiered on, catching his breath while Leapstryke strode purposefully toward him. There was no more fluidity in the body. The form was becoming absolute. Leapstryke's legs lengthened to mirror the legs of his old body — long and slender, feet and ankles, walking on toes like a cat or dinosaur. Each toe ended in a massive blade-like claw. The torso was finely muscled and human-like, but his hands ended in long, razor-like fingers. Leapstryke's face was featureless and white, like the mask he wore when he killed. This was the form he chose; not human, something more terrifying, something more deadly.

Tim struggled to his feet, looking up at the suddenly taller Leapstryke who grabbed him around the throat and lifted him to eye level. "I hate people like you. You think you're better than me," Leapstryke spat out while cutting Tim across the chest deeply. "You had everything, a wife and kid who loved you, a father who didn't hate you, a home to return to; I deserved those things too. I could have had a chance for most of it, but you took all that away from me." Leapstryke drove a pointed finger into Tim's heart, not a killing blow for men like them, but painful and debilitating. Leapstryke dropped Tim to the floor and started pacing in a circle.

"This all my father ever left me; did you know that?" Leapstryke explained. "An empty warehouse. He hated that I went into the service. Said I wouldn't hack it as a Marine. And he was right, I didn't. But the CIA liked what they saw."

Leapstryke turned and faced Tim, adding, "You know, you remind me a lot of him. You're better looking, but your attitude is the same. You know what he really hated?" Leapstryke asked rhetorically. "He hated it when I slit his throat." In a quick motion, Leapstryke swung a razored hand across Tim's neck, deep enough to cut the artery on the left side. Tim grabbed his neck and dropped to one knee. Another blow that couldn't kill him, but blood loss would slow him down. He just needed a little more time.

"You don't even know why I left, do you?" Leapstryke asked gravely.

"I know enough," Tim whispered loudly, working to repair his neck. "You've always taken care of number one. I assumed someone made you a better offer."

Leapstryke laughed in his creepy, malcontented way. "I gotta say, Whiteboard, for being slow on the uptake, your instincts are amazing. I always admired how good your guesses were. Yeah, I suppose I did get a better offer."

"What could the Chinese offer you?" Tim asked, still raspy. "Money? Power? You never seemed to care about those things. Was it just an endless supply of people to kill?"

Leapstryke ran up startlingly fast and kicked Tim so hard in the face that it dislocated his jaw. Tim slid a few yards across the concrete floor, smashing into the nearby boxes. "Like I said, good instincts, but so fucking slow."

"No," he continued, "China didn't offer me anything I couldn't get here. I didn't run away to China, I was sent. How could you not know that? I guess Pappy always was a dick about sharing intel. Now I work for someone else. Someone like me; someone interested in chaos. Someone as broken as I am. Someone who's very interested in meeting your precious little Lambchop."

"You stay…away from her…you monster," Tim struggled to speak through ragged breaths and excruciating pain. It was all starting to make sense, and he hated that he hadn't seen it earlier. This was all a trap to get Emma: the story about the Diner, the cyborg at the apartment, she was always the target.

"She looks a lot like her mama, don't she?" Leapstryke goaded, mimicking Nate's accent. "Aww, are you trying to get in *her* pants too? Setting up for a family plan? Or did you already?" Leapstryke asked, feigning disgust and shock. "Whiteboard! She was just a child!" he said mockingly.

"Shut up!" Tim spat out, still fighting to get the words out.

Leapstryke had been walking slowly toward Tim and pushed him onto his back with a heavy foot, pinning him and pressing his clawed toes deep into Tim's chest. "Aww no, you're too noble for that, aren't you? But I know about you and her mother. You kept it all a secret. Did your buddy know? Here, you can tell him now!"

Leapstryke jumped across the room in a single massive stride, then jumped back, landing right on Tim's chest again, causing him to cough up blood and gasp for air. Leapstryke leaned over and held Nate's disembodied face right over Tim's. Manipulating the jaw, he perfectly mimicked Nate's voice. "What do ya need to tell me, buddy? Ya got something to get off your chest? You can tell me anything!"

Leapstryke placed Nate's head on Tim's chest. Tim looked into the clouded dead eyes of his best friend. How did it come to this? So much lost time. So many wasted years. So many things that didn't get said. Nate risked everything for Tim, more than once, and his reward was a humiliating death at the hands of a psychopath. Tim failed Nate like he'd failed Claire and failed his family.

"Cat got your tongue, Whiteboard?" Leapstryke asked derisively. "You don't even know what's coming. Let me tell you what's going to happen next. Ying Qi's cyber monkey over there is going to kill the old man, and the little teacher's pet. Probably the big…whatever that blurry bright spot is too. And you're going to watch them all die. Then I'm going to grab pretty little Lambchop and take her back to my *real* boss. I don't think it's going to end well for her. I'm not going to kill you, though. Not yet. You're going to have to live with your failure first. And after you stew in that for a decade or two, then, maybe, I'll come and finish what I started. But know this; you will never, ever, love anyone again. Because if you do, I'll kill them. I'll kill them in front of you. And you won't ever be able to stop me."

Looking into Nate's eyes, Tim couldn't deny that he didn't have a lot of success when it came to saving the people he loved. He always blamed himself for Claire's death. That feeling had been so strong, it broke through all the memory manipulation Samuels and his team had done. And now he failed his best friend. He could feel Nate's lifeless eyes staring at him accusingly. This wasn't part of the plan. Now everyone was in danger, and he couldn't help them. He *had* to finish this. He had one more task. Then he could rest; no, then he could start.

"It's now or never, Colonel," YVE said resolutely. "Let's go to work."

Chapter 40

Drake was feeling his age. He hadn't battled a foe so fierce since the Saxons ruled England. This was his worst fear made manifest; a Harmer made too powerful to manage. Even Bathael was struggling to make any blow count against the massive creature. This had to be something more than just a typical Harmer. The way it could so easily deflect magical blows was unreal. He noticed, though, that it wasn't attacking them, it was only keeping them from getting to Sarah, or past her to Tim. That made him even more uneasy.

After another glancing shot, he motioned for Bathael to take a step back. "We're not getting anywhere," he said in frustration, catching his breath. "How did this thing get so powerful?"

"I do not know, Drake Sullivan," Bathael said, not showing any sign of fatigue. "It has likely been trapped here since the Shattering, feeding on human souls. I expect it is one of the Named."

Drake just sighed heavily. "One of the Named? What good are you if you can't prepare me for these things *before* they are so critical?" he asked with annoyance. "How are we going to find out its name? We can't defeat the thing without it."

"Have faith, Drake Sullivan," Bathael reassured him. "Everything is happening as it must."

That was something less than reassuring to Drake. He'd learned ages ago that 'things happening as they must' was often a code for 'prepare for disappointment.' He needed to get to Sarah; her wound was grievous; she was unconscious and bleeding badly. He wasn't prepared for the disappointment of losing her, nor did he want to be. It was time to change tactics.

"You! *Mashl'khim*!" Drake called out, holding up his sword. "I've killed hundreds of your kind, and yet you fight me to a stalemate. Do you not fear my blade?"

The voice of the Harmer was nearly as shadowy as its form. It was filled with scratching noises and unheard whispers. It was the sound of discontent and malice. "I fear nothing, especially a blade of the Aetherium."

Drake's eyes widened a bit at the revelation. "That's right, child. I know that which you wield. I know who your companion is as well. You are not Enoch of the line of Seth. I name you Ba'ath'El, and by the power of your true name I command you to kneel!"

Bathael stopped cold and dropped to one knee as if compelled. Drake shot Bathael a worried look and put aside his weapon for a moment. Drake had been around long enough and killed enough Harmers to be known among them. Drake hadn't been careful about his true name, but it was so old, and he was so seemingly unimportant that very few knew it. But no creature on the Planes should have known Bathael's true name as a *Be'elohim*. As far as he knew, only the members of the Aetherium and the Creator knew. He hadn't even known until that moment.

"You are surprisingly well-informed," Drake replied after clearing his throat, trying to hide his unease. "You seem to know things you shouldn't. I wonder how that is."

"I am ancient beyond your reckoning," the creature replied. "I know many things your kind do not. I have forgotten things you race have never even learned, child," the creature added with its unsettling laugh.

Drake was unphased. He always knew a lie when he heard one. He'd told too many not to. "No, I don't think that's it," he replied confidently. "You're undoubtedly old. That much is certain. You were probably feeding on humans before they had a proper language. Which makes me wonder how you got trapped here by the Shattering. All of the properly powerful *Mashl'khim* were in the Nether, leading legions, feeding on the work of their lessers. But you were here, fending for yourself."

The Harmer hissed at the implications Drake was making. "I am here because I enjoy hunting your kind. Your fear is sweet, your despair delicious, and your sadness fulfilling. I have devoured millions; I am not a thrall of a higher power. I *am* the higher power," the creature growled out, menacingly.

"Of course, you are," Drake said with a patronizing tone. "I bet all the other little hell spawn look up to you."

The Harmer took a menacing step forward but still did not attack. "I am the reason humans fear the night. Their names for me are as innumerable as the stars. And I am the last thing you will see before you die!"

With that final declaration, the talking was over, and the massive Harmer moved to attack. Drake, having had time to recover, brought his sword up in a flash and blocked the incoming blow. He was old, but he still had the body of a man in his twenties. Bathael stayed on their bent knee, unable to continue in the fight. Drake was on his own, but the Harmer had given something very critical away.

"Your hubris will be your undoing, Nether beast," Drake called out as he deflected blow after blow. "You will be the last thing I see before I die? I think not," he chided, thrusting forward with his sword to put the creature on the defensive.

"I know you, creature of darkness. I name you *Achlys*, the Death Mist. The blackness that consumes men as they perish. I know you and you have no power here!" Drake cried, stabbing the Harmer through a space in the armor at the creature's shoulder.

There was a blood-curdling screech from the monster as the flaming blade plunged deep into the shadowy blackness that was the Harmer's true body. Before Drake could withdraw the weapon, though, the Harmer twisted its torso, pulling the hilt out of Drake's hand. That left him open for the Harmer's next attack, which sent him flying into the boxes a dozen yards back away from where he'd been.

The Harmer roared and extended a massive shadowy and armored arm to pin Drake to the floor. "I will eat your heart, old man, but not before I devour the essence of your young protégé and destroy the living body of your Aethereal servant. You will watch them suffer and perish before you succumb and become my slave."

Nearby, behind a large wooden crate, Emma was hidden, watching the fight unfold. She was terrified, but not because of the Harmer. She'd been warned by Sarah and Drake after the attack on her apartment, so she was surprised that she didn't feel anything but contempt for the creature attacking her friends. Her fear was completely rational; she didn't want to get accidentally killed.

She hadn't seen everything happen, though. She hadn't seen what happened to Sarah because she was instructed to hide before the fighting began. Merlin had been with her, but he padded off after Darke and Bathael when the Harmer first appeared. He was over in a dark corner sleeping now; she passed him to get to her current hiding spot. If anyone could sleep through the Apocalypse, it was Merlin.

Emma inched back toward the clear part of the room and peeked over one of the shorter crates. She watched Drake and Bathael striking the armor of the reanimated cyborg, and heard the Harmer speak. It was like listening to nails on a chalkboard. Why was Bathael kneeling now, she wondered. Drake seemed to have things under control; the creature stopped attacking. She started to relax and breathe slower.

"They need you."

Emma looked around for the source of the voice. But she didn't see it. "Are you talking to me?" she asked quietly, but aloud.

"Yes, Emma, I'm talking to you. They need you," came the insistent reply. The voice seemed familiar, but at the same time not.

"Who is this?" she asked looking around. All she could see in the dim light was Merlin's shaggy form, head raised. He barked at her once, just loud enough for her to hear.

"What? No," she scoffed in disbelief. "I refuse to believe that a dog is talking to me telepathically."

"If it helps you accept it, I'm not really a dog," Merlin replied directly.

"That's not helpful at all!" Emma retorted.

"There's no time for this, little one," Merlin replied impatiently. "All will be explained once your work is done. But they need you. You need to be who you were born to be, and you need to be that person now."

"I don't know what you're talking about," Emma replied abruptly. "There's nothing special about me. I'm not even that smart. I'm nothing like my mom. I'm just a plain woman."

"Oh, little one," Merlin comforted her, "you are anything but plain. You are more special than you can know, and you are exactly what this world needs right now. Go, join them. Please."

When Emma was a little girl, she often dreamed of being special like her mother. She tried all sorts of things, even lying to say that she knew an outcome of something after the fact. But she never manifested power of any kind, let alone precognition. Claire, for her part, always loved and supported her, and never showed any disappointment in her daughter. Emma felt enough for both of them.

"You're wrong. You don't know me," she answered. "I'll just be in the way, putting them in danger."

She could hear Merlin snort behind her, but he didn't say anything else. She watched intently as Drake conversed with the Harmer. Did he just look at her before he stood up again? What was that he said? Some sort of weird name. Whatever it was really seemed to enrage the Harmer. She watched in helpless horror as the monster struck Drake and sent him flying, pinned him and snaked a smoke-like tendril around his throat. She listened to the beast gloat and saw, for the first time, that Sarah was lying motionless on the ground behind it. Special or not, she couldn't stand by while this creature destroyed her friends.

Summoning all the courage she could muster, she stood up and marched toward the Harmer. "Hey, dickhead!" she shouted. "Are you looking for me?"

The Harmer was clearly not expecting this intrusion, and it stopped what it was doing to turn toward the new voice. "Who is this, old man?" it asked Drake with genuine interest. "Another one of your acolytes? Is she ready to lay her life down for you as well? Let's find out. Wait! I have a better idea."

The Harmer lifted Drake up by his neck and then lifted Sarah off the floor through the hole in her chest. It dangled them both in front of Emma and laughed his horrible, hollow laugh. "Choose, human."

"What are you talking about," she asked, unsure if the creature was seeing through her false bravado.

"Choose which of these mortals will die first," it replied. "I was going to make the old one suffer by watching the others perish, but I think your pain and fear will taste better than his."

"I'm not afraid of you," Emma said truthfully.

"Do you have any idea how many times I've heard that from mortals like you?" the Harmer asked rhetorically, chuckling. "Everyone fears me. I *AM* fear, young one."

"Maybe you hear it a lot, but I'm really not feeling it. I mean, the whole get-up, the smokey tendrils and the raspy voice, I suppose it could work. But not for me. I'm not afraid of you," she said again, more firmly. She was tired of feeling out of control of her own life. She was no one's pawn.

The Harmer roared and charged at Emma, throwing Drake and Sarah off to the side roughly. Emma knew in that moment she would die. But maybe she could save the others. Maybe she could occupy its attention long enough for Drake to recover. They all had to live. She needed them all to be OK. No one else was going to die today. She closed her eyes tight and waited for the killing blow.

The Harmer stopped cold in its attack, hissing loudly. "What is this? What are you?" it asked frantically, screeching.

In Emma's head, she started to hear the voices of those around her. Loudest of all was Merlin. "There you are. You have found yourself, and your power. You just had to find your courage first. Now end this."

Emma opened her eyes, and her world was completely different. She looked down at her hands, and they glowed with a bright multi-colored light. She could hear the fish out in the bay swimming under the boats. She could smell the blood from Nate's crumpled body. She could feel the secrets of Creation seeping into her mind and became keenly aware of how the universe was ordered. She was connected to all the Planes, where moments before, she didn't even know they existed. She was overflowing with power.

Emma reached out her right hand, and she felt herself connected to the blade buried deep in the Harmer's essence. Reaching out the other, she connected herself to the cybernetic bits and armor that it carried from its former host. Making a fist with her left hand and then opening it quickly caused all the armor to fly off the beast and into the far corners of the warehouse. She flicked her right hand to the side and sent the sword flying through the creature, around and into her hand.

The Harmer writhed on the floor in agony, screaming out, "Who are you? What are you?"

Emma lowered the blade at the Harmers face and replied flatly, "Don't you know fear when you see it?" before stabbing it in the face.

Emma pulled the sword out of the concrete where it was embedded from her attack. There was nothing left of the Harmer but a slight smell of sulfur and burnt flesh. She ran to Sarah's side to check her wound. Both sides of her shirt were soaked in blood, though it looked like the bleeding was slow. Sarah's breathing was short and ragged, and her lips were turning blue. Emma checked her pulse, and her heart was beating a mile a minute. She needed immediate and urgent medical assistance.

Emma looked over her shoulder to Bathael, who was slowly rising, using their sword for leverage. Drake was similarly struggling to get to his feet, rubbing his neck where the Harmer had held him. "Does one of you have mystical healing powers or something? I'm not a paramedic, but if we don't do something soon, I think we're going to lose Sarah!" she pleaded.

Drake hurried, as much as he could, over to where Emma was kneeled and looked Sarah over. He looked over at Bathael who just shook their head solemnly, and replied gently, "She requires healing beyond our power."

"What do you mean? Aren't they an angel? Can't it cry on her or something? ANYTHING?" Emma asked frantically as she continued putting pressure on Sarah's chest.

Drake placed his hand on Emma's and looked at her with softness in his eyes. "Some things are just lost," he remarked sadly. "Don't you think we would heal her if we could? It's something that just can't be done anymore. If only we could...," his voice trailed off, "...things would be very different now."

Drake patted her hand and stood up slowly. He turned away from Emma and walked over to check on Bathael, who was noticeably struggling. "Fine then, give up. Mom always told me that I couldn't count on you when it mattered." Drake stopped walking and turned his head slightly as if he were going to speak.

But he didn't; he just absorbed the insult and continued toward Bathael with his typical slight frown.

Emma looked down at Sarah's unconscious form struggling to breathe. She felt strange; angry and sad and powerful all at once. It was different from how she felt attacking the Harmer, but the same too. It welled up inside her and she felt it overflowing from her hands. "If you won't help her, I will," Emma said, determined and driven.

Emma placed her hand on Sarah's chest and closed her eyes. She could feel the power flowing through her hands and into Sarah's body. The whole world faded into the sound of rushing water as she focused all the energy she could on repairing the grievous wound in Sarah's chest. Merlin barked loudly, calling Drake's attention to what was happening behind him. As Drake looked, Sarah and Emma were surrounded by a bright, greenish-gold light, and it was moving from Emma and into Sarah.

There was a bright flash that knocked Drake off his feet and caused Bathael to stumble. Sarah sat up with a loud gasp, breathing fast, almost panicked. She looked around, then reached up to feel the wound on her chest. She winced in pain and recoiled her hand, but the bleeding was stopped, and the damage was mitigated.

"What…. What happened?" she asked, looking around frantically. "Where am I?"

Emma smiled and hugged her friend in relief. "Relax, Sarah. We're still in the warehouse in San Francisco. You need to rest. You were badly injured."

Bathael stepped over and helped Drake to his feet. Drake shook the cobwebs from his head and hobbled over to the women. "You were more than wounded, Captain," he said frankly. "Young Miss Thibodeaux, here, just pulled you from the firm grasp of death quite literally."

"But how…?" Sarah started to ask before Drake stopped her.

"It doesn't matter, and I couldn't explain if I wanted to," Drake said impatiently. "We can discuss it later. Right now, the Colonel needs our help."

We are such stuff / As dreams are made on,
and our little life / Is rounded with a sleep.
- The Tempest, Act IV, Scene 1
- *William Shakespeare*

Chapter 41

Years of being rebuilt and the endless training that followed never could have prepared Tim for the battle he was in at that moment. As hard as it might have been to face a tank, or even cyborgs, facing off against another Cytotechnic Augment was exceptionally difficult. He'd been in fights that were tests of skill, fights that were tests of strategy, and even fights that were tests of strength; this was a test of purpose, and Tim wasn't sure he could win. How do you win against someone whose purpose is chaos? But he knew he had to.

"Colonel, we'll need to maintain the connection with the other frame for 5 full seconds to start the transfer," YVE said directly.

"I'm trying, damn it," Tim said in his head, lost in the fight. "You're welcome to take over if you think you can do better!"

"I think we both know that's a bad idea, Colonel," YVE snapped back.

"Then shut up!" Tim shouted aloud.

Leapstryke laughed and continued throwing wild punches and kicks, keeping Tim off balance. He was always the better fighter. None of Tim's squad had ever been close, even Tim. "I don't know who you're talking to, Whiteboard, but I love where the conversation is going," Leapstryke said gleefully. "You know, they say that talking to yourself is the first sign you're going crazy. Maybe we can get adjoining rooms at the asylum," he added with another chilling laugh.

"It's cute that you think you're going to get out of this alive," Tim spat out while blocking a kick.

"It's cute that you think I won't," Leapstryke joked. "You don't even know what you're dealing with. All your planning, all your whiteboard drawing and you still just run in blind. That's what I love about you. A blind, reckless, savior complex that I will love beating out of you." To accentuate the point, Leapstryke landed a massive blow to Tim's gut, followed by a left cross that dropped Tim to his knees.

Tim spat out a mouthful of blood and wiped his lip. He waited for Leapstryke to step forward, then grabbed his foot and pulled, sending Leapstryke onto his back in sprawl. He tried to grab the foot again, to make the connection, but Leapstryke was prepared and came across with his other leg which sent Tim flying to side. He leapt through the air, but instead of landing on Tim, he swept his foot up, sending Tim flying into the far brick wall, which shook the foundation and knocked mortar dust all over.

Tim took a moment to glance down the length of the warehouse to see that the large creature had gained the upper hand against Bathael and Drake. He needed to put a stop to this and help them. He just needed to find a way to get the upper hand. His old nemesis wasn't going to make it easy. He never did.

"I gotta say, Whiteboard, you disappoint me. When I found you in that cabin, and saw your new threads, I thought you'd be…I don't know…better? You're still the same old Andrews, only best at being second best. You were always so boring," Leapstryke said with disgust, walking over to Tim with purpose. "It's time to stop playing."

Leapstryke stretched his arm and grabbed a large piece of heavy transfer equipment and held it over Tim tauntingly. "Time to die, Whiteboard."

Leapstryke slammed the heavy steel down onto Tim's body over and over with such force that he was being driven into the concrete floor. Tim hardened his body against the blows, but it wasn't going to be enough. Tim struggled to roll to the side, but the divot he was lying in kept him from escaping. He knew Leapstryke was going to trap him for the killing blow.

In the distance, between the crashing blows, he could hear Emma screaming, but he couldn't make out what she was saying. He was going to fail her. He was going to fail them all. He tried to raise his arms to stop the blows, but they buckled under the force. Leapstryke threw his bludgeon to the side and stood over where Tim was half buried in the rubble of the floor.

"Any last words?" Leapstryke asked with a wry smile.

"What's that?" Tim asked weakly, looking toward a growing light.

"How stupid do you think I am?" Leapstryke asked coldly before a wave of greenish-gold light washed over them both, causing Leapstryke to look toward the blinding flash and shield his eyes.

Tim knew this was the chance he'd been waiting for. While Leapstryke was distracted, Tim grabbed him around the ankle and held tight, focusing all his energy into keeping a firm hold. He produced the cable from inside his arm, where he'd been holding it, and jammed it into Leapstryke's foot. After five seconds, just as YVE said, the transfer began.

"This is your chance," Tim said to YVE silently. "Make it count. For all our sakes. How long do you need?"

"I'll only need about 30 seconds, Colonel," YVE replied directly. "This frame was made for me. Until we meet again," she added as she started the transfer.

"Until then," Tim said to himself, since he could feel that YVE was fading from his mind. He just needed to hold on a little longer.

As the light faded and Leapstryke recovered, he tried to take a step and realized he was held fast. Looking down, he noticed Tim's hand firmly locked around his ankle. "Whiteboard, I didn't know you cared," he said derisively as he struggled to get free. He pulled as hard as he could, but he couldn't lift his foot at all. As he tried to free himself, he found Tim effectively countering every move. A dark realization started to settle in; Tim had been stalling to get his guard down.

Leapstryke started to get angry as he began hitting and slicing Tim's hand and arm to no effect. No marks, no bruises; it was like trying to punch through steel with a sponge. How was this possible? "What's going on here? Why won't you let me go? This isn't fair! I was winning and you were going to die! What's happening?" he asked frantically as he did everything he could to try to escape Tim's grasp.

Once thirty seconds had passed, Tim released his hold and stood up quickly. He set himself in a defensive stance, preparing for an attack that never came. Leapstryke looked at his useless hands with confusion and pain. "What did you do to me?" he asked Tim, stepping forward with halting steps. "What's going on? Who's that?" he asked aloud frantically.

Tim relaxed his posture and watched intently as YVE began her work in earnest. "I'd like you meet Yvette Young, the late wife of the man you kidnapped and tortured," Tim explained. "She's the reason you and I exist, and that's her body you're in. I think she wants it back."

Leapstryke looked down at his hands again, the bladed fingers disappearing into more conventional looking hands. His feet, too, were reconfiguring into a more recognizable shape. "No, no, no, no, NO!" he screamed. "You can't have it! It belongs to me now! He told me that he'd changed it so it would work right. It's mine!"

Tim knew what was happening. YVE was attacking Leapstryke in his own mind, taking away his control of his body, piece by piece, as he had with Matthew. Off in the distance, Tim could see that Sarah was back on her feet, which was a relief of its own, and the whole group was moving toward him. He held up his hands to stop them from approaching too close.

Leapstryke put his head in his hands, screaming and cursing while his body started to shift uncontrollably.

Looking up, the face now held a distinctly feminine look. "Colonel, I have run into an unforeseen situation."

"Shut up, bitch!" The same face said while morphing back into the white featureless face of Leapstryke.

"Colonel…" came a weak call from near the large roll-up door. Matthew was awake, but only barely. Tim wouldn't have heard him were it not for his augmented hearing. Tim kept one eye on the internal battle in the Cytotechnic frame as he rushed to Matthew's side.

"Hey Doc," Tim said quietly. "I thought we'd lost you. We're going to get you some help, ok?"

"Colonel…" Matthew repeated weakly.

"Shh, don't try to talk, you're in pretty bad shape," Tim explained.

"You need to know…," Matthew continued, "I modified… the frame…"

"Relax, Doc. I brought YVE with me. She's in there taking over the frame right now. It's going to be all right," Tim reassured him.

Matthew's eyes widened in horror at the revelation. "No!" he tried to shout, but only a weak protest came out. "She can't! I modified the frame with his DNA. I had to…make it work for him. Colonel…he's going to…you have to get her out!"

Tim wasn't sure what was going on, but he knew panic when he heard it. He waved over to others, motioning for them to come and help Matthew. Leapstryke was over near the far side door, struggling to keep one shape over the other. At this point, it was difficult to tell who was winning.

"YVE," he called out, "We have to get you out of there. Matthew said…,"

"Yes, I know," she said forcing the words out in a mingled voice. "I know what he did, and now I know what needs to be done."

"What are you talking about?" Tim asked urgently.

"You're distracting me, and time is short, Colonel," she replied in a voice more her own. "You need to get everyone to safety at once. I don't know if I can get enough control to get far enough away from you. There's a block of cells that have been reconfigured at the atomic level. In about sixty seconds, they will create enough energy to level this building and everything within 100 meters of it. I am working to contain the impact of the explosion, but I can't stop it. You need to go now!"

Just then the face changed again, and Gino's grinning face appeared, just as he was before. "You don't have enough time, Whiteboard. If I'm gonna go, I'm gonna take all of you with me." Saying that, the frame reached out and grabbed Tim's arm, holding firmly with a massive force. Tim looked over to the others sadly. He wasn't going to fail them. Not this time. Never again.

"Do what you need to do, Colonel," came YVE's soft voice.

Looking back to the frame, he saw her lovely face, smiling gently at him with understanding eyes. "Do what needs to be done. Please."

Tim recalled silently the last time these players were all on the same stage. Last time, his mistakes affected everyone else's lives. He worried that there wasn't enough time to get the blast far enough away from the whole group. He had to try. He'd already lost too much. No more.

"All of you, start running now!" He cried out. Before anyone could argue, he changed his tone enough to be taken seriously, even by Drake. "Do it! Now!" Drake just nodded and gathered everyone up, all of them running to the far side of the building.

All he could hear now was Leapstryke's hair-raising laughter. The maniacal cackling of a broken man driven beyond insanity. "You don't even know what's coming. You'll never know," he could hear Leapstryke say as the grip tightened. Tim looked back over his shoulder and saw the far doors open. They would all be safe.

"And neither will you," Tim said he pulled hard on his right arm, separating the joint at the elbow. The wet sound of snapping sinew and muscles echoed in the warehouse as Tim weakened the joint enough to pull free of Leapstryke's grasp.

"Tell Matthew I will always love him," came YVE's final plea.

After pulling back, Tim spun around with all his augmented might, launching the frame through the open door and into the water of the bay beyond. No sooner had the body touched the top of the water than there was a massive release of energy, exploding out with an unbelievable force.

Tim prepared himself for the blast. Everyone was safe. everyone who could be at least. He'd found himself again, and he'd made sure that Gino paid for Claire's death. And even if he hadn't found Claire's killer, he could rest easy now. His work was done. Everything was moving in slow motion. He saw the blinding flash through the door, followed by the searing heat. He could see the bricks and mortar giving way under the force, exploding in showers of red and grey rubble. But the end never came. Just the sound of dull thuds as the building collapsed against a solid structure.

Looking around, Tim noticed that he was surrounded by a smokey green light. He saw the blast wave from the explosion crash against the light and move around it, like water around a rock in a stream. Looking to the side, he saw Emma standing to his left and slightly behind. He hadn't noticed that she didn't run with the others.

"I thought I told you to run, Sunshine" Tim said with an annoyed tone.

Emma just smirked and replied, "Yeah, but then I remembered that you're not the boss of me, so I decided to stay and save your life. Losing one friend was enough today." He noticed a tear running down her cheek as she added, "Will it ever stop hurting?"

"No," Tim replied softly. "But I don't think it's supposed to. I think if it did, we'd stop seeing them in our dreams, and honestly, that's the only thing that kept me going."

Emma kept the shield up until the dust cleared. As they looked around, there was nothing left of the warehouse but a massive pile of rubble with a large circular clearing near one end.

"That's going to make things a bit more difficult. How are we going to find a book in all this mess?" Tim said, sighing.

"You mean this book?" Emma asked, pulling a book out from the back of her waistband.

Tim grabbed the book and looked at the flowing cursive on the front cover, instantly recognizing Claire's writing. "I found it while I was hiding," Emma explained. "It was in a box marked *trophies* sitting right on top. Something told me this is what we needed. I didn't need a letter this time."

Tim grabbed Emma by the back of her head and kissed her forehead. "She'd be really proud of you, you know that?"

"Yeah," Emma replied, "I think I do." She hugged Tim tight, then as she pulled back, she asked, "What's wrong?"

Tim looked down at her confused, then felt something cool on his cheek. He wiped away a single tear, and replied, "Nothing. Nothing at all."

What we call the beginning is often the end.
And to make an end is to make a beginning.
The end is where we start from.
- T.S. Eliot

Epilogue

Li Fong sat on a jetty on the opposite side of the inlet where the warehouse had been. By the time the blast from the Cytotechnic frame got to him, though, it was little more than a rush of warm air. With his expanded senses, he watched the events in the warehouse unfold. He'd seen Gino take over the frame, kill Nate Lange, and fight Tim. He could have intervened, like he had when he shot Claire, but he wanted to see how events would unfold. Besides, he had no desire to pull Gino from the fire if he didn't need to.

As he watched with curiosity at the appearance of Emma's shield, he heard someone approach from behind. The light, almost floating steps were familiar to him, and he didn't bother getting up from this seated position. Instead, he invited his visitor to sit.

"I was wondering when you'd show up," Li Fong called out into the night. "You nearly missed the interesting part."

Samuels sat down next to Li Fong, eating popcorn from the nearby carnival. "I saw it as I was walking here. Those two always put on a good show. The end was a bit unexpected, though. Popcorn?" he asked, offering the bag toward Li Fong who just held up a hand to reject it. "Well, I don't think you risked calling me here just to watch this. What did you need?" Samuels asked directly.

"Emma Thibodeaux found the book, and she has Awakened. I fear this will complicate things," Li Fong explained.

"I don't think the book matters," Samuels said while continuing to eat. "And being Awakened doesn't make her invulnerable. You should know that better than most. I'm more concerned about what to do with the remains of our dear friend, Mr. Lorenza."

"Our deal still stands, Stephen," Li Fong replied flatly. "We will split whatever is recovered by my team, who are already in the water. You can expect delivery in 48 hours. My main worry is what my brother will do when he hears of this loss."

"He'll suck it up," Samuels offered plainly, "or he won't. Throwing a tantrum about it won't change what happened."

"You don't understand what's going on. My brother expects his American general to deliver the Thibodeaux girl to him personally. I could have done so in his place, but she's beyond our power now," Li Fong explained. "I fear that my brother's Master will not take the news well. All of this is their will, not my brother's."

Samuels stopped chewing at the revelation. "Master? What do you mean 'Master?' What haven't you told me?"

Li Fong struggled to answer. He'd already been pushing the limits of his brother's trust being in America in the first place. He had intentionally disconnected himself from his brother's mind only a few sparse times in the past, usually to communicate with his counterpart in the American government, Samuels. The pair had an arrangement, one of which Ying Qi would not have approved. But it kept the peace, and it allowed China access to advanced cybernetic designs.

"Since he was a young man, my brother has been working to summon a powerful creature from beyond our Plane," Li Fong said. "Early on, he came to the belief that this creature was a powerful supernatural being known only as the *Nadach*, a Hebrew word meaning Outcast."

"I'm familiar," Samuels proffered returning to his popcorn.

"Soon after I left, he was successful in summoning the creature using the power of its true name," Li Fong continued, "and forcing it into the body of a small boy."

Samuels raised an eyebrow and set aside his snack. "An intriguing set of events, to be sure. Do you happen to recall the name he used to invoke the creature? I have some knowledge in these things."

"I believe he called it Shakra'el," Li Fong answered. "But if I'm being honest, I worry that my brother is under the influence of something too powerful for even him to control."

"Oh, of that you can be certain," Samuels interjected. "He is absolutely in great peril."

Li Fong turned toward Samuels in alarm. "How do you know this? You must tell me so I can help him!"

"Well," Samuels answered, "I don't know who your brother is dealing with or talking to, but if it needed a ritual that took decades to complete, it's something far more powerful than a fallen angel. Besides, I know of no being with the name Shakra'el, and if there is, it certainly isn't the *Nadach*"

"How would you know this? Only my brother has these secrets," Li Fong demanded.

Samuels just laughed and started eating his popcorn again. "I know because *I* am the *Nadach,* and my name isn't Shakra'el, It's Sammael. Your brother is in deep shit. I think we all are."

To Be Continued…